WHAT
DIES
INSIDE US

TONY J FORDER

A DI Bliss Novel

DEDICATION

For Peter Reisiger, who fought the good
fight and went out on his own terms.
I don't believe in an afterlife, but you
left this one with dignity.

dignityindying.org.uk

Death is not the greatest loss in life. The greatest loss is what dies inside us while we live.

Norman Cousins

THE BEGINNING OF THE END...

Bliss looked on in horror as the slender young girl backed up onto the rooftop ledge. Her face, twisted by a dozen creases of anguish, flushed red from tears as she stared at the man who had once been her saviour.

'I'm sorry,' she whispered, barely loud enough for him to hear above a low rumble of thunder and the hiss of traffic passing by on the wet streets below. Her white nightdress glowed like a shimmering apparition against the background of a roiling granite sky. 'I guess in the end we can't help being who we are.'

With that, she stepped off the ledge.

Bliss rushed forward with both hands outstretched, his fingers grasping flimsy material slick with rain. He made a pair of tight fists, his grip as powerful as it could be, but the girl's momentum wrenched her from his grasp.

'Molly! No!' Bliss cried.

He looked on in impotent horror as she tumbled through the air, unable to avert his gaze while a cry of icy dread died in his throat. Molly's features transformed into an horrific mask of terror, her lips forming a silent scream without end; not even when her shattered body lay on the ground in an ever-expanding pool of blood. Her eyes remained open, almost as if she continued to gaze upon him, but for the first time since he had known her they finally looked at peace.

Bliss sobbed, slumping forward to his knees as he cried out her name one last time to an uncaring world. He leaned out over the edge with his arms extended as if still attempting to rescue her, reaching further and further until he also surrendered to the inevitable pull of gravity and fate.

ONE

JIMMY BLISS JOLTED HIMSELF out of the unbearable daydream. No slick roof beneath his feet, no leaden sky above, no shattered bodies oozing precious lifeblood across the pavement. He was in his own living room, Molly sitting by his side; the waif he had prevented from killing herself more than three years earlier when she was just fifteen; a girl he had come to love as if she were his own daughter; the young woman who reciprocated out of more than mere gratitude for his having saved her life.

Until the darkness inside his head led his thoughts astray, the pair had been engrossed in watching the Pink Floyd Pulse DVD. Between them on the sofa lay Max, a Golden Labrador who finally seemed comfortable in the presence of people having been rescued from his abusive previous owner. On a wide flatscreen, David Gilmour exhorted his Fender guitar to produce yet another melodic phrase that made it sound as if the guitar itself were emotionally exhausted, strings bending almost to snapping point. Molly sat with her mouth hanging open, tongue lolling. Beside her, Max did the same.

As the band launched into the final stretch of *Sorrow*, a discordant ringtone spoiled the moment. Bliss groaned and hung his head. Reached for the remote to pause the disc, before digging into his trouser pocket for the phone. He flashed Molly an apologetic look.

'Sorry to call you, Jimmy,' Detective Constable Gul Ansari said to him when he answered. 'I tried my best not to, but ended up not having a choice. I got lumbered because Bish called in sick.'

'Again?' This was the third time in as many weeks that Detective Sergeant Bishop had taken a day off. 'I do hope it's nothing trivial.'

'I know what you mean, boss. But to be fair to him, he did sound rough. Not that it would have mattered in this case. I am sorry, though.'

'It's okay, Gul,' Bliss said, entirely used to having his down time interrupted by the demands of his job. He checked his watch and saw that it had just turned 10.30pm. 'What have you got for me?'

'An odd one.'

'They usually are.'

'True. This time, we have a homeless man in the interview room who claims to have witnessed a murder at Cuckoo's Hollow Park in Werrington. Says he chased off the attacker and tried resuscitating the victim before realising it was too late. Our witness has no phone, so he made his way to a local pub, who called us after they heard his story. Only when the response unit arrived on scene, there was no sign of a body, no sign of a struggle. Nothing out of the ordinary at all. They quizzed the bloke, suggesting he might be confused due to being a bit inebriated. Apparently, he reacted badly to that, got a little aggressive, insisting he saw what he saw. They brought him in, expecting to just stick him in a cell and let him sleep it off, except that he demanded to speak to you.'

Bliss frowned. 'He asked for me by name?'

'He did. I went down and had a word, to see if I could pacify him and get him to talk. But he wouldn't have any of it. Refuses to speak to anyone other than you, boss.'

'Did our homeless witness give a name?'

'He did. Roger Craig.'

Bliss ran the name through his memory banks, but came up with just the one hit. 'I know of a Roger Craig who was a running back for the San Francisco Forty-Niners. But unless our witness is a six-foot, sixty-something black bloke from Iowa, I have no idea who he is.'

'Well… you got the height and skin colour right, Jimmy. But our man is more forty-something and sounds to me like a Brummie.'

With a reluctant sigh, Bliss said, 'Okay. Give me ten minutes, Gul.'

'You want me to give Penny a bell?'

DS Penny Chandler was his regular partner, only she wasn't on call, either. 'No, don't bother her,' he said. 'I can handle this one on my own. Shouldn't take too long.'

When he ended the call, he found both Molly and his dog looking at him with pitiful longing in their eyes. Behind Molly's lay mischief, a deliberate ploy to make him feel bad for leaving her. As for Max, he seemed to be learning bad tricks fast.

'We'll pine for you,' the girl told him.

Bliss raised his eyebrows as he levered himself up off the cushion. 'Of course you will. I'm sure your heart will bleed.'

'It will. I genuinely don't know if I'll survive.'

'I think you'll manage. Just try not to make a mess on my carpet. If you feel the blood leaking out, go and pass out in the garden.'

Molly extended a clenched hand in his direction and slowly unwound the middle finger. He shook his head in faux exasperation. 'Remind me why I invited you to stay with me?' he asked, patting his pockets in search of his car keys.

'Because you had a desperate need to be insulted?'

'Yeah, like I don't get enough of that from Pen.'

'Clearly not. And I bet she doesn't give you the finger.'

He found his keys on the arm of the recliner, the seat of which also held his thin leather jacket, which he slipped into. 'No, Pen prefers the traditional British two-finger salute.'

'See. Now you have something different to look forward to in your old age.'

'Yeah, thanks.'

'You going to be back in time to finish watching Floyd?'

Bliss shrugged. 'I have no idea. I've seen it plenty of times before, so watch the rest of it if you want to. And if you go up to bed, make sure to lock the front door first, but don't leave the key in it or I won't be able to get in.'

Molly sniggered. 'That'd be fun,' she said.

'So would me waking you up by kicking the bloody thing in. Oh, and give Max his walk before you turn in, will you, please?'

'Of course.' She drew the dog closer to her, both arms draped around his neck. The animal accepted the embrace without fuss.F   Bliss nodded. 'Sorry about this, Molly. I arranged not to be on call tonight, but we're a man down and this shout sounds personal.'

She shook her head and waved a hand. 'No sweat, Jimbo. Truly. Truth is, I'm knackered after all the travelling today. Plus, we have all weekend to catch up. Well… hopefully, that is.'

He nodded. 'I promise. Whatever this is, I'll sort it tonight and make sure somebody covers for me until Monday morning if necessary.'

Bliss winked and left the house feeling guilty as he closed the door behind him, though reassured that Molly genuinely understood. He drove to the station with his own words echoing inside his head. How many times had he made similar promises to his late wife and subsequent female friends? Always with the best of intentions, but also with one eye firmly on the job in hand.

TWO

DC ANSARI WAS WAITING anxiously for him when he entered the body of Thorpe Wood police station from the car park. She regarded him warily, but he gave her a smile instead of the irritated grunt she might have been expecting.

'No need for another apology, Gul,' Bliss said, raising a hand. 'If the only way to get this bloke to cooperate was to call me out, then you did the right thing.'

'Thanks,' she said uneasily. 'But I also know you don't spend as much time with Molly as you'd like, and I hated having to bother you. How's she doing, by the way?'

'Terrific. Mind you, I only picked her up from the station a couple of hours ago, so I'll tell you more next week. Right now, what's the situation with this Roger Craig bloke?'

'Nothing further since we last spoke. Like I told you, he's homeless and has recently been getting his head down over at Cuckoo's Hollow, off Skaters Way. He's ex-forces and although he's down on his luck he comes across as confident and composed. He admits to having had a couple of beers but doesn't seem to be drunk. Says he's not taking anything stronger, and I'm inclined to believe him.'

Bliss thanked the DC and said he'd find her again before he left. He used his lanyard card to buzz himself through a security door. The corridor beyond led to the interview rooms. The moment he entered IR1, his olfactory senses were assaulted by a variety of odours, the combination of which caused his nose to twitch. There was no stench of urine or faeces, for which he was grateful, but the man was ripe with neglect.

'I'm told you requested me by name, Mr Craig,' Bliss said, studying the man closely. Shaved head. Weathered face. Full beard and moustache, neither wild nor ragged; clearly, he maintained himself whenever possible. He wore a thin raincoat over a denim shirt and navy jogging trousers, the clothing soiled and threadbare. A beanie hat lay squashed on the table beneath a pair of black gloves.

'If you're Bliss, then yes.' Craig's voice was deep, and as Ansari has intimated sounded as if he originated from the Birmingham area.

'I am. Forgive me, but do we know each other?'

The man shook his head, the slick dome picking up a reflection off two recessed ceiling lights.

'So how come you asked for me by name?'

'I know you by reputation only, Inspector. A few years back an old mucker of mine was beaten to death in the city centre because he was homeless and vulnerable and because the lads who did it thought nobody would give a damn. That kind of news doesn't take long to spread between us rough sleepers. I was in the library shortly afterwards reading about the investigation in the local rag and thinking that somebody cared after all.'

'I remember it well,' Bliss said with an empathetic nod. 'Adrian Summerby. A tragic end and so unnecessary.'

Craig set his jaw and nodded. 'See. You even remembered his name. That sort of thing impresses me. Article in the *Telegraph* said you took a personal interest in finding the bastards who did it.'

'It was a team effort.'

'A team led by you.'

Bliss regarded him shrewdly. 'And because I wanted to see a homeless man's killers behind bars, you thought I'd be more inclined to listen to you.'

Craig folded his arms beneath his chest and stretched out his legs. 'That's exactly right. A lot of people, some police officers included, see the likes of me and find it easier to dismiss what I have to say because of the way I look and smell and occasionally behave after a few too many drinks. From what I read, you're the kind of copper who'd be willing to hear me out.'

'I'm sure the officers who responded would have if there'd actually been a body found where you told them it was, Mr Craig.'

The man's lips twisted, and his nostrils flared. 'I don't know what to say about that. But I stand by what I saw.'

'Tell me about it,' Bliss said, sliding onto a chair at the table. 'Take your time.'

'Not much to tell. I'd made camp for the night and was sitting there minding my own business when I heard something. It was away in the distance and muffled, but it sounded like a struggle of some sort. I was tucked out of the way in amongst the trees, but when the sound came again, I could tell it was somewhere over by the bridge spanning the narrow end of the lake.'

'You could tell all this from where you were?'

Craig leaned forward and gave a broad reflective smile that contained no humour. 'When you're on the desert basin in Helmand you learn to listen to the breeze drifting in off the mountainside as it creeps along the edges of the valley. Out there, the difference between hearing what it had to say and not could decide whether you lived or died. There were too many predators crawling around out there for my liking, but by far the worst of them were human. And whereas the creatures were silent in their approach, those scurrying on two legs looking to pop off a shot at you with a sniper's rifle were not always as quiet as they thought they were.'

'Must have been tough out there,' Bliss said. It was no idle comment; he had a huge amount of respect for those who served. 'What unit were you in?'

'Two Para. And yeah, it was no picnic.'

'You came home wounded?'

'Nope. Did three tours in all before deciding enough was enough. Left to take up a job working close protection security with an old mate of mine who'd set up his own business. It was all going smoothly when one day while on the job I heard the rattle of firearms and the concussive pounding of explosives. At the same time, I clocked that me and my protectee were surrounded by Taliban fighters swarming in off a hillside with us as their only targets. They weren't there, of course. Not physically. And none of what I saw and heard at that precise moment actually happened.' He paused to tap his temple. 'It was all inside here. On a positive note, because we're not allowed to be armed, I never killed anybody who happened to be standing close by. On the downside, not only did I lose my job, I also lost my reputation.'

Bliss could only imagine what the man must have gone through. 'I'm sorry to hear that, Mr Craig. And I apologise for using your own words against you, but is there a chance that what you saw earlier tonight never really happened, either?'

The homeless vet responded with a nod and a tight grin. 'I understand why you might think that. Difference is, this time I wasn't back in Afghanistan inside my head. And it wasn't insurgents that I saw. I came bursting out of the trees on the run, and on the path by the bridge I spotted a man choking the life out of another man with a length of cord or rope or something along those lines. I shouted out and started heading towards them. The attacker legged it. I ran across the bridge after him, but by then he'd disappeared into the trees. I turned and jogged back to the poor sod lying on the deck, but it was already too late. He wasn't breathing. I checked for a pulse, did a bit of CPR, but he was too far gone.'

Nodding, Bliss prompted him to explain further. 'Okay. So you found yourself in an awkward situation. What then?'

'I… I don't really know why, but I took off my heavy overcoat and covered him with it. As you might imagine, I don't have a mobile, but I knew the closest place to get help was probably the Ploughman pub, over by Tesco. I got there as quickly as I could, told the girl behind the bar what had happened. They gave your lot a bell. The landlord was kind enough to calm me down with a splash of brandy, even though I thought I was handling myself okay. Then your lot turned up, drove me back to the park, and we walked through to the bridge.'

'But the victim… the body, was no longer there.'

Craig shook his head almost in wonder. 'Just my coat. It was like he'd vanished into thin air while it was still draped over him. The two coppers looked at me as if I was bloody insane. That or just pulling a fast one. But I told them straight. I didn't imagine it. I wasn't screwing around with them, and I wasn't looking for a night in the cells. I saw somebody being murdered. I saw a dead body. I tried to save him, and when I couldn't, I covered him with my coat. In fact, when you find the body, it'll probably have a couple of broken ribs from me being too heavy handed with the resus attempt.'

'Can you describe the assailant?' Bliss asked.

'No. Not really. There aren't any lights by the bridge, so it was dark other than the moonlight. Impression I got… six feet plus, heavy set, and the way he moved, not a kid.'

'And the victim?'

'White. About the same height as his attacker, but younger and wiry. One of those awful chin beards; you know, a scruffy growth right on the point of the chin. There was also something over the bridge of his nose which might have been a scar. No tattoos that I could see.'

Bliss smiled. He'd expected the ex-paratrooper to have good physical recall. Craig also came across as both truthful and sane. 'And how was he dressed?'

'A plain sweatshirt, its hood pulled over his head. T-shirt, I think. Jeans and trainers.'

'And he wasn't familiar? You said you'd been sleeping in the park over the past few weeks, so is there any chance you'd seen him before?'

Craig gave a firm shake of the head. 'No. Not that I can recall.'

'Okay. So what do you think happened to the body?' Bliss asked.

'Me? I think the killer clocked me running off in the opposite direction, circled back, and probably disposed of the body in the lake.'

Narrowing his gaze, Bliss said, 'I find that unlikely. I mean, it stands to reason that anybody investigating a possible murder that close to a lake is going to search it for the missing body, right? So why risk returning to the scene only to shift it a few yards into an obvious place?'

Craig spread his hands. 'You're the detective, Inspector. I'm just an old self-medicating paratrooper. Could be they dumped it in the lake hoping the water would screw with your forensics.

But like I say, you're the detective. The one thing I do know is that a dead body didn't just stand up and walk out of there on its own.'

Bliss acknowledged this with a nod. 'That, my friend, is one thing we can agree on,' he said. 'Now, let's go over the whole thing one more time.'

THREE

DC ANSARI WAS SITTING in the Major Crime Unit working her way through CCTV footage from an ongoing case when Bliss entered from the second-floor corridor. The young constable looked up from her screen and raised her eyebrows.

'How'd it go?' she asked him. 'All sorted?'

'That is a good question.' He chewed on his bottom lip before slumping into a chair opposite and relating the broad strokes of the interview.

'So, what do you make of it?'

'I find myself in four minds, Gul. Tell me what you think. One: everything happened exactly as he says it did, and the killer returned to claim the body. Two: everything happened exactly as he says it did, only he got it wrong about the assault victim being dead. Three: he had some kind of PTSD episode and imagined the entire event. Or four: he made the whole thing up for reasons we don't yet know.'

Ansari considered the options for a moment, before saying, 'I'm inclined to rule out the first and last. The killer coming back to remove the body after being discovered would be a first for me. And Mr Craig didn't give me the impression of being a liar looking for his fifteen minutes of fame.'

Nodding, Bliss said, 'I'm with you. Neither of them sounds or feels quite right. I'm also not buying the PTSD argument, mainly because everything he described was set here and not in the desert. The killer and the victim he saw were regular people, not Taliban and some local Helmand tribesman. That leaves me with one solution. But Craig was once a trained soldier. He knew how to check for a pulse, carry out CPR, and genuinely believed the man was dead. So much so that he even took time to drape his own coat over the body before running for help. All of which makes me think my third option can't be right, either.' He paused to take a deep breath, exhaling slowly. 'But it may just be more right than wrong, because he's not infallible and he could have made a mistake.'

'Hmm. What do they call that, Occam's Razor?'

'That's the one. Basically, the simplest solution is usually the right one. But what does that leave us with?'

'Okay. Not a great deal clearer, then. So how do we proceed? Or do we? Without a body or the slightest sign of struggle, isn't this something to toss back to uniform?'

'Not yet, no. Because even if we don't like those options, it could be any of them and we have to make certain allowances.'

'And once made, we have to act.' It was as if DC Ansari could read his mind.

'Indeed. It's a puzzle. But it's one I'd like you to solve. I'm going home, but I'm leaving you with a list of jobs to organise.' Bliss paused, eyeing Ansari keenly. 'Where's Alan? Isn't he on lates as well this weekend?'

'He is. The duty inspector needed one of us to attend a burglary, so we tossed a coin and he won.'

He gave a sly grin. 'You and DC Virgil seem to be getting on rather well lately. I notice how he worked a change in rotation with Phil so that he'd be partnering up with you.'

Ansari regarded him with suspicion. 'What are you trying to suggest, Jimmy? You have something you want to ask me?'

Bliss shook his head innocently. 'Not at all. Just saying what I see and wondering out loud, that's all.'

'For your information, Alan and Phil swapped rotation at Phil's request. With his wedding coming up soon, the changes worked better for Phil and his fiancée. Alan didn't have a problem, and neither did I. Anything else you'd like to know?'

It was probably time to back off, but that wasn't Bliss's style. 'As you're asking,' he said, 'are you and Alan seeing each other?'

'He's not in my command line, so why does it matter?' the DC replied indignantly.

Chuckling, Bliss said, 'Easy there, tiger. Who said it mattered? I'm asking not as your boss but as a friend.'

Ansari closed her eyes for a moment, perhaps seeking to calm herself. When she opened them again, she looked chastened. 'I'm sorry, Jimmy. The truth is, we've been out together a few times. I don't know how ready I am for dating him, so it's baby steps at the moment. My family won't be pleased, that's for sure.'

'Because he's not Muslim or because he's a copper?'

'A bit of both,' she admitted. 'They can barely stomach *me* working for the police, so bringing home another officer who also happens to be a white Christian… If one of my brothers brought home a white girl, my parents wouldn't like it, but they would at least accept it. I don't see them making the same allowances for me, particularly my father.'

'I'm sorry to hear that, Gul.'

'Don't be. My father loves me, but he's unlikely to overlook his faith in favour of me. That's just the way things are. He actually might not be overly troubled by my dating Alan, but a father looks to the future, to a wedding, grandchildren somewhere down the line, and that will be his greatest challenge to overcome.'

Bliss nodded. He patted Ansari's hand. 'Trust me when I say I have no intention of adding to the drama. But I won't be the only one to have already noticed. In fact, I'm usually slow on the uptake when it comes to relationships, so I'm probably lagging way behind the others. As far as I'm concerned, you two are professionals and I trust your work will not be compromised. Mind you, it's time to think beyond me and how your next DI might react.'

Cupping her face in both hands, Ansari said, 'Please, don't. I can't even begin to think about that right now. It's impossible to imagine someone else sitting in your office. By the way, any word on who that might be?'

'Not yet. They interviewed two candidates but rejected them both.'

'There are strong rumours about DI Bentley wanting to move over from CID. Please tell me that's not going to happen, boss.'

Bliss noticed the look of angst on his colleague's face. He knew her fears would be shared by others in the team. Bentley was a good copper and he got results, but his methods and manner were questionable at best. He'd been known to throw colleagues under the bus in the furtherance of his own ambition and was widely disliked because of it.

He shook his head. 'Not going to happen, Gul. Not on a full-time basis, at least. Word coming down from further up the chain of command is that his career has plateaued unless he moves to another area. All my recent discussions on the subject have cen-tred on the possibility of persuading either Pen or Bish to step up.'

'Either of them would be great.' She checked her enthusiasm. 'Not that we want to lose you, Jimmy. But if we must, then con-tinuity is preferable.'

He made no immediate reply. DS Olly Bishop's recent behav-iour and attitude had started to concern him, something he intended to address in the coming days. Also, Bishop had previously enrolled in the Detective Inspector promotion training framework and had undertaken an acting DI role for a period of time, but had later stepped back out. The powers that be were likely to frown upon that and question his temperament and suitability. And when it came to Penny Chandler, she had no ambitions aimed at promotion; she was too busy living her best life as a DS.

'I agree,' he said eventually. 'But those two have their own lives to consider. I won't try to influence either of them, so I wouldn't count on it if I were you. But look, you know our senior leadership as well as I do. They won't bring in anyone who might throw a spanner in the works. Anyhow, the clock is ticking. Those jobs I mentioned...'

DC Ansari snapped off a mock salute. The action reminded him of another colleague, long gone and greatly missed. 'Yes, sir. Your word is my command.'

He gave a vague smile before continuing. 'I think we are obliged to treat this as if something actually did happen out there, Gul. But not to the point where I feel it's necessary to pull everybody in, because we have no real evidence to suggest there's a victim missing and a killer to hunt down.'

'Sounds about right to me.'

'So, here's what needs to be done: the uniforms who brought in Roger Craig had the presence of mind to bag up the man's overcoat. I want you to get that off to forensics ASAP. Fibres, skin cell transfer, DNA, the whole shebang.'

'And Mr Craig himself?' Ansari asked.

Bliss gave the question some thought. Judging by their conversation in the interview room, Roger Craig was not in the midst of some form of delusional breakdown. There was no reason to detain the man any further. It was an awkward situation, but not one that threw any suspicion on the ex-paratrooper.

'Ask him for his prints and a DNA swab,' Bliss told Ansari. 'He'll provide them without argument, I'm sure. Written statement, too, before he goes. In reference to the victim, let's have an initial uniform search of the surrounding area, including the fringes of the lake. If we get nothing from those sweeps, stick an underwater search team in there.'

'Are you sure about that, boss? That's a major call given we have no body.'

'It is, but the body could be in the water. Mr Craig suggested the killer might have returned to drag his victim into the lake, although that's not what I'm basing it on. I think that if the victim recovered consciousness, was perhaps disorientated as a result, they might easily have staggered into the water by accident.'

The young DC was looking quizzically at him. 'You really think that's likely, boss?'

He grinned. 'At this stage of my career, I'm not concerned about covering my own arse, but wouldn't we all look like prize pricks if we dismiss this one only to have a floater pop up in front of a bunch of kids feeding the ducks.'

Ansari arched her eyebrows. 'You have a point. Should I bring in PolSA?'

The Police Search Advisor team was good, but costly to any investigation due to the manpower – or person power as he was probably supposed to think of it these days. But in this case, the thought that their victim might have wandered away in a daze was all the nudge he needed. 'Yeah, go for it,' he said. 'If we're going to do it, let's do it properly. I'll authorise, you liaise, and we let the experts do their thing.'

Bliss turned to leave, then spun back around. 'One more thing. Have a word with the SSAFA. I'm not sure if it's still there, but they used to have an office in London Road at the Army Reserve Centre. Find out if our man was known to them, and if so, what they knew.'

'Sorry, the SS…?'

'It's the Soldiers', Sailors', and Airmen's Families Association. A charity for our service men and women. And before you ask, Gul, I just want to know this man better than I do at present. And when you're done with him, sort out a car to take him wherever he wants to go tonight.'

He left Thorpe Wood less than ten minutes later. He instructed DC Ansari to bother him only in the event of a result, before popping back to the interview room to arrange a meeting with Craig by the park bridge on Monday morning to go over the events as the man had experienced them.

'I'd just like you to walk me through it as you remember it,' he said.

'I'm free to leave?' Craig asked, somewhat bemused.

'Of course.' Bliss nodded. 'You always were. My DC is coming down in a few minutes to have a chat and take your statement. I'll make sure you get a ride back to the park afterwards to grab your things and then have them take you wherever you like. We have no choice but to move you on because it's a potential crime scene, but I'm sure you have other places to go. I'd let you stay here, but it's Friday night, so I don't think they can spare you a cell.'

'No problem. I'd rather be outside.'

The two men shook hands. 'See you Monday morning,' Bliss said.

He drove home unsatisfied with the outcome, not quite knowing what to believe or expect of the next few days.

FOUR

MONDAY MORNING AT 7.30AM found Jimmy Bliss at a desk poring over ongoing caseload files to see if any fresh information had been unearthed over the weekend. No movement on any of them meant he and the team would spend the first briefing discussing outstanding and future actions. Crime was a growth industry in Peterborough, with a dramatic increase in serious and violent crimes over the past decade. Not every investigation got the time it deserved, but there were only a certain number of hours in the day. Swingeing budget and staffing cuts were partially responsible, but the societal impact ran far deeper than that.

He had approached and entered the building earlier with a curious eye. It had been a long time since he'd taken notice of his surroundings in terms of the police station in which he worked, and perhaps because this was the start of his final week as a card-carrying police officer he was acutely aware of every creaking, groaning, eyesore inch of it.

The austere facade never looked anything less than grim, with its dirty-sand bricks and water-stained lintels. The style was typical of buildings thrown up in new towns and developing cities across the country during the seventies; lacking in architectural flair, imagination, and without the finances to strive for better. The interior had seen some cosmetic improvements and modifications while ignoring the more fundamental need for improved plumbing, heating, air-conditioning, and electrics. But what Bliss saw when driving in was an exterior that probably hadn't so much as been cleaned since the final brick was first laid.

The offices and open plan working areas such as the one he sat in were functional and no more. New carpeting and decorations improved the look and feel, and the once almost overpowering fug of smoke was, of course, long gone. The biggest change had come about with the introduction of new technology, with monitors on most desks, the computers themselves hidden away. It was a dour and bland building, but then Bliss believed the inspiration had always come from the people who worked within.

Over the next ten or fifteen minutes the room gradually began to fill up around him. In between slurps of black tea from the flask he'd brought from home, he called out a greeting to each member of the Major Crime team as they came within earshot. He was especially pleased to see that DS Bishop had recovered well enough to come in, though the big man appeared more than usually dishevelled and not altogether present. When Detective Sergeant Penny Chandler breezed through the doors, she immediately sought him out.

'Morning, Jimmy,' she said brightly, shedding her jacket and perching herself on the edge of a nearby desk. 'How did it go with Molly this weekend?'

The young woman he'd spent the weekend with had been no more than a child at her lowest possible ebb when she entered their lives. Bliss had prevented her from jumping from a hotel roof, and in the days that followed, the kid who had already lived the lives of ten people touched their own in an indelible way. Having subsequently been relocated, fostered, and later adopted by the same family, Molly had grasped her second chance at a decent future with both hands. Her particular affection for the man who both stopped her from taking her old life and encouraged her to settle into a new one had endured. The two often talked on the phone, he had made several trips down to Torquay where she lived with her new family, while Molly had also visited him on a couple of occasions after the city had once again been deemed safe for her to return to. Nobody questioned the disparity in their ages or their fondness for one another, for nobody regarded his role in her life as anything other than either paternal or avuncular.

Bliss smiled at the more recent memory. 'It went very well, thanks. But far too quickly for either of us, so she decided to stick around a while longer. She already prefers to spend time with Max than she does me, so it works out well for both of them my being at work today.'

Chandler laughed and dismissed his observation with a flap of a hand. 'That is not true, and you know it. That girl adores you, Jimmy. None of us can understand why, not unless she has a thing for grumpy old buggers. But even a dog as lovely as Max isn't going to take your place in Molly's affections.'

'Well, either way, she's welcome for as long as she wants to be here.'

'She might as well stay until your retirement do this Saturday.'

The reminder caught him unawares, hitting him like a punch to the midriff. With the way his shift rota had been scheduled and allowing for annual leave days he was owed, he knew all too well this was his last full week as a Detective Inspector. Even so, he was startled anew every time the dying embers of his career as a police officer were stoked. He swallowed down some tea to buy time and cover the abrupt shift in his mood.

'Good idea,' he said. 'No reason why she shouldn't.'

'I'm sure it'll be nice to have her around.'

He tilted a hand one way and then the other. 'We'll see. She shows me about as much respect as you do.'

Chandler sucked air between her teeth. 'Ooh. That bad, eh?'

Bliss nodded dolefully. 'I sometimes wonder why I bother with either of you.'

She chuckled. 'Simples. Because you love us. Anyhow, I heard you had a shout on Friday night. Anything we need to talk about?'

He gave her a thumbs-up and briefly outlined the details. 'We may need to spend some time with it today,' he told her. 'There was no further movement over the weekend, which means POLSA did not find a body. Nor any evidence to suggest there ever was one. I'm not quite sure if that's a good or bad thing under the circumstances.'

'Gul said the witness asked for you by name. Did you know him?'

'No. He knew of me from the Adrian Summerby case a few years back. Seemed to think that meant I had some kind of sympathetic ear for the homeless.'

'And do you? I mean, what was the deal there?'

Bliss shrugged. 'I genuinely don't know, Pen. You remember the case?'

'How could I not? He got beaten and kicked to death by a bunch of scumbags. As I recall, Bish was even more fired up about it at the time than you were.'

'I think that's because he was also ex-forces. Serving in some capacity runs in Bish's blood, so it doesn't take much to stir him when a veteran is involved. Me, I reckon it's a crying shame that we don't take better care of them. And nobody deserves to end their days the way Summerby did.'

'The fact that you called in PolSA tells me you believed this Mr Craig.'

Reclining in the office chair, Bliss said, 'Yeah. As it happens, I did. I'm meeting him at around ten by the bridge over at the lake, which is approximately where he says the murder took place. He's going to walk me through it stage by stage. I genuinely don't know if we have a case yet, and I could see nothing in the weekend reports to suggest we have a relevant misper on our hands. I'm hoping something more will come to him today. Whether that's recalling the incident in greater detail or realising it never happened, I suppose we'll see.'

'I can understand why you gave it the necessary time, but to be honest his story looks pretty weak in the cold light of another day.'

Rising to his feet, Bliss gave a reluctant nod. 'It feels that way, Pen. I'm currently unconvinced, but still curious. Let's get morning prayers out of the way and then we'll go over it one more time.'

Bliss was ten minutes into the briefing when DCI Diane Warburton entered the room. 'Sorry to interrupt, but this can't wait,' she said. 'Jimmy, we need to speak to you upstairs in the conference room. Hand off to Bish or Penny, please.'

Before he could react, she was gone again, the door thumping closed behind her. Bewildered by the brusque interruption, he wound down the set of actions he'd been discussing, before passing the baton to DS Bishop. He'd been surprised by his boss's absence from the meeting and couldn't help but wonder what had been so important. He walked to the end of the corridor and took the stairs up to the third floor, past Detective Superintendent Marion Fletcher's empty office, only to find her in the conference room with Warburton and the recently promoted Detective Superintendent Alicia Edwards seated either side of her.

'Morning, Jimmy,' Fletcher said. 'Park your bum and make yourself comfortable for a few minutes.'

WHAT DIES INSIDE US

Bliss took a seat opposite. The DSI's voice was warm but reserved. So, no bollocking, but not good news, either. 'What's up?' he asked apprehensively.

Fletcher's face turned serious. 'On Friday night, you were called in by DC Ansari at the request of a man by the name of Roger Craig. Is that correct?'

'It is. He claimed to have witnessed a murder in Werrington.'

'Indeed, he did. But no body, no victim at all, was discovered. Yet you requested a PolSA team, so you must have given credence to his claim.'

He wondered what was going on, concerned by the line Fletcher was taking. 'Not entirely,' he admitted. 'But neither could I dismiss it out of hand.'

In the silence that followed, he felt a twist of anxiety. He met his DSI's focussed gaze. 'Marion, what's going on here? What is this meeting about, and why does it involve me?'

'It involves all of us because the immediate issue is one of accountability. At the end of the month, I move up to replace DCS Feeley, while at the same time, Alicia here gets her feet under my desk. There's also the question of whether you want to tackle a murder op this close to retirement.'

Shifting uncomfortably in his seat, Bliss looked down his nose at the question even being put to him. 'You really have to ask? Of course I want it.'

Fletcher nodded, linking her hands together on the table. 'I suspected as much. Jimmy, am I correct in saying you had no prior connection to this Roger Craig?' she asked.

'That's right, yes. He asked to speak with me because he'd read about an old case of ours in a newspaper article.'

'What was your impression of him?'

Bliss took a beat or two to answer that one. He thought back to their meeting, Craig's deeply intelligent eyes and earnest voice.

'An honourable man brought to his knees by a system that let him down. From what he told me, he returned from service with PTSD, but because it failed to manifest itself immediately, he never received the support or treatment he needed. He lost everything and wound up sleeping rough. Though less rough than others, I suspect, given he'd spent time in the desert and all that brings.'

'So… not the kind of man to tell tall tales? To report a murder he had not actually witnessed.'

'Not deliberately, no. Not with any malice, at least. But he wasn't well, and although not drunk, he'd clearly had a couple of beers. Add to that the lack of a victim and him admitting to me that he'd had prior incidents where he'd hallucinated, it was a tough one to call. Look, I'm sorry for being so blunt, but what the bloody hell is going on? Are you going to tell me there was a victim after all, that we somehow missed a dead body on Friday night?'

Superintendent Fletcher cleared her throat. 'Jimmy, I'm sorry to tell you this, but earlier this morning the body of a man fitting the description of Roger Craig was found by a couple taking a walk through Cuckoo's Hollow park. He'd been murdered.'

Bliss felt an icy chill whisper over his exposed skin. Suddenly, all he could hear was the high-pitched screech of tinnitus raging in both ears. Bile rose up into his throat, and he swallowed it back down with a grimace.

'How?' he asked.

'We don't have all the details, but the first officers on scene reported blood loss resulting from a possible stabbing.'

'Please tell me it didn't happen while we had a police presence in the park.'

'I can't guarantee it at this stage, not without the post-mortem results and time of death. It's not likely, though. Cuckoo's Hollow is not a large park, and neither is the lake. Both searches were over before sundown on Saturday evening. We couldn't justify keeping officers at the scene or people out of the park when we were unable to confirm a crime had taken place. We therefore believe the murder took place sometime yesterday.'

Bliss rubbed the scar on his forehead. Craig had been moved on from his spot on Friday night. Why had he returned two days later?

'You said he fit the description. Who described him?'

'The woman who made the call mentioned the victim looked homeless. They also mentioned his skin colour. The car that caught the shout picked up a local PCSO on the way to attend. The community officer knew Mr Craig reasonably well.'

Bliss ran both hands across his face, exhaling over steepled fingers. His mind was racing, yet his thoughts were clear. 'This is no coincidence,' he said dejectedly. 'Roger Craig did witness a murder, did attempt to prevent it, and did chase off the attacker. But that same attacker not only returned to remove the body, they also came back for our homeless veteran. The killer knew he'd been seen, and therefore could potentially be described. Whoever it was covered their tracks by murdering our only witness. And I let him go back out there to die.'

FIVE

BLISS WAS QUIETER THAN usual during the drive to Werrington. He silently questioned if he could have done more to prevent Roger Craig from being murdered. While his head told him he couldn't have anticipated what would become of the homeless veteran, his heart refused to give up on the notion. Logically, it was hard to think of anything he might have overlooked, said, or done, yet the nagging doubts persisted. He wondered if his determination to spend more time with Molly had distracted him.

As they arrived at the scene and spotted onlookers standing outside their front doors or gathered together on the pavement in small, animated pods, Bliss huffed angrily. 'Look at them,' he sneered. 'There's a fairly broad line between curiosity and morbidness, and this lot are on the wrong side of it.'

Chandler gave him a sidelong glance. 'The only difference between this and any other crime scene we've attended is your mood,' she said. 'Gawkers gotta gawk, Jimmy. Same way they do at the twisted wreckage following a road traffic collision. It doesn't usually bother you.'

He accepted her point with a shrug. 'You're right. I just can't help feeling that our victim didn't have to die. He came to us… came to me, and I sent him away.'

'Bollocks! You heard him out. You couldn't have known he was in any danger. Enough with the self-pity, Jimmy. Let's do what we do and find the bastard who murdered him.'

Bliss parked alongside a line of liveried traffic vehicles. It was an unseasonably warm late-April day, the increasing moisture-laden heat prompting him to loosen the knot of his tie and undo the top button of his shirt the moment they exited the car. He took a deep breath before looking at his partner.

'Sometimes I hate this bloody job,' he said.

Chandler peered at him over the rim of her sunglasses. 'And yet we don't seem to be able to get rid of you.'

'Like you could cope without me.'

A uniformed officer made a note of their presence at the scene before allowing them to pass beneath an entrance cordoned off by taut ribbons of fluttering tape. Bliss didn't know the park well but had been told to expect a heavily policed area due to the number of entrances into Cuckoo's Hollow. The pair were directed off the pathway into the trees towards a small gathering of white-suited crime scene investigators. The area CSI manager was on holiday, so today his deputy, Lydia Keene, was in charge. As they approached the tent erected over the body, she handed each of them a bag of protective clothing.

'Good morning, Lydia,' Bliss said cheerfully. 'How's your luck?'

The woman rolled her eyes. 'You tell me,' she replied. 'Over the weekend I finally got a date with the pleasant young Barista chap from the coffee place I go to every day. Ten minutes into our date I discover he's neither overly pleasant nor a man.'

'What?!'

'That was my reaction, too. Evidently, *he* happens to be a *she*. And I mean, she still has all the bits I do. So, when she drops this into our conversation, I go into panic mode. Not so long ago you could just tell someone there'd been a mistake, that you didn't swing that way. There's me almost having a fit over whether it's somehow offensive to reject a person these days just because they're not the sex you happen to favour. And just at the point where I told myself I was being silly, she proved me wrong.'

'Wait, what?' Chandler said. 'Are you telling me this woman threw a wobbly over you rejecting her because she wasn't a man?'

'Just about. She turned quite nasty because, even though she looks like a man, dresses like a man, walks and talks like a man, but is actually a woman, I'm supposed to ignore all that and date her anyway.'

Unable to help himself any longer, Bliss started to laugh. 'I'm sorry, Lydia. Only you could get yourself into a scrape like that.'

Keene scowled at first, but then saw the funny side. 'I ended up feeling dreadful about it. I told her I was sorry, but I was into men so couldn't go ahead seeing her because she was a woman. And that was the thing… she *was* still a woman, actually identified as a woman, only she chose to present herself as a man. So, go on then, you tell me how my luck is.'

Bliss pulled his best sympathetic face. 'On the whole, not great,' he admitted.

She grunted at him. 'I tell you, Jimmy, it's a minefield out there in the dating world.'

'He's too decrepit to care about that sort of thing anymore,' Chandler remarked.

Ignoring his partner, Bliss started climbing into the white suit. He nodded at the clipboard Keene held in one hand. 'How far along are you?' he asked.

'We're getting there. The victim has some shocking wounds. I'd say cleaver or machete over carving knife or similar.'

Bliss winced at the thought of the man he'd spoken to on Friday night suffering such a brutal attack. 'Any defensive injuries?'

Shaking her head, Keene said, 'Nothing obvious in respect of the bladed weapon. You might have to wait for the pathologist, but whatever we find will be in my report.'

'In that case, I'm betting he was grabbed from behind. Mr Craig was an ex-Para, and still had his wits about him. I don't see him getting caught cold by a frontal attack.'

'I'd say you were spot on, Jimmy. Though there are signs of a separate attempt. The skin around his throat was scuffed, possibly by some kind of cord. I found similar markings on the palms of both hands and on his fingers, as if he had grabbed at it to wrench it free. Again, the post-mortem will tell you more, but I think he might have shrugged off an initial attack, which resulted in his killer resorting to using the blade.'

The first thing Bliss noticed as they entered the tent was Craig's face. One thing he had learned over the years was that death had an impact on expressions, with violent passing resulting in the widest variety. New recruits expected masks of pain, terror, or horror, forever etched into the creases and folds of flesh. But the truth was, most appearances were mere empty shells. Life extinct was often how the dead were pronounced, and he thought it best summed them up. In Craig's case, the man looked almost resigned.

As if he had somehow accepted his fate.

As if he had perhaps welcomed it.

But not like this, Bliss thought. Although the worst of the wounds were hidden beneath the folds and creases of slashed clothing, a gaping maw had been opened up across the face from just below the nose, reaching almost to the top of the ear.

'Surprisingly, not likely to be the one that killed him,' Lydia Keene said, following his gaze. 'There's a deep laceration along the inside of his right arm. I suspect the brachial artery was severed and he bled out from that. The pathologist will confirm, of course, but that's my take.'

Bliss frowned. He wondered if the cut had been accidental or deliberate. The latter would suggest a more skilled assailant. Despite his lack of nourishment and natural muscle wastage from living on the streets, Craig would not have surrendered easily.

'How many wounds in total?' Chandler asked the crime scene deputy manager.

'I've not examined the body in detail as yet, but so far I've counted four. All deep and long. Applied with some force.'

'So, a man?'

Keene nodded. 'I'd say so. A strong woman with a very sharp weapon might be capable, but again, you'll know more after the PM.'

Having found his gaze wandering back over Roger Craig's face, Bliss couldn't help but recall their conversation on Friday night. The way he had described having to listen to the breeze in order to stay alive was chilling, and it was hard to believe that same man had been taken by surprise. At least, not by somebody who lacked the necessary training.

But then he reminded himself that words were cheap, and time could be the fiercest of adversaries people ever had to encounter. In an active war zone, men like Craig were mentally and physically attuned to their surroundings. During moments when a single lack of concentration might cost you your life, it was only natural for instinctive defence mechanisms to function at their peak. Back here in the real world, weakened by circumstances, perhaps enshrined in a false sense of security or possibly even apathy, Craig had become vulnerable.

'I know it's the pathologist's job,' he said to Keene, 'but any idea on time of death?'

She gave him a knowing smile. 'Unlike my boss, I'm willing to be flexible. I can be, you know, given the right circumstances. The body was in full rigor when I arrived, so I'd say our victim has been dead for at least eight hours.'

Bliss thanked Keene, and after discarding the protective garments headed out of the trees, back onto the path towards the bridge. Chandler hurried after him. There were two wooden bridges traversing the lake, one at each end. Their homeless veteran had described the longer of the two as the spot where he had seen the attack taking place and had subsequently administered CPR to the victim. There might be nothing to see, but Bliss wanted to not see it for himself.

The bridge provided little of interest. Slightly convex and basic in structure, about two dozen paces in length, it was functional and no more. Swans and ducks lingered in the still water below, perhaps anticipating food. Bliss turned to face the trees. If Craig had been in roughly the same place when he heard the scuffle as he was when he was murdered, he would have appeared in the open about fifty or sixty yards away from the two men. Illuminated only by the moon, it was entirely understandable that he had not been able to identify the attacker.

'What are you thinking?' Chandler asked him.

Bliss looked up. 'I'm asking myself what was so important about the victim Roger Craig tried to save.'

'Important?'

'Well, not only did the killer make sure to remove the body, but they also came back to silence our homeless vet. I'd say that means the first victim was significant in some way. To whoever murdered him, at least.'

Nodding, Chandler said, 'Whoever that victim was, somebody has to be missing him by now.'

'You'd think. But no relevant mispers have been reported.'

'Maybe he wasn't local.'

This time it was Bliss's turn to nod. 'You could be right. We have to extend our enquiries. I want to know who he was, why he was here, and why somebody wanted him dead.'

'If they wanted him dead.'

'What do you mean?' he asked.

Chandler surveyed the scene and shrugged. 'We still don't have a body, remember? I'm not saying things didn't go exactly as you described, Jimmy, but let's not get ahead of ourselves.'

SIX

As THE PAIR TRUDGED back into the heart of Thorpe Wood station, a female uniform urgently waved a hand at them as she spoke into the phone. She jabbed the mute button and said, 'We have somebody waiting to talk to you two. A woman reporting her husband missing.'

'Sounds positive,' Bliss said. 'Or negative, depending on your point of view, I suppose. Where is she?'

'I put her in the public interview room myself ten minutes ago. We were given notice of the situation at Cuckoo's Hollow Park during the morning briefing and told to keep our ears open for a misper fitting the description. I think this could be our man's wife, Inspector.'

'Name?'

'Sharon McKenzie.'

Bliss thanked the officer, before he and Chandler walked over to a separate room attached to the reception area and stepped inside. The woman waiting for them on a two-seater sofa looked up in alarm. She was thin and frail and mousey, lank hair tied up in a large bun that covered her scalp. She wore sizeable, hooped earrings, a short denim jacket over a pale yellow dress, and was barelegged, her feet tucked inside flat-heeled canvas shoes. As Chandler closed the door behind her, Mrs McKenzie's left hand shot to her mouth, at which point she began nibbling on chipped fingernails.

Bliss and Chandler introduced themselves before taking a seat on either side of the sofa. He flashed a warm smile and said, 'Mrs McKenzie, I believe you're here today to report your husband missing.'

'Um, yes. Yes, that's right. My husband, Stuart.' Her accent suggested she was locally born and bred.

'I'm sorry to hear that,' Bliss said gently. 'When was the last time you saw or spoke to him?'

'Friday. Just after lunch. He said he had a bit of business to take care of. That was it.'

'No phone calls or text messages since?'

She shook her head vigorously. 'No, nothing at all.'

'I assume you've tried to contact him?'

'Of course. I called his mobile, left voicemails, sent texts and WhatsApp messages. I contacted his parents, his sister and brother, and the friends I know. None of them have seen him or heard from him since he walked out of the house.'

Bliss leaned forward. 'Was he angry or distressed when he left? Had you two been fighting at the time?'

'No. We hardly ever quarrel.'

'In which case, you must be extremely concerned.'

'Of course I am. I'm frantic with worry.'

'Understandably so. Might I ask, then, Mrs McKenzie, why you left it almost three days before reporting your husband missing?'

Waving aside the question, the woman said, 'Because three days is his limit. Look, let me explain. Stu has often gone out and not come home again for a couple of nights. But not to come back by now or call me is unlike him. So I phoned around, and the people he usually hangs about with hadn't even heard from him, let alone seen him. That's when I started to worry. I've never known him go off on his own before.'

Bliss wondered what kind of relationship these two people had when one of them could be away from home for days without saying why beforehand. As unlikely as it seemed to him, perhaps it worked well for the couple. He regarded McKenzie closely as he considered the next step.

'Did you leave a description with the officer who took your details?' he asked.

'Yes, I did, but she told me you'd want me to go over it again.'

'If you would. Please. Let's begin with height and build.'

'Six-two, but scrawny with it. You could probably snap him in two.'

Bliss ignored the comment. 'Ethnicity?' he asked.

'British. White. Whiter than most, as it goes.' She smiled at her own feeble attempt at humour.

He could tell she wasn't anticipating never seeing her husband alive again.

'Any significant features? Does he wear glasses or a hearing aid? Does he have any facial hair? Any scars or tattoos? Is he disabled in any way?'

Sharon McKenzie rocked back in her chair, puffing out her cheeks. 'Blimey. Well, no specs or hearing problems. He has one of those chin beards; you know what I mean, the stupid tuft of hair on the end of his chin. Ink on both arms. Oh, and a small scar over the bridge of his nose.'

Bliss's heart sank, but at the same time it began to pump furiously. It was starting to sound as if Roger Craig hadn't been hallucinating after all. 'Do you recall what he was wearing on Friday, Mrs McKenzie?'

She shook her head. 'Sorry, no. Usually in decent weather he's a T-shirt and jeans man. Probably a hoodie, too.'

'If he had decided to go away for the weekend, wouldn't he have come home to pack at least an overnight bag.?'

'Not necessarily. He always kept a change of clothes at the office or in the boot of his car.'

Studiously avoiding exchanging glances with Chandler, Bliss said, 'I am going to need you to complete a missing persons report when we're done here. At this stage, however, I have to advise you of my concerns. Before I begin, please understand that we have no more details than those I'm about to give you. A great deal is still unknown to us, but I will tell you what we have so far. Are you ready, Mrs McKenzie?'

She blinked at him, fearful. 'I… I'm not sure. I don't like the sound of this. Has Stu got himself into trouble? Has he been arrested? Has he been hurt?'

'Let me explain, and then we can both ask our questions. Before I begin, can you think of any reason why your husband might have been in Cuckoo's Hollow Park on Friday night?'

'No. I don't even know where that is.'

'It's in Werrington.'

'We live in Longthorpe.'

'Might he have been in that area on business?'

'Not that I can think of.'

'To visit with friends or family, maybe?'

'Again, no. I don't think we know anyone there. Look, please tell me what's going on. I'm bricking it here.'

Bliss nodded and got into it. 'On Friday night, a homeless man reported intervening in a fight between two men. He chased off the attacker, attempted to resuscitate the victim, but on believing him to have died went in search of help.'

'Oh my God!' McKenzie cried, clutching a hand to her chest. 'Are you saying my Stu is dead?'

'No, I'm not,' Bliss said firmly. 'And for one specific reason, which I'll come to. The description you gave closely matches the one provided by our witness. To that extent, we can reasonably assume something happened between your husband and this other man, who remains unidentified. However, when both the witness and our officers arrived back at the scene, there was no body to be found. What I'm saying to you, Mrs McKenzie, is that while I do believe your husband was involved in an altercation with somebody else that night, we have no indication as to what became of him afterwards. There have been no reports made to us, and a check of the hospital came up negative.'

'So… you don't know if he's dead or alive, or stumbling around somewhere injured and maybe hurt so badly he doesn't remember anything?'

'That's about the size of it, I'm sorry to say. We searched the park and the pond itself and are doing everything we can at this stage to find him. I can't tell you we're launching a murder enquiry because we have no physical evidence to justify that. But we are treating it as a major crime and we'll be conducting a thorough investigation. I'm hoping you can help with that.'

Visibly distraught, McKenzie gathered herself together enough to nod and splutter, 'Of course. Whatever you need.'

'Good. Then let me tell you how we'll approach the next few hours. To begin with, we will work on the presumption that Stuart is alive. We'll obtain a list of family and friends from you, known haunts, information connected to his work, in short as much detail about his life and your lives as a couple that we consider useful. At the same time, we will analyse in more detail the incident itself, at which point we'll consider alternative outcomes. I don't want to alarm you, Mrs McKenzie, but neither am I about to offer false hope. The situation is as I said before, in that we are open-minded about what took place on Friday night and are considering all eventualities.'

After a few moments, the terrified-looking woman jerked her head up and said, 'What about this witness? The man you say tried to help Stu. How much help has he been?'

'We wouldn't know anything about this incident if it weren't for him coming forward,' Chandler said. 'He heard the scuffle. He ran towards it, which most people wouldn't. He called out and chased off the attacker. He then applied CPR, after which he ran to get help. He came willingly to the station to give us a full statement. He was about as helpful as he could be.'

'When did you last speak with him? On Friday night?'

'Yes. Into the early hours of Saturday morning.'

'So he might remember more now, right? I've heard that can happen.' There was a desperate edge to her voice, and hope burned in her eyes.

This time, Bliss and Chandler did look at each other. He gave his partner a nod and steeled himself for Sharon McKenzie's response to finding out that the only witness to the possible murder of her husband was also dead.

SEVEN

THE RIVER WAS BEAUTIFUL at that time of year. Chandler's apartment complex was too close to traffic and the hustle and bustle of people crossing the old town bridge for the location to be regarded as idyllic, Bliss mused, but you couldn't knock the view. The water was high after recent heavy rainfall, but its languid flow beguiled all those who paused long enough to notice. It was almost crystal clear, as it often was in early spring. A variety of waterfowl peppered the surface, the cacophony of noise they created with their calls not at all unpleasant. Their presence caused great excitement in young children spread out along the embankment.

The two detectives gazed down at the Nene while they ate ham sandwiches prepared by Chandler in her tiny galley kitchen. Both sipped iced water drawn straight from the fridge.

'I like it here,' Bliss said contentedly, wishing his drink also contained various grains, hops, and yeast. 'I've been thinking about moving and watching the river sliding by gives me the urge to do something about it.'

'What, into *this* building?'

He laughed while clutching a hand to his chest as if wounded. 'Don't sound so horrified by the prospect.'

Chandler nudged him with her hip. 'No, I didn't mean it that way. It just doesn't seem like an upgrade from what you already have.'

'That's true. Which is why if I do move, it won't be to here. So, consider yourself safe. Property values won't drop, and you won't have a neighbour problem to deal with. No, I think I'd want something a bit more secluded, away from the city centre. Somewhere quiet but overlooking the river further downstream. Or upstream.'

'What's stopping you?'

'Sad to say, but it's the garden. A lot of time, effort, and money went into its creation. It's my oasis of tranquillity. That's harder to find than you might imagine.'

'Jimmy, you can put in a pond and bring your fish with you wherever you go, provided you buy something suitable. The plants and rocks and bamboo bridge and all the other stuff can be pulled out and recreated no matter where you move to. Blaming your indecision on the garden is a load of old tosh.'

Bliss hated it when Chandler was right. The truth was, while he wanted a more peaceful place to live, which was also easier on the eye and not so close to neighbouring homes, the thought of packing up the contents of his house and moving filled him with dread.

'Can you imagine ever not being part of the chase?' Chandler asked him, a wistful note to her voice.

Bliss cocked his head. 'What brought that question on?' he asked, surprised by the abrupt change of direction.

'I don't know. It sounds to me as if you're talking about a place to retire to. And I mean proper retirement, not this half-arsed one you've worked out for yourself. Don't get me wrong, I'm happy you've extended your time with us in your new role as a civilian worker, and being part of the new unsolved unit as well is a great move for you. But I know you, Jimmy. Before long, you'll come to regard it as a postponement of the inevitable – if you haven't already. And in doing so, you'll ask yourself what comes next, at which point your mind will get stuck in that loop.'

Bliss sighed. 'Pen, I'm already as old as dirt. And if I ever happen to come across as a little maudlin, let's assume it's the Irish in me. When the time comes, I'll be ready for it. By then I'll be clapped out and fit only for afternoons measured out with coffee spoons and TS Eliot, as the *Crash Test Dummies* so succinctly put it.'

'I don't think I know that one.'

He gave a sniff of lofty superiority. 'Molly would.'

'That's because you've indoctrinated the poor girl. You've carried out some form of Psy-Op on her and brainwashed her into thinking music from the seventies and eighties is somehow superior to anything that's come since.'

'Don't forget the sixties,' Bliss reminded her.

'What's the song about, anyway?'

'Growing old and passing our time differently than we once did, while we wind down the clock.'

'Apt then, in your case.'

Bliss nodded. 'Definitely so. And on that note, care to share your thoughts on this bizarre case of ours?'

Chandler puffed out her cheeks. She used a fingernail as a temporary piece of dental floss before polishing off her drink. 'If I had any thoughts, I would. To be honest, I'm mystified. I think we have to accept that it was Stuart McKenzie who was attacked. What became of him after that… who knows?'

'And where to begin looking for answers? It's all very well me pacifying his wife by telling her how we're going to deal with the incident, but going about it is another matter entirely. As angry as I am about what happened to Roger Craig, I'm thinking we have to put his murder to one side, because if we find who attacked Stuart McKenzie, then we find the man who murdered our homeless vet.'

'I agree.'

Bliss frowned. 'You do?'

'Yes. Why, is that a problem?'

'Not as such. I just get worried when you agree with me.'

Chandler hissed between her teeth. 'Don't say that. Great minds think alike, remember?'

He ignored the dazzling smile she followed up with. 'I do. But I also remember that fools seldom differ.'

'Typical. Jimmy Bliss. The original *glass is half empty* man.'

He snorted and shook his head. 'Pen, sometimes I don't think you know me at all.'

'Oh? Why?'

'Because that's not me.'

'It's not?'

'No. To me, there was never anything in the glass to begin with.'

EIGHT

THE EASTERN INDUSTRY DISTRICT of Peterborough was pretty much as described. The industrial hub of the city vibrated with well-honed activity. Few people strolled the pavements even on such a balmy day, but the roads were clogged with traffic. Second-hand car dealerships littered the area, though Bliss estimated there were fifty percent fewer than when he had first moved up from London. Emerging from the welcome but brief shade of a flyover into Fengate, he turned onto the forecourt leading to Platinum Standard Cars and parked in the area designated for customers.

The pair followed signs for the reception, which led them to a single-storey building, its bright green apex roof hard to miss. Bliss showed his warrant card to a young girl of no more than eighteen or so who sat behind a scruffy wooden desk littered with scraps of paper, wallet folders, Post-It notes in a myriad of colours, and a black laptop on which she was intently focussed.

'We'd like a word with the owner, please,' Bliss said. 'If they're not in, the manager will do.'

She barely glanced at his credentials. Without looking up from the computer screen, she said in a disinterested monotone voice, 'We have three owners. Which of them would you like to speak to?'

'Whichever is available?'

'That would be none of them, then.'

The young woman was messing with him, but Bliss remained calm. 'Then the manager will do just fine, thanks.'

'He's busy.'

'We can wait.'

Still not looking up, she said, 'He could be a while. Why don't you give me your name and make an appointment?'

'Tell you what, why don't you drag yourself away from playing Solitaire or whatever you're wasting your life doing and tell your boss the police are here to talk to him about Stuart McKenzie?'

The venom in his voice seemed to snag her attention. Her eyes flickered before meeting his. 'Mr McKenzie *is* one of the owners.'

'That's not news to us.'

'What's this about?'

The deep frown of concern wrinkling her forehead told Bliss it might have been more than his abrupt tone that had prompted her to take an interest. 'It's about us wanting to speak with your manager,' he said coolly. 'It's also about me getting somewhat irritated with you mucking us about. Now, are you going to get your manager, or do I have to thump my fist on every closed door in this place?'

The girl clicked her tongue, which she then rolled around the inside of her cheek. After a brief stand-off, she picked up the receiver on her desk phone and tapped a number. 'Some people are here in reception looking for you, Jacob. They say they're the police, but I'm not convinced.' She tossed Bliss the sweetest and most insincere of smiles.

Before she could replace the handset, a door directly behind the reception desk opened and a large, balding man beckoned the two detectives into his office. As they stepped beyond the desk, Bliss caught the girl's eye and winked. 'You'll go far in life,' he said. 'But you'd better hope you never cross my path again.'

The man introduced himself as Jacob Nash and gestured for them to sit. Bliss pulled over a chair and took up his usual position to the left of Chandler.

'What can I do for the police?' Nash asked pleasantly enough.

'We're here about Stuart McKenzie,' Bliss told him. 'Tell me, would you normally have expected to see him in the office today?'

Other than a faint smile, the man's reaction gave little away. 'Not… not normally, no.'

'You say that as if him being here would be a rarity.'

'As one of the owners, Stuart is free to come and go as he pleases.'

'Of course. Exactly how often would he do that?'

Nash ran a hand down his face, making a show of considering his response. 'Half a dozen times a year. Maybe. When he and the other owners had one of their *board meetings*.' He wrapped air quotes around the emphasised words.

'Sounds to me as if you're implying they were owners in name only,' Chandler said.

'I'm not *implying* anything, Detective. They own the business and run it the way they see fit. I manage the day-to-day operations and they allow me to do that without constant micro-managing, for which I am grateful.'

'I'm sure you do a fine job. Though you could do worse than get rid of your receptionist,' Bliss suggested.

This time, Nash chuckled and shook his head. 'The majority of people who work here are either related to or friends of one or other of the owners. Our Natalie on the desk is one of them. Unfortunately, she would prefer not to be here, and she doesn't care who knows it.'

'Is she one of Mr McKenzie's relatives?' Bliss asked. 'I thought I noticed a flicker of concern when I mentioned his name.'

'Yes. Distantly, I believe.' Nash spread his hands and looked pained. 'Look, I'm sorry to press you, but I do have a busy day ahead. What is this about?'

'We're here this morning because Mr McKenzie has been reported missing,' Bliss told him.

'Missing?' The manager appeared genuinely surprised. 'Stuart? Since when?'

'Friday. His wife reported his absence earlier this morning. I don't suppose one of those board meetings happened to take place on Friday, did it, Mr Nash?'

The question provoked a firm shake of the head. 'No. I've not seen any of them here for a while. But we did get a call on Friday morning from somebody asking to speak to him.'

'Is that unusual?' Chandler asked.

'More like unheard of.'

'Did they leave a message? Did you get their name?'

'No to both. I didn't think anything of it at the time, though. Look, you have to understand, other than not getting much of a say when it comes to the hiring and firing around here, I run this business. Technically speaking I'm the manager, but in reality, I'm responsible for the place. Stuart, Mickey, and Grant put the money in and over time they take the money out again. The rest is down to me.'

'That places you in a position of considerable trust. So does that make you a friend or family member?'

Nash lowered his head, running a hand over his glistening scalp. 'Yeah, all right. The nepotism extends to me. I'm friends with all three of them. Have been since we played football together for the same team when we were in our early teens.'

'You know Stuart McKenzie well, then,' Bliss said. He watched in fascination as a single bead of sweat made its way slowly down from the man's wrinkled forehead. 'Is it unusual for him to go missing like this?'

'It's not unheard of for him to take off with the others, no. They'd go on benders, usually on a whim. Mostly they took a train down to London and spent two or three days there.'

'You said you were all mates. How come you didn't go with them?'

'Who said I didn't?'

'Well, did you?'

'Sometimes.'

'Why not this weekend?'

'Because it never came up. We rarely make arrangements in advance. More often than not, we'd wing it. But it didn't happen this time. In fact, I had a lunchtime beer on Saturday with Mickey and Grant.'

Bliss nodded. Mrs McKenzie had already spoken about her husband's two co-owners of the car business. Michael Banks and Grant Dixon were next on the list of people he and Chandler wished to talk to, and they'd hoped to find both men here.

'Just the three of you?' Chandler queried.

'Yes. Grant said he'd given Stu a bell but had got no answer. He left a message, and now that I think about it, we were a bit surprised not to see him turn up there later on.'

'Did you attempt to contact him yourself, Mr Nash?'

'No.'

'Not even when he failed to show?'

'No. It's not as if we'd made arrangements. It wasn't always the four of us. We've all got families, other shit going on in our lives. I just assumed he had something else to do with Sharon and the kids.'

Bliss chewed that over. He didn't get the sense that Nash was lying, nor that he was unduly alarmed. 'Between you, us, and these four walls,' he said, lowering his voice. 'Did Stuart have a bit on the side? Could he be with another woman?'

'Not that I know of.' The reply was immediate and unequivocal.

'Did he have any worries… that you know of?' Bliss persisted.

'If he did, he didn't tell me.'

'And when was the last time you spoke to him?'

Nash gazed up as he gave the question some thought. 'Just over a week ago. Weekend before last.'

'And what was that conversation about?'

'A motor. He wanted me to keep an eye out for a decent SUV for a pal of his. And before you ask, no, he didn't give me a name.'

Nodding, Bliss said, 'So to clarify, sir… you don't know where he is, and you don't know where he's been since Friday. Nor are you aware of any reason why he might be missing from home. Is that about it?'

'That's exactly it. If I had an inkling I'd tell you, if only for the sake of Sharon and the kids. She must be worried sick. I mean, sure, we'd occasionally decide on the spur of the moment to shoot off somewhere, and not everybody is good at calling home, if you know what I mean. But three days is a long time even for Stu. I won't pretend I'm frantic with worry just yet, but if he doesn't show up today then I reckon something has gone badly wrong.'

Bliss looked at Chandler. He hadn't fully made up his mind about Nash, but he agreed with the man's final statement.

NINE

THERE WAS NO FORMAL briefing that evening. Instead, DCI Diane Warburton summoned the team together to go over the progress made so far. She began with Bliss, who walked them through the steps he and Chandler had taken that day. He ended by summarising their efforts as both enlightening and frustrating.

'Identifying the victim of the attack was a good break,' Warburton said.

Bliss nodded. 'Yes. That was the enlightening part. The frustration came about in still not having a handle on why he was attacked, and more importantly, what became of him afterwards.'

'Any further thoughts on that? Did the wife seem genuine?'

'She seemed legit enough to me.'

'Me, too,' Chandler agreed. 'Her reaction when we mentioned the altercation was real enough.'

'Overall impressions, both of you?' their DCI pushed.

Chandler opened up first. 'We spoke to one of Mr McKenzie's close friends. He claims to have had no contact with our victim at all. We still need to have words with the remaining two men from their little foursome, but if they tell the same story, then I think we're probably looking at a second murder, boss. Well, technically, the first of two.'

'I'm with Pen on this one,' Bliss said, looking around the Major Crime area at familiar faces. 'We haven't officially identified Stuart McKenzie as our victim, but it's him. Nobody has laid eyes on him since Friday night, he hasn't been treated at the hospital, and he's not contacted his wife or mates. I'm still struggling with this notion of his assailant returning to the scene and carting McKenzie away, but it remains the most likely scenario.'

'He could be lying low,' DS Bishop suggested. 'If he recovered from the assault and sloped off into the night licking his wounds, he might have gone into hiding in fear of his attacker coming back to finish the job.'

Bliss nodded. 'That's clearly one of several alternatives to consider. Me and Pen happened to discuss the very same possibility on the way back from visiting the car place in Fengate. I'm open to persuasion, but I get the impression he would have contacted somebody by now if that's the way things were. If not his wife, for whatever reason, then one or more of his close friends.'

DCI Warburton scribbled a few notes, then tapped the pen against her teeth. Her eyes flitted between Bliss and Chandler. 'So, you're going to follow up with these remaining friends, right?'

'Unless something more urgent crops up, yes. I doubt we'll get any further, but we should hear what they have to say. We're also following up on Roger Craig. I'm of the opinion that we'll solve his murder by finding McKenzie's attacker. His wife had the presence of mind to provide us with his comb and toothbrush for DNA testing, both of which will help when the time comes. That said, I'd like to dig a bit deeper on our dead witness.'

'I have those details you asked for the other day about the SSAFA,' DC Ansari piped up. 'I'll let you have them afterwards.'

Bliss nodded his thanks. Warburton then turned her attention to Ansari. 'What do you have for us, Gul?'

The young DC flipped over a page on her notebook and began to read from it. 'Okay, I spoke with forensics. Evidently it was a busy weekend so the coat Roger Craig left behind has not yet been tested. They hoped to get to it later today or tomorrow morning at the latest.'

CSI Keene had joined the team to provide an update. She read from notes attached to a clipboard. 'As you're all probably aware, we got zero from the first alleged scene of crime. We pulled fibres from the second crime scene, and we've sent off a number of DNA samples, but I strongly suspect they will prove to be from our murder victim. On the plus side, we might just have a partial boot print that did not match those worn by our homeless vet. Tomorrow should produce more answers for us.'

'Thanks, Lydia,' Warburton said. She then turned to DS Bishop. 'And Bish?'

His rumpled clothing had not improved during the day. Neither had his sour disposition. 'Alan and I have been focussing on the park itself. No CCTV so far, and although you can access the park from Fulbridge Road, which is on a bus route, the last bus might fall a smidge outside our time window. There are no ANPR cameras in the area, either. I'm waiting on dash cam and in-bus footage, but don't hold your breath.'

The lack of Automatic Number Plate Recognition cameras close to the park came as no surprise to Bliss; they were rarer than people imagined. 'What else?' he prompted.

'As per usual, we've asked cab companies for footage from any fares that took them out that way. We've also arranged an appeal for private dash cam footage to go out on our Facebook page, and we can extend that to the *Evening Telegraph*. Finally, door-to-door is in hand and we're also asking for doorbell camera and other private security video. It's a large area to cover, so it's a big task, as you might imagine.'

'Nice job, the pair of you,' Warburton said, nodding in DC Alan Virgil's direction. She glanced around the room. 'Does anybody have something else to ask or offer?'

'We got the plate for Stuart McKenzie's car,' Bliss said. 'It's a 2021 F-Pace Jaguar. That's an SUV in white. Who wants to take on the job of looking for that?'

Ansari's hand shot up, as Bliss had suspected it might. 'Cheers, Gul,' he said. 'Try Jaguar's InControl Tracking Centre. You might have to liaise with Jacob Nash at Platinum Standard Cars in Fengate. If a stroppy teen by the name of Natalie gives you a hard time on the blower, mention McKenzie's name; they're distantly related, so there's some concern there.'

'And why might I need to speak with Mr Nash?' Ansari asked.

'McKenzie's wife wasn't sure whether her husband or the dealership owned the motor. The Jag people might want the manager's approval before running a GPS track. Meanwhile, let's have the door-to-door officers keep an eye out for it parked close by.'

'All of which leaves us where?' their DCI asked, looking harried.

'I'd say today has been a good step in the right direction,' he replied. 'The golden hour didn't do us many favours, but we're not entirely short of ideas. And in respect of our likely first victim, we're really only just starting to get to grips with Stuart McKenzie. The moment Pen and I got back I ran him through PNC. He's no stranger to us. Five interviews, three arrests, no convictions.'

'What was he arrested for?' Bishop asked, his tone remaining sullen.

Bliss ignored the attitude and answered the question. 'The unholy trinity: theft, robbery, and burglary. He was pulled the first time in connection with the theft of vehicles when he was a teenager. The impression was he was stealing them to order, but it went nowhere. The robbery allegedly took place at a warehouse in Woodston. They got close to charging, but the CPS decided we didn't have enough on him. Finally, we have an arrest for aggravated burglary. This was a gun shop on an industrial estate in Whittlesea. In the end, no evidence was offered against him.'

'Suspected accomplices?' Warburton asked.

'Not with the cars, but the warehouse and gun shop, yes. No other arrests were made, but the names of Michael Banks and Grant Dixon came up during the investigation. They both co-own the car place with McKenzie.'

'A rogues' gallery with not a day of time served,' DC Virgil observed. 'Might they have had something to do with the attack on their friend? A falling out of thieves, maybe?'

Bliss shrugged. 'It's possible. For all we know, that's all it was supposed to be – an attack. Perhaps whoever did it intended to rough him up, not kill him. But if we're going to go at these men we need to do it gradually. As I mentioned earlier, me and Pen want an informal chat with them about their pal. We'll go at that softly softly, see if there's anything to pick up on. Meanwhile, we'll gather the case files on those arrests and find out what we can discover in the finer details. My guess is they're just mates who happen to be bent, but I'm discounting nothing at this stage of the game. I do think we should look into their personal and business finances, see if they're in trouble. If they are, it might be due to something McKenzie did.'

'Good, good,' Warburton said with a vigorous nod. 'We'll divvy up the actions at morning briefing.'

'One last thing,' Bliss interrupted. 'We also ought to discuss our overall thinking regarding Banks and Dixon. I'm happy for me and Pen to still make the initial approach in both cases. But if we decide to go in stronger later on, I think it would be better to split them between two teams. Also, we can't forget that the manager at Platinum Standard Cars is a close mate of theirs.

Neither me nor Pen got the sense he knew anything more than he told us, and his name doesn't come up in connection with McKenzie's arrests. Even so, he might be worth a second look.'

'Can it wait until morning?'

'Absolutely.'

Warburton seemed happy enough. She told them the investigation into Roger Craig's murder had been assigned a name, and Operation Sandpiper, as it was to be known, would encompass the incident by the lake as well.

They were done for the day and Bliss was about to leave for home when he received a phone call from the hospital. A doctor's personal assistant first apologised for calling but then went on to ask if he would attend a meeting to discuss an urgent situation that had arisen concerning a young female patient brought in suspected of having taken an overdose. One of the two paramedics who first treated her at the scene and then subsequently brought her in as an emergency told hospital staff she believed there was more going on than first appeared. She had provided Bliss's name when suggesting a call to the police, claiming the incident might be taken more seriously if they also mentioned the name of the paramedic.

'It wouldn't be Kelly, would it?' Bliss asked, a smile thinning his lips.

'That's her. A real livewire, apparently. She was… insistent, and I was asked to make the call.'

Bliss requested further details and told the woman he'd be there within the next twenty minutes. It used to be said that almost anywhere could be reached by road in Peterborough inside ten, but the congestion caused by a major programme of roadworks and bridge strengthening had virtually doubled that estimate.

He nosed his pool car in the direction of the Thorpe Wood Interchange. As he inched his way towards the massive island roundabout and flyover, his thoughts drifted to the paramedic. He had first met Kelly following a car chase, which had resulted in him throwing himself out of the door moments before his vehicle launched itself into a public lake. She had flirted a little while treating him, and he recalled how she and Chandler had ganged up on him. The paramedic, young enough to be Bliss's daughter, had flirted with him again when he happened to bump into her and a colleague in the Emergency department. He hadn't taken it seriously, but he respected the job she did and her obvious intellect and insight. If she believed there was more to this apparent overdose, then there probably was. He didn't need another case on his hands, but he was intrigued. He also hoped Kelly was still at the hospital; he could do with a laugh at the end of a day like this one.

TEN

BLISS CALLED MOLLY TO let her know he'd be home a little later than anticipated. She told him not to worry about her; she and Max were enjoying the warm evening in the garden. He asked her to feed the fish and take Max for a walk and that he'd bring food home with him. At the hospital, he found a parking space close to the wards and soon found his way to an office set aside for this specific meeting. To his disappointment, the paramedics had declared themselves clear and available and were already on another shout. Two men and one woman sat waiting for him. One of the men stood to greet Bliss.

'Hello, Inspector. Thank you for coming. I'm Doctor Kapoor.' A neat and tidy man, he wore a snazzy waistcoat in some kind of herringbone pattern, and his moustache was thick and healthy. Kapoor turned to indicate the smartly attired woman occupying a chair to his right. 'This is my PA, Jan, whom you've already spoken to.'

Bliss shook the doctor's hand and gave a nod in the direction of the PA, who looked exactly as he had imagined she would; round cheeks, bright observant eyes, and wearing conservative clothing. The third person then also got to his feet and extended a hand. 'Inspector Bliss, I'm Peter Alinson from Adult Social Care?'

If he hadn't stated his occupation, Bliss would have guessed it, anyway. The painfully thin man dressed down, wore frameless spectacles, his hair long, and the end of his beard was knotted and fastened with a wooden toggle. His presence in the room had come as a surprise.

'ASC?' Bliss frowned, confused. 'I was told this meeting was about a young girl?'

'Ah, yes. Sorry for the confusion. I'm here today on behalf of the family, having been alerted to the reported incident. Her mother being my actual case client, the girl in question has been on our radar for some time, and we thought it best if we were involved at this early stage of any investigation you might decide to run. I will, of course, be feeding back to relevant child protection services.'

All three men took a seat. Bliss noticed there was an extra chair. 'Are we waiting for someone else?' he asked.

No sooner had he spoken when there was a sharp rap of knuckles on the door and a female uniformed police officer entered the room. She smiled and introduced herself as PCSO Lauren Halliday. After sitting beside Bliss, she took a notebook from her breast pocket and set it down on the large coffee table they were clustered around.

Doctor Kapoor coughed into his hand and suggested he begin. 'Earlier today a young girl by the name of Nora Bell was rushed into our emergency department, which had been pre-alerted by the ambulance crew. The paramedics had attended her home following a 999 call from her sister. They treated Nora at the scene, but the girl was largely unresponsive. I am the senior doctor responsible for taking care of her needs here. Treatment has gone especially well, and Nora is currently recovering in her own room within a ward. However, while they were here, the paramedics reported a serious concern relating to the incident.'

'Which was?' Bliss asked.

Kapoor clasped his hands together, steepling his fingers. 'Before we get to that, Inspector, it may be of help for you to understand the location of the child's home and the conditions she and her family may be facing. PCSO Halliday has already been briefed, having been asked to attend this meeting as the area is well known to community officers.'

'All manner of officers, actually,' Halliday insisted. She angled herself better to meet Bliss's gaze. 'Inspector, the Bell family live in Millfield. I probably don't need to tell you how high the crime rate is there. Anyhow, we've got to know the place and its people quite well. In fact, I'm familiar with the family from previous dealings and have met all three of them at various stages – the father isn't on the scene, it's just Mrs Bell and her two daughters.'

Bliss was more curious than puzzled, but he already didn't care for the direction this was heading in. 'Okay. Good. So, you can provide some useful insight into who and what we're dealing with.'

'Yes, sir. I believe I can. You should know that the patient in question, Nora, has Cerebral Palsy. She is fourteen, but extremely vulnerable given her mental state is that of a child. The family first came to our attention when Mrs Bell reported that she and Nora were being bullied by neighbourhood kids. They would taunt the pair of them as Mrs Bell pushed Nora in her chair or if they caught sight of Nora in the front garden. Some of the kids used paint to daub horrible stuff on their front door and shoved dog sh… faeces through the letter box.'

Nodding, Bliss said, 'Okay. Sounds as if they felt under siege.' He thought he knew what was coming next, but hoped he was wrong.

'Yes,' Halliday agreed with a nod. 'But I'm as convinced as I can be that it's much worse than that, Inspector. I'm confident they're being cuckooed.'

Bliss closed his eyes, for once despairing of being right. 'You're saying some of the locals are using the Bell home from which to run a drugs business.'

'I am. We've seen the comings and goings. We've made our reports and we walk our patrols down their street as often as we can. I even confronted Mrs Bell with my suspicions, but she denied it. I could tell she was lying. She wanted to open up, but the poor woman was terrified. I can only imagine the threats these young thugs have made against the family. Her and Nora, especially, but her other daughter, Patricia, as well.'

Bliss heard the outrage in PCSO Halliday's voice. He admired the officer for it, but he also pitied her as well. She was far too young and enthusiastic to be carrying around such a burden of awful experiences and empathy for victims.

'All right,' he said. 'That's given me a good idea of the background. Who's going to tell me why we're gathered here today?'

'I think knowing their story is essential, Inspector,' said the man from ASC, Alinson. 'It'll help you better understand the dilemma.'

'Okay. I get that. But can we move it on?'

PCSO Halliday took up the sorry tale once more. 'The paramedics are often nervous going into this particular area. They've been lured there before only to find youths trying to break into their vehicle with the intention of stealing drugs. But Kelly's colleague recognised the address and remembered attending Nora Bell previously. On that occasion, the poor girl had experienced severe difficulty breathing. This time when they arrived, the streets were unusually free of young people. Kelly asked me to emphasise that point to you, Inspector. Nora's sister opened the door to the crew – her mother was in the city centre and not answering her phone. These days Nora's bed is in a converted room downstairs, and as soon as the paramedics walked in, they realised they had a life-threatening situation on their hands. Once they had established that the overdose had been a cocktail of sleeping tablets and co-codamol, Kelly administered Narcan to help remove the opioid aspect. Nora remained largely unresponsive, so they made the call ahead, intubated the child, and got her here as quickly as possible. Shortly afterwards, a tragic medical incident became something else entirely when Kelly raised her concerns.'

'Which were?'

Halliday explained that she and her PCSO colleague had stumbled upon the scene quite by chance just as Nora was being placed inside the ambulance. Before the paramedics left, Kelly asked the officers if they would make their way to the hospital as she had some doubts as to what had taken place inside the house. When they arrived, they took her to one side and asked for an explanation.

'According to her, something about the sister's reaction and the scene inside Nora's bedroom felt wrong. Kelly had her wits about her even under the pressure of attending to the girl. Initially, she couldn't understand why two boxes of strong medication were on Nora's bedside cabinet and not kept well out of reach. She then noticed that the girl had somehow managed to pop open two entire strips of blister packs. She queried her colleague about it, and the response left Kelly to question whether Nora lacked the manual dexterity to do it all on her own.'

'This is where my department was brought in,' Alinson commented.

Bliss visualised the incident as the PCSO described it. He nodded and said, 'So we're potentially looking at somebody assisting her to take her own life, or perhaps going so far as to force those tablets down her throat.'

WHAT DIES INSIDE US

The nods of agreement in the room told him the small group had already reached the same conclusion. 'Is it possible to know precisely when she ingested the tablets?' he asked.

Dr Kapoor cast his gaze upwards as he considered his response. 'Not precisely, but possibly close enough for your needs. If we work backwards as we consider, we begin with the time Nora was brought in. The paramedics will have recorded their time of arrival at her home, and control will have the exact time the emergency call was made. Once we've collated those details we ought to be able to provide a narrow window for you.'

'You're wondering if we can identify who was inside the house at the time,' Halliday said to Bliss, who nodded.

'Yes. It was the sister who made the triple nine call, the sister who answered the door to the crew. But she might not have been alone when Nora took those pills.' He left it there for a few seconds, running the sequence of events through his head. Then he looked at the PCSO and said, 'I don't suppose you thought to collect the medication packaging, did you?'

He was rewarded with a wide smile. 'No, sir. By the time we got there, they were all about to leave and the house was locked up. Plus, we didn't know at that stage what might have happened inside. We heard overdose and that was that.'

'I see. Then why so happy about it?'

'Ah. Well, the other paramedic did think to bag up the packets and bring them in so that the staff here could check out the medication for themselves. Which means they are still here somewhere.'

'Forgive me, Inspector,' the doctor said, 'but we already know the type of meds our patient ingested. I'm not sure how the packaging itself can be of any help.'

Bliss raised his eyebrows. 'Prints and DNA,' he said simply.

63

This time it was Halliday who voiced her surprise. 'But surely we'd expect the packets to be covered in prints from both Nora's mother and sister, sir.'

Nodding confidently, he said, 'Naturally. I'm thinking more in terms of whose prints won't be on them if the girl didn't feed them to herself.'

The penny dropped, encouraging further nods of agreement.

Keen to learn, Halliday wondered if the police were allowed to take the medication packets and boxes away with them as evidence. Bliss pointed out that as per section 19 of PACE, the items were lawfully available at new premises and as such could be seized.

'Do you think you have enough for you to mount an investigation?' Alinson asked.

'There will be eventually, I'm sure. I'll need the paramedics to provide us with a statement. A report on Nora Bell's condition, specifically anything that evidences her inability to pop those blister packs. Together with the timings and medical reports on today's events, if that all adds up to assisted suicide or attempted murder, then yes, we'll get to the bottom of it.'

'Do you see the importance of the background to all this?'

'In what way?'

The social worker shifted in his chair. 'If – and to my mind there's still a big question mark hanging over what transpired – either Nora's mother or sister helped the girl to take those pills, we must make allowances for their potential mental state at the time. None of us can imagine the life this family has endured. Mrs Bell was already struggling with Nora's disability as well as Patricia's unruly behaviour when the bullying and taunting began. If they have now been... cuckooed, for want of a better description, every day must be intolerable.'

This prompted Bliss to think of something. He looked up in alarm. 'If Mrs Bell did this to save her daughter from a living hell, her absence from the home might be telling. She may well be considering taking her own life. Perhaps she already has.'

'You're right,' Alinson said urgently, leaning in. 'The kind of pressure that drives mothers to protect their offspring in such an extreme manner often results in them seeking to end it in the way you describe.'

'I'll get uniform and my team on it the moment we're done here. We'll distribute photos and obtain Mrs Bell's mobile number to see if we can trace her. We'll need to speak with Patricia as well. I take it she's here, with Nora?'

'She is,' Dr Kapoor said. He looked uneasy. 'But Inspector, I do have something else to tell you. So far, we have naturally focussed all of our energies on Nora's health and recovery, and then how she became so ill, but in carrying out a whole raft of tests we uncovered a quite dreadful discovery.'

Something crawled inside Bliss's stomach. 'What is it?'

Kapoor shook his head slowly, eyes fixated on both hands, which were clutched together on the table. 'The blood and urine tests we ran came back with one surprising result. I hate to be the bearer of worse news, but Nora Bell is pregnant.'

ELEVEN

'YOU ALL RIGHT, JIMBO?'

Molly's voice percolated into his thoughts. Having eschewed a takeaway in favour of a few drinks and pub grub, he'd first driven home from the hospital and shortly afterwards they walked the short distance to the Windmill. A handful of regulars greeted Bliss with a nod or a raised glass, but he barely made eye contact. He and Molly ordered and then ate in relative silence, exchanging minimal small talk. He was on his second pint and already thinking of a bottle of Connemara single malt sitting in his kitchen cupboard when he realised he was being spoken to.

'Sorry,' he breathed, avoiding her direct gaze. 'I'm not great company tonight, Molly.'

She snorted. 'You're no company at all. But I've seen this side of you before, remember? It saved my skinny arse back then, so I'm hoping some other lost soul in desperate need of a friend is about to benefit from the Jimmy Bliss effect.'

Despite himself, Bliss laughed. The girl had that way about her and could always find a corner of his veneer to peel back and sneak beneath.

'You sound so much wiser than your years,' he told her.

'I don't know about that, but I'm not wrong. Am I?'

'No. It's been a bastard of a day,' he admitted, taking a long draw from his pint glass. 'It began with one horror and ended with another. There's still plenty of pure evil in this world, Molly. I know you've seen more than your fair share of it. It's not always this hard to take, but today is one for those memory banks we keep locked away in the shadows.'

Molly gave an empathetic nod. 'I won't ask because I know you won't tell me. But you can if you need to. Always. If not, forget about keeping me amused. I'm fine. It's you I'm worried about at the moment.'

'I'm fine, too. Or… I will be. If the sun comes up for me in the morning, then I'd've lived to fight another day.'

They fell into sombre silence for a few minutes. Bliss finally looked up, caught her unswerving gaze, and said, 'You would tell me if anything was wrong in *your* life, wouldn't you?'

Her forehead crinkled. 'You really have to ask?'

'I just wanted to make sure that you know you can aways come to me. Day or night. You can tell me absolutely anything. I'll never judge you, Molly. If anyone ever bothers you or bullies you or does something horrible to you, I'm there. I'll do everything in my power to make it right.'

Molly's frown deepened. 'I know that, you dummy. What's going on with you tonight? Jimbo, you already know my worst secrets. You know my worst nightmares, my worst actions. Believe me, you'll know all about it if my life ever looks to be drifting away from me again. I mean, I can say any of it to Mum and Dad as well, because they know a lot about what happened to me before they took me in. Not as much as you do, but more than most. So I'm covered, believe me.'

Bliss smiled. 'I like to hear you call them that.'

'Well, they are my mum and dad.' She cracked a smile. 'I have the legal documents to prove it.'

'I'm so glad you feel that close to them. It helps me function better when I know you're doing well. Mentally, physically, and emotionally. So, tell me what's new, young lady.'

Molly's laughter was warm and genuine. 'I've never thought of myself as a "lady" before, but I think I like it. Um, did I tell you I started my own YouTube channel?'

He shook his head.

'You do know what YouTube is, don't you?'

Eyebrows raised, he said, 'I'm not that much of a Luddite. YouTube can be an interesting platform.'

'Then you know all about channels, too?'

'Not really. I'm guessing it's your own space, where people can find your videos.'

'Well done.'

'Please just tell me you use it for something worthwhile.'

'I do reviews of songs from the sixties, seventies, and eighties. All the music you introduced me to, plus loads more. I've been down the rabbit hole with Yes, Genesis, It Bites, Dream Theater. Plus The Kinks, Small Faces, Badfinger, and AOR bands like Journey and Strangeways. It's amazing, Jimbo. Seriously, I don't think it's possible to live long enough to play every great song out there. But I'm introducing people my age to all the bands we both love, and they're loving them, too. I tell them what you always say to me: there's no need for ProTools when you have pro musicians, and in the years before AutoTune was invented, people had to actually be able to sing properly. Most of them agree.'

Happy to see how energised Molly was by this new venture, Bliss nodded along and threw in a few more band names, songs, and albums for her to try. For a few precious minutes, he escaped from the maze-like prison his mind had created. The terrified kid he had first met on a sodden rooftop standing in the freezing December rain was long gone, replaced by this bubbly and bright young woman living the dream. Did either Nora or Patricia Bell have the same opportunities to escape from their nightmare lives? It was hard to see how.

Perhaps having noticed the change in his mood, Molly's features softened. 'Something else on your mind, Jimbo?' she asked. 'You thinking about Friday?'

He wasn't. but it was difficult not to. Days like this one made him wonder why he hadn't handed in his warrant card years ago. But days like this one also answered the casual question for him: it was almost impossible to bear, but it was actually impossible to turn his back on it. It had taken a compulsory retirement order for him to accept the end of his police career, and yet he had immediately sought ways in which to return, albeit as a civilian.

No doubt he was feeling his age. His medical condition showed no sign of improving, though its progression was not aggressive. Meniere's disease had taken a lot out of him, but his essence remained. Managing vertigo and imbalance required constant attention, but there was nothing to be done about the accompanying hearing loss in both ears. He doubted he would become completely deaf in the time he had left, but with enormous reluctance he had recently looked into hearing aids. He needed a stronger prescription for reading glasses every couple of years. Coaching boxing kept him fitter than he would otherwise be, but the resulting aches and pains had begun to insist he start winding down. In his younger days he'd not questioned his coach injecting cortisone into damaged knuckles and hadn't known about the long-term effect on cartilage. His fingers screamed a reminder at him every day, and he found himself rubbing the joints more often. Amateur sportsmen and women tended to suffer from a lack of professional treatment, and his more competitive years had certainly done a number on his knees, ankles, and hips. Apart from all that, he was in great shape.

Bliss groaned, angry with himself for becoming maudlin. As he often told people, putting up with the ageing process was better than the alternative. He polished off his drink and looked across the table at the beautiful young woman opposite.

'This isn't the me I wanted you to see this week,' he said. 'Believe me when I tell you I'll be fine. Friday holds no fears for me because it's just another day. Come June I'll be back at Thorpe Wood, working alongside Pen, Bish and the others in much the same way. I'll also have new colleagues to irritate, so that'll be fun.'

Molly nodded. 'Oh, I'm sure you'll lap that up. Not so certain they will.'

He chuckled. 'That's their problem. No, facing up to retirement hasn't thrown me, Molly. And I'm not so much troubled by growing old and becoming less than, either. But I will admit that in recent weeks and months, I have asked myself if I've made a difference.'

Molly opened her mouth to voice an objection, but he raised a hand to silence her.

'Let me finish. I speak to you on the blower or face-to-face as we are now, and I have my answer. Then along comes a day like to today and I realise mine is not a finite profession. I'll never solve every case, never answer every question, and never stop the conveyer belt of misery from coming around without a fucking cuddly toy anywhere in sight. If you ever need to cite an example of perpetual motion, it's criminal activity. And don't ever believe anyone who tells you things are improving, Molly.'

Rolling her eyes, she said, 'Hmm, well, that's not at all grim.'

'Grim, perhaps. But true. People are in our faces insisting we live in a progressive society, but I struggle to think of anything that has genuinely improved. The way I see it, the important things in society have taken massive steps backwards just when we were on the verge of achieving some kind of success. Crime has changed, but it hasn't gone away and there's a different tragedy to be found on every street corner.'

'And now we've gone from grim to horrific. Keep talking, Jimbo. No sleep for me tonight. I might even slit my wrists.'

Bliss's face hardened. 'Don't ever say that. Not even in a joke.'

Molly laughed it off, but Bliss sensed his sharp rebuke had pierced her thick skin. He sighed and shook his head. 'Since when have you ever taken notice of anything this sad old git told you? Ignore me. I'm trying to claw my way out of the deep pit of misery I've dug for myself, but all I'm doing is pulling more soil back in to weigh me down. Look, forget tonight ever happened. Tomorrow I'll be out of this funk and back to the jolly japester you know and love.'

Molly reared back. 'Jolly? Japester? You?'

He smiled. 'Fair play. Whatever my more moderate versions of those are, then. I'm horrified that I've brought things down for you, and you must wish you'd gone back home. I promise the rest of the week will be better. Okay?'

'If you say so. But it's really not a problem, Jimbo. Honestly. I get it. I lived the misery you're talking about. I know what it looks like from the inside, remember?'

Bliss recalled the awful daydream on Friday night before Gul Ansari's phone call. A terrible image of Molly falling from his grasp took centre stage inside his head. He shook it off and nodded. 'Impossible not to. I just want to know that you feel safe. And happy. You are happy, aren't you, Molly?'

'Can't you tell?'

'Why do you always answer a question with another question?'

'Do I?'

The look of delight on her face told him she was doing fine. As happy and safe as she had ever been in her entire life; not that the childhood bar had been set very high. He nodded and said, 'Promise me you'll make the most of your second chance. I love the sound of your new YouTube venture, but don't make your living as some kind of online influencer or whatever they're called. Be something special. Make a genuine difference.'

Molly sniggered. 'As much as I love you to bits, Jimbo, do you really think I'm going to take online advice from an old man who doesn't even have a Facebook account?'

Bliss pulled his phone from his trouser pocket and held it up. 'See this? I could sit and post all kinds of crap on social media, or I could make use of its original purpose and call people. Speak to them. What a concept, eh?'

'I talk to people.'

'Yeah, who?'

'Well, there's you, and there's... others whose names I can't immediately think of.'

'As I suspected. I know I come across like an old codger who can't appreciate modern communications, but all I'm saying is you should experience both worlds. Enjoy your channel, make money from it if you can. But do it for enjoyment on the side. You can be so much more than that, Molly.'

He realised he had stepped way beyond the line, but he had no regrets. He wasn't the girl's father. Not family at all. In truth, he didn't really know how best to describe their relationship, other than as kindred spirits. He loved the idea of her introducing younger people to older music, having them experience something entirely different. He also understood that people earned a living in a completely different way to his generation. One thing he knew for certain was that Molly was her own person, and nobody was going to knock her off whatever course she set herself.

'When are your exams coming up?' he asked, shifting the conversation.

'Later this month. We're on study leave.'

Bliss was extraordinarily proud of Molly's ambition and achievements. With virtually no worthwhile schooling behind her she had knuckled down, and although she was repeating her final year she had caught up to the point where her adoptive parents were expecting many good results.

'Thought about what you might study if you go on to uni?'

'Well, I did once convince myself I was going to join your mob. But then I realised I'd never cope with having to deal with the public, because people are so fucked up. I'm doing well in chemistry and biology, though, so I thought maybe forensic science.'

'Really? In a lab or working scenes?'

'I want to be hands-on, not stuck in a lab.'

He was surprised, but took it in his stride. 'Sounds like a plan. You sure, though? Other than the emergency services, the CSI team are first on scene with bodies and believe me the reality is far worse than TV or films ever show. The smell alone can be reason enough to give you pause. But it also gets graphic, Molly. Grotesquely so at times. A few months ago, we were at a scene where a mother and her two kids had been bound to the dining room furniture and stabbed over and over again in a frenzied attack. The father had his face taken off with a shotgun. That's a crime scene you never forget.'

Molly huffed and gave a weak smile. 'You think I've never seen a dead body before, Jimbo?'

That pulled him up short. The question had never occurred to him. 'I... to be honest with you, I hadn't given it much thought.'

'Well, I have. Overdoses, plus a stabbing and a gunshot.'

An involuntary shudder rippled all the way between Bliss's shoulder blades. 'I sometimes forget the horrors of the life you once led.'

'Believe me, I don't. So yeah, it's a job I think I might be good at.'

'Have you checked out the courses? You do know you'll most likely have to attend a uni away from your usual support system?'

She nodded. 'I have, and I do. There is one in Bedfordshire, so that's a possibility.'

Bliss was pleased to know she had been looking ahead, planning her future. He wasn't sure that he liked the idea of her working crimes, but it was her life, and she had studied hard to put her in a position to have choices.

'Come on, let's go home,' he said. 'Show me your channel.'

'You want to vet my choice of tunes?' she asked with an easy grin.

'Of course. Social media I may not know much about, but when it comes to music, I am your Sensei.'

As she got to her feet, Molly treated him to a mock bow. 'Yes, master. And I am your more than willing student.'

TWELVE

THE FOLLOWING MORNING, AFTER the actions were agreed upon and allocated, Bliss held the team in place to inform them of his hospital visit. 'I'm not sure what this is yet,' he admitted. 'But there's so much wrong with everything I heard yesterday. I want to follow up after Pen and I are done with Stuart McKenzie's business partners. Whether this was an attempted suicide, an attempted assisted suicide, or attempted murder, it's rotten to the core and I want a piece of it. On top of that, the poor kid was raped, because she's only fourteen. And I'm told she's mentally and emotionally much younger.'

DCI Warburton wore a look of disgust. 'It's repugnant is what it is. And I agree with you, Jimmy. Dig deeper. We can cope without the pair of you for an afternoon, so you tackle it as best you can together. Because of the cuckooing allegation, have a word with the drugs team to make sure you won't be trampling over a clandestine op they might be running.'

'What the fuck is happening in the world today?' Bishop said, shaking his head miserably. 'Raping a fourteen-year-old kid is bad enough, but a kid with cerebral palsy? You have to be one sick bastard.'

'If it is only one sick bastard,' Gul Ansari offered dourly. 'Who knows how many of the local shitheads have paid a visit to her room?'

Bliss closed his eyes. For a moment, he felt physically sick. He hadn't even considered the possibility. Now he knew it was all he'd be thinking about for the rest of the day.

'I'll make sure there's nothing in the works regards the cuckooing,' he said. 'While I'm at it I'll familiarise myself with whose patch it is and gather some names and faces. Me and Pen can do a drive-by and take a quick shufty at the gaff they're using. I really want to get into this one quickly. We'll also visit the hospital for a follow-up, but it's important for us to talk to Nora's mother as soon as possible.'

'I take it she eventually turned up safe and sound?' Ansari said.

'She did. Uniform did their best to locate her, but it was the eldest daughter who finally managed to get hold of her on her mobile. Because at this stage we can't be certain what happened, I arranged to have a FLO close at hand, with a warning to keep watch on everybody who goes near the poor kid who overdosed.'

'Good thinking,' DCI Warburton said. 'Sounds as if Nora Bell is in need of our protection.'

Bliss nodded. Having a Family Liaison Officer close by was the best he could do for the time being. 'I want to know what's been happening inside that house, and of course we must also establish how those pills ended up inside Nora Bell.'

Warburton eyed him candidly. 'I got a sense you weren't ruling the mother out, Jimmy. I understand why, because the pressure she's been living under must be intolerable. But tread carefully. If she didn't do it, knowing that it happened and then learning that her daughter is also pregnant, might well push the woman over the edge.'

'Will do. I have to say, I was worried about her state of my mind when I first heard about this whole sorry mess. Perhaps we can separate the mother and the older sister, and I'll speak to her on my own while Pen has a go with the girls. But meanwhile, let's also make some progress with this… I was going to say murder, but we still don't know what became of Mr McKenzie, so I won't close my mind on that one, either.'

Leaving Chandler to locate contact details and additional relevant information on Michael Banks and Grant Dixon, Bliss left the room and took the short walk around to the other side of the building on the same floor. In the area allocated to the drugs squad, he scanned the room before picking out Detective Sergeant Jordan Higgins, uninspiringly known to all he worked with as 'Hurricane', after the famous snooker world champion. The DS, a youthful-looking Mancunian whose attire was somewhere between M&S and Armani, spotted him coming and lurched to his feet. The two men shook hands.

'Congratulations on the retirement,' Higgins said with a warm smile. 'Though I hear you're coming back as a civilian SIO.'

Bliss was happy to nod confirmation. 'That and working cold cases with a few other retirees.'

'You must be insane.' Higgins puffed out his cheeks. 'When my time is up you won't see my arse for dust, my friend. Mind you, surely you could've gone donkey's years ago.'

'Could have. Some would argue I should have. But I've got bugger all else to do with my time at the moment, so yeah, I've signed on the dotted line for another year to begin with.'

'Rather you than me, Jimmy. But I wish you all the best. Anyway, what can I do for you?'

Bliss explained his interest. Higgins immediately raised his eyebrows. 'Good timing,' he said. 'Millfield is an area of particular concern to us of late. That whole patch on the eastern side of

Bourges Boulevard, extending out to Eastgate and up to New England, has recently undergone some major changes in the background. We knew of two main crews distributing, supplying, and dealing over there, but at the back end of last year we got word of a new face carving out some territory.'

'Are we looking at a large outfit?'

'Big enough to worry about. And from what we can tell, heavy enough to have taken over the entire patch with very little bloodshed. Same crews are still in place, but currently they answer to somebody else and are strictly dealing from a new supply.'

'You have a name of this new Mr Big?' Bliss asked.

Higgins shifted uneasily. 'Possibly, but not for definite. Not that I'm complaining, but when you helped bring down Eric the Eyeball's empire a few years back, it didn't take long for these smaller gangs to step up. There was a void, and they filled it. Trouble was, they were splintered and not terribly well run, so we've had our work cut out for us. Then all of a sudden everything stopped, and when it restarted, things were completely different. They're organised, operate in smaller cells reporting to middlemen, so there are more links in the chain.'

'Do you have anybody with an in working undercover?'

'Yes, and quite close. The intel coming back to us from him is that a man by the name of Saad Ali slipped into the area from Leicester and is running the show. We have little to go on, and he doesn't have a record. A great deal of suspicion and local knowledge passed across to us, but nothing by way of good evidence.'

'So, definitely a man close to or even at the top,' Bliss observed. It was usually the way; the lower-level workers were the ones who turned up on the corners and working out of houses, took the hits, paid their fines, and served their time, while further up the chain the people holding a thumb on the scale bearing the real balance of power were often seen and heard of yet were elusive and stayed out of reach.

'We've definitely got an eye on him. Meanwhile, I'll admit we've been distracted by all these changes, so some things are bound to have slipped through the net.'

Higgins walked back to his desk and sat down in front of his computer. He logged on to the network and brought up a database. Bliss noticed a familiar hunt-and-peck style of typing, but before long the DS was scrutinising something on the screen. After a moment he looked up. 'Does the name Patricia Bell mean anything to you?' he asked.

'It does.' Bliss nodded, unsurprised. 'She's Nora's older sister. I thought you might have her on record. Dealing, using, or both?'

'Using. Caught twice. Two warnings. Nothing on the mother, Frances Bell, and nor do I have any mention of their home being used by a crew. You sure about the cuckooing intel?'

Bliss thought about that. He was confident in the officer who had been forthright when outlining her suspicions. 'Pretty much,' he answered. 'PCSO Halliday and a colleague know the area well and they both picked up on it. I think Halliday said they'd reported their observations.'

'Recently?'

'I believe so, yes.'

Higgins turned back to the keyboard and brought up a different file. He scanned a list and eventually nodded. 'Yes, here we go. This information is marked TBC, so it has yet to be confirmed and clarified, which is why it's missing from our main intel database. We keep them separate to avoid mixing verified data with speculation. But I can see the joint report made by the PCSOs. It looks promising.'

'My main objective in coming here was to make sure we didn't trample on anyone's toes,' Bliss explained. 'But as you have no specific ops running in connection with either the address or the residents, I assume we're free to look into this in greater detail?'

'Of course. I'd appreciate some feedback. The more we know the more we can act. The cuckooing is a big deal, naturally, so if you discover evidence of that I'd appreciate a heads-up. We could then work together, but at the very least I'd want to make our UCO aware of it. He might even be close enough to find a way inside.'

'I understand,' Bliss said. Working as an undercover officer in the drugs world was precarious and dangerous, but their capacity to provide deep intelligence was often the difference in making a raid and subsequent arrests more successful. By their very nature, such operations were delicate and fraught with sensitivities, the main one of which was not to expose the UCO in question.

'Pen and I are initially approaching this from a different angle,' he told Higgins. 'A young kid may have been harmed with the intention of killing her, and she was definitely raped. That's our first line of enquiry. If the cuckooing is connected, which is looking extremely likely, then we'll be taking an interest in that as well. The abuse of the girl is the priority, but if there's the kind of overlap into your field of expertise as expected, then we'll all sit down together and consider our options. That okay by you, Jordan?'

'I'm obliged,' the DS said, standing once more. 'You think you can put this to bed before clocking off on Friday?'

'Who the fuck knows? I'll give it my best shot.'

Higgins winked and clapped him on the arm. 'Let slip the dogs of war, Jimmy.'

Bliss grinned and said, 'Count on it, mate. Count on it.'

THIRTEEN

THOSE WHO LIVED IN south Bretton always made the distinction. What separated much of it from the rest of the township developed in the early seventies was the amount of private housing. The Peterborough Development Corporation had wisely used the land formerly owned by the Milton Estate to establish its first new local authority housing estate to the north, but if your house was below Bretton Gate, then you made sure people were aware of that fact.

Michael Banks's house lurked behind closed wrought-iron gates in the centre of a tiny close. What had probably once been a significant two-car garage had been converted to become an extended part of the home itself. The block-stone driveway held no vehicles, and ringing the bell on one of the gate pillars drew no response or sign of activity from inside the dwelling.

A short drive away stood the equally impressive home of Grant Dixon. No gates barred the way this time, and three cars stood on the drive. Bliss reversed to find a parking spot further along the road. A couple of minutes later, he and Chandler stood in the lengthy porchway having rung a bell that offered a pleasant chime. The man who yanked open the door was a big unit, taller and broader even than Olly Bishop. Bliss had to take a small step back and crane his neck to meet the man's puzzled gaze.

'Mr Dixon?' Bliss asked, holding up his warrant card. 'Detective Inspector Bliss. I'm here today with Detective Sergeant Chandler. We'd like a word with you if we may about Stuart McKenzie.'

The man's features softened, but his shoulders were at odds and seemed to set firm. 'What's that old rascal got himself into this time?' Dixon asked, hinting at a laddish smile.

'May we talk inside?' Bliss asked. 'The conversation could get a bit delicate.'

'We have guests, so no,' was the man's brusque response. He stepped outside, closing the front door behind him. His presence made the porchway feel claustrophobic while his suspicious gaze darted between the two police officers. 'What's this about?'

Clearing his throat, Bliss said, 'You asked what Mr McKenzie might have got himself into this time. May I ask what you mean by that?'

'I think you just did.' Dixon drew himself fully upright. 'It's just an expression. I didn't mean anything by it.'

Bliss maintained eye contact. 'Fair enough. So, tell me, when was the last time you saw your friend?'

The man scratched the back of his head. 'Last week sometime. Wednesday, maybe.'

'And the last time you spoke with him?'

'Same time. I tried to get hold of him on Saturday, but he didn't answer. I left a message. Look, what's going on here? Stu isn't just a mate, we're also business partners. Why are you here asking questions about him?'

'Were you aware he was missing from home?' Bliss asked, hoping to catch Dixon out in a lie.

'Well, yes and no. I knew he *was*. Sharon called yesterday morning to ask if we'd seen or heard from him. Tell the truth, I didn't think much more of it. Stu disappears every so often, generally a long weekend. I suppose I assumed, as I never heard back from her, that he'd turned up, sheepish and offering an apology by way of a bouquet as per usual.'

'The way we hear it,' Chandler said, 'you and Michael Banks usually join Mr McKenzie on these jaunts. London was mentioned as a particular favourite destination.'

'That's true to a certain extent. But not always, and not this time. If I need to prove where I was then I can. And some of that time I was with Mickey, so I know he wasn't away with Stu, either. I gather the reason you're here is that he still hasn't shown his face or even called?'

'You gather right. Tell me, Mr Dixon, when you do travel south, do you stay in the same hotel in London? Do you visit the same places? Or does it vary?'

The big man widened his stance and folded his arms. If his aim was to appear more menacing, his body language worked a treat. 'Yes, yes, and no. We hit a few casinos. Mainly the Hippodrome in Leicester Square or the Sportsman in Marylebone. As for where we bed down, that's normally either the Langham or Holmes.'

Chandler made a note of the hotel and casino names. 'And if he didn't want to be found...?' she asked.

The question seemed to stump Dixon for a few seconds. Eventually, he shook his head. 'I wouldn't know. But if he was looking to go on a bender away from home, he would have told me. Me or Mickey. I don't see him doing the usual if he felt like slipping away on his own.'

Bliss thought of something. 'Does Stuart have a little place somewhere? A place his wife knows nothing about?'

'You mean somewhere he might take a bit of skirt?' Dixon coughed up a laugh. 'No. Stu wasn't like that. Yeah, now and then we take in a strip club, and he'd have the occasional lap dance, but he doesn't fuck around on Sharon.'

'No escorts?' Chandler asked.

Dixon paused. Colour crept into his cheeks. Bliss could guess what that meant. He lowered his voice, 'Sir, all we're interested in is finding your friend. What you all get up to when you're away from home is nothing to do with us. Frankly, I couldn't give a toss. But if Mr McKenzie did have a bit on the side, someone he saw on a semi-regular basis, then we need to know about it.'

'No.' The man's shake of the head was firm. 'Not Stu. Him and Sharon are solid. Don't go looking there, because you'll be wasting your time. If he's still AWOL, then pound to a penny it's not anywhere the three of us have been together. If he's taken off and doesn't want to be found for a few days, then my guess is he's put a pin in a map and just set off on a whim. That said, I've never known him stay away from Sharon for this length of time before.'

'So, you have no idea where he might be or why he might have gone off on his own,' Bliss clarified. 'His wife tells us things were fine at home. How about business, Mr Dixon? Everything all right there?'

'Sound as a pound.' Dixon's eyebrows arched. 'Though I suppose a quid ain't as sound as it once was. No, you're barking up the wrong tree there, mate. Business is good, better than it has ever been.'

'What kind of business are we talking about?' Chandler asked. 'Is it just the car place in Fengate?'

The big man's eyes sparkled as he chuckled. 'No, no. We've got a lot of fingers in a lot of pies. We're what you might call entrepreneurial.'

'Does that require a lot of speculation?' Bliss asked him. 'You know, speculate to accumulate, that sort of thing.'

'Of course. But if you're asking if we've bitten off more than we can chew, the answer is no. We never put in money we can't afford to lose. That's why we're successful.'

'Is it possible that Mr McKenzie had anything going on the side? Did you ever suspect him of… speculating elsewhere?'

The question clearly bothered Dixon, who cleared his throat and ran a meaty hand across his head. 'No. Can't say I did. Look, I think I've been patient enough and answered all your questions. You've got me worried now. Has something happened to Stu? Is he involved in something you're keeping from me?'

Bliss was about to reply when the front door opened and somebody on the inside beckoned Dixon over. A conversation took place between him and a woman, their voices hushed. Moments later, the man stepped back out, and this time he was clearly unhappy.

'Sharon's just been on the blower,' he said. 'Why the bloody hell didn't you tell me about the fracas in Werrington, or that you suspect Stu might be dead?'

'That's not the way we work,' Bliss explained, disappointed to have been rumbled. 'We're here to ask questions and gain information. We choose what we give away in return.'

Dixon took a step closer to them, stooping to lower his face. 'Well, if you think you're asking any more, think again. We're done here. Got it?'

'We'd prefer to talk to you here rather than back at the station,' Chandler said. 'We won't be much longer.'

'You won't be *any* longer. This is my house, and you two are no longer welcome on my property. And stick your threat of dragging me over to Thorpe Wood where the sun don't shine. You weren't honest with me, so you can do one.'

Chandler met his stern gaze with one of equal measure. 'Why has your attitude become so negative since you found out about

Mr McKenzie? If anything, I'd expect you to be more cooperative, not less.'

Dixon took a deep breath, his barrel chest rising and falling inside his pale green polo shirt. 'Do I have to call the police on the police?' he asked, hands spread. 'Is that what it's going to take to shift you two?'

'Not at all,' Bliss said. 'We'll go. Though, like my partner, I find it puzzling that you no longer wish to help us. Your friend is clearly in some sort of trouble and yet suddenly you don't want to talk to us.'

Holding up a hand and pointing a finger, Dixon said, 'Because you're lying bastards, that's why.'

'Neither of us lied to you, Mr Dixon,' Bliss said, not backing off. 'We simply didn't tell you the complete truth.'

'Right. Well, that's the same thing as far as I'm concerned. My mate is in schtuck, and you stand here asking all kinds of questions about how he makes a living and who he might be seeing on the side. It ain't right. So please do as I asked and leave, because I'm going back indoors.'

With that, the man spun on his heels, stepped inside the house, and slammed the door behind him. As they walked back to his car, Bliss felt eyes on their backs. 'What do you make of that?' he asked Chandler, clicking the key fob to release the locks. 'Bit of a turnaround, don't you think?'

As she wrenched the passenger door open, Chandler grimaced and said, 'I'm not so sure. He seemed genuinely put out about us keeping things from him, so maybe it was a natural reaction.'

Bliss laughed. 'Don't tell me you feel guilty about it.'

She responded with her own laughter. 'Of course not. Just saying I understand the change of mood, that's all.'

'Maybe. You say natural reaction, I say overreaction. Hopefully we'll find out which another time.'

As he climbed into his seat, Bliss turned to look back at the house. He saw nobody at the windows, no curtains twitching. Yet still he felt watched, and he wondered what that might mean.

FOURTEEN

I N REPLACING THE EDITH Cavell Hospital with the new Peterborough City Hospital, around £340 million had been spent on creating some absurdly long walks. Bliss felt his calf muscles cramping by the time he and Chandler reached the ward. As he'd previously indicated to DCI Warburton, he took the mother to one side in the family room while his partner kept both daughter's company. The woman was bowed and beaten down, her appearance slovenly with a wan and waxy complexion, though he reminded himself that he was seeing her at what was probably the worst time of her life.

'I'm sorry to meet you under such difficult circumstances,' Bliss told Frances Bell after introducing himself. 'I realise this can't be easy for you. But I'm here to find out what went wrong, and to help if I possibly can. I'm not here to pry, but if I do then believe me, it'll be because I consider it necessary if I'm to do my job properly.'

The issue he wanted to concentrate on initially was the overdose. He began by asking Bell where the family's medication was usually kept and how it had come to end up in Nora's room. She'd had plenty of time to come up with a reasonable story, and Bliss was unsurprised when she confessed to having made a terrible mistake. Ahead of going out into the city centre, she told him, she had changed handbags while chatting with her youngest daughter. After emptying and sorting the contents, she had inadvertently left behind a number of items that she had intended to either dispose of or relocate. Among those items were the tablets Nora had later swallowed.

'But your daughter didn't just swallow them, did she?' Bliss quickly pointed out. 'They had to be pushed free of their blister packs beforehand. From what I've been told, Nora didn't have the manual dexterity to do that for herself. So if everything you've told me so far is true, only her sister could have removed them, because at the time they were taken you were already out shopping.'

Bliss had half expected the mother and elder daughter to play one against the other, creating reasonable doubt in the minds of the police. But Frances Bell surprised him by declaring a habit of popping all tablets from their strips upon opening the boxes.

'I took everything out of my old bag when I made the change,' she explained. 'I intended to put the pills in the new bag's zipper pocket and then drop the packets in the bin afterwards, but I was in a hurry, and I must have forgotten. In all the rush, I obviously also left behind the pills themselves. I know it's still my fault, Inspector, but it was just a terrible oversight.'

Sceptical to the point of disbelief, Bliss pursued the incident more fully. 'What you're claiming, then, is that in amongst all the other mess you'd discarded from your bag, Nora somehow found the pills and then just fed them to herself one after the other? Has she done that kind of thing before?'

'Not with pills, that's for sure. But she does have a habit of putting stuff in her mouth and eating things we haven't actually given her. With all the meds she takes for her CP, Nora doesn't have a good sense of taste, so it's all much the same to her. The pills would have been like gobbling down little sweets, I'm sure.'

The woman's awareness belied her general demeanour. Her brain had been working overtime, allowing her to create this wild fantasy inside her head. Bliss was certain of that but not entirely sure if she was covering for herself or her elder daughter, Patricia. The story she had concocted was absurd, but not altogether impossible.

He wanted to take a look at the scene for himself and asked permission to enter the property. It came as no shock when she refused, but he was torn as to why. He couldn't decide if she didn't want the police checking out her home in case they uncovered evidence of the cuckooing, or because they might focus on the overdose and catch her out in a lie.

'This isn't only about collecting evidence,' Bliss assured her. 'If we are allowed to enter your home, then we can install surveillance devices. This will allow us to observe and listen in to whatever occurs inside the property.'

'Why do you want to do that?'

'Because I think you know as well as I do that not long after you all return, so will they.'

'I'm not giving you permission to do any such thing,' Bell responded sharply.

'Why not?' he asked. 'Why wouldn't you?'

She regarded him with cunning in her eyes. 'Because there's no need. Like I told you before, Inspector, there's nothing going on inside my home.'

'If you force my hand, I can apply for a warrant to enter and search your entire house, Mrs Bell,' Bliss told the woman, though he knew full well any application would be rejected without additional evidence of wrongdoing.

'Then that's what you should do,' she replied, turning her head away from him.

He felt his forehead bunch up. 'I don't understand. All we're trying to do is help. Though you refuse to admit it, we know drug dealers have been working out of your home, and we genuinely believe that has occurred very much against your will. Then there's the rape and resulting pregnancy to consider. Why would you not want to help us help you, Mrs Bell?'

She regarded him for some time, perhaps searching for signs of deceit. Her face clouded over, and fresh tears glittered as they became trapped in her lashes.

'I dare say you've seen more than your fair share of such ugliness,' Bell said in a voice no louder than a whisper. 'But whatever you've witnessed as an outsider will never compare to what goes on behind those walls. You've no idea what it's like to live in fear of your life day in, day out.'

'And you do?' He edged forward. 'You're finally admitting it? If so, tell me more. Please. Let me in and I'll do my job.'

With a determined shake of the head she said, 'I'll admit nothing to you, Inspector, nor will I agree to any request you make. But for the sake of it, let's just say you're right. Knowing what you know about these evil little bastards, why do you imagine I would potentially make life even harder for me and my own by spilling my guts to you?'

'Because we can help,' Bliss insisted, leaning closer still and softening his voice. 'We can protect you and your girls if you'd only let us.'

Bell shook her head. 'I'm sorry but I can't be sure that's true. And if I'm not sure, then I can't take the risk.'

'Even when the result of not taking the risk is to perpetuate a life of misery?'

Her lips curled. Pain flashed in her eyes; a lifetime of experience caught in a single, terrible look. 'Yes,' she said simply. 'And I'll tell you why, Inspector Bliss. Because when we discovered Nora had CP, I didn't think my life could get any worse. But then her father left us, and it did. And when she and I – all three of us, actually – became the victims of a campaign of horrible, vicious taunts, and physical acts of anti-social behaviour, I stupidly thought once again that our lives couldn't get any worse. But they did when those same brutal thugs stepped up their actions in defiance of my complaints to your lot. Now my poor baby is lying in a hospital bed and has no idea she has a child inside her, nor how it got there or who did it to her. So, you'll perhaps forgive me if I don't accept that life can't get worse than it already is. Because it can. For the likes of me and my kids it always can, it always does, and it always will.'

FIFTEEN

B EFORE HEADING TO MILLFIELD, they stopped for a drink and a sandwich at a small café in Mancetter Square close to the Brotherhood Retail Park. The food was excellent, the service friendly. It was one of Bliss's favourite places to grab a quick bite. There was no disguising the odour of hot grease wafting in from the kitchen, but he could testify to how good their all-day breakfasts went down. As they munched their way through a cheese and ham salad on seedy wholemeal, the two discussed their relative conversations.

'At first it was so unnerving,' Chandler explained. 'There's this fourteen-year-old girl who is well-developed and looks six years older, but who speaks and behaves six years younger. I admit it took me a while to adjust. But the moment I did, it just about broke my heart, Jimmy. Regards the rapes – and I'm convinced we are talking plural – to Nora it was nothing more than a bunch of boys playing games with her. She said it hurt the first couple of times, but after that it was just them mucking around, and they were all very nice to her. They gave her sweets and crisps. Little treats so's she'd look forward to their visits.'

Bliss found it difficult to swallow. He closed his eyes to block out the mental image, but it only increased in clarity. 'And the overdose?'

'When it comes to the tablets, she told me her mummy gave her ice cream with lots of sweets sprinkled over the top. If hers is the true account, then Patricia is out of the frame. But of course, that's where this all breaks apart, because no prosecutor will ever agree to Nora testifying. As awful as this sounds, she'd do more harm than good in a witness box, even if she gave evidence in camera.'

'That might depend on whether her verbal account is the same as a recorded formal statement, which we have yet to take.'

Chandler grimaced. 'You remember I just said her sister might be in the clear? Well, according to the nurses attending Nora, the girl has recounted two additional versions to them. In the first, it was Patricia who fetched her the ice cream, and in the next she did it all herself after she'd eaten the ice cream. She's an unreliable witness, Jimmy. It's as simple as that, I'm sorry to say.'

Bliss accepted his partner's position and talked about his conversation with the mother, whose version of events made no mention of ice cream whatsoever. Chandler heard him out before offering a helpless shrug. 'That's rather sly of her, don't you think? She accepts the blame for making a mistake while at the same time excusing herself for it.'

'Not that I believed her. Not for one moment.'

'And not that it matters what you believe. None of the accounts we've been given so far add up to a worthwhile charge.'

'Perhaps, but they do warrant an in-depth investigation. The only reason I'm not going harder at this is because of Nora Bell's condition and the emotional cloud hanging over all three of them.'

Chandler nodded. 'I agree with you, Jimmy. But if we can't rely on a statement from Nora, I'm sure Frances and Patricia will get their stories straight.'

'Not necessarily. It depends on how angry they are with each other.'

From behind the counter came a clatter of dishes as a stack crashed to the ground on their way into the kitchen area at the back. The café fell into silence for several seconds before the customers picked up their conversations once more. Bliss had time to note that a similar accident in a pub would have been met with a loud cheer followed by raucous laughter and maybe even light applause.

Chandler responded to his observation about the anger between mother and her first born. 'While what you say is true, family is family, and loyalty often backs that up. And as far as the cuckooing is concerned, and the boys who visited the poor kid to play *games* with her, if neither the sister nor mother own up to it, we're left with little to go on.'

Bliss felt his face stiffen, jaw tightening. 'Leaving Nora's rapists and the woman who tried to murder her own child to walk away as if nothing happened? No, I'm not having that.'

'But that's my point. You say Frances Bell tried to murder Nora, but it could just as easily have been Patricia.'

'Either way, they're not getting away with it. Nor are those scumbag rapists.'

'Perhaps one of them won't. Certainly not the father, we must hope. But the overdose is both clear and muddy as hell, and that's exactly how it would come across to a jury if it ever made it into a courtroom.'

Indignant, Bliss said, 'We're saying that because of her disability, this poor girl can't obtain justice for the very worst acts human beings are capable of? That's unacceptable, Pen.'

'It's reality, Jimmy. And you're usually the first to acknowledge it. Still, I suppose there's always a chance of Frances Bell caving in to the pressure and admitting to the part she played, but I wouldn't bank on it.'

He shook his head. 'No, me neither. The whole shitty mess is sickening. We have to find a way to do better, Pen. We just have to.'

'We can give it a bloody good go, but Nora is still confused,' Chandler told him, jabbing the air with her food. 'She doesn't understand why she can't be at home or why, and she clearly doesn't fully recall why she went to hospital in the first place. All she remembers is having a tummy ache after eating her ice cream. Normally I'd wonder if she was being reserved because her older sister was in the room with us, but in her case, I think she lacks the guile.'

'In other words, her confusion is genuine.'

'I think so, yes. I was asked by a nurse not to touch on the subject of her assault and definitely not the pregnancy itself. They also suggested I steer clear of the overdose as they consider her recovery to be at a fragile stage. Basically, we can only talk around the issues and listen to her responses.'

Bliss huffed. 'Which couldn't have left much to discuss.'

'It didn't. She seems like a lovely kid, but I still say she'll be of no help to us.'

He paused, biting into what was left of his sandwich. This was new territory for them all. Theirs was a difficult enough case to mount under normal circumstances, and even harder to prosecute. But take a girl with Nora Bell's mental age and limited capacity, and every single aspect became that much tougher.

'And Patricia?' he asked eventually.

'She bothers me,' Chandler confessed, sipping diet cola from a glass through a paper straw. 'I spoke to them separately as well, of course. I found her to be unafraid, confident, seemingly unruffled, and a po-faced liar. According to Patricia, she knows nothing about dealers, and certainly her home has not been commandeered by them. As for the overdose, that was all down to Nora. The girl looked me right in the eye and reeled it off.'

Bliss flared his nostrils. 'The whole thing stinks. At some point soon, we will have to interview Nora in the presence of a child psychologist. And we're going to have to ask some difficult and extremely awkward questions unless her mother or sister owns up. As for those two, we need them in the room with social and child welfare services. We ought to have all relevant reports by close of play today, so let's arrange a meeting for tomorrow in a family room at the hospital.'

'You want me to sort that?'

'Please. When we're done here, we'll get eyes on the Bell property and the surrounding area. I asked for the PCSOs to keep tabs on the place, as it's empty. I want to see who's hanging around, though.'

'Do we want to get inside?'

'I already broached that subject with Frances and got nowhere,' Bliss confessed. He drained his mug of tea, then wiped his mouth with a serviette. 'Assuming Patricia and Nora were not home alone yesterday when the overdose took place, the crew will have moved their stash out before the older sister made the triple-nine call. We have the meds packaging in evidence as well, so without permission to enter the property and install some surveillance, I think we need to consider going covert.'

'What d'you mean?'

'The drugs squad will by this stage have the house on their radar. I'll have a word with them, but they might want to mount surveillance if they can get a team in one of the neighbouring houses. I just wish we could get CSI in there under some pretence to gather evidence without any of the local scumbags being aware of it.'

'Surely they will have been scared off after this? Even if it's only temporarily.'

Shrugging, Bliss said, 'I'm not so sure. The Bells are easy prey, and if this crew thinks they've got away with it then they might well return as soon as the family does. You never know, they might even crawl back anyway and not bother waiting. By this stage in their cuckooing, they must be able to come and go as they please.'

It was Chandler's turn to pay, which she did at the till. Out in the car park, she suddenly grabbed Bliss's arm without warning. 'Jimmy,' she said, her eyes wide and gleaming at him. 'Do you realise what you said back there?'

'Probably not. I'm old and past it, remember?'

He got an elbow in the ribs for his trouble. 'No, you silly sod. So far, we've been looking at either Frances or Patricia Bell for overdosing Nora. But as you rightly said a few minutes ago, they were unlikely to be alone inside that house at the time it happened. So, what if one of the crew slipped her those pills? And what if the little twunt who deliberately overdosed her is the same little twunt who raped her?'

They discussed the possibilities as Bliss drove to Millfield. He was having a hard time understanding why one of the nesters would decide to take the young kid's life, especially in such a cold and calculated way. If they wanted rid of the girl, smothering her was easier and more certain. Chandler agreed with his misgivings but refused to rule out the possibility. Bliss agreed to bear it in mind and bring it up with the rest of the team.

He turned onto Stone Lane from Lincoln Road. The street was narrow, a mixture of early twentieth century two-up, two-down terraced homes on one side, and new-build apartments and three-storey houses on the other. The deeper they progressed the more it changed back to homes that were standard fare for the area with piss-poor parking opportunities. A lot of the houses had been designed with only two windows at the front, which gave them a somewhat skewed appearance. Many outer walls remained natural brick, while others had been cladded or rendered over and painted. A large number sprouted satellite dishes, vast saucers clinging on for dear life. Alongside every few properties ran alleyways leading to back gardens.

The house they were most interested in stood opposite a gated new-build block. Bliss paid no attention to it as they drove past, but noted a complete lack of potential miscreants lingering close by. No hooded cyclists turned lazy circles, acting as lookouts or information gatherers. All was eerily quiet, as if the street itself was holding its breath in fearful anticipation of what was to come.

'Paramedic Kelly made sure to mention how unusually quiet these pavements were when they arrived yesterday,' he said to Chandler. 'I think she was telling me that the crew running this area had scarpered because they knew precisely what had happened.'

'She's astute that one,' Chandler said. 'Way too young for you, though,' she added with a derisory sniff.

He ignored the jibe, still regretting not being able to enter the Bell property and having no justifiable reason to do so without a warrant. At the first junction, he turned left, then first left again. Here they encountered two rows of mainly semi-detached properties, a major step up from what they had just driven through. Pockets of older kids littered the pavements, their eyes drawn to the unfamiliar vehicle.

'We might as well be in a marked car with blues and twos going off,' Chandler muttered. 'It's as if they can smell us in here.'

'Bacon?' Bliss asked.

'In my case. You're more like crackling.'

'Tasty, in other words.'

Rolling her eyes, Chandler said, 'If you insist.'

'You reckon the fucktards we're after are among that lot back there?' he asked, glancing in the rear-view mirror.

'The majority of them certainly don't look as if they belong on this road.'

'That's what I was thinking.' He shook his head in wonder. 'Just a street away, but it might as well be another world entirely.'

The thought drew him back to his own teenage years. It had been much the same in and around Bethnal Green. Street gangs were not so much turf-driven in those days, but you still didn't want to stray too far off your own manor if you were on your own. A hundred yards could feel a lot longer than it was if you found yourself heading in the wrong direction. You wouldn't necessarily find dealers on every corner back then, but most areas had their share of tough nuts looking to demonstrate prowess with their fists and boots. Some of the scraps were legendary, but by the time he was old enough to do any real damage, Bliss was learning self-discipline in the boxing ring. That and having a police sergeant for a father prompted two kinds of reactions: other kids were either wary and so avoided him or looked to make a name for themselves by giving him a hiding. It hadn't been an easy path to navigate, but he won more battles than he lost and along the way he thought he might have earned their respect.

'What was life like for the mid-teens Penny Chandler?' he asked as he nosed the pool car back onto Lincoln Road.

'Not like this place,' she said, wrinkling her nose in distaste. 'I'm a rube, remember?'

'Of course. All webbed feet, interbreeding, and hasty fumbles in rural hay ricks?'

Chandler's smile was reflective. 'Pretty much. East Anglia felt like the entire world at the time. Going into Peterborough and

Norwich seemed exotic and exciting. A week in a caravan in Sunny Hunny or Cromer was the dream holiday. I suppose we thought it was how everybody lived if they weren't lucky enough to reside in a big city. It didn't take me long after moving here to realise we were the fortunate ones growing up.'

Nodding, Bliss said, 'So if you'd not joined the Job you reckon you'd still be there? A farmer's wife, maybe?'

'Why not the farmer?'

'Why not indeed?'

'I think you're right, though. If I hadn't got myself tubbed in my teens, I almost certainly wouldn't have felt like I needed a career. So no, I probably wouldn't have become a copper.'

'Which would have been our loss.'

Chandler smiled and gave him a playful nudge. 'Ah, you're just a big old soft cuddly bear really, aren't you?'

Bliss ignored her, saying, 'I've been thinking a lot about you lately, Pen.'

She glanced across, feigning shock and horror. 'Uh-oh. You're not about to confess your undying love for me, are you?'

'Not even close. I'm telling you I think this is the right time for you to step up. You or Bish, perhaps even both of you, are perfectly positioned to make yourselves as close to irreplaceable as you can get.'

Chandler groaned, thrusting her head back. 'Not this again. Promotion? Really?'

'Yes. Promotion. The unit needs a bloody top-notch DI. You and Bish are ideal. Bish less so if he doesn't get his shit together, though I'll be having a word in his shell-like before I leave. But you, you are in your prime and ready for this challenge. Let's face it, Pen, if I held you by your ankles and flipped you upside down, a little piece of me would fall out.'

Chandler shuddered. 'Ugh! That's an unpleasant thought.'

He reacted to her comment with a wry grin. 'Very droll. But the good thing is, some modern policing would also end up in a big heap on the floor. You have a bit of both inside you. You're a… a hybrid.'

'Hmm. A hybrid copper, eh? There are worse things to be called.'

'Worse things to be, full-stop.'

She shrugged. 'We've talked about this before. Becoming a DI is not in my stars.'

'If not one of you two, then before long some fast-tracked book-thumping graduate is going to be flailing around up there between you lot and Diane Warburton, completely out of their depth.'

'What you're really trying to say is you're the irreplaceable one. That without you the team will fall apart.'

'You know me better than that,' Bliss scoffed. 'I'll be forgotten as quickly as yesterday's headlines. But if it doesn't sound too conceited, I am worried about my legacy. By pure chance, I've helped create a dynamic, insightful, and relentless team. All the moving parts are exactly right and mesh together perfectly. My moving to SIO changes that, because a DI will have to step in to fill the void. But you and Bish can make sure that's a temporary glitch. You can make sure that when I finally turn my back on Thorpe Wood for the last time, I can do so knowing either or both of you are running the show.'

Chandler huffed out a sigh. 'I just don't know if I'm cut out for the job.'

Bliss switched lanes and navigated around a slow-moving panel van. He must have pulled back into the nearside lane too quickly because the van driver flashed its lights. Ignoring both, Bliss drove on and said, 'Then find out the hard way. You can only do that if you give it a go.'

'It's Bish who's had the training,' she argued. 'He's already been part of the framework, so he has the advantage.'

'If he gets over the slump he's in, then maybe so. But everybody has to start somewhere, Pen. I'm not going to be around forever, but while I am, I can help you. Before long, they'll start making use of you as an acting DI and if you show your worth during that period, it's you who can make that position yours.'

Chandler turned to him, frowning. 'So you're discounting Bish?'

Bliss indicated to take the off-ramp at the Thorpe Wood interchange. He shook his head and said, 'Not at all. You're right in saying he'd get there before you. If he puts his mind to it. And perhaps he then gets to fill my shoes instead of you. But Pen, there are some shakeups coming. Changes at the top have already been decided, but look around you at the team. Before you can say "promotion ladder", both Phil and Gul are going to be sergeants. The SCU will then justify having two DIs again. Just make sure you're one of them.'

SIXTEEN

BACK AT THE FACTORY, Bliss was pleased to see everyone in their regular positions. Later, they would regroup into a Major Incident Room for a formal briefing, but he was eager to catch up on developments and swiftly gathered the team together for an ad hoc update meeting. He made sure to include the DCI, and as soon as Warburton joined them he fed them details relating to the Bell family.

'In a moment of previously unheard of inspiration,' he said, glancing sidelong at his partner, 'Pen noted that while we've been focussed on the mother or daughter slipping those drugs to Nora, in all likelihood they were not alone in the house at the time. Odds are that one or more of the nesters was also there. Personally, I doubt any of them had sufficient motive to kill the girl, and if they did I don't see them doing so in such a contrived way. I suspect they'd be far more direct and would leave nothing to chance. Nonetheless, for once in her career, Pen made a good point, and we can't rule it out.'

'My soon to be careerless boss is right to have his reservations,' Chandler shot back, giving him daggers. 'They can't possibly know about the pregnancy, so it's hard to think of a motive. And like Jimmy says, are they likely to do it with a stack of tablets? It's just another line of enquiry to consider, that's all.'

Bliss agreed and suggested they move on to the events at Cuckoo's Hollow. He gave DS Bishop the nod to get the ball rolling. 'What have you and Gul got for us regards CCTV and mobile data?' he asked.

Bishop hesitated too long, and the ever eager DC Ansari spoke up in his place. 'I've put the request in for data and hope to hear back later today. What I can tell you so far is that there has been no activity from our supposed victim's phone since late Friday evening.'

This came as no surprise to Bliss. In gathering the phone data, he was hoping to achieve three things: track the phone mast and GPS positioning in order to plot Stuart McKenzie's movements in the days leading up the incident at Werrington; check to see if there were any incriminating or potential leads in text form or on WhatsApp; and to listen to stored messages in the hope that one or more might prove useful to the investigation. This prompted him to remember something he had overlooked.

'Thanks, Gul,' he said. 'I completely neglected to ask Mrs McKenzie if we could search their home and collect any other devices that her husband might have used. Will you sort a warrant for me, please? Just in case she gets bolshy and refuses.'

'Will do, boss. I'll see if I can get it signed later today.'

'And CCTV?' Bliss asked, turning his gaze to Bishop.

The big man's response was rapid this time. 'First of all, we found Mr McKenzie's motor. It was parked in a side street a fair distance from the park. For whatever reason, I imagine he didn't want to be seen arriving or leaving. Anyhow, we had it towed into the yard at Huntingdon and the vehicle techs are swarming all over it as we speak. As for security footage, we're still in the process of gathering. I can tell you there won't be much in the way of CCTV, but we might get luckier with doorbell cameras. Footage obtained from cabs and buses will dribble in as per usual.'

'So basically, we're no further on,' Bliss remarked.

'Other than locating the car, no.'

Bliss nodded in DC Virgil's direction, gaining his attention. 'What about you, Alan? Did you get anywhere with their financials?'

The Major Crime Unit's most recent recruit leaned back in his chair and uttered a booming groan. 'It's like wading through treacle, boss. Their personal accounts are simple enough, but the business side is labyrinthine. I lost count of the companies they own, and those are the legit ones. I found myself in the middle of a company shell game, but as they are all rerouted abroad, I'm obviously going to have to approach the search in a different way. I've been on the phone with forensic accounts techs at Hinchingbrooke, who have been very helpful. I'm doing my best, but it takes time.'

'Okay. Good. Thanks. Could you do with another couple of bodies?'

Virgil grinned. 'I'm not going to refuse. In fact, what would help is if I could get a few people working on things for me here while I shoot over to county HQ. It'll speed up the process if I'm in the room with the forensic accounts people.'

Bliss raised an upright thumb. 'Fine. Organise that. Anything else I need to know?'

'I have something from forensic science,' Warburton said, referring to notes made on her phone. 'After a few moans and groans, they put a rush on Roger Craig's overcoat. To my astonishment they were able to pull some skin cells off the inside lining that weren't his. A short while ago, they confirmed a match to Stuart McKenzie, based on the material they scavenged from the comb and toothbrush his wife provided. This lends even more credence to Mr Craig's account of what happened on Friday night.'

'Yeah, and while all this is happening how much effort is going into testing and finding results from his own murder scene?' Bishop growled. 'I don't suppose a homeless man, veteran or not, will be dealt with as a priority.'

'That's where you're wrong,' the DCI told him, adding a little edge to her tone. 'They understand the two cases are closely connected, so Mr Craig is next on their list. A long list, I'd remind you.'

'Thank you, Diane,' Bliss said, keen to get between the two. He then flashed Bishop a warning look. 'Whatever gripe is circling that massive nut of yours, Bish, don't let it become a distraction.'

When there was no reply, Bliss said, 'Is that understood, Sergeant Bishop?'

'Yes… boss.'

He let it go. It wasn't worth arguing about here and now in front of a captive audience. The obvious disrespect in the way Bish had delayed calling him "boss" would once have been a big deal, but Bliss knew his colleague was going through a rough period and hadn't intended to appear contemptuous.

'Thanks, everyone,' he said. 'Pen and I managed to speak with Grant Dixon. It was hard work but became impossible after he received a call from Sharon McKenzie, who told him about our investigation.'

'Didn't you specifically ask her not to do so?' DCI Warburton asked.

'I pretty much instructed her not to. Seems she wasn't able to keep it to herself for long. Anyhow, Dixon spoke quite freely about their regular jaunts away. They like casinos, apparently, and when the mood strikes, they indulge themselves. He was adamant that Stuart wasn't seeing another woman and claims not to know where he might have gone. He says there is no reason why his friend might be hiding from anyone and has no idea why he would have been the victim of an attack.'

'And your impression of him overall?'

Bliss thought about it. 'He was good. Able to think on his feet. No real panic. For me, what we got from him was two parts truthful to one part bullshit.'

'Penny?' Warburton asked his partner.

Chandler, arms folded, nodded, and said, 'I'd have to agree. Dixon was definitely hiding something from us. Maybe even several somethings. He told us the truth when it didn't matter, but lied through his teeth when it did.'

'And the other partner… Michael Banks?'

'Not at home and not answering the only phone number we have for him. We'll drop by later on and see what he has to say for himself, but his mate Dixon will get to him first, so it'll probably be like listening to an echo.'

'Okay.' The DCI spread her hands. 'Do we think these business partners are at all involved in the attack on and subsequent disappearance of Stuart McKenzie?'

Bliss was keen to explain why he didn't think that was the case. 'Nothing points to it at this stage. Their financials will tell us more and might provide a possible motive, but in the absence of that, I'm not seeing one. No, if we are right about Dixon skirting around the truth, it's more likely to be because he knows a reason why McKenzie was targeted rather than being directly responsible. My guess is that reason involves both him and Banks. I wouldn't discount the car sales manager, Jacob Nash, either.'

Warburton seemed pleased enough with the progress made. 'Sounds about right. So where are we? We have evidence to endorse Mr Craig's eyewitness statement. I'm happy to go along with everything he told us. What we still don't know is if McKenzie recovered and walked away under his own steam, or if his attacker returned to move him.'

'That still sounds wrong to me,' DC Virgil said. 'Why take such a massive risk?'

'To buy time, maybe?' Chandler suggested. 'No body means no ID.'

'But whoever did it must have known he'd be reported missing and that we'd eventually put two and two together.'

'How? We had no body to compare any misper identification against.'

'Which is where Roger Craig comes in,' Bliss said. 'The bloke who carried out the attack will have seen him run off after trying and failing to resuscitate McKenzie. If it were me, I'd assume he'd gone for help. I'd note that the homeless man got a good look at the victim and could therefore describe him. In fact, I think there's every chance he went looking for Craig not necessarily to kill him, but to question him. Craig reacted unexpectedly, leaving the attacker no option but to silence him for good.'

'He would surely have known he wasn't buying much time by moving McKenzie away from the scene,' DC Virgil persisted.

'But he did buy some. And maybe that wasn't the only reason for taking the body. It's much harder to prove a murder took place when there's no victim. Look how much more difficult it's already been. At this stage, we're not even certain there is a body for us to find.'

There were nods of agreement all round.

'Why can't anything be easy?' Ansari grumbled. 'Man A kills Man B, witnessed by a dozen people, and Man A is caught still holding a bloody axe in his hand. Job's a good'un and we all go home happy. This one is already doing my head in. Is it a murder, isn't it a murder? Is there a body, isn't there a body? Are we after a killer or just an attacker? And where the hell is Stuart McKenzie if he isn't dead?'

Bliss blew out a rasp of air. 'We've tackled our fair share of simple jobs,' he said to placate her. 'They're not all like this one.'

'I know. Just letting off some steam, boss.'

'Understandably. These cases take their toll. On this one, we have to nail down why both these men were in that park on Friday night. I keep coming back to that, I know, but it's critical.'

'Yeah, and we're getting nowhere with it,' DS Bishop said, his knuckles showing white as he gripped the edge of the desk he was sitting on. 'Let's face it, if we don't find a decent lead on his mobile, then we're stuffed.'

'Not necessarily,' Bliss said, more placidly than he felt in the face of such negativity. 'There's still the human element to fully explore. Let's go back to what coppers did before technology took over. We get out on the streets, and we ask questions. Stuart McKenzie was in that park for a reason. Odds are he was meeting the man who ended up killing him. If somebody doesn't know precisely why the two were together, they might have a rough idea.'

'And who is this somebody?' Bishop challenged.

Bliss stared him down. 'I don't know, Bish. But our missing man has a wife and business partners. One or more of them knows more than they've said so far. And we still have one to question. But I have a good idea where to start next.'

'I'll make a note on the calendar, boss,' Virgil said, drawing laughter from most people in the room, Bliss included.

He pointed at the young detective and said, 'Just for that, the cakes are on you, Constable.'

'What? Why? I didn't volunteer for anything.'

'No, but you did take the piss out of the boss. It's bad form, and it warrants a forfeit. Anyhow, back to my brilliant idea. Pen and I will pay a visit to Mrs McKenzie. Because I reckon she's got her husband's mates round there as we speak. If they know something, they'll be circling the wagons, putting their heads together and coming up with answers to cover their arses.' He got to his feet. 'Cakes later, DC Virgil. Me and Pen are off to rattle some cages.'

SEVENTEEN

BLISS PERSUADED CHANDLER INTO fetching him a bottle of water from the canteen while he had a quick word with DS Bishop. But the moment his partner closed the door behind her he walked across to the desk at which DC Ansari was sitting and asked her to text him the McKenzie home address.

'When Pen gets back, tell her I decided to go on my own,' he added, before leaving the unit, making his way along the corridor and taking the stairs down to the car park. It was only when he opened the door of the Mondeo and slid inside that he became aware of the figure already sitting in the passenger seat.

'Jesus!' he cried, putting a hand to his chest. 'You almost gave me a Connery, Pen. What the bloody hell are you doing here?'

An insincere frown flitted across her face. 'You never lock up when you park here. I mean, why would you? If it's not safe here, it's not safe anywhere, right?'

'I didn't ask you *how* you were here. I asked what you were doing here?'

Chandler shook her head and this time her glare was heartfelt. 'How long have we worked together? No, forget that. Too long, that's for sure. I'm only glad it will come to an end on Friday. But for the time being, remember that I can see your every move coming a mile off. I knew you were going to dump me before you even thought of it yourself, Jimmy. Because I know you don't intend to follow the rules when you get to McKenzie's place.'

Bliss was silent for a moment. Then he started the engine. 'Did you at least get me my drink?' he asked.

'If I had, you'd have been long gone. Besides, that was all part of the ruse. I mean, since when do you drink water?'

He nodded in agreement. 'It bothers me that I can no longer surprise you.'

'It bothers me that you still try. After all, aren't you the man who once told me it was unsporting to have a battle of wits with someone who was unarmed? I've got news for you, old man, that person these days is you.'

Wincing and sucking in air, Bliss said, 'Ouch. That one actually hurt.'

They bickered for three further minutes, all the time it took to reach Grove Lane, which ran behind and to the side of the Fox & Hounds pub in Longthorpe. Bliss whistled as they pulled onto the drive outside Stuart and Sharon McKenzie's modern-build home. Clearly the couple had done well for themselves, and as he parked he could see between buildings to the garden beyond. A circular summer house lurked in one corner, while halfway along the edged border stood a raised, stepped half-moon circle of patio. A rattan-style table in the centre was populated with more people than the three gleaming new cars on the gravel driveway implied.

'Those were two nice gaffs we saw earlier today,' Bliss said to Chandler. 'But this is another step up altogether. Looking at this place, I'm beginning to wonder if their slices of the pie are even.'

He tried the front doorbell, and moments later a voice called out from the back. They walked around the side of the house, past the parked cars. When Mrs McKenzie opened the garden gate and saw who it was, her face immediately clouded over. She stepped out onto the gravel shaking her head.

'No, no, no,' she said determinedly. 'Now is neither the time nor the place.'

Bliss continued on until he was within a couple of paces of the woman, who looked decidedly more kempt than she had the previous day. 'Is your husband still missing, Mrs McKenzie?' he asked as if perplexed by her attitude.

'Yes. I would have said so otherwise.'

'Then as far as I'm concerned, this is precisely the right time and place.'

'But I have family here,' she protested. 'There are children in the garden.'

'Don't forget your friends, Mrs McKenzie. Grant Dixon and Michael Banks are here too, yes?'

As if on cue, Dixon approached the gate. 'What's going on here?' he demanded to know as a second man appeared close at his heels. 'What do you two want?'

'Sorry, but is this your home?' Bliss asked pointedly.

'You were at mine this morning, so you know it isn't.'

'Then it's none of your business what we're doing here. I'd advise you to stay out of it… until I'm ready to ask you further questions.'

His eyes switched to the other man. He was shorter than Grant Dixon but with a powerful, sturdy build, smartly dressed in what Bliss guessed was golfing apparel. 'Mr Banks, I assume?' he said. 'We tried your place earlier today, but I'm sure Mr Dixon here has brought you up to speed.'

'He did, which is why we're here. Sharon and the kids need our support at this time. And I can only reaffirm everything he told you. I have no idea where Stuart is. None of us do.'

'Is that still true, Mrs McKenzie?' Chandler asked the woman, whose anxiety levels seemed to have increased in the presence of the two family friends.

'Yes. I've already said.' The nod she gave looked half-hearted.

'Did you, though? My boss here asked you if your husband was still missing. My question was quite different.'

After a moment of charged silence, Sharon McKenzie took a deep breath and said, 'Look, can't you leave me be for the time being? This is all very distressing. I'm overwhelmed at the moment, and I have my guests to attend to.'

'I wouldn't have thought any of that was as important as your missing husband,' Bliss persisted, jumping back in. 'There are still a few things we need to make you aware of. Things we need to know from you, too. I suggest you talk to us first on your own, then we'll invite both Mr Banks and Mr Dixon to join our conversation.'

McKenzie looked up at him with hope in her eyes. 'You have news about Stu?'

'We do. A confirmation of sorts. Believe me, you will want to hear what we have to say, so where can we speak?' Bliss was firm, his demeanour implying there was no alternative and that he would not take no for an answer.

*

The three of them sat in the summer house, one quarter of which was decked out like some kind of Tikki bar, its Polynesian décor too garish to even pass for kitsch. A colourful rendition of Waikiki beach in Oahu hung on the wall behind the bar. Sharon McKenzie and DS Chandler occupied a padded bench seat, while Bliss arranged a fold-out camping chair so that he could keep an eye on the two men without having to turn his head. He didn't think either of them would make a run for it, but he couldn't be certain. Keeping his voice low, he explained the result of the DNA swab of Roger Craig's coat.

McKenzie looked at the two detectives. 'What does that mean?' she asked. 'Are you telling me Stu is dead?'

'No, not at all. As I said, the DNA swab picked up skin cells, not blood. Our forensic people tested the result against DNA taken from the items you gave us yesterday morning. This matches the statement provided by the homeless man who attempted to resuscitate your husband. As a consequence, we're reasonably confident that Stuart was attacked. As you know, Mr Craig, believing him to have passed away, covered the body with his coat before seeking help. However, as we mentioned last time we spoke, Mrs McKenzie, since the body was gone when our officers arrived, we have no way of knowing what became of it… your husband. But he was there, that much we're certain of, and we believe events transpired as described to us.'

It took the woman a few beats to respond, leaning back with a hand to her throat as she gathered her breath. 'Well, obviously I'm relieved you're not here to tell me my Stu is dead, but what happens next?'

Bliss recalled the items he had neglected to ask for the previous day. 'The first thing we'd like from you is your agreement for us to remove any electronic devices used by your husband. By that I mean mobile phones, tablets, laptops, computers, game stations, even if he only shared them with others.'

'I assume he has his phone on him. Why on earth would you want those other things?'

'It's our job to look into anything and everything that your husband was involved in during the days leading up to and including Friday,' Chandler explained patiently. 'With so much of our lives involving technology today, Mrs McKenzie, the information we require might well be sitting on one of those devices. Now, we will also need to search your home, but I promise you we won't tear the place apart. That is, provided you grant us permission.'

Sharon McKenzie's head came up with a jerk. 'And if I don't? I'm not saying we have anything to hide, but I'm sure there might be things neither of you would want others to have access to on your own devices or in your own home. Private, personal things.'

'I understand your concerns. But we'll be both quick and discreet. Our only interest is information that might lead us to your husband or the man who assaulted him.'

Neither spoke for a few moments. At which point, Bliss intervened. 'I have to tell you that, as we speak, one of our sergeants is obtaining a warrant. If you force us to use it, I can't promise you the same level of care and attention when conducting the search.'

McKenzie gave a curt nod, which Bliss took to be a tacit agreement. He then allowed his gaze to drift, jerking his head in the direction of the patio. 'How well do you know your husband's business partners, Mrs McKenzie?'

'Grant and Mickey? I've known them both almost as long as I've known Stu. Why do you ask?'

'You trust them?'

'Why wouldn't I?' She appeared affronted by the question.

'Do you trust them?'

'Yes. I trust them. Of course, I do. Why would you even ask me that? What are you suggesting?'

Bliss deflected her own queries. 'What do you know about their business dealings together?'

Sharon McKenzie pushed herself deeper into the bench's padded cushions, crossing one leg over the other. She wore light blue casual trousers, and sandals on bare feet. Her dangling foot twitched to an unheard beat. 'Virtually nothing,' she said defensively. 'The three of them own a number of companies together. That's all I know. It's all I need to know.'

'And does your husband have any sole business interests? Any companies he runs on his own?'

'Not that I know of.'

'Do you think you would if he did?'

She gave a shrug. 'Probably not.'

'So as far as you're aware it's just the co-owned ventures. You say you know virtually nothing about them, but you must be able to tell us something.'

The woman blew out an exasperated blast of breath. 'Look, as I've already explained, Stu is in business with his friends. What they do and how they do it is their world. Mine is taking care of this place and our kids.'

Bliss picked up on something in her flat statement. '*His* friends?'

'All right then, *our* friends. As for the companies they own together, some I'm aware of, some I'm not.'

'Then talk to us about the ones you are aware of.'

Shaking her head irritably, McKenzie counted off on her fingers. 'There's the small casino here in Peterborough. It's not much more than a shop in the city centre, with physical gambling machines people use. I know about that because investing in a larger one is their latest brainwave and it's been discussed a lot lately. Then there's the long-established car sales business over in Fengate. They also have interests in importing and exporting, but don't ask me what because I don't know. I think they own a media company as well.'

'You were never curious enough to find out more? Not at all interested?' Chandler asked sceptically.

'No. There's never been a need for me to be involved, so I do my best to keep out of it. That way, I can focus on taking care of the home plus Stu and our children. Why are you keeping on with this line of questioning? You think what happened to my husband has something to do with work? With Grant and Mickey?'

WHAT DIES INSIDE US

Bliss cocked his head. 'As it happens, I think it might. But let's get the pair of them in here, shall we? See what they have to say for themselves.'

He got to his feet, caught Dixon's eye and beckoned him over, extending the invitation to the man sitting alongside him by jabbing a finger in his direction. The newcomers each took a stool by the bar. When they were settled, Bliss kicked things off.

'Before we crack on,' he said, 'are you two gentlemen able to provide me with your whereabouts on Friday night? Between 6.00pm and midnight.'

'Why do you want to know?' Dixon asked gruffly.

Shaking his head, Bliss said, 'This always goes better if we do the asking. It was just a few days ago, so it should be a simple enough question to answer.'

'I was at home,' Banks told them. 'I spent the first part of the evening with my wife and kids, then later went online in my office.'

'Presumably your wife can vouch for you?'

'Of course.'

'Same here,' Dixon said with a heavy shrug.

'What, you also went online in your office later that same night?' Chandler challenged him.

'Yes. That's precisely what I did. Me and Mickey both enjoy a flutter every so often. Poker and Blackjack mainly, and occasionally we even sit in on the same game.'

'Okay, thank you. Our working hypothesis,' Bliss began, 'is that Stuart went to meet someone at Cuckoo's Hollow on Friday night. At some unknown point during the meeting, things clearly turned violent, and Stuart was attacked. We don't know by whom, nor why. And clearly, we still don't know what became of Stuart afterwards. If I had to guess, I'd say nobody here was directly involved. However, I do believe one or more of you might know why somebody would assault Stuart. I'm therefore giving all three of you the opportunity to speak up.'

Bliss sat back and let his eyes do the work. Looks were exchanged between the three of them, each shiftier than the last. He made the decision to add to their obvious discomfort. 'Perhaps I wasn't clear enough before. So let me clarify. If DS Chandler and I leave here none the wiser, you will all be drawn deeper into our investigation until we are certain as to the extent of your involvement. We'll turn your lives and your homes inside out and upside down. Your business and personal finances, too. We'll also ask our friends at HMRC for their forensic accounting assistance. My guess is none of you want that.'

He turned his attention to their victim's wife, suspecting she would be the one to break first. When their eyes met, Bliss knew he'd been right.

EIGHTEEN

J ACOB NASH PACED THE hotel room. By this point, he had almost worn a furrow in the carpet. Given his bulk and physical condition, he was prone to sweats, but today it was as if his glands had sprung a leak. He'd already had one shower since booking in, and less than an hour later he felt the need for another soap and soak. He couldn't recall ever having been this nervous before in his entire life. But then he'd never done anything like this before and hadn't imagined the experience would be so stressful.

On several occasions over the past few days, he had come close to calling the whole thing off. Yet whenever he drew his mind to why he was doing this at all, he knew he couldn't walk away. This was not only his first time, it might well be his last. But it was an urge he had been unable to fight off in recent months, and he'd been looking forward to today for so long that the thought of turning his back on it right at the death twisted his insides all the more.

He jumped as if scalded by hot liquid when his mobile pinged. This particular phone was known about by only one person, and their number was displayed on the screen. The text message he'd been salivating over had finally arrived.

I'm here. In reception.

Swallowing thickly, his hands shaking and his heart tumbling like rocks in an avalanche, Nash typed a response.

I can't wait. But you must remember what we discussed. When you see me you come and hug me right away and call me BIG BROTHER!

Time seemed to slow. It felt too long. Then: *I know. Hurry. I can't wait either.*

Nash drew in a deep breath, adrenaline shooting through the entire mass of his bulky frame. He was jumpy, nervous, terrified even. But he was also hugely excited. He tapped his pockets, making sure he had the key card on him. Then he left the room and made his way along the ground floor corridor around to the entrance at the front of the building. He exited the passage with a winning smile on his face, which was immediately wiped off the moment he saw the reception area was empty.

Well, not quite empty. But there was no sign of the young man he'd been expecting to see standing there, waiting to dash into his open arms like long-lost siblings as they'd discussed. Confused, he walked across to the entrance, stepping outside to survey the car park when the doors automatically slid open. No movement. No man. Puzzled, he took out his phone.

Where are you? I'm here but you're not. Then a thought occurred. He typed some more. *Please don't tell me you went to the wrong hotel.*

It didn't take long for his reply to come in.

Look behind you.

Jacob Nash spun on his heels, the smile already back in place.

The woman who'd been sitting on the reception area's only sofa stood facing him in the hotel doorway, her dark sunglasses reflecting back the sunlight. The look on her face snatched the smile away from his.

'Invite me to your room, Jacob,' Danielle Halford said in a soft unflustered voice.

'What?!' The big man's narrowed eyes spoke of wariness and fear. 'Who are you? What do you want?'

'Who I am is none of your business, Jacob. Clearly, I know who you are, which is as it should be. As for what I want, I'm here to do you the biggest favour of your entire life.'

'Do what? Is this some kind of joke? Look, whatever you're selling I'm not buying, sweetheart. Okay? If you'll excuse me, I'm waiting for a guest to arrive, and I'd like you to stop giving me grief.'

'Oh, I'm terribly sorry. If you're waiting for somebody that makes all the difference.'

'Well, I am. Please, whatever your scam is, try it on the next moron to come along.'

'Would that be twenty-year-old Tommy you're waiting for, Mr Nash?'

A sudden pall of fear seemed to cast the large man's face in shadow. His mouth opened and stayed that way, no sound emerging from his lips.

Halford took a step closer. 'Invite me to your room and we can do this in private. It's the only way you retain some measure of control over the situation. Please understand, either we do this now and do it my way, or what I know about you goes straight to your family.'

Nash was horrified, but from somewhere he found his balls and it seemed that even he was surprised to note they were intact. 'And if I choose to put you in the ground instead?' he threatened, spitting the words out as if they were poisonous.

Halford chuckled, her narrow shoulders juddering. She wore a tailored trouser suit with pinstripes, platinum earrings in the shape of a bow hung from both ears and rising and falling against her cleavage lay a matching pendant. She looked the part for every role she played.

'I think not, Jacob,' she said in that same gentle whisper. She appraised him before shaking her head. 'No, you won't do that. To be honest, you couldn't even if you tried. And I'd strongly advise you not to because if you think you're miserable now, I promise I can make matters so much worse. Instead, take the uncomplicated route. Invite me inside and let's get this over with. I'm sure you don't want Marie or Josh and little Annie to learn about this mid-life crisis escapade.'

The man broke at the mention of his wife and children. He splintered and fragmented inside his head where it counts most of all. Halford saw it clearly, the ultimate disintegration of a person's very soul. Nash closed his eyes and gave a simple nod of wordless acceptance. He was hers to do with as she liked.

She followed him back inside the hotel and into the small room the man had rented. A room rendered squalid by Jacob Nash's intent. Taking a seat at the small circular table wedged into the far corner of the room, she crossed one leg over the other and said, 'You've been such a bad boy. A naughty little pervert almost caught with his trousers down, so to speak. Using a male prostitute behind your wife's back is just so gauche.'

Nash remained silent, staring at her defiantly. As if he still had a say in what was to come.

Halford smiled at him. 'This will only go well for you from this point onward provided you don't lie to me. If I hear the truth coming out of that fat gob of yours, you get to walk away free as a bird. Imagine that, Jacob. Here you are caught red-handed, trapped in a small room with your accuser, but you can emerge with no stain on your character. No disgrace. No humiliation. If not, if you tell me porkies, I throw you to the wolves and your family and friends find out what kind of arsehole you really are. Am I making myself clear?'

Perched anxiously on the edge of the bed, Nash nodded mutely. He was bowed, crushed, and barely able to breathe. Halford got to her feet, took two steps towards him and without any warning slapped the man hard across the face with a stinging blow. 'Answer me properly by using your words,' she snapped. 'Or next time I'll knock your fillings out.'

His head jerked up, cheeks flushed, eyes glazed. 'Okay, okay. You made yourself clear.'

Digging a hand into her jacket pocket as she returned to her seat, Halford took something out and placed it on the table between them. 'Tell me about this,' she said, gesturing towards a single glittering diamond.

This time it was Nash who shot to his feet, shaking his head wildly. 'No, no, no!' he cried in protest, waving both hands across each other. 'They have fuck all to do with me! I have fuck all to do with them!'

Halford remained quite calm. Waited a couple of seconds for the ire to drain out of the man. 'I know that, Jacob. Believe me I do. But that's not the point of this little chat. Okay?'

'Okay,' Nash panted, rooted to the spot.

'Good. Then sit your fat arse back down and tell me what you do know.'

The petrified man's legs buckled and he collapsed onto the bed as instructed. His forehead creased as he said, 'So... let me get this straight. You know I'm not involved in the diamond business?'

'Let me put it this way, I understand why you might not think so. Except... actually, you are. I'll explain further as we go along. First, tell me how deep it runs.'

Seemingly confused by the exchange, Nash was keen to talk this time. 'All right. It all started when the three of them went to Amsterdam one weekend without me. I think I was away on holiday somewhere with my family. Anyhow, when we all got together again, they asked me how close I was to my uncle Ted. He's a wholesale jeweller in the diamond district down in London.'

'This would be Edward Foster of Hatton Garden.'

Visibly shocked by how much she already knew, he nodded and said, 'That's him, yes. He's my late mother's brother. My friends asked if I would procure some diamonds from him on their behalf. Cheaper the better, and at cost price. You know, family rates.'

Halford offered an encouraging smile. 'Go on.'

'So, I did. Didn't see any problem in it. By then, they'd told me they were bringing diamonds into the country and moving them on for a small taste. I didn't ask for any details, and they didn't feed me any. It was one of their business deals, and none of mine. What they did with the diamonds I bought for them I have no idea. I got a small buyer's fee for each transaction, and that's all I know.'

Processing the information and matching it against what she already knew, Danielle Halford was convinced. 'I believe you. So let me fill in a few gaps for you. Your friends weren't satisfied with their cut for smuggling diamonds into the country. Their job was simple enough, but they thought it was worth more. The process saw them given x number of diamonds in Amsterdam, which they brought back with them into the UK. They, in turn, handed over those diamonds to a local contact in exchange for an envelope stuffed with cash. The problem for them... and you, as it turns out, is that not all the diamonds they moved on were the same as those they were given. See, the main buyer spent top money on purchasing diamonds with a quality cut, clarity, colour, and carat. But while most of what he received in return was worth what he paid, a handful of diamonds on each run fell far below the anticipated quality. Are you with me so far, Jacob?'

Nash gave a hurried nod, desperate to be done with the situation he found himself in.

'As you've probably already figured out for yourself, Jacob, I work for that buyer. The poor quality of some of the gems got noticed. Between us, we took time to explore the Amsterdam end of the deal. We then did the same with the contact end back here. Satisfied with their explanations when put under enormous duress, we turned our attention to the smugglers themselves. Which is where you come in.'

'But I don't!' Nash protested vigorously. 'You said yourself that I didn't do any smuggling.'

'Please don't interrupt me, Jacob,' Halford said, lowering her voice to a deep rasp. 'See, the way we look at it is, it's a skim they couldn't pull off without you. Well, they wouldn't make quite so much money from it, shall we say? They simply take a few pieces from each run and replace them with the cheaper gems you provide. That's stealing. What's more, it's stealing from the wrong person. The wrong people, to be precise.'

Nash's face blanched once more. He shook his head. 'No, no. You can't pin anything on me. I didn't know. I wasn't part of the skim.'

She raised a hand to settle the man down. 'Do you think it matters to my boss whether you knew or not? Maybe you did, maybe you didn't. I'm giving you the benefit of the doubt, remember? But that's not the point, Jacob. It's not why we're here today. Instead of you running your hands and whatever else over a stud of a young man, we're sitting here having this chat because my boss has diamonds provided by you rather than the ones he bought. So, to him, you *are* part of the problem. Very much so. And if you are to him, then you are to me as well. You understand?'

'But that's not fair! How the fuck is that right?'

'Life's not fair, my friend. Life's not always right. Whatever you knew or didn't know, you were the go-between. You bought those diamonds, you moved them on to your mates. You had to know the deal you were making was dodgy, but you didn't care so long as you got your cut. I'm guessing you care now, though.'

Nash made no reply. He sat and fumed, rocking back and forth, his eyes wide and brimming with panic.

'So now you know the situation,' Halford told him. 'But not what comes next.'

The big man pulled back, hands raised defensively, fearful of an immediate reaction.

Halford waved his concerns aside. 'Don't worry yourself, Jacob. You haven't lied to me, so our deal is still in place. But there is a second part to it. Thing is, before I take any... permanent action against your friends, my boss wants to know more about their side of the arrangement. In particular, he wants to know where the original stones are, because he knows people who know people and he doesn't think the merchandise has been moved on. Not all of it, anyway. This is where you get the chance to be lucky. Because if you find out what's what and you tell me something useful, our business is concluded, and you never have to look at my ravishingly beautiful face again. Are we clear?'

Nash swallowed. 'You want me to grass on my friends.'

Grinning, Halford said, 'There you go. I knew you had to be brighter than you looked.'

'And if I don't, you tell my wife all about this arrangement with my escort.'

'You mean prostitute. And yes, your wife, extended family, friends, and let's not forget your children. I should say at this point, Jacob, that I personally have nothing against homosexuality itself. But paying for sex with a man less than half your age in a hotel room is so terribly seedy, wouldn't you agree? And the things you suggested the two of you get up to in this very room today were… sordid and depraved, in my opinion. Water sports are bad enough, but coprophagia is, for want of a better word, distasteful in the extreme.'

Jacob Nash closed his eyes and allowed his head to hang. His shoulders heaved as he began to sob. Halford sat unmoved. Eventually, the man managed to lift his flabby array of chins. 'I suppose I don't really have a choice.'

'Well, you do. But granted it's not much of one.'

'What if they won't tell me anything?'

'Then you get them to talk anyway you can. Your future depends on it.'

'I'll try. I promise I will.'

'Oh, I know you will. But try hard, because there's a lot riding on what you have to tell me next time we meet.'

'Okay, but can you just tell me one thing?' Nash said after a lengthy pause. 'What happened to Tommy? I hope you didn't hurt him.'

Halford regarded the obese man carefully. 'You know, I take back what I said about you being bright,' she said. 'In fact, for a businessman, you're pretty dim. Jacob, nobody hurt Tommy.'

'They didn't?' Whether it was because the prostitute was safe or in his twisted mind it made him available for a second shot, Nash's voice betrayed genuine relief.

She shook her head. 'No, they didn't. Fact is, they couldn't. Because Tommy never existed. That virile young boy with the oiled six pack, biceps to die for, and a dick that went on and on, was actually little old me, Jacob. It was you and me who had those online conversations. The photos you saw were from a porn site.'

'What?' The man appeared devastated.

'I know. Sneaky of me. But that, if nothing else, ought to convince you we do our homework. We seek out people's weaknesses. We were close by when you visited several gay strip clubs. And we were watching your online activities after dumping spy software on your devices. The moment we observed you checking out gay prostitutes, I came up with Tommy for you.'

With a husky chuckle, Halford got to her feet, walked across the room and opened the door to find its frame filled with the bulk of a stern-looking figure in a black suit. She nodded once and then glanced back over her shoulder with a slow shake of the head. Jacob Nash was a simple man in many ways, and there was no doubt he'd betray his friends to save his own skin. But even though Tommy had never been real, the perv's sordid intentions were more than enough to warrant some form of punishment. Halford unzipped the bag the man in the hallway held out to her. After rifling through various knives, hammers, pliers, hacksaws, and rolling aside a butane torch, she took out a mallet with a thick rubber end, used for tamping down stone slabs, and handed it over.

'Bones only,' she said quietly. 'Show him this and make the threat to begin with. If you think he's not taking you seriously, use it. A digit at a time if you have to. If he gets completely out of order, cut him. But leave him alive and able to walk and talk. The poor sod has some difficult work ahead of him.'

NINETEEN

'HOLD ON A MOMENT,' DCI Warburton said at the evening briefing. 'What exactly did Sharon McKenzie admit to, and did she incriminate Banks and Dixon?'

Bliss and Chandler between them had just finished relaying the details of their meeting. As was their habit, the initial run through was to the point. Now it was time to fill in any gaps.

'She admitted knowing about her husband's involvement in a smuggling operation,' he confirmed. The faces looking back at him were bright and eager, with the possible exception of DS Bishop, whose demeanour Bliss hoped spoke more about a lack of awareness than his disinterest. 'She said she only knew about it because he had become quite anxious in recent weeks. According to her, he was showing signs of paranoia, saying he was being followed everywhere he went. When she asked if the police had him under surveillance, he scoffed at the suggestion and told her there were worse things to worry about. He was cryptic about it and refused to discuss the matter any further.'

'And his business partners?'

'Denied all knowledge. According to them both, they weren't involved and didn't know anything about it.'

'And your take…?'

Bliss gave a firm nod. 'They were involved. They knew everything about it.'

'In which case, we dig deeper into those two,' Warburton stated flatly.

'Without question. But this does represent our first solid lead. We were scratching around for motive, and this may well be it. Smuggling can be a dangerous business. You buy from somebody crooked, you sell to somebody crooked. If it goes tits up, you've got trouble. Stuart McKenzie might have stepped into a mess not entirely of his own making.'

'And found himself unable to escape the blowback,' Chandler finished. 'The boss and I discussed it on the drive back. We popped into the hospital first to see how things were there. We asked Mrs Bell if she had changed her mind about the surveillance techs going in to place their gear around the house.'

'Any progress?' Warburton asked.

'None. She stuck to her story. No need for surveillance, because nothing was going on. Eventually, we're going to have to bring her in, but she's not going anywhere. Anyway, going back to our businessmen, we thought that perhaps McKenzie had attempted to settle some kind of disagreement on his own. Jimmy posed the question why he would choose to do so, and between us we decided it could be because he did something his friends weren't aware of. Or possibly were aware of but disapproved of.'

'Makes sense.' The DCI nodded, surveying the team around her. 'If they were all involved in some kind of scam, why wouldn't they all respond together at the same time?'

'That's precisely the conclusion Pen and I came to,' Bliss said. 'Of course, the alternative is that McKenzie was the only one to be contacted. He might have been trying to keep his mates out of it for their own good.'

'Either way, it's finally something for us to get our teeth into,' DC Ansari said. 'Any progress is good progress.'

Bliss agreed. 'With Banks and Dixon keeping schtum, our next move is to find leverage against them. We have to get them to open up. Sharon McKenzie knew the what, but not the when, how, why, and more importantly, the who. If they are involved, and Pen and I are convinced by their reaction that they are, then Michael Banks and Grant Dixon are the only people who can steer us in the right direction.'

'This smuggling op is pivotal, then.'

'It is, Gul. In my view, it's where we'll find all the answers we need.'

'What kind of smuggling?' DC Virgil wanted to know.

'Diamonds.'

'I guessed as much. Is Amsterdam too obvious?'

'Could be from further afield,' Bliss replied with a shrug. 'Maybe they're coming in directly from Africa.'

'Or Russia,' Warburton suggested. 'They're big players in that market these days.'

Taking his time to consider the options, Bliss eventually said, 'I had the distinct impression that McKenzie's role was hands on. Which suggests the same for Banks and Dixon. I'm not ruling out any country, but Amsterdam seems like an ideal location for these men and their weekend jaunts. And now that I think about it, another person we need to add to the mix is our car sales manager. Mr Nash might not have been in business with the three amigos, but he's friends with all of them. He might just know something useful, and I got the impression he could be a weak link if pressed harder.'

The DCI confirmed with a nod. 'Sounds like a plan. Okay, think on and we'll sort the actions in the morning. Where are we on Stuart McKenzie's devices?'

Chandler chuckled. 'Jimmy found a way beneath the wife's skin. She agreed to a search and seizure of all requested items. I walked around their house with her and together we agreed on a list. I took photos of each item, then made arrangements for them to be collected and brought over to the techs at Hinching-brooke for analysis.'

Warburton smiled. 'That's good. I won't ask what methods you used to persuade the poor woman, Jimmy.'

'That's probably just as well,' he said. He then turned to DC Ansari. 'I don't suppose we've got that phone data yet, have we, Gul?'

'McKenzie's? Not yet, boss. I'll give them a bell before I leave. What do you want me to do about the others involved in this case?'

Bliss turned his thoughts to Sharon McKenzie, Michael Banks, and Grant Dixon. Their victim's wife had given up everything she knew. He was confident about that. And although he was equally certain that the two men had lied when questioned, it would be hard to justify a RIPA authorisation. Although the template forms were easily altered to suit all Regulation of Investigatory Powers Act requests, it would be difficult to rationalise in respect of Banks and Dixon. Their right to privacy would be weighed against evidence produced by the police. In this case, he knew his team had none to offer against either man, other than suspicion based on experience. Over the years it had become commonplace for superintendents to sign off on a RIPA request more as a fishing expedition than a genuine need for the data. The governing body, at the behest of its opponents, had warned against such practices. In this instance, while the data might certainly help the enquiry, the reasons behind asking for it were at best speculative.

Shaking his head, he finally told DC Ansari to compile the request should he later decide to pull the trigger.

'Which leaves me with two things to cover before end of briefing. Bish, do you have any positive news for us concerning CCTV and other video feeds?'

His expression unaltered, Bishop shook his head. 'We're getting nowhere fast. I'm not expecting to come up with any critical evidence from our searches.'

'Okay. Which leaves me to move on to our interest over in Millfield. I haven't had time yet, but I will be asking for the meeting I mentioned earlier today. I'm of the opinion that we can't allow Nora Bell to go back to the family home without either her mother or sister admitting to us what's going on inside those walls. Mrs Bell might wake up with a different perspective tomorrow morning. If not, then hopefully we can persuade her just how bad things might get if she remains silent. I'm pretty sure child services will agree to my protests where the vulnerable child is concerned, but we can't expect the hospital to keep her once she's out of danger. A nurse on the ward suggested to Pen that Nora Bell was likely to be discharged as early as lunchtime tomorrow. By the time the paperwork goes through, and travel arrangements are made, my guess is she'll be there until the evening at least. By then, our meeting must have taken place and agreements reached.'

'You think Mrs Bell will relent?' Warburton asked.

'I think she'll want to,' Bliss allowed. 'But she's hard to read. Also, I'm not absolutely certain which way she'd like it to go. I don't believe she wants to be parted from her daughter, but at this moment, in Nora's condition, and with the crews likely to return to the family home shortly after the family does, she might just decide that being kept in care is the best thing for the girl as things stand.'

'I see what you mean. In which case, you have no leverage.'

'That's what I'm thinking. But there's still a mother's outrage to use against her.'

'In what way?'

'She didn't know about the pregnancy. She didn't know about the rape. She might not want to put Nora in such a vulnerable position again, but neither is she going to forget that one of those despicable excuses for a human being sexually assaulted the kid. For all we – and she – knows, more than one of them was involved. The anger she must be harbouring is something for me to exploit.'

'Rather you than me, Jimmy.'

Bliss sighed. 'One of the perks of being in charge, Diane.'

She frowned. 'Uh, I thought that was me.'

'You want the job?'

Hands up, Warburton shook her head. 'No, thank you. It's all yours.'

'Yeah, cheers,' he muttered. 'This is turning out to be some final week.'

TWENTY

T HE MOMENT HE ENTERED the station the following morning, Bliss sensed an atmosphere. An enjoyable evening spent with Molly and Max had been followed by a decent sleep for a change, so he was in a good mood until he walked through the doors and felt a tingle of anticipation in the air. Not exactly fear, not exactly excitement. More a dramatic release of adrenaline associated with something having kicked off. A couple of the uniforms he had greeted responded not with nods but with deep looks of suspicion. He couldn't recall anything he might have done to earn their disfavour. Narked by this, he was on the point of retracing his steps to confront the pair when a breathless DCI Warburton rushed along the corridor towards him.

'You're needed in the conference room,' she panted, gulping down a lungful of air. 'Now.'

Bliss liked to use the stairs as often as possible, but on this occasion he rode up in the lift with his boss, assessing the mood. This was one of the strangest beginnings to any day in recent memory. 'What's this about, Diane?' he eventually asked. 'Am I in trouble? Did I fuck up? Did the team fuck up?'

Warburton opened her mouth as if to reply when the lift came to a juddering halt and the doors shuffled open. 'It might as well wait until we're all together,' she said, her voice almost a whisper.

'Is it serious? Tell me that, at least.'

'Yes,' she said as they strode towards the conference room. 'And it could get a lot worse.'

Waiting for them and already seated were both Detective Superintendent Fletcher and DCI Edwards, neither of whom had officially taken up their newly promoted positions. Their expressions were equally grim, and Bliss understood this was bad.

'We have a situation, Jimmy,' Fletcher said. The only emotion she displayed was a hint of sympathy, which confused him. 'One that has to be nipped in the bud before it is out of our sphere of influence.'

'Okay,' Bliss said, eking out the second syllable. 'Is one of you going to tell me what's going on?'

Fletcher and Edwards exchanged looks. The Super nodded, but it was the DCI who took up the story. 'Jimmy, there was an altercation in the station a short while ago between two officers. The brief version is this: Detective Sergeant Bishop attacked Police Constable Brewer. Bishop grabbed the man first by the collar and then by the throat, slamming Brewer back against a wall. Other officers were on hand to intervene before any punches were thrown, but from what I hear it took several of them to pull DS Bishop off, with a minor scuffle ensuing as they attempted to calm him down.'

'And the full version?' Bliss wanted to say he was shocked, but given the way his burly colleague had been acting lately, an explosive outburst irrespective of who it was aimed against came as no great surprise.

'On his way into the station, DS Bishop overheard a conversation between PC Brewer and a fellow officer. Apparently, Brewer was ridiculing homeless people, disparaging them about the smell, the way they begged, the way they drank so heavily, and the way they lived in general. He then mentioned Roger Craig by name, calling him a disgrace for falling so far, especially having been a paratrooper.'

Bliss closed his eyes and groaned. 'Which is when Bish kicked off, right?'

'Yes. Witnesses say he gave no warning, just went for PC Brewer, shouting and swearing at him, telling him how he wasn't fit to lace the boots of someone like Roger Craig and calling him a lousy excuse for a copper. Asked him what he had ever risked... you get the picture.'

'Sadly, I do. Bish's background and his connection to the armed forces is a point of pride. He's often mentioned his disgust at the way our servicemen and women are treated, especially the veterans.' Whatever the provocation, his friend had overreacted, leaving his career on the line. Bliss wet his lips and nodded. 'What do you want from me?' he asked.

Fletcher stepped in at this juncture. 'First of all, have a word with Bish. We tucked him away inside your office, letting him cool off and making sure nobody sniffed around to poke the bear.' She glanced across at DCI Edwards. 'Alicia and I will meet with PC Brewer and a representative from the uniformed ranks, possibly the duty inspector. We'll begin with humble apologies, explain the trigger, and insist on Bish making a full and unreserved apology. If that doesn't do the trick, which is to say that if the constable tells us he plans to escalate the matter all the way to disciplinary measures, then we will change tack. At that point it might be advisable to point out to PC Brewer that his own comments fell far short of what we would expect from a serving police officer.'

Bliss nodded. 'Unless he's a complete dick he'll accept it for what it was and shake hands on it. I drew a few sideways glances myself when I came in, so uniform in general are not happy. I'm sure you can smooth things over, though. Meanwhile, I'll have words with Bish. Are we done here?'

'For the present,' Fletcher said, as Bliss was in the throes of levering himself up. He nodded at all three women and got out of there quickly before any of them tried to offer him advice.

It was the last thing he needed because he was already furious with himself. He'd been intending to speak with Ollie Bishop, but had kept putting it off. That might not have mattered had the situation not deteriorated, but it had. If push came to shove he'd tell his bosses that the earlier brawl could have been prevented had he acted without delay, but that would not resolve the more immediate problem.

When he reached the Major Crime Unit, Bliss ignored the looks from those members of the team who had already arrived, and instead marched tight-lipped across to his office. He pushed open the door, met Bishop's gaze, then jerked his head back the way he had come. 'Car park,' he said, spinning and walking away. 'Now.'

A man Ollie Bishop's size and stamp doesn't pull off sheepish very easily, but a few minutes later the robust DS made a half decent attempt as he came through the doorway from the station. As he made his way over to where Bliss stood leaning back against his pool car, he held up both hands up in supplication.

'I know, I know,' he said in a flat, regretful voice. 'I lost my rag. Sorry, boss. I'm sure it'll all blow over soon enough. I'll apologise and offer to shake hands and buy him a few pints. Main thing is it won't happen again. I thought Roger Craig and those who are forced to live their lives just like him deserved more respect, that's all.'

'I have no doubt you're right about that,' Bliss said, folding his arms. 'But not the rest. If you genuinely believe that codswallop, then you're neither the man nor the officer I thought you were. This won't be pulled back so easily. You've set off a chain reaction, Bish. You physically assaulted a fellow police officer.'

'Oh, and I'm the first to do that, am I?' Bishop glared pointedly at him.

'If you're referring to me and Sergeant Grealish all those years ago, then okay I won't be a hypocrite on that score. The difference is, we're talking about a very different time and level of scrutiny, plus I didn't do so in full view of witnesses.'

'Is this for real?' The DS regarded him in astonishment. 'Are you really bollocking me over this?'

'Me? No. It's not about bollocking you. It's about trying to defuse the situation. As we speak, plans are being discussed to make a case for you. Your bosses – my bosses – are stepping up on your behalf. They'll try smoothing the waters, no matter what the cost or number of favours they have to call in. But what certainly won't happen is this thing blowing over of its own accord or on the promise of a drink or two.'

'What does that mean? I didn't thump the prick, which I could have and probably should have.'

'Have a word with yourself, Bish' Bliss told him, shaking his head in despair. He stood up straight to face his friend. 'If you had landed a punch, you'd be lucky only to lose your job. You might well have faced charges. You still could if Marion and Alicia between them can't work their magic.'

'Oh, come on. That's nonsense. It got heated, but it'll cool down. I'll go and have a word with Brewer and make it right.'

Bliss wasn't having any of it. 'No. No, you won't. You'll steer well clear until you or I hear otherwise. You may not be able to see dangerous ground when it's right beneath your plates, but you stray over it at your peril, old son.'

Clearly still angered and unimpressed, Bishop complained, 'It's a fuss over nothing. You'll see. But I'll do as you suggest and keep my distance. So what next?'

'Next? The truth is, we need to talk, Bish. About whatever is going on with you.'

'I don't think this is the right time, boss,' Bishop said with a dismissive shake of the head.

'You're bang on about that. The right time was a couple of months ago. Trouble is, I was so wrapped up in my own future I lost sight of my team. My colleagues. My friends. You in particular, because I could see all was not well. Before I leave, I need to put that right if I can.'

Bishop sighed. 'Okay. If you say so. Just not right now. Not today. Not at this precise moment. I'm just not up to it, Jimmy. And we have work to be getting on with.'

Bliss noted the look of regret in his colleague's features, but he was not backing down. 'I get that, Bish. I genuinely do. And I blame myself for letting things drift this long, so I'm stepping in to take matters out of your hands.'

Shaking his head, Bishop said, 'No way. This mess has got bugger all to do with you, Jimmy. It's on me. I admit I've been struggling of late, but I'll put it right. Just trust me a bit more.'

'Jesus, Bish, look at the state of you mate. "Struggling?" "Trust you?" Have you had a good look in the mirror lately? When was the last time you had your barnet cut? Or even put a comb through it? And as for your clobber, I don't know where to begin. Your whistle's hanging off your bones like you're a bloody scarecrow. Your shoes are scuffed and unpolished, and do you even remember the last time your mush felt a razor over it?'

The big man stood there for a moment, open-mouthed but silent. When he found his voice, he said more softly, 'What's this all about, Jimmy? I thought we were mates as well as colleagues. How can you have a pop at me like that today of all days?'

'Because I *am* your friend, you Muppet,' Bliss said. 'And because today is the day you came close to decking a fellow officer and getting yourself thrown out of the job. That's what it's about. Talk to me, mate. Tell me what the fuck is going on.'

For a few seconds he thought Bishop would refuse, to pretend all was well. But then, with a massive venting of breath, his friend and colleague nodded and came to lean against the car alongside him.

'Life hasn't turned out quite the way I imagined,' he admitted. 'I'm currently kipping in my sister's spare bedroom. I moved out of the family home about a month ago.'

Bliss snapped his head to one side, wincing. How had he not seen it? Was he already detaching himself from his colleagues before he had even retired? 'What happened?' he asked. 'What went wrong?'

'All down to me, Jimmy. I've changed. That's one of the reasons I walked away from the promotion training. My head is seldom where it needs to be these days. When I'm at home, I think only about work, and when I'm at work, I think only about home. About the sodding mess I've made of my marriage.'

'But in what way? How are you treating them differently?'

'In every conceivable way. I'm not there for my wife or my kids. Even when I'm in the room with them. I can't sleep, can't eat properly. I'm as moody as fuck. I can drink, though. Yeah, I can manage to work my way through the booze. And you're right, boss. I've become sloppy in my appearance and the way I do my job. This one here as well as the one I'm supposed to do in taking care of my family.'

Replaying his friend's words, Bliss latched on to one important point. 'If you're staying at your sister's place, then it's a temporary measure, right?'

'For the time being.'

'Maybe, but it's something to cling to, Bish. Tell me, did you jump or were you pushed?'

'A bit of both,' Bishop said after a time.

Bliss took a breath. The situation didn't appear to be terminal. But it also sounded as if it could become so if the problems were not addressed and resolved. 'Tell me what's going on inside that thick head of yours,' he said. 'You've listed the symptoms, but what about the cause?'

Shrugging, Bishop said, 'It's precisely what you might imagine, boss. My mood is in a constant downward spiral. It's been that way for a long time, and I can't seem to find my way through it.'

'You're depressed.'

'I'd assume so. But we don't like to discuss the "D" word, do we? We certainly don't admit to suffering from it. People look at you differently afterwards, no matter how much better you get.'

'Not on our team they don't. I won't have that as an excuse. You're suffering from depression, and we both know what kicked that off.'

'It's really not one thing, Jimmy. You know better than most how this job scars you. The things we see, the people we deal with… what are we all doing to ourselves? I wish I could forget whole swathes of my life. Just scrub it raw. But then I realise that if I do that, I'll also forget anybody who ever meant anything to me, and all the good memories I still have.'

Feeling a huge wave of empathy crash over him, Bliss said, 'Bish, this has been building for quite some time, mate. And time doesn't always heal all wounds, no matter what songs might tell us. Quite simply, you're not over Mia's death. But it's worse than that, because you're still carrying survivor's guilt around with you. To the point where it's become a burden you can no longer bear.'

Their former colleague, Mia Short, had been murdered by a madman with a shotgun. The whole team had been devastated by the loss, but Bishop had been alongside his pregnant colleague at the time. His pain was, therefore, different and more acute.

Bishop hung his head, and when he looked up again, his cheeks were slick with tears and his eyes were voids of hopelessness. Bliss took a step and drew the much larger man into his arms. He held his now sobbing friend, weeping right along with him. They maintained the embrace for several minutes.

'I just can't get her out of my head, boss,' Bishop finally admitted, cuffing his face as he drew away. His voice had risen by at least an octave. 'Every time I catch a glimpse of myself in the mirror I see a man who shouldn't be here. It's me who ought to be ashes, not Mia. So, yes, I did survive, and yes, I do feel guilty about that. But that's my water to carry, as I will do until my dying day because I got to live, and she didn't.'

Bliss understood his friend's despair all too well. It was an issue he himself had thrashed out with a therapist, whose constant prodding and poking had made a huge difference. He looked into his friend's eyes and said, 'You think Mia would approve of the state you're in right now, Bish? You think she'd want you carting all this sorrow around and blaming yourself? Mate, this is going to sound terribly harsh, but you do her memory a huge disservice. She would be so disappointed in you. My friend, you're on the verge of a full mental and physical breakdown. It's as clear as that fat nose on your ugly boat to everyone but you. I should have spoken up sooner, but I'm here for you this time.'

'I know that, Jimmy. I've always been able to count on you. But this isn't just about Mia. It's the cumulative effect of all the horrors I've seen over the years. This job... it takes, takes, takes, and then takes some more. More than we have to offer, if the truth be known.'

'I agree. Every new obscenity we face drives that nail deeper into our flesh, and there's a toll to pay. We all have to cough up at some point. No denying that, Bish. But add that to your survivor's guilt and depression and you have a devastating cocktail of mental ill-health leaving you teetering on the edge.'

'You make it sound terminal.'

Bliss shook his head. 'Not quite. But you're done, Bish. Hopefully not for good, but at least for a while.'

Bishop's face crumpled as he realised what he was being told. 'Boss, please don't take me off the case. That might be the final straw. I'll get help. I will. I'll sort myself out. Just please don't take me off the case.'

Bliss continued shaking his head. 'Hate me if you have to, Bish, but you're not only off the case, you're off the shift roster, too. As of this moment, you're on sick leave.'

The big man reeled. 'For fuck's sake, Jimmy, you can't do that to me!'

'I'm not doing it *to* you, mate. I'm doing it *for* you. At some point I hope you understand and appreciate the difference. Now go home. Spend some time with your wife and kids. Tell them everything you just told me. Every single word. You'll only get through this with their help. Then you rest. Recuperate. Regain your strength. And I'll make sure you see someone who will help you through this difficult time.'

'But boss… this is all I have. It's all I am.'

The desperate, pleading look in his eyes was almost too much to bear. But Bliss had to be strong for his friend's sake. 'And what does that say about your state of mind?' he said gently. 'If you were thinking straight, you'd never have said that, not when you have a family at home waiting for you. The real you, I mean. I've been there, and I can tell you from experience that it's not a place you want to linger for any length of time.'

Bishop's pained expression burned right through him. 'You did all right, Jimmy. Look at everything you've achieved. Why deny me the opportunity to make amends?'

Bliss felt his shoulders starting to sag. He felt wearied by the conversation but had one final point to make. 'It all came at a cost I didn't need to pay, Bish. Too high a cost. I know better than most people how much you're suffering and the unseen ways in which you're struggling. It's taking bites out of you from the inside because you care. About the job, your colleagues, and our victims and their families. I've come to regard that as a positive thing, and I think you will as well. In time. Either way, my friend, this is no longer a debate. This is happening. I'm not denying you the chance to make amends, I'm simply postponing it. You go away and get yourself well again. And when you're ready, you come back and do what you're best at. This team won't be the same without my mate Bish in it. But he's been absent for quite some time, wouldn't you agree?'

The shattered nod Bishop gave just about broke Bliss's heart.

TWENTY-ONE

THE REST OF THE morning passed off without any further drama. Bliss took his team aside to inform them of his decision to bench DS Bishop. Not even his regular partner, DC Ansari, raised an objection or so much as voiced a concern. Their thoughts were for the popular sergeant and his recovery, but there were also investigations to be getting on with. By the time Bliss and Chandler left for the hospital, they had made no further progress with either case.

A family room had been set aside for the scheduled meeting. When the two detectives arrived, Mrs Bell and her daughter, Patricia, were already waiting, along with their caseworker, Peter Alinson. Bliss wasted no time in apprising them of his intentions.

'Thank you for your time,' he began. 'I felt this meeting was important so that we could clear the air and begin to get an official handle on this case. Today, this moment is the time for honesty and cutting out any lies or omissions. We have to establish some trust if we are to make progress. I believe, and I hope you all agree with me, that we owe it to Nora to resolve this matter as quickly as possible.'

There were nods all around the table at which they sat, but nobody volunteered any further information. Bliss waited, his attention fixed on the young victim's mother. When she continued to avert her gaze, he carried on. 'Rather than wasting time by going around in circles, let me tell you what we suspect. First, we're as certain as we can be that your property, Mrs Bell, is being used by drug dealers and that they have taken over your home to use as they please. The most common term for this is cuckooing, and our intel suggests you and your daughters have been exposed to an extreme form of this over the past few months. Before I go on, do either of you have anything to say to that?'

His eyes swept between mother and daughter. Patricia engaged, but remained silent while anxiously chewing her nails and tapping one foot on the floor. Her mother simply stared at the top of the table they were sitting at.

'Okay,' Bliss said, adding a harder edge to his voice. 'At least this time there were no denials, which is progress of sorts. But there's no avoiding the matter of Nora's overdose, which is something we need to deal with.'

Silence. Bliss felt irritation scrabbling inside his chest at their unwillingness to talk. Infuriated, he said, 'Mrs Bell. Please do me the courtesy of looking at me when I'm talking to you. This is not going away, so you can't avoid it by ignoring me. We're here today to give you the opportunity to speak with us. If you'd prefer we did so in private, that can be arranged. If you'd prefer to speak to my colleague alone, that's not a problem. But you have to understand that you continuing to say nothing is not an option. Nora is your daughter. She lives in your home with you and Patricia. She is your responsibility. As her parent you have your own duty of care. I would both hope and expect you to speak freely here, or elsewhere with DS Chandler, if you prefer. Believe me, I'd rather that than having to arrest you for neglecting and failing to protect your child. But if you continue down the path you've chosen, if you do not speak up, I promise you I will do precisely that and I will charge you. You have this chance to defend yourself, so please use it wisely.'

He sat back to allow his words to sink in. He had noted Mrs Bell becoming more animated, agitated even, the longer he spoke. It was clear to him that she'd had no idea she might be arrested, and nobody had thought to warn her of the possibility. In a situation of such intense vulnerability, making a threat was the last thing he wanted to do. But he'd felt the need to push ahead and reveal his intentions.

Alinson broke the silence to suggest he speak with Frances Bell on his own, offering to counsel the woman and her elder daughter if necessary. But Bliss shook his head, refusing to consider the proposal. 'That really won't do,' he said. 'We can't know if this so-called counselling will be for or against Mrs Bell complying. Besides, that's not your job here. You're her caseworker not her priest.'

'I must protest,' Alinson responded, looking shocked. 'Mrs Bell is considered a vulnerable person, and as such it is very much my job to advise her on all matters of protection. And in case it needs explaining to you, Inspector Bliss, that protection also extends to Mrs Bell's children.'

Bliss shook his head. 'No, you didn't need to explain that. And of course, you are free to offer guidance to Mrs Bell when my colleague and I are finished with her. Which we are not.' He turned to face Bell once more. 'Please look at me, Frances. I need to know that you fully understand the situation you are facing. I am not unsympathetic to your dilemma. I realise you are scared of reprisals should you reveal precisely what's been going on inside your home over the past couple of months. That's something we can address as a separate issue. My immediate priority is Nora. I simply must find out who did this to her, and in my opinion that means you have to open up and be honest with me. Do you understand?'

Bell glanced at Alinson, and then nodded after turning her attention to Bliss.

'Good,' he said. 'Then walk me through it. Step by step. From the initial taunting and bullying, to the first time they commandeered your home, to the current state of play. You can do so without naming names if you must, though we will eventually need to know everybody involved. You can leave the identification process until we take a formal statement from you if that helps, if you'd rather not speak about them individually. For the time being, just start at the beginning. We're all on your side, Frances.'

And so the deeply troubled woman opened up about the tragedy that had befallen her little family. It had begun the way such atrocities often do. In Bliss's childhood, kids who looked different, walked different, were different, found themselves reduced to being called names like 'Spaz', 'Flid', and 'Mong'. Other kids had no idea what precisely was wrong with those who were branded sub-normal, nor did they much care. If you couldn't talk properly or walk properly or worse still lived a life that was a combination of the two, then you were regarded as less than and consequently became fodder for the dull-witted to sharpen their so-called humour on. A couple of those awful terms remained, along with 'Retard'. All of them were familiar to Frances Bell after pushing her daughter's wheelchair through the streets of Millfield.

However, it was Patricia's habit that had drawn the family's tormentors closer to home. A teenager herself, at times the girl loathed Nora for making the Bells the centre of the wrong kind of attention, but mostly she abhorred the local troublemakers who doled out the abuse. To make matters worse, some of those same brutes sold the drugs her body craved. An awful way to live for anybody, let alone a young girl struggling to survive adolescence.

'The verbal abuse wasn't aimed only at Nora,' the girl's mother admitted. 'I've never been the sharpest tool in the shed. I've let myself go, don't have money for new clothes or getting my hair done, so I know what I look like to these mouthy little bastards.'

'Thank you for opening up to us,' Bliss said. 'It's a good start.'

Wiping away a stray tear, Bell sniffed and said, 'I now understand the need to. I'm sorry about before.'

'Please, there's no need to apologise. How about you, Patricia?' Bliss asked, hoping to encourage the girl to tell her side of the story. So far, they had only her mother's words to go by where the dealers were concerned. But it was Mrs Bell who once again spoke up on behalf of her daughter.

'They called her all kinds, too. They as good as suggested she slept around with all sorts, so you can imagine the language they used. None of it was true, but that didn't stop them.'

Bliss gave that some thought. Had one or two of the lads entered the house thinking they were going to get their end away with Patricia, only to decide her younger sister would do instead when she refused to put out?

'Patricia?' he prodded once more. 'We'd like to hear your version of events. I'm sure some of them at least have been different from what we've heard so far.'

Eighteen with a fifty-year-old's knowing eyes, the girl eventually shrugged and said, 'It's my fault. It's always my fault.' She threw a spiteful glare at her mother then put her head back down and fell into silence once again.

Bliss gave a despairing look at his partner, who nodded and slid her chair back. 'How about you and I have a chat in private, Patricia,' she said, her soothing voice in stark contrast to his own.

'What, so's my Mum can bad mouth me even more?'

'That's not what I'm doing,' Frances argued, her voice rising sharply. 'These people asked for the truth. That's what I'm giving them.'

'Oh, right,' the girl sneered. 'Because you're all about the truth, aren't you?'

'Patsy!' The two syllables rang out around the room.

Chandler got to her feet. 'Come with me, please,' she said to Patricia. 'Before this gets out of hand.'

The pair left without another word. Bliss half expected Mrs Bell to apologise on behalf of her daughter, but instead she said nothing at all.

'This must be weighing heavily on her,' he said. 'After all, she was the one who discovered Nora, who had to deal with the paramedics and the doctors here until we were able to inform you.'

'She's not far wrong, though,' Bell suddenly blurted out, thumbing tears away from both eyes. 'I do blame her for bringing those bastards into our lives. And it's not often I don't remind her of that. I know it's wrong, I know I shouldn't. Because the only one to blame is me.'

Peter Alinson leaned in and broke into the conversation. 'I fear I must shoulder my own portion of blame,' he said, looking distraught. 'I should have noticed more. Should have asked more. Should have done more to protect you all.'

Frances Bell shook her head. 'You weren't to know, Peter. We kept it from you. We knew precisely when you were due to call in and they made damn sure to make themselves scarce when you did. You couldn't possibly have known. You've been kind and caring towards all of us, which is more than most can say. No, as the only adult in the household, there's only me to blame for what happened to both my girls. I'm weak minded and pitiful.'

Bliss responded in a softer tone. 'In all the ways that count, I don't think any of that is true,' he said. 'These dealers seek out the vulnerable. Some of them had already abused you verbally, and it was a short journey from there to them deciding to take over your home. It didn't need Patricia's habit to coax them, and I understand why you stood back and allowed it to happen. It's a scary world out there, and these lads can make lives a misery for people if they put their minds to it. You're not to blame, Mrs Bell. Neither is your older daughter.'

'Somebody has to be responsible,' she replied sharply, cocking her head to one side.

He nodded. 'Of course. The lads themselves. Their parents. A lack of discipline in schools. A lack of police presence on the streets. The law not punishing offenders in the way we might. It all adds up, and there's blame enough to go round. But I'm a great believer in focus, Mrs Bell. How you and your daughters ended up in this situation isn't anywhere near as important at this very moment as finding out who sexually abused Nora. We strongly suspect one of the dealers – at least – forced himself on her during the period of cuckooing. We can't know for sure how many of these lads did so, nor on how many occasions. But Nora *is* pregnant, so she has had sex but isn't of age to consent. Let me be blunt: we are talking rape. We can't change what happened, though we can and will punish whoever is responsible. But as you are surely aware, we must also address the overdose and how that could possibly have occurred.'

Peter Alinson injected himself into the conversation once again. 'I fear we're going around in circles, Inspector Bliss. I think Frances has been extremely brave in telling you how the cuckooing began, in admitting that it went on at all, for that matter. But here we are back at the point where you will want names relating to the abuse Nora suffered, yet the fear of repercussions remains the sticking point.'

'What would you have us do?' Bliss asked him. 'Ignore the matter? A fourteen-year-old girl was raped in her own home. A teen who is still really no more than a child, who could not defend herself even if she realised what was happening. She subsequently suffered a drugs overdose. Are you suggesting we turn a blind eye?'

Alinson recoiled. 'No. Of course not. I feel sickened by what happened to Nora. It happened on our watch, too, remember? I want the boy or boys responsible to be arrested and charged and heavily punished every bit as much as you do. True, I don't have any suggestions as to how you go about identifying them without help from the Bell family, but one thing I know for certain is that long after your investigation is done it'll be me and my department who will be the only ones around to help pick up the pieces. That's if there are pieces to pick up when the friends of those you arrest and charge have finished dishing out their own form of punishment.'

Wanting to argue the point, Bliss reeled himself back in. Alinson was right. In reality, the police could not protect the Bell family twenty-four hours a day, seven days a week, fifty-two weeks a year. For naming names, Frances, Patricia, and Nora Bell would suffer the consequences in unimaginable ways. He wanted to believe that a mother would risk everything to point a finger at the person or persons who took advantage of her disabled child, yet the risk was not hers alone to shoulder.

'Is that how you see it?' he asked the woman. When she offered a sullen nod, he said, 'Believe it or not, I do understand. I wish I could offer you assurances, but the only way we can do so is if you agree to enter the witness protection scheme. Is that something you'd be willing to consider if I can persuade my bosses to make the offer?'

Frances Bell narrowed her gaze. 'You mean sending us to another part of the country, changing our names, giving us a home and jobs… all that?'

Bliss scratched his chin. 'Not quite. I'm not the type to sell you on a false promise. Witness protection isn't everything it's cracked up to be. It's not as if we hand over vast sums of cash and you get to live the dream, Mrs Bell. Also, it's only in exceptional circumstances that we'd consider providing you with a new identity. But what we would do is remove you from this area to negate the intimidation and potentially more severe responses and actions.'

'You'd do that for us?'

'Specifically, it's the National Crime Agency who would make all the arrangements. But yes. You'd have named contacts, and they would find accommodation for you until your house could be sold, after which they would help you find another home. If you're on benefits, then you'd remain on them unless you chose to get a job, and again your NCA contacts would advise and assist you as much as possible in that regard. You would have to agree to testify in court, allow us to carry out internal surveillance by planting covert devices around the house, but once you're in the programme, you wouldn't be allowed to communicate with friends or family at least until the relevant court case or cases are over, and even then it would depend on conditions and agreement by all interested parties.'

'But me and my kids would be safe if I agreed, right?'

Bliss saw the first rays of hope flickering like flames in Bell's eyes. 'Yes,' he said. 'Provided you stick to the terms of the agreement, nobody you testify against nor any of their crew should ever be able to find you. I won't say never because coincidences occur, and if one of them happened to move to or visit your new location then of course you might run into each other. But if you compare your odds against those if you choose to remain here, then witness protection is surely worth considering.'

'And what about those odds if I tell you nothing more?'

Bliss gave a reluctant shrug. 'Not as good as you'd like them to be. The thing is, Mrs Bell, you do know them. You can name names. I don't want to frighten you more than you already are, but it's only right that you know what's what. These kinds of people… they don't always hang around for a situation to react to. There might come a time when they regard you as expendable, to get to you before you get to them.'

'Really, Inspector?' Alinson said with a shake of the head. 'Just how likely is that?'

Bliss gave him a sharp look. 'It happens. It happens all the time. I'm not scaremongering. This is the reality of the world the Bells live in at present. The moment they return home they become vulnerable, and the bottom feeders will be back. Put yourself in the mind of the lad or lads who raped Nora. He or they will know by now that she was taken to hospital, but what he or they won't know is what was said in these rooms. When life itself is of so little consequence to these people, how do you imagine he or they might react?'

He paused, turned to Frances Bell once again. 'I realise you have a great deal to think about. If you decide you want to nail the kid who did that to your daughter, you let me or one of my colleagues know. If you want us to put you in touch with the NCA, that's easily arranged. But in my opinion, it is not safe for Nora to return home when she is released, which could be later today or tomorrow at the latest. So, take your time, because it's not an easy decision to make. Discuss it with Patricia. We can include her in being relocated, though at eighteen she has the right to opt out. But don't take too long about it. As I said at the beginning, we have to resolve this matter and we have to do it soon.'

Silence reverberated around the room. Bliss gave it a few more seconds before intruding once again. 'With all that in mind,' he said, 'we must also address the other issue of priority to me and my colleagues. Nora overdosed, and I've yet to hear a satisfactory explanation as to how that might have happened. She has told both us and her nurses a variety of stories, though all of them involve a bowl of ice cream with some pretty unsavoury toppings. Before we go any further, Mrs Bell, I want you to take us through your version of events one more time.'

TWENTY-TWO

THEY ATE LUNCH AT the Chalkboard on Embankment Road next to the Key Theatre. Parking was brutal, but Bliss spotted a van pulling out of a space just as he was about to give up. After leaving the hospital, they had first paid a visit to the local branch of SSAFA, the charity supporting war veterans and families. There they spoke with a volunteer who knew Roger Craig. The ex-Royal Engineer was saddened to hear of the man's murder, but unsurprised that it might be related to him trying to help somebody. According to him, Craig remained a dutiful and honourable man long after he'd left the service. Bliss gave the veteran his personal mobile number and promised to keep in touch about whatever arrangements might be made.

During the short drive to the embankment, Chandler steered the conversation to the elephant sitting in the back seat of the car. 'That was rough with Bish earlier,' she said casually, gazing out of the side window. 'I understand why you made the decision to send him home, but it can't have been easy.'

'No,' he said, shaking his head. 'It was far from easy. Besides you, he's my closest friend and ally. Removing him from the case was bad enough, but ordering him out of the building was gut-wrenching. But the way I see it, I didn't have a choice. My last few days as his boss or not, the hard decisions still have to be made.'

'What did Diane have to say to you about it?'

'Not much. Neither of us had time to discuss my decision at length. She accepted it and said we'd talk later.'

'She'll back you up. As for Bish, while he won't be thanking you any day soon, he'll understand and accept you did the right thing.'

Bliss nodded. He wasn't about to break his friend's confidence about a disintegrating marriage, but he had plenty to say otherwise. 'The poor sod's burned out, Pen. Too much going on inside that massive head of his. He got help to cope with Mia's loss the same way we all did, but he'll always have to live knowing how close it came to being him.'

'He still blames himself? Bish? That's such a Jimmy Bliss thing to do.'

'It's not that. Not *just* that. What I really think gets to him in the darkest hours is a deeper knowledge. One that he probably believes reflects badly on him and makes him feel like shit every time it crosses his mind.'

Wearing a deep frown, Chandler said, 'Okay, you really have to finish that thought. Don't leave me hanging, Jimmy.'

'You asked for it. You're right, of course, because he does still blame himself. He also has survivor's guilt, which is a heavy burden to carry. But worse, much worse, I think he's also grateful it wasn't him. That's the part that shreds him to pieces.'

Bliss felt Chandler's eyes drilling into his skull. He shrugged. 'But what do I know? I'm no psychoanalyst.'

When they were seated inside the Chalkboard, he ordered eggs Benedict and Chandler opted for the Red Leicester and spring onion sandwich. Unlike the Mancetter Square café, this eatery smelled of roasted coffee beans and cinnamon, which was fine by him. While they waited, she told him about her trouble-some conversation with Patricia Bell.

'The proverbial blood from a stone would have been easier,' she said with a shake of the head. 'It really was like pulling teeth. She's a typical smart-arsed and sullen teen with plenty to be sullen about. With some coaxing, I did manage to get something out of her, though.'

'I'd have expected nothing less,' Bliss said, peering out of the glass frontage at the hardier diners who had chosen to sit outside on a mild but breezy day. 'Rather you than me with that one, so thanks for taking her on.'

'Stroppy, sour, and sullen or not, I couldn't help but feel sorry for the kid. Her life has taken so many strange and disturbing twists. It's barely begun, but she thinks of it as being over. The teasing and taunting were hard to take, but she had her own shields to hide behind. In that way, she appears to be mentally strong. But drugs have been her weakness for many years, and she definitely blames herself for bringing the dealers closer and eventually inside her home.'

Nodding, Bliss said, 'I told Mrs Bell the cuckooing was inev-itable from the moment the vermin identified their prey. It had nothing to do with either her or her older daughter. They were just a vulnerable family ripe for exploiting.'

Chandler smiled. 'That's pretty much what I said to Patri-cia. I told her these drug dealers are like hyenas picking off the stragglers of the herd. I'm not sure if I sold her on the idea, but she did at least relax a little. She was at great pains to insist the things the lads said about her being a slut there for the taking, were all rubbish.'

'Did you manage to get her talking about Nora?'

'Yes and no. She admitted hating Nora at times for the teasing and abuse they had to endure, and in turn despised herself for hating her sister. But she also loves the girl and feels protective towards her due to her illness.'

Bliss tilted his head. 'I think it's understandable. She's not much more than a kid herself, so she must feel confused by these wildly different feelings she has about her sister. Did you get the impression she genuinely knows nothing about the rape?'

'Put it this way, I neither saw nor heard anything to make me think she does.'

'How about her mother? There's clearly friction between the pair of them.'

Chandler fidgeted with her hair as she was prone to do when speaking, a nervous mannerism he had never once mentioned. 'Patricia feels bitterness towards her for what she sees as giving in too easily, too readily to the nesters. She thinks Frances should have stood up to them, been more protective of her daughters.'

Bliss snorted. 'She's an angry teenager. She'd probably be angry even if her home wasn't being cuckooed. It's no wonder she considers her life to be over. What does she have to look forward to except more of the same?'

Their food arrived and they broke off the conversation until they'd both consumed some of it. In Bliss's case, he was almost finished when he said, 'It's a bleak outlook for all of them if we can't convince Frances Bell to act. I discussed the possibility of witness protection with her. There was a spark of interest, perhaps even hope. I didn't force the issue, but I was pretty blunt about their chances if she did nothing.'

'Do you think she'll go for it?' Chandler asked before biting into her second triangle of sandwich.

'I think she might. I'm just not certain she's brave enough at the moment to reveal the names of the dealers doing business out of her home. That said, I'm hopeful she can be persuaded provided her daughter is on board. Do you think Patricia will want to go with her mum and sister?'

Waiting until she's swallowed down the masticated food, Chandler nodded forcefully and said, 'She'll jump at the chance to extricate herself from the situation she's in. Despite everything, she adores her sister. I'm reasonably sure she feels the same way about her mother. But yes, she wants out and a fresh start would be an ideal way to move forward with her life.'

Bliss thought about the opportunity being offered to the family. In his opinion, it was a good and fair deal, but one that still had to be played just right. 'If Frances Bell gives me everything and is willing to stand up in the witness box and confirm her statement, I'm sure we can swing it with the NCA. Nailing drug dealers is always a win, but drug dealers who are also child rapists… that's a major bonus in anyone's book.'

'But then we come back to the reason why Nora is in hospital at all,' Chandler said, eyeing him keenly.

He finished his glass of sparkling orange before saying, 'Of course. And I brought that up, made it clear that until we'd resolved the overdose scare, we really couldn't move forward.'

'And what did she have to say about that?'

'She stuck to her most recent claim. Leaving the tablets opened up and close to Nora was an accident. A terrible and thoughtless one, but still accidental. The ice cream the kid kept mentioning came earlier in the day, evidently, which she later got confused about. Frances is adamant when she says she's not covering for Patricia and refuses to believe her youngest daughter deliberately tried to off herself. She claims the girl had no conception of what she was doing, and I believed that at the very least.'

'Did you mention our suspicions?' Chandler asked.

Bliss nodded as they both rose and headed towards the main counter and tills. 'I told her that if she remembered otherwise in the next twenty-four hours, then we might understand and be willing to overlook a single slip brought on by the overwhelming pressure and stress of her situation. She understood what I was saying.'

He paid the bill and, on the way back to the car, took a call. 'Well, hello there,' he said breezily. 'I can't believe it took you so long. This case is into its third day, slacker.'

Sandra Bannister, a journalist with the local city newspaper, blew a loud raspberry and said, 'For your information, I've been away. Some of us take a holiday when the old batteries need to be recharged. I just got back from California yesterday and I'm wiped out by jet lag.'

He knew the Bell case had been kept under wraps, but the murder of Roger Craig had garnered a degree of local attention. So far, the disappearance of Stuart McKenzie had not attracted any interest outside of family and friends, and Bliss wanted it kept that way. Even so, he decided to throw out a baited hook.

'You'll be wanting to catch up on our murder, then,' he said.

'If there's anything to catch up on. Or is this just another gang of thugs getting their kicks with one of our homeless people?'

'You make that sound as if it would be beneath your lofty position to report on such an incident. Would it not be considered newsworthy?'

'Sod you, Jimmy! You know I didn't mean it like that.'

He smiled to himself. He did know, but he also enjoyed pushing buttons. Recalling the official media statement, he remained within its boundaries. 'We're still investigating. I can't say more than that at present, other than to suggest you bide your time. There might be more to it than first appears.'

'Oh, you little tease.'

'I know. I just can't help myself sometimes, Sandra.' He winked at Chandler as he said it.

'All right. I'll bite. You'll let me know the moment you know more?'

'If I can. My plate is already full, and if this moves it could do so quickly.' Bliss thought about the circumstances of the murder and the link to McKenzie. One of the benefits of an arrangement like his with a local journalist was that the newspaper often had details on people the police did not have access to. In return for him feeding her updates ahead of her more immediate competitors and the wider media, she had no qualms about sending him whatever intelligence the *Peterborough Telegraph* had on file. On a whim, he made a quick decision and said, 'You might be able to help me with something else we're looking into.'

'Different case?'

'Yes. I'd like to know if you have anything on a company called Vantage Holdings.'

There was a pause. He assumed she was writing down the name. 'Vantage?' she repeated back.

'Yes.'

'Okay. Nothing springs to mind, but I'll have a look. Can you give me any more to go on? Some context, perhaps?'

'Not at this time,' he replied. 'It could be something, maybe nothing. Whatever you do, don't go off on your own looking into them. If they get to hear about your interest, it could make them jumpy. Just let me have what you've got, and if it pans out and becomes more than a hunch, I'll let you know.'

Bannister agreed to email him with anything she found, by which time he and his partner had reached the car. Satisfied with the conversation, Bliss pressed down on the key fob to unlock the doors.

'What was all that about?' Chandler asked. She was familiar with her partner's dealings with the reporter, despite them being off book. 'Vantage Holdings?'

He nodded. 'Remember the name came up in our search? It's the umbrella company run by McKenzie, Banks, and Dixon. The company that owns all the other companies – before you drill down into the shell game, that is.'

'So technically you're having her look into the three of them, but without having mentioned them by name? Isn't that a bit dangerous? What if she gets wind of McKenzie's disappearance?'

'I see no reason why she would.'

'She's a reporter, Jimmy. You don't think she's going to dig around a little bit?'

'On the contrary, I know she will. But she'll be mindful of what I said to her. She won't want to burn me as a resource. Nor will she be happy with half a story.'

'Why not? What better time with you leaving?'

He shook his head. 'Because first, I'm not exactly leaving. Second, as and when I do go, she'll want me to suggest a replacement insider. I have no doubt she'll take a look beyond whatever her paper has on file, but not too deep. She won't hear about McKenzie being missing because it's not widely known beyond family.'

Chandler appeared to accept his reasoning. 'Speaking of our missing person, shall I call in? Somebody might have made progress while we've been tied up.'

Bliss gave her the nod. He sat back without starting the engine and said, 'Put your phone on speaker so's I can hear and react.'

Not wishing to disturb DCI Warburton, Chandler called DC Ansari, as with Bishop at home, Gul was the most experienced colleague in the office. The first item they discussed was Stuart McKenzie's phone data.

'Nothing we didn't already know,' Ansari said with regret. 'If McKenzie and his attacker were in contact, it wasn't via the phone we know about.'

'He might have had a burner,' Bliss suggested, which they all agreed was a possibility.

'Anything yet from tech at HQ about his other devices?' he asked.

'Nothing yet, boss. Last I heard they hadn't even started; they're backed up with requests and we're way down the list.' Ansari's frustration was evident in her tone of voice.

'How about the deeper dives into these three men?' Chandler asked.

'Don't forget Mr Nash as well,' Bliss reminded them both.

'I haven't,' Ansari assured him. 'Look, I'm not complaining, but we are a man down. Two, if you count Phil still being away. I spoke to Diane earlier about additional civilian or uniform help but have heard nothing back so far.'

'Just do what you can, Gul,' Bliss told her. 'I'll make an official request for more warm bodies from around the county. Meanwhile, nobody is expecting miracles. I realise you and Alan are holding down the fort, so just give me what you have, and we won't quibble.'

'Fair enough.' The DC sounded relieved. 'Alan and I have split our enquiries into two. He's taken Grant Dixon and Jacob Nash, while I have Michael Banks and Stuart McKenzie in my sights. Unfortunately, we're not having a great deal of luck. There are plenty of rumours about these men, and in one way or another they are all known to us. But not a single conviction between them, and nothing to report on at all in the past decade.'

'I'm not surprised by that,' Bliss admitted with a grunt. 'I reckon they upped their game and started to work together more professionally. That's roughly the time they began to hide their business interests under a single umbrella. They got wise knowing if they didn't, they were bound to make a mistake.'

'We're still hard at it, Jimmy. Regards McKenzie, I'll do what I can to find out if he had use of another phone. I'm going through his financials so I'll see if I can spot a purchase. I'm guessing he paid cash if he bought a burner, but we'd never arrest some of these criminals if they didn't make stupid mistakes.'

When she ended the call, Chandler shifted in her seat to face Bliss. 'This thing you have going with Bannister… do you genuinely never have qualms about it?'

He shook his head without pause. 'Not at all. What I give her is simply a head start on her competitors. I break no real confidences and have never compromised an op. I make no personal or professional gains from our relationship. I've always accepted the potential repercussions if I'm caught, but the truth is she's been extremely helpful and has never regarded our exchanges as breaking any laws. Rules, perhaps, but lots of coppers have media insiders. Why do you ask?'

'I don't know. Just thinking ahead.'

Bliss nodded. 'You can trust her, Pen. Not that I expect her to be with the *PT* much longer. She's too good not to move on to bigger and better things.'

Chandler seemed to relax, accepting him at his word. 'What if we're wrong about McKenzie's disappearance being connected to his business ventures?' she asked, changing the subject. 'It could just as easily be personal. Somebody he pissed off so much they laid into him and allowed it to go too far.'

Bliss exhaled softly. 'You're right. There's no reason I can think of why it couldn't be something along those lines. But we'd better hope not. Because whoever did it covered their tracks very well, and if it was personal, we might never find out the motive. That's why we have to bank on it being connected to business. Because it might be the only way we have to discover the truth.'

TWENTY-THREE

WITH A CHALLENGING EIGHTEEN holes designed by the Scottish golfer and renowned architect, James Braid, the Peterborough Milton Golf Club had been established in 1938. Set in the grounds of the Fitzwilliam Estate, with tree-lined fairways, well-guarded greens, and a large lake dividing the first and eighteenth holes, the course was hugely popular with its members and their guests.

Both Michael Banks and Grant Dixon were members, and when Jacob Nash asked for a private meeting, they decided playing the back nine would provide them with the appropriate amount of time and privacy required. Nash had sounded apprehensive, which in turn worried his friends. They suspected the subject of the meeting would involve their missing business partner and perhaps business itself, a discussion best dealt with in full view of others but also from a great distance.

Nash was hardly a novice at the game, but he was the weaker of the three players with a club in his hands. He did manage to find the first fringe on the tenth hole, a 416 yard par 4 off the red tee, but even with a kind skip and bounce his ball landed a good fifty yards behind those struck by his fellow players. They began their awkward conversation as they made their way up the fairway.

'Is this about Stuart, Jacob?' Banks asked, keeping his eyes pointed ahead. 'You have concerns?'

'Don't you?' Nash replied testily. 'This isn't like any of the other times he's gone off on his own. Something is wrong. Badly wrong. I… I feel like I'm out of the loop, so I was wondering if you two knew more than I've heard.'

'That depends on what you've heard.'

'That Stu is missing. That he went out on Friday and hasn't been seen or heard of since. That's the total sum of what I know.'

'Join the club,' Dixon said, hands in pockets as he strode purposefully.

'And you aren't worried about him? The man's our friend. If something has happened to him, if he's in trouble or injured or worse, then I'm concerned it might have something to do with the nature of our business.'

Banks stopped in his tracks. He glanced back towards the elevated position they had just vacated, but there was nobody waiting to tee off. He gave Nash the full force of his steeliest of glares. 'The nature of *our* business? The nature of our business with you, Jacob, is that you earn a decent living selling cars on our behalf. That's it. Or do you know something we don't?'

Nash swallowed. It was another warm day, but he felt uncomfortably hot, sweating profusely and fearing pit stains appearing on his polo shirt. He couldn't help but wonder if the others had noticed. 'No, no,' he said quickly. 'We're doing fine and it's all sweet on that score. Look, we're all mates is what I'm getting at. I realise you three are closer and you run your empire as you see fit, but I've always known the other side of the legit ventures. You both know I was always worried about this diamond smuggling deal, though. I had a bad feeling about it right from the off, which is why I didn't ask to be included other than providing the stones from my uncle. But with Stu going missing, I have to ask if the two are connected in some way. Surely, you've both had the same concerns?'

They walked on and each played their second shots. None of them hit the green, and as before, Nash's ball remained the closest to them as they continued forward. This time it was Dixon who spoke first. 'Jacob, mate, while all three of us are grateful to you for negotiating the purchase of those diamonds, your involvement ends there just like you said. Even if me and Mickey had our issues, I'm not sure what business it is of yours.'

He was prepared for the question, having rehearsed any number of likely scenarios within the safe confines of his garden shed where he did his best thinking. 'It's my business because Stu is my friend as well. I thought I made that clear. Whatever deals you three made, whoever you've screwed along the way, I don't care. At least, I didn't. But if Stu is in trouble because of it, then I reckon it's become my business whether I wanted it to or not.'

Nash hoped his earnestness had overcome the bluster. He wasn't good at winging things. He could run the words over and over again inside his head, but his body always let him down when he had to put them into practice.

They finished with the tenth and had played irons off the eleventh tee to the green just over 100 yards away. All three avoided the bunker to the left, and to his surprise Nash's ball had come to rest less than thirty feet away from the pin. They were making their way down the hill when Banks said, 'I think we find ourselves in a grey area, Jacob. We've always accepted there are three aspects on the go between us. First and foremost, there's our friendship. Then there's the business we do with you at the dealership. But there's also the business we do without you. To be honest, that's by far the larger part, which means there's an awful lot you don't know, don't need to know, and shouldn't want to know. We're in that little part in the centre where they overlap. Like a Venn diagram.'

Nash understood he was being fobbed off, but somehow found the strength to fight his corner. 'And that means I can't worry about my friend? That I can't raise awkward questions with you two? Look, if you know or even suspect that his disappearance is to do with your other types of business, then I want to be in on it. I wouldn't expect or ask you to tell me everything, but if one of you was missing, I'm certain Stu would confide in me.'

'In that case,' Dixon said firmly, 'what will it take for you to believe we don't know or suspect anything? Mate, you're treading a fine line here. That said I do take your point. Listen, we're all worried about Stu. Of course we are. But I'm telling you, neither of us has any idea where he is, what happened to him, or why. He's a big boy and he can look after himself.'

'So, it's definitely got nothing to do with the diamonds?'

Dixon rounded on him this time, anger pinching his cheeks. 'Why the fuck are you banging on about the diamonds, Jacob? You seem to be fixated on them, and I have to say that bothers me.'

Again, Nash was ready for the question, and he thought he could pull off his pre-prepared response. 'You really have to ask me that? Too true I'm fixated on the diamonds, Mickey. Because I'm not involved with any of your other shady dealings, so they can't come back to bite me. But I am where the diamonds are concerned. You dismiss my involvement by saying I buy them on your behalf as if that counts for nothing. Well, it does. To me it does. You couldn't pass them on if I didn't obtain them for you in the first place. Or to put it another way, if somebody has an issue with you three over those diamonds, then they probably have an issue with me as well.'

'They don't even know you exist,' Banks argued.

'Not by name, no. Not who or what I am. But they know you get the diamonds from somewhere. And it's a bloody short path from you lot to me, Mickey.'

He knew he'd blown it the moment he closed his mouth. Both men were giving him deeply curious looks. 'What did you mean by that?' Dixon demanded, taking a step closer to Nash.

'By what?' he asked, swallowing thickly.

'You said they know we get the diamonds from somewhere.'

'Did I?'

'Yeah, too right you did, Jacob. First of all, who is this *they* you're talking about? And second, what precisely do *they* know? The whole point of our scam is that nobody knows we have our own supply of our own diamonds. Come to think of it, I'm not sure we ever told *you* what we did with the ones we bought from you.'

'Now that you mention it, I don't think we did,' Banks said urgently. 'What the fuck is this, Jacob? What's going on?'

Nash felt trickles of perspiration leaking from his hairline. He had to think quickly and walk it back. 'Okay, okay. I misspoke. You know me, speak before I think. Stu told me what you were doing with the diamonds. I admit curiosity got the better of me, so I asked and he explained.'

'We all know what curiosity did to the cat,' Dixon said menacingly.

'For fuck's sake, Grant,' Nash replied, stepping away. 'Do you have to be like that with me? I kind of had my suspicions, so all Stu did was confirm them. He saw no harm in telling me. Don't worry, he didn't give me any details. I never knew who you were doing business with. I think I just assumed that whoever you hand the diamonds off to got wind of it and that's what led to Stu vanishing off the face of the earth. It's why I asked to meet with you. I suppose I… I assumed you were aware something had gone tits up but were keeping it to yourself.'

He could tell they were torn. Neither seemed convinced by his protestations, but his was a feasible story. He knew they'd treat him with suspicion from now on and were unlikely to open up, but to his astonishment Grant Dixon did so.

'All right, calm yourself down,' he said, glancing around. There was still nobody waiting to play behind them, so he continued. 'It doesn't matter if Stu told you or what he told you. What I can confirm is that as far as Mickey and I are concerned, the third party involved in the smuggling deal has no idea we're passing off your gems as the ones we bring in from Amsterdam. And I'm sure we would know all about it if they did. It's an arrangement all three of us are part of, and in fact I'm the main point of contact. It makes no sense for them to go to Stu first.'

Relieved to have got away with the subterfuge, Nash decided to call it a day. Better to come back at them when he was calm again rather than risk saying anything else so stupid. It was hard juggling what he knew with what he was supposed to know since his encounter at the hotel. If Stuart appeared out of nowhere, more questions might be raised if he discovered the lie Nash had just told. But he couldn't risk making any further mistakes. One more slip of the tongue could do untold damage.

'Fair enough,' he finally said with a nod to both friends. 'I hope you understand I had to ask.'

'Yeah,' Banks said, his hard eyes unblinking. 'You had to make sure your own arse was covered.'

'That's not it at all, Mickey. Yes, part of my concern was what might spill back in my direction. But I genuinely thought you were both more clued in where Stu is concerned. I realise the truth is you don't know any more than I do. To be honest, I'm not sure if that makes it better or worse.'

'I know,' Dixon agreed, his lips twisted as if tasting something bitter. 'Because at the end of the day, Stu is still gone and we're no closer to understanding why.'

TWENTY-FOUR

BECAUSE THE UNIT WAS understaffed and Bliss felt a little guilty for half the problems that created, he and Chandler teamed up with DCs Ansari and Virgil for the remainder of the afternoon. After a while they were joined by DCI Warburton who offered some hands-on assistance, but the going was hard and slow. She and Bliss had a short, private conversation regarding DS Bishop, but as Chandler had suggested, his boss came firmly down on his side. It was a challenge working a murder enquiry with two detectives out of the picture, especially with a relatively small team, but they all agreed the shortage left them no further behind given the lack of worthwhile intel to action.

Nonetheless, Bliss felt bad and offered to stand a round of drinks after work. They called it a day at five-thirty, and after an hour in the pub he drove home. He'd called Molly to ask for her choice of takeaway, but she told him not to bother as he'd find a surprise waiting for him. What he'd expected was pizza on the table courtesy of Molly's own money, but instead he walked into a kitchen smelling of home cooked food.

'What's this?' he asked after greeting Molly and Max in turn. The latter treated Bliss to an irregular show of dancing around in circles, which Molly attempted to replicate while cooing at the dog as if it were a baby.

'It's meat pie, mash, veg, and gravy,' she told him. 'With a few roasties on the side.'

'You cook?' he said, stunned by the discovery.

'I can and do,' she said with an air of disdain.

'So how is this the first I'm hearing about it?'

'Because you never asked.'

'And you decided to lay all this on for just us two?'

'It certainly looks that way, Jimbo, though I could do without the third degree.'

Bliss bowed and made a gesture suggesting he was not worthy. 'I apologise, Molly. I had no idea. Thing is, I know damn well I didn't have most of the ingredients for this spread.'

'Other than the butter and milk I used for the mash, you had none of the ingredients I needed. But you know what, in addition to being a pretty good cook, I can also find my way to the shops on my own. And when I get there, guess what…? Yeah, I can choose stuff from the shelves and then buy it. Fancy that, little old me going out into the world hunting and gathering at the local shops. Whatever next for us young women folk?'

He took the sarcasm well while reflecting on how often he dished it out. The food was surprisingly tasty, and he told her how delicious it all was. She beamed with pride and delight at the compliment. He washed up afterwards – well, rinsed and put into the dishwasher. He faffed around for five minutes trying to remember how to work the machine, only to admit defeat and have Molly step in to rescue him.

'I don't know,' she said, shaking her head at him. 'What are you like? How the bloody hell do you cope on your own?'

'I keep cooking to a minimum. It's easy when you know how.' He suddenly remembered something and flashed a wide grin. 'Hold on a sec, I've got a few things for you.'

Bliss trotted off into the hallway, opened up the cupboard under the stairs, and took out a carrier bag. He waited for Molly to join him in the living room then handed it over. 'I popped into a little record shop in Lincoln Road last week and got you these,' he said, eager to see her excitement up close rather than speaking on the phone when he introduced her to something new.

Molly's eyes grew wide as he pulled out three vinyl albums still in their original cellophane sleeves. 'Steve McQueen is Prefab Sprout's finest hour,' he told her. 'And Drops of Jupiter by Train is theirs. I know you're going to love them both. For balance I threw in Blue Oyster Cult's Fire of Unknown Origin, and if you haven't heard of them, then this will blow your socks off.'

They were three tracks into the Train album when Bliss's phone rang. He didn't recognise the number, but as it was his work phone, he had no choice but to answer after lifting the stylus off the record. 'This is DI Bliss,' he said. 'Who am I speaking to, please?'

'Oh, Inspector. Thank God I managed to get a hold of you. It's Peter Alinson. Frances Bell's case worker.'

'Yeah, I remember. What can I do for you? Is there a problem with Nora?'

'No, no. Nothing like that. I'm calling to let you know that Patricia ran away and isn't answering her phone. Not to calls or texts.'

'What happened?' Bliss asked, annoyed by the girl's actions.

'Frances contacted me. She spoke to Patricia about the possibility of moving out of the area under witness protection. They argued, and when it started getting out of hand, Frances told her about Nora. The rape, the pregnancy. Patricia evidently had some kind of meltdown and stormed out. There's been no word from her since, and with everything that's been going on, her mother is naturally deeply concerned.'

Bliss took a breath. He had an idea where the girl might be. 'All right. Well, given her age and the fact she's not been absent too long, this really isn't a police matter as things stand. I suspect Patricia might have returned home ahead of her mother and sister to confront the lads responsible for the rape. If I'm right, then I'll make sure we get involved. Give me an hour and I'll get back to you.'

He looked across at Molly. 'I'm sorry,' he said. 'You heard?'

She nodded. 'Sounds like a kid in trouble. Your speciality.'

Bliss chuckled. 'Not quite. Damsels in distress are not usually my thing.'

'What the fuck is a damsel when it's at home? Isn't that some kind of jam?'

This made him laugh harder still. 'I think you'll find that's a damson. A damsel is an old-fashioned term for a young woman.'

'Then just say that next time. Don't confuse me. It's easily done.'

He couldn't avoid drawing the parallels between Molly and Patricia. There were many differences, Molly's experiences fundamentally worse on the horror scale. But they were both young women who had been exposed to the seedy underbelly of society at an early age. Perhaps what set Molly apart was her indomitable spirit, or perhaps she had simply been the recipient of a large slice of luck when she needed it most. He was struggling to differentiate between the two, but he felt a trickle of fear at Patricia's current state of mind.

Bliss leaned over to plant a peck on Molly's forehead. She smiled. He smiled back. 'I have to go,' he said. 'I won't be long.'

'Take as long as you need, Jimbo. Me and Max will be fine. I'll finish listening to the vinyl. I'm loving it so far.'

'I'm happy about that. Make sure you cop an earful of *Bonny* and *Appetite* on the Prefab Sprout album. And finish off the A side of Drops of Jupiter. As for BOC,' he said with a grin, 'they might be a bit too scary for this time of night.'

'I'll listen to them all. Don't worry. And if I decide they're all shit, I've always got Taylor Swift to listen to on Spotify.'

Bliss winked, got his things together, and headed out. It didn't take long to reach Millfield. Nowhere was ever too far away in the city. He drove straight to the Bell home, not bothering to scout the area first. With the sun having set, the street took on a more threatening presence. He felt tension leaking from the bricks and mortar of every building. There were more youths around this time, and as he parked and got out of the car one of them cycled up to him, circling around like a shark weighing up its prey.

'You lost, mate?' the kid asked on one of his passes. The evening was reasonably warm with little breeze, yet the cyclist wore a puffa jacket over his sweatshirt, its hood pulled up around his head and his features lost to darkness.

Ignoring the question, Bliss continued on through a gateless entrance into the postage-stamp front garden. Tall growths of patchy grass fought for space in an area choked with weeds, a straggly hedge bulging with angry thorns forming the only barrier between the pathetic lawn and the pavement. He'd already clocked the downstairs windows and noted they were unlit, but he knocked on the door anyway.

'There's nothing for you there, mate,' the cyclist called out. 'Better move on while you still can.'

Bliss glanced back over his shoulder. The kid was resting with one foot on the ground, his bike angled across the road. His face remained lost inside the shadow of the hoodie, but the voice sounded not long broken.

Taking a couple of steps back, Bliss looked up at the windows on the first floor. No lights. No sign of movement. He turned his head to the left and right, then headed back towards the car. As he hit the pavement, the kid said, 'Oi, fuckface. Don't ignore me, man. You disrespect me, you pay a toll. You feel me, yeah?'

Bliss was going to walk on. Should have. Instead, he stopped, then moved sideways and stepped in closer until he had invaded the cyclist's personal space. 'Listen to me, little boy. You want me to ignore you. You need me to ignore you. Because if I don't, then I'll be taking notice of you instead. And you really don't want that. A lack of respect will be the least of your concerns if that happens. You feel *me*?'

He didn't wait for a response. He simply walked across the road, got into his pool car and drove away. At the junction, he turned right, and then first right again. The moment he did, Bliss knew he'd chosen correctly. The sense of dread that had permeated the road in which the Bell family lived was deeper and more profound here. Up ahead in the distance, he saw a yelling and cheering crowd spilling out across the street. His gut gave a lurch. It looked as if a fight was taking place and he immediately knew Patricia was at the heart of it. He sped up until he was only yards away from whatever was going on and was almost out of the vehicle before he'd activated the handbrake.

Bliss felt sick with worry. If the girl had come back here looking for trouble, she might well have found it. As he barged his way through a shouting, screaming mob baying for blood, he paid no attention to where his elbows landed. Through the melee, he saw a body lying on the road like a broken marionette.

No! I'm not going to lose this one.

Desperate not to be too late, he forced a passage through into open space, expecting to have to throw himself at Patricia's assailant. Instead, he stumbled upon her standing over a bloodied figure lying face down on the potholed tarmac. She was panting hard, and in her right hand she clutched a length of iron pipe.

She stood hunched over like an animal, wild eyed, hair hanging down over her face. 'Come on you fuckers!' she screamed. 'I know there's more of you out there!'

In that moment, even though Bell looked physically unharmed, Bliss knew he was already too late to save her.

TWENTY-FIVE

H E CALLED FOR AN ambulance and requested backup from his uniformed colleagues. Two response vehicles arrived shortly afterwards, but the volatile nature of the mob made it seem far longer as time slowed to a crawl. With more officers from the Emergency Response Team on the way to carry out crowd control, he decided to remove Bell from the scene as soon as a pathway had been cleared. His head churned with all manner of dreadful possibilities, and a couple of minutes into the drive he reached a decision he hoped he would not regret.

'From what I saw, you did some serious damage with that iron bar,' he said. Patricia Bell stared at him in silence from the back seat, barely blinking. After arresting the girl, he'd secured her hands in front of her with a set of Plasticuffs taken from his equipment bag in the boot of the car. Detaining a person with handcuffs is regarded as a use of force, in this case warranted by Bell's actions and loss of control. He didn't believe she presented a danger to him, which is why he had cuffed her wrists to the front, but it was hard to read her current state of mind.

'He was still out of it when we left the scene,' Bliss continued, still assessing her demeanour in the rear-view mirror. 'His brain could be swollen. Might even have a bleed. It's impossible to know what damage you've caused, but we can at least be thankful he's not dead. Or maybe you're disappointed about that.'

Still nothing. She was a tough little nut. He knew he shouldn't be talking to her, but it wasn't the same as asking her questions. Which he was about to do.

Bliss shook his head. 'Patricia, we don't have long before we reach my nick, so let's not fuck about. I need you to listen to me, and then I need you to respond when I ask questions. I'm going to assume that the kid you just assaulted is the one you believe raped your sister. Let me start by saying that while I understand why you did what you did, you're in a shitload of trouble. You're ours for a minimum of twenty-four hours from the time I book you in, and we will keep you for that entire day. We can then request extensions, and we'll get them. By the time we're done with you over the course of two or three days, we will have consulted with the Crown Prosecution Service to decide on charging. I can guarantee there's enough evidence, so you *will* be charged. We'll wait it out until we know precisely what that charge will be, because it could yet be murder.'

This time he got a reaction. The teen's eyes widened and grew serious, her quivering lips parting to draw in air. She was close, but needed a final push. 'Listen to me, Patricia. Your best chance is if we decide not to charge you. The way things are, I don't see that happening. So, the reality is your next best chance is if you present a problematic defence. Problematic for us, that is. I advised you of your rights when I made the arrest. So far, you haven't asked for legal representation. That needs to change. You demand your right to a solicitor the moment we reach the custody suite. Do you understand me?'

Bell nodded but said nothing. He regarded that as progress. She was listening to him, which was important.

'Good. Later, after your solicitor has arrived and you've had a chance to meet with them, you're going to put on a show. If you're as smart as I think you are, you'll do as I tell you. But before any of that can happen, you have to speak to me. I have just one question to begin with, okay? I need to know where you got the iron bar from. Did you pick it up elsewhere along the way or did you find it in the street close to where you carried out the assault?'

Initially, he didn't think she was going to speak, but when he also remained silent, the girl seemed to reach a decision to trust him. 'I picked it up on my way there,' she told him in a faltering voice. 'There's a builder's skip not far away, and I knew I'd find something inside it that I could use.'

Bliss briefly glanced back over his shoulder and shook his head. 'Wrong answer, Patricia. Let that be the one and only time you tell anybody where you found the bar, because you've just admitted to premeditation. You repeat that same story to anyone else and it will earn you a prison sentence. Now listen and listen closely. This is the time to take on board everything I have to say, because I'm your only hope. When my colleagues interview you, tell them you have no comment to make. Until, that is, they ask you to explain what happened. At that point, you open up. You admit you have no recollection of anything from the moment your mother told you about your sister's ordeal until I took the bar from your hand. Do you hear me? No memory whatsoever. After that you answer with a no comment to every question they put to you.'

The girl regarded him with a mixture of suspicion and scepticism. 'I... I don't understand. Why don't I just say nothing throughout?'

'Because you're establishing a defence, Patricia. Given you have no legally reasonable explanation for your actions, it's best to have no explanation at all. Look, when your solicitor arrives you tell them the exact same thing. Don't worry if they believe you or not. It doesn't matter. Your brief will quickly realise it's perhaps your only way out of this mess, so you just have to stick to your guns.'

After a slight pause, the young woman said, 'Why are you doing this? Is it some kind of trick?'

Bliss shook his head. 'Am I right about your reason for taking that bar to this particular kid's head? Is he the one who raped Nora?'

'Yes,' Patricia said, whipping her head away in disgust.

'Okay. Then I'm doing this because I understand what triggered you. And if this kid you assaulted did what you say he did, then perhaps on some level he deserved his punishment. That might win you the sympathy vote, but the law is the law. You'd still be charged, and the chances are good that you'd be found guilty for it. So, your only real approach is to establish from the beginning some form of mental and emotional breakdown. Basically, you accept that you may well be guilty of what we're accusing you of, but you didn't know you were doing it at the time.'

She seemed to catch on. 'All right. Say that's true. I still don't understand why you'd want to help me.'

Bliss assembled his thoughts before speaking. 'I believe in natural justice as well as the law. I also think you and your family have been through enough strife to last a lifetime. If things go the right way, all three of you could be settled elsewhere very soon. What you did to that kid hasn't helped, I won't lie. Your mother and sister can't go home at the moment, that's for sure. I reckon there's a crew of angry young men already circling, just waiting to take revenge in any violent way they can. But I do have one more important question, Patricia.'

'Okay. I'll answer it.'

'This kid whose head you caved in... back at the scene you said his name was Zander Hirst... how certain are you that he is the one who raped Nora? That he fathered the child she's carrying?'

'Completely. It was him.'

'But how can you know that? You weren't even aware it had happened until a short while ago.'

Bell turned her head to one side, looking away. 'Because he tried it on with me first. I kept knocking him back, until eventually he said it didn't matter because if he couldn't have me, he knew who couldn't refuse.' Patricia lowered her chin and began to sob, her shoulders heaving. 'I thought he meant my mum. I had no idea he was talking about Nora. I mean, who would do something like that? How fucking sick do you have to be to even think like that? If I'd known he meant my sister, I would have let him do anything he wanted to me rather than touch her.'

Bliss pressed himself back in his seat and let the girl cry it out. Even if she kept to the plan the most likely outcome was that she would be charged, and that charge would depend on Zander Hirst's condition. But the story he had insisted she stick to might buy her something. Perhaps not her freedom, but a reduced sentence was a genuine possibility. And if she could convince a jury that she had been experiencing some kind of dissociative fugue at the time she had swung that metal bar, then with the testimony of a favourable doctor any result was possible.

'Patricia,' Bliss said softly. 'I want to switch things around to discuss something entirely different. I want to know who fed Nora those tablets.'

The girl dropped her head, and she shook it. He couldn't see her eyes, but he guessed there were tears in them as she said, 'I came home and ten minutes later my mum went out. She told me Nora was sleeping and that I shouldn't disturb her for an hour or so. But then…'

'Go on,' he said encouragingly. 'You can trust me.'

'She did something she hadn't done in, I don't know, maybe ten years.'

'And what was that?'

'She gave me a hug. Then she kissed me on the forehead and told me she loved me. She's never that emotional, so I knew something had to be wrong. But I'd never have guessed… not that. Never that.'

Bliss took the young woman at her word. From the moment he'd learned of Nora's inability to both fetch and open the pill containers, he had suspected the girl's mother. A life of chaotic desperation and poor choices had caused the woman to snap. He believed her intention had been to end her own life as well, and Patricia's account seemed to confirm that theory. Whether Frances Bell had changed her mind because of her older daughter, or had simply regained her reason, might forever remain unknown. In some ways, he hoped it did. Not that it mattered, his suspicions superfluous with the woman's statement having been accepted.

'Are you worried about the future?' he asked, turning his thoughts back to the two daughters. 'For Nora, I mean?'

She shook her head. 'Not if we're still allowed to move away from this place. If my mum did what I think she did, that wasn't the real her. That woman is gone. She'll never allow life to get this bad for us again. I really believe that. I can see it in her eyes when she looks at Nora. She's so grateful for this second chance. And if you're asking me if Nora is safe from my mum, then yes, she is. And if the baby is aborted, she might never realise what happened to her. My sister won't ever be well, and she's unlikely to live a full life. But I have to believe we can all be happy again. Because without that, what's the point in any of us carrying on?'

Bliss swallowed back his own emotions, a sob dying in the back of his throat. This poor kid. Only just eighteen and with the full weight of an unjust and despicable world upon her shoulders.

She could bring herself to admitting what her mother had done, but not to saying it out loud. That would make it real. It would make it true. But for as long as it remained unsaid, it might never have happened. And she could live with that.

Though troubled, Bliss said no more about it. He thought about the case, and while the circumstantial evidence pointed to Bell having taken it upon herself to end her younger child's life, there wasn't enough to charge her with. And at the end of the day, what would that really achieve? Removing her from her children's life could only do more harm than good. He agreed with Patricia's convincing argument that their mother would never be desperate enough to repeat her crime. Only that didn't make it true. What's more, wasn't what Frances Bell did yet a further abuse on a child who had already suffered?

'Have you told anybody else what you suspect about your mother?' he asked.

'No. It was a terrible thing that she did, but I know her better than she knows herself. She'll be fine. We'll be fine.'

'She may yet be charged, Patricia. Her version of events makes for a nice story, but that's all it is.'

'Unless I back her up. I could easily have been in Nora's room when my mum swapped stuff between handbags and accidentally left a pile of things behind.'

'You'd lie?' Bliss asked, surprised that he was surprised. Their conversation could never be used against either of them, so he thought he might as well pursue it.

'Who says it'd be a lie? Maybe it's something I'll just remember.'

It was all so confusing. He had to give the situation more thought. But he also had other matters to attend to. 'Look, putting your mother and Nora to one side, what you did to that lad wasn't right,' he said after a while. 'I meant what I said about natural justice, and sometimes I think that if you live by the sword then you can't complain if you also die by it. But there are other ways to punish young men like him without giving up your own liberty, although emotions often understandably take over. Your problem is the law doesn't see it the way you do. Nor the way I do, for that matter. Vigilante justice is frowned upon, but it's a grey area for many of us. If you weren't of sound mind at the time, then you might not be held fully responsible for your actions. But it's going to help your case if you're right about Hirst, Patricia. And even if you are, I still have to prove it.'

'It was him. I know it was.' Her face was buried in her hands, but even through the tears her tone was defiant.

The last thing Bliss wanted to do was ask the next question, but there was no way to avoid it. 'I'm sorry if this distresses you further,' he said, 'but is there a chance, just a chance, that even if Zander Hirst did force himself on Nora that the baby might not be his?'

Bell's head shot up as she recoiled in horror. 'What?! What are you saying? You think my sister would –'

Bliss shook his head. 'No, that's not what I'm implying. I'm saying that with all the lads going in and out of your house over the past few months, it's surely possible that Hirst wasn't the only one to have access to your sister.'

The girl cupped both hands around her mouth. 'Oh, my God! I think I'm going to be sick. Are you... is this... am I going fucking mad? Am I? Is this what insanity feels like?'

'Hey, hey. Calm yourself,' he said in a soothing voice. He was glad the roads were relatively quiet, given the attention he was paying to his prisoner. 'I could be wrong. I want to be wrong. But you have to admit it's possible. I just want you to prepare yourself for that eventuality, Patricia. If it's Hirst, then we'll have the prick for it, no matter what his condition. And I understand your reasoning, I really do. All I'm saying is, life doesn't always work out that way. Solutions don't often come wrapped up in a bow. Sometimes life coughs up nasty surprises, bitter disappointments. Remember that. And Patricia… it goes without saying that this conversation never happened. Understood? Neither of us uttered a single word the whole way to the station. You walk in with me, you demand your solicitor and stick to everything we just discussed, and let's see how things go. Okay?'

She nodded, sucking in air as she rubbed her tear-streaked cheeks. 'Okay. And Inspector Bliss, thank you. I didn't expect this from you.'

'Understood. And no problem. You can do this, Patricia. You have the strength, that much I do know. Now all you have to do is use your brain. Think you can handle that?'

'Of course. This isn't the first obstacle I've had to overcome in my life.'

Smiling as they headed into the Thorpe Wood Police Station staff car park, Bliss caught her gaze in the mirror and winked. 'Good luck to you,' he said.

'If I didn't have these cuffs on, I'd give you a hug,' Bell said.

'Let's see what the outcome of all this is. You might change your mind.'

'The hug has nothing to do with the outcome. It's for the intent. I know what I did was wrong. And the thing is, I'm actually not all that clear on the specifics. So maybe I did have some kind of breakdown. Either way, I do appreciate you trying to help me. I'll never forget it.'

Bliss eased out a sigh as he parked the car. Many people would frown upon his actions in potentially providing this angry teen with a way to avoid prosecution, or at the very least some prison time. He might end up questioning it himself if Zander Hirst died or was left brain damaged. But if the boy had raped Nora Bell, a vulnerable and severely disabled child, then was his brand of evil worthy of a humane response?

The boundary lines between right and wrong were drawn and known to most, but they were not easy to remain within.

TWENTY-SIX

T HE LAST THING BLISS did the following morning before heading off to work was to call Sandra Bannister, the *Peterborough Telegraph* reporter. She seemed to think he was chasing her up for the information on Vantage Holdings, but stopped her rant in mid-flow when he said he had something else for her.

'Are you aware of the events in Millfield yesterday evening?' he asked.

'No. I've not so much as glanced at the online updates this morning. Why, what happened?'

'A young lad is in hospital after being beaten with an iron bar. I'm pretty sure he'll be painted by some as an innocent, loveable kid who happened to be in the wrong place at the wrong time. Don't bite. I checked him out, and he has form. Well known to us as a street dealer. He's brutal with it, thought to be behind a couple of stabbings and the vicious torture of a mule who tried to tuck him up.'

'Thought to be?'

'By that I mean we have good intel, but no proof. Nobody will testify against him. Not even the torture victim who wound up being hospitalised.'

'Okay. If I'm reading you right, Jimmy, you're suggesting my slant when or if I get around to writing a piece on it should be this is not a good kid caught up in somebody else's mess, but one who emerged from his own on the wrong side of it.'

Bliss was impressed. 'That's pretty much word for word what I was about to suggest.'

He had hoped she would go for it immediately, but Bannister was her usual contemplative self despite her jet lag. 'Hmm. The thing is, if you don't have any proof then neither do I.'

'That's not a problem for a wordsmith like you. Imply rather than state. Suggest the information came from a reliable source.'

Bannister was not convinced. 'I don't know. How badly was this lad beaten?'

'Ah, well this is where it might make your job a bit tricky. He was hit pretty hard two or three times around the head. He's suffered a bleed to the brain and hasn't regained consciousness. I called the hospital just before dialling your number and there's no significant change overnight.'

'He's in critical condition, then. In the Intensive Care Unit.'

'That's correct.'

'Okay, so there will be an outpouring of sympathy for him and outrage against the person who struck him. Do you have him in custody? Do you know the reasons for the assault?'

'Her. The attacker is a young woman, still a teenager herself. Sandra, I can't tell you why she did it, only that at the time she believed he deserved it. And if she's right about what the little prick did, then any sympathetic response towards him will be restricted to family and close friends. Perhaps not all of those, either, when they hear just how bad it is.'

Pausing to consider, Bannister then said, 'My angle, then, is that his crime may be far worse than hers and that people ought to wait for the result of the investigation.'

'Yes. Perfect. The overall approach you take is obviously up to you, but the main thing is to get something out there that stops the news from being one-sided behind the victim.'

'Okay, I can see the angle. Tell me, is your assailant pleading guilty?'

'That's still to be determined.'

Bannister took a long breath. 'I'll look into it,' she said finally. 'How confident are you that the kid who got pounded is actually the real villain of the piece?'

Bliss gave that a moment, then said, 'My confidence is high.'

'And the girl's name? The one who did the beating?'

'No, you can't know that without calling in and asking questions first,' he said. 'There are only a few of us who know her and precisely what caused her to flip. But the attack took place in front of a whole load of kids, so there's bound to be phone footage of it floating around on social media. I'm sure the story will interest mainstream media as well, so you might need to make your assessment quickly.'

'But I'm the only one with insider knowledge, right? The only one who knows there's a better story behind the obvious one.'

'Of course. Provided you get in before the media briefing, the time and details of which have yet to be decided.'

When Bliss ended the call a couple of minutes later, a voice from the kitchen doorway piped up. 'I suppose that's what you couldn't tell me about last night?'

He snapped his head around, surprised to have been caught out like a thief in the night. 'You weren't supposed to overhear any of that. I was just about to wake you.'

'Max already did that job for you,' Molly said, knuckling her eyes and yawning. She wore a lightweight dressing gown over purple pyjamas, her feet snug in fluffy slippers.

'He's good like that,' Bliss admitted. 'Did he pounce and slobber or sidle up and sprawl all over you?'

She chuckled and squatted to rub the dog's head. 'He kicked off with the old sidle and sprawl routine. Then, when I wouldn't budge, he pulled out the pounce and slobber.'

Bliss nodded, looking down at Max. 'Yeah, he's effective, I'll say that for him. Anyway, I have to get going. Ignore what you just heard, okay. It never happened.' Bliss realised it was the second time in less than twelve hours that he had said those words to a young girl.

Molly drew an invisible zip across her mouth. 'You going to crack this one, Jimbo? Before tomorrow night, I mean?'

At first, he frowned, then he remembered. And nodded. 'Yeah, we'll get there,' he said with more confidence than he felt. 'Clear two cases in two days. No problem.'

Walking into the office ten minutes later, he felt eminently more stressed and apprehensive about his chances of ending the week with two wins behind him. After delivering Bell to custody the previous evening, he had placed calls to DCs Ansari and Virgil. He'd asked them to run an initial interview with the girl, but had also revealed his strategy.

'Hold on, let me make sure I have this right,' Ansari had said to him. 'You're going to advise her to ask for a brief, and to shut us down entirely other than when we ask her to tell us what happened.'

Bliss first confirmed that he had already made his recommendation, before explaining why. He'd sensed his colleague struggling with the notion, but evidently not to the point of balking at it and openly disagreeing with him. Given that he'd had them interrupt their own time to carry out the interview, he'd not expected to see either of them in the office prior to the morning briefing, but they were both at their desks working on their laptops when he walked in.

'Good morning, Gul. How did it go last night?' he asked Ansari.

She looked up and nodded at him over the top of her monitor. 'Pretty much as you hoped, boss.'

'She stuck to the story, then?'

'Oh, yes, she did. Not only that, but she was also remarkably convincing.'

The point of the quick, late-night interview was for Patricia Bell to establish her lack of memory as early as possible into her arrest period. It was now part of the record, and from this point on would be the focus of attention for the team. Bliss believed that was crucial, as a night in the custody cell might have wrought havoc with the girl's emotional and mental state. As it was, both the prosecution and defence knew precisely where they stood as the clock wound down.

Bliss sensed something off in Ansari's tone. He leaned across her desk and placed both hands flat on its smooth even surface. 'Do you have anything you'd like to say to me, Gul?'

Ansari shrugged. 'Not at the moment, boss.'

'Do you have a problem with anything I did last night?'

'It's not for me to say.'

'Not true. It's very much for you to say. If you disapprove, tell me. If you have something to say, say it.'

Her eyes met his. 'You had your reasons. If I'd disagreed strongly enough, I would have said so last night. It's on me now, boss.'

Bliss nodded and stood straight. He thanked his colleagues once again. He felt sure they both had questions but was quietly confident they would remain unspoken. He neither asked nor expected his fellow detectives to feel the same way he did about the vagaries of the justice system or how often true victims never saw it work in their favour. In truth, he was not always certain about it himself. He struggled with the idea of justice by any means. After all, it was his job to uphold the law, irrespective of the motivations. Patricia Bell had taken the law into her own hands, acting as judge, jury, and potentially executioner. Legally, perhaps even morally, the girl was completely in the wrong. The correct path would have been for her to give the police Hirst's name and tell them what she knew. An arrest would have been made, an investigation launched, after which the judicial system would have taken over.

But the system didn't always get it right. From time to time, it spat out people like the Bells, affording them no justice and leaving them as victims twice over. He understood why people often decided to seek retribution of their own design. Outwardly he could not condone it, as a warranted officer of the law his job was to ensure law breakers were prosecuted. But the other part of him, the individual, the person behind the badge, had some sympathy for those who elected to do things their own way.

Elements of the situation facing the Bell family swam carelessly in his thoughts, but the moment he entered the Major Incident room and locked eyes on the boards at the far end of the room, he became focussed on the murder of Roger Craig and disappearance of Stuart McKenzie. They deserved his full attention, and he gave it to them.

'Where are we?' DCI Warburton asked, facing the team. She gestured at the boards. 'Any updates at all? Any thoughts? Suggestions?'

'There are no updates,' Bliss confessed. 'We've covered all the usual bases with tech and forensics, carried out a series of interviews, waded through financial records and asked all the obvious questions we can think of. So we might need to get creative.'

Warburton's eyebrows arched. 'Meaning what, Jimmy?'

'I have no idea. But I think we need to start looking beyond the usual parameters. Clearly, we're getting nowhere following our usual trains of thought. We're not getting help from CCTV or phones, no witnesses worthy of the name, but we still have one man dead and one man missing, presumed dead. Working on the assumption that the same person or persons is or are responsible for both, we're still back at square one. For my money, this has always been about who attacked McKenzie. No, I stand corrected. It's about *why* he was attacked. The why gives us the who.'

'If we're back at square one, then what's our next step?' DS Chandler asked.

'To retrace our previous steps.'

'I'm sorry,' Warburton interrupted, 'but how is that getting creative or thinking outside the box?'

'It isn't. Before I say what's on my mind, do you agree with me that we don't have sufficient evidence against Stuart McKenzie's wife and business partners to sign off on the RIPA request?'

'Yes. We're nowhere near the standard required to request their phone data.'

'Right. To date, then, we've spoken to Mrs McKenzie and Stuart McKenzie's business partners informally. On their terms. I'm of the opinion that one or more of them knows more than they are saying. I'd also include the car sales boss, Jacob Nash, as well.'

'And so, our next approach should be…?'

'We take off the gloves. The lack of evidence means it's earlier than I'd have liked, but let's admit to the suspicions we have. Make requests of each of them to attend for formal interviews here. Light a fire under them, see which of them sits the most uncomfortably.'

Warburton was reluctant. 'And when they refuse? Because they will if they have anything about them.'

'Even that would tell us something. But I'm sure you're right. Mrs McKenzie and Nash might come in, but I'm pretty sure both Banks and Dixon will advise them against it. That shouldn't stop us from making the requests. And if they tell us where to stick it, we offer inducements.'

'Such as?' DC Ansari asked.

'Finances. Specifically, business finances, because that reaches across all four of them. We drop hints suggesting that in the course of our investigation into Mr McKenzie, we came upon a number of discrepancies and issues relating to Vantage Holdings and their various companies. We hint at considering a more forensic examination. I think that will be enough to get them in a room with us.'

'With their briefs,' DC Virgil stated flatly.

Bliss agreed. 'I'd expect nothing less. But if we get them in the room, then we can start to exert some pressure.'

'But you still haven't told us how,' DCI Warburton said.

He gave a dejected sigh. 'That's because I don't know. Not yet. I'm opening it up to everybody, people. No suggestion is a bad one, and more to the point...' his voice trailed off as his eyes found and rested on DC Virgil. 'On this one special occasion, nobody has to buy cakes because they said something stupid.'

TWENTY-SEVEN

WITH TIME TO FILL and no actions assigned, Bliss suggested he and his partner return to the scene of crime. Originally an area of pastureland surrounded by dykes with Werrington Brook running through its centre, the area of Cuckoo's Hollow was excavated to create the lake and shape the site in the late 1970s, after which the trees and shrubs were planted, and the two bridges built. It had since become a breeding ground for many swans, ducks, and other waterfowl. At dusk, bats could be seen skimming the water, and otters had been known to take up short-term residence.

"This is a nice park,' Bliss said, squinting against the sun. It was another sunny morning, with no sign of the rain forecast for later. 'I have to say, I'm still not a fan of the housing they put up here in the 70s, but the developers did well to leave places like Bretton Woods relatively untouched and build recreational areas such as this and Ferry Meadows.'

Chandler's eyebrows rose and fell. 'You realise you just mentioned three murder scenes we've worked?'

He gave a wistful nod, picturing each of them. 'People are responsible for that, Pen, not the locations themselves.'

'Yes, oh wise one. So, tell me why we're here.'

Bliss breathed in some fresh air. 'To get a feel for the location since it's returned to normal, with no tape flapping and without our lot traipsing all over the gaff. I felt a prickle on the back of my neck last time we were here, and the scene of crime is where it all began, so it might have something to tell us.'

She chuckled. 'Now you're just trying to sound philosophical.'

With a grin, he said, 'Possibly. On the other hand, if you consider me enlightened then why not listen and learn?'

'Yeah, fat chance, old man. Just get on with it.'

'You philistine. Anyway, the SOC is a good place to start again whenever you feel stuck.' He paused, then added, 'Getting bogged down is something I find happening more frequently. I had hoped that was due to the cases themselves being so complex, but maybe it's more a case of me losing a step or two.'

If he'd been expecting his partner to argue, he was going to be disappointed. Perhaps he was right and even his colleagues were second-guessing him. They found themselves at the first bridge having approached from Skater's Lane, which is where Bliss stopped walking. He turned to look back the way they had come, then over to the approximate spot in the trees from which Roger Craig would have emerged, before finally turning his attention once more to the wooden structure traversing the lake.

Over the water on the other side, the path was bordered by more trees and underwood crowding in. The attacker needn't have moved too far into them to become lost from sight, especially allowing for the darkness that night. Craig had admitted that he hadn't given much of a chase, his focus riveted on the victim.

'Come on,' Bliss said, his shoes already clattering on the boarded walkway. 'Let's see what's over here.'

The treeline was dense and gloomy but took only fifteen seconds or so to walk through before the pair emerged into the sunlight once again. The path they were on would take them deeper into the park. A distinctly shorter trail cutting left led to a street of large, detached homes. He stopped and put both hands on his hips.

'Huh,' he grunted, shifting his body to study his surroundings once more. 'I just realised what that skin-prickling was all about.'

'Were you having a mini stroke?' Chandler joked.

'Do you want a mini slap?'

Chandler scoffed. 'Yeah, you and who's army?'

Bliss shook his head and thought back to their first visit. 'Something niggled me last time, but I couldn't put my finger on it. Seeing it afresh has opened my eyes. It isn't a long walk from the entrance we used, but it's far enough. I think my instincts were screaming at me to ask how the attacker dragged or carried our victim all the way out of here before presumably bundling them into a waiting vehicle. But if they were parked here, on this side of the bridge, it looks easily doable.'

Chandler made her own assessment. 'Still a dead weight to move,' she said. 'No pun intended.'

'True. And none taken. But although he was tall, Stuart McKenzie was evidently all skin and bone. It could be done.'

She agreed. 'Not that it gets us any further. We were only considering a single attacker, anyway.'

'I know. I didn't say it helped us. Just scratched an itch for me.'

'Are you satisfied, then? Has this visit to the scene improved matters in any other way? More to the point, has it assisted us in our investigation?'

'I'm not sure,' Bliss admitted with a drawn-out shrug. 'Probably not. But it can't hurt. Just standing here in the middle of it all makes me wonder why anybody would choose this place. It's an odd choice for a meeting.'

'If that's what happened,' Chandler pointed out.

His partner was spot on. They still didn't know for certain.

'Good point, well made,' he said. 'On the other hand, it's relatively secluded.' He proceeded to swear and thump a fist against his side. 'How can we still know so little about this case? Did McKenzie die here or didn't he? Was it a chance attack or premeditated? Did he provoke it somehow? Did McKenzie arrange to meet his attacker here, or was he followed? And where the bloody hell is he now?'

'I still think the answers we've come up with are the most likely,' Chandler said defiantly. 'It all fits, Jimmy. Maybe this time we don't need to look around the corners to find alternative explanations. McKenzie was murdered here and was then removed from the scene by whoever killed him. We just don't have a Scooby who did it or why.'

Bliss accepted his partner's explanation, but he wasn't happy about it. He still believed somebody knew more than they were saying, which left him feeling disgruntled. His mind was still churning it over when his phone rang. The call from Sandra Bannister took Bliss by surprise until he remembered he had asked her for information on Vantage Holdings. He sensed the enthusiasm in her voice the moment she started speaking.

'The men running this company are very interesting,' she told him. 'It seems fairly obvious that they're doing something iffy and worth hiding, but whatever it is they're doing it extremely well because we've not managed to dig up any real dirt on them. Nothing damning, at least.'

'We're in the same boat,' Bliss confessed. 'All rumour and speculation with no firm leads.'

'Which is to be expected of businessmen with fingers in so many pies. It's only natural for people like us to wonder how they've achieved so much without being bent in some way. Perhaps that says more about us than them.'

Bliss stared off into the distance, enjoying the sunlight on his face. 'No, I'm not having that. They're dodgy. I know they are. I've looked them in the eyes, remember?'

'But you can't prove it. And neither can we. However, there was a note made by one of our researchers which I followed up on myself. Did you know Vantage Holdings had applied to the Gambling Commission for a licence to operate a major casino in the city?'

'No. Though all three partners enjoy the casino life, and they already own one of those tiny machine-based shops. I suppose it's not a big stretch to imagine them expanding into that area.'

'Fair enough. Maybe it's nothing. But I think you might be interested to learn that a fourth partner is listed on the licence application, and even more intrigued by who that person is.'

'Go on then,' he said. 'Don't leave me dangling.'

'Hector Karagiannis.'

Bliss felt a chill whisper against the back of his neck. He gave an involuntary shudder. What the hell would a main player like Karagiannis be doing with such small fry operators as McKenzie, Banks, and Dixon? It didn't make a great deal of sense, not unless they were looking to move up in the underworld.

'Are you certain, Sandra?' he asked.

Bannister chuckled. 'I knew you'd be interested. These men working with a known villain like him pretty much seals the deal on them being bent in some way, wouldn't you agree?'

'I would.'

He said it in that distracted way people do when they're lost in thought. Something else was stirring in the back of his mind, and he felt his flesh tingle. The Karagiannis family were heavy hitters in the Greek Mafia, with interests in every conceivable sordid and criminal enterprise imaginable. This included something that was regarded as old school and fast going out of fashion:

jewel smuggling. These days, all manner of gemstones from right across the world found their way into the country via any number of different routes, but one of the main connecting cities was still the Dutch capital. And Amsterdam was a destination the three Vantage Holdings entrepreneurs might have visited on a regular basis.

When he was finished speaking with the *PT* journalist, Bliss placed a call to DC Virgil. He asked the young officer to look at the crime book to see if doorbell footage had been requested from Lakeside residents, which lay off the Fulbridge Road and led directly into the park.

'If not, make gathering it a priority,' Bliss insisted. 'If we have it, start checking through it as soon as possible. I think McKenzie's attacker might have parked there. I also want you to call the NCA to ask for everything they have on the Karagiannis family operations here in the UK. When you're done with them, contact Europol. From them, we want any records on the same family's dealings in Amsterdam. If Hector Karagiannis owns casinos in Holland, I want to know if any of our Vantage Holdings co-owners ever stayed there and if so, when.'

The eager detective constable responded quickly, wondering what the thinking was and in which direction he expected the answers to take them.

'I'm not sure,' Bliss admitted. 'Just a suspicion I have, and in all honesty, any additional information we can learn about them will be better than anything we've had to date.'

TWENTY-EIGHT

Shortly after he and Chandler returned to the unit, Bliss sat down with DCs Ansari and Virgil. He wanted to know how their second interview with Patricia Bell had gone. Alan Virgil turned to look at his partner, offering no opinion.

With a derisory sniff that implied her displeasure, Ansari told Bliss that it had panned out pretty much as he had expected. The woman had stuck rigidly to the story concocted in the car on the way back from the incident. 'You'd have been proud of her,' she told him. 'And her solicitor certainly seemed happy enough with it. I think we can safely say there will be no change over the remaining custody period.'

'How do you propose we move forward?' Bliss asked, overlooking the curt tone.

'Isn't that for you or DCI Warburton to decide?'

'You ran the interview, not us.'

'Did you not have the next stage already mapped out, boss?'

He ignored the remark, but felt a prickle of irritation. 'Your proposal, Gul?'

Ansari huffed out a sigh. 'If it matters, I say we get her in a room with a psychiatric specialist. This... memory loss of hers ought to be evaluated by somebody trained and experienced. The CPS will want that report anyway if they're going to consider charging.'

Bliss kept his focus on Ansari. She plainly disapproved of her role in what amounted to his deception. He understood, but opted to push back. 'I realise you're not exactly turning somersaults over this, Gul, but why are you so pissed off with me?' he asked.

Her response was immediate. 'I'm not pissed off. If anything, I'm more disappointed than annoyed.'

'What are you upset about and disappointed in?' He sensed his DC's reluctance to vent, but knew she had enough about her to speak up in defence of her opinion. She regarded him with cool detachment.

'All right. Since you asked. This young woman hit a lad her own age over the head with an iron bar. She put him in hospital. He's yet to recover consciousness and may well be in a coma following the bleed to his brain. He's got broken bones in both hands, and severe bruising to his shoulder. Personally, that's not the kind of behaviour I believe we ought to be encouraging.'

'You think that's what I was doing? Gul, that girl had just found out that her baby sister, a fourteen-year-old girl with cerebral palsy, was raped. She believes the lad she assaulted is the sick bastard who got her sister pregnant. Patricia has no prior record of violence, and I also suspect she will never encounter those specific set of circumstances again to set her off. Should that be the case, I doubt she'll ever be *encouraged* to strike anybody else.'

Ansari shook her head vigorously. 'I get that what he did – if it was him – was a shocking, appalling, and disgraceful crime. Perversions beyond my understanding. But has justice been meted out, boss? His punishment for the rape of a disabled minor is potentially to have brain damage, the kind that turns you into a vegetable. Does that sound just to you? Does it seem right?

Should that level of retribution be acceptable to us as police officers?'

He conceded the point, but after a moment, Bliss said, 'Let me turn it around and put it to you in a different way. What she did was not right. Neither was it acceptable. You'll get no argument from me on that score. Had I arrived there a few minutes earlier I would have intervened to prevent it. But I didn't and so it happened. We can't put the toothpaste back in its tube. Any debate over what punishment he might have deserved ended there and then because as things stand it can only ever be a retrospective discussion. You have to move on and deal with the event in front of you, which is all that I did.'

'Then maybe I'm disappointed in the way you handled it.'

'Which is fair enough. You're entitled to disagree with me, Gul. But you asked if what happened to this child rapist was right, just, or acceptable. Now ask yourself those self-same questions about the young girl who did it to him. Does banging her up on remand sound just to you? Is it right to charge and convict her and to send her to prison for a lengthy sentence? Is it acceptable to punish her so severely for a momentary and entirely understandable lapse?'

'What if it is?' DC Ansari argued. 'It's the law. A law we're sworn to uphold. But perhaps we tend to regard things differently when we feel sympathy for the aggressor – of any specific incident, not just this one? That doesn't change the rights or wrongs, it's just a different point of view.'

Bliss held up both hands. The debate was getting them nowhere, and he called a halt before it got heated. 'Okay. Then we agree to disagree, but we move on to more important questions. What information are we pulling in from the scene itself?'

'Such as?'

'Such as witness testimony. There were plenty of people there.'

DC Virgil, who had remained close by but silent throughout, finally spoke up. In his view, the response was as they might expect from that particular area of Millfield. Most bystanders claimed not to have seen a thing. Those who did admit to witnessing the disturbance said their attention had been drawn to the assault moments after it had happened. However, uniform had gathered witness statements at the scene from six lads who each gave similar accounts, insisting the attack was unprovoked and cowardly.

'You won't be surprised to learn they are all KAs of Zander Hirst,' he said with an irritable shake of the head.

The young DC was correct; Bliss was not at all surprised. Known associates feeding the police a one-sided story was a common practice in the world of casual violence. 'What about footage?' he asked. 'There were phones out all over the place filming the attack.'

'We found plenty uploaded to YouTube, boss. Here, let me show you...'

He took out his phone, selected a couple of options, before turning the screen to Bliss. The background voices were mostly muffled, but a shrill voice cried out a warning just as their camera swung around. By the time it did and obtained a focus, the first blow had already been delivered. Hirst could be seen staggering away, bent double, both hands clutched to the top of his head. Looming over him, Patricia Bell's face was twisted with rage as she swung again. The bar came crashing down on the boy's hands with a sharp crack that could be heard above the din, and when he slumped to the floor, her third and final blow landed on his shoulder. The second and third swings accounted for the broken bones in Hirst's hands and the deep bruising to his body.

Bliss winced. The assault was vicious. He asked if any footage prior to the attack had been handed in or gathered up at the scene.

'Not that we've seen so far,' Ansari replied, her voice returning to its natural timbre. 'It's like they all reacted to that first strike, but nobody captured it quickly enough on film. If they had, I'm sure it'd be up online by this time. We'll keep searching, though.'

It was still incriminating enough to damn Patricia Bell, Bliss thought. 'What I'm seeing here suggests the initial blow came out of nowhere. Which accounts for nobody filming it.'

'Sounds about right. That was our thinking, too.'

Bliss nodded. 'How about those actions I put you two on earlier? Where are we with them?'

Virgil immediately brought up an app on his phone and read from the notes he had made. 'We have some doorbell camera footage, and some dashcam film from parked vehicles, but I have officers there as we speak trying to collect more from those homes where the residents were not in first time around. I have two people sifting through what we do have, but nothing of note so far. To be honest, it's not much to go on as most of the houses don't have those types of doorbell. But we might still get lucky. As for this Hector Karagiannis character, I've spoken to both the NCA and Europol who have assured me they'll gather their intel today and get their files across to me this afternoon. The Europol officer is looking into casino hotel room registers and whatever they obtain they'll forward on as soon as possible.'

Bliss thanked him. 'Good job,' he said, patting his colleague on the shoulder. He told DC Ansari the same and meant it despite their earlier dispute. He asked if a further interview had been arranged with the solicitor and Patricia Bell. Ansari's response was to ask if he would prefer to take over for the duration.

'No need,' he said. 'I'll have a word with her before a charging decision is made. If she's released, she needs to know the strength of feeling out there towards her. I can't imagine this Hirst kid's crew letting it go.'

'You think release is likely?' Ansari asked.

Bliss shrugged. 'I think it's probably fifty-fifty. But if whoever assesses Patricia Bell confirms that she likely doesn't know what she did, or at the very least doesn't remember, then I don't see the CPS agreeing to a charge. They tend to put their weight behind dead certs, and despite the damning video footage, this is anything but. There's a good chance they'll decide it's something we can revisit at a later date, and she's hardly a flight risk.'

'And what if Zander Hirst dies?'

'Well, then you can remind me I got it wrong,' he snapped.

Ansari closed her eyes for a moment. Took a breath before saying, 'Jimmy, I really don't want to fall out with you over this. I genuinely understand why you did what you did. I also sympathise with Patricia Bell. I can't honestly say I wouldn't have done the same thing in her shoes. I just can't help but have my doubts as to whether this is the right way to go about things.'

He gave an unconvincing grin. 'That's easy enough to answer. It isn't. Not by the book. You're right to have doubts on that score. You'd be a poor copper not to. So, make yourself comfortable with how you feel about it, Gul. Stand by your own convictions. There are all kinds of right and all kinds of wrong. And to be fair, I'm still not sure which side of them I'm on.'

TWENTY-NINE

A LTHOUGH THE STRATEGY TO lure Sharon McKenzie, Jacob Nash, Michael Banks, and Grant Dixon to Thorpe Wood for interviews under caution worked surprisingly well, it also gave Bliss and his team an unforeseen headache. In what looked like a pre-planned tactic, all four arrived at the station within minutes of each other, their legal representation walking in with them. Given the preference was usually to conduct interviews as a pair, DCI Warburton hurriedly gathered together what remained of the Major Crime Unit.

They had earlier discussed a common approach, which was to apply pressure and make each interviewee aware they were suspected of wrongdoing. A list of specific questions had been drawn up and shared out between them, but the DCI had also made it clear that everybody would have to be alert and think on their feet. The object was to learn more than they gave away, which meant the ability to lay verbal traps was essential. An easier task when paired, as Warburton pointed out.

She argued in favour of the familiar, with two pairs taking two interviews each. DS Chandler voiced her concerns that the waiting time might result in one or more of their interviewees choosing to leave and perhaps not return. The others agreed, insisting they'd be fine having a shot on their own.

Warburton turned to him for answers, and Bliss considered their options. He elected to go for it and allocated his detectives as he saw fit. Previously, Grant Dixon had not only made his physical presence count, he'd also been the more talkative. Yet Bliss had a sneaking suspicion that it was the slightly more diminutive and quieter Michael Banks who was the real alpha. Where Dixon had been all brash bluster, the remaining business partner had come across as studious and thoughtful. The sign of a leader. He was Bliss's pick.

Interview Room One, with its olive-green soundproof panel walls and glass brick window placed on the other side of an alley in which cannabis plants were stored after being salvaged in police raids, generally felt overcrowded with four people clustered around the table on which the recording device sat. Bliss immediately felt more comfortable walking into the room in which only Banks and his solicitor were already seated. Between them, they completed the formalities, including applying the caution despite there being no arrest. It had been a while since Bliss had conducted an interview, but the routine and protocols soon came flooding back. The lawyer announced for the record that his client was attending on a voluntary basis and threatened to call a halt if he didn't like the questions being posed.

'Why exactly was my client asked to be here, Inspector?' the solicitor, Brian Armstrong, asked.

'To help us with our enquiries,' Bliss replied.

'More specifically…?'

'As your client is already aware, one of his business partners, a Mr Stuart McKenzie, is missing having not been seen for six days. Our evidence suggests that Mr McKenzie was physically assaulted on Friday night. The man who witnessed the attack believed the victim to be dead, yet when my colleagues arrived at the scene no body was discovered. Two days later, a body was located. It was that of our witness, and he'd been murdered. Your client briefly spoke with me and my partner on Tuesday about Mr McKenzie's disappearance. Upon reflection and closer examination, I found the meeting to be unsatisfactory and decided to explore and develop that conversation further today.'

'Inspector Bliss,' the solicitor said. 'Prior to this interview I asked you what crime my client was suspected of and you declined to answer. Will you please provide us with one now?'

Bliss huffed. 'For the record, I think you'll find I did not decline to answer, Mr Armstrong. I informed you that our investigation was gathering pace and that we had reached the point where we felt it would be beneficial to speak with a number of people of interest in a more formal setting.'

'Which tells me you are fishing with a hand grenade. Or do you actually have a genuine line of enquiry?'

Bliss liked the line. 'The latter. As you'll discover if you allow me to ask my questions. After all, it is why you're both here.'

He took a moment to compose himself. He remembered the items on the list of agreed questions without having to refer to it, but he was feverishly trying to decide on the best way to approach asking them. Several lines of enquiry appeared to have similar appeal, and eventually he plumped for one.

'Our main area of focus is on the business partnership between your client, Mr Dixon, and Mr McKenzie. We've found a number of enterprises all sheltering beneath the umbrella of Vantage Holdings. In the absence of an obvious motive, it is our working hypothesis that the disappearance of Stuart McKenzie is somehow linked to how he makes a living. That's where your client comes in.'

When the solicitor made no reply but instead merely nodded, Bliss continued by turning to the suspect directly. 'Mr Banks, which of your businesses would you say is most open to exploitation or abuse?'

Armstrong reacted as expected. 'You don't have to answer that question, Michael,' he told his client.

Banks briefly raised a hand to suggest he was in control. 'As the Inspector indicated, we're here to see if we can help find out where Stu is or what might have happened to him. I'll answer anything I can. However, in direct response to that one, I have to say I don't believe any of our companies fall under that category.'

'Really?' Bliss put all the scepticism he could muster into the single word. 'We'll come to the many company names that tell us nothing about what business is being operated, but let me begin with a few I'd certainly call into question. As you're aware, we're also interviewing Jacob Nash, who runs your second-hand car dealership. That's a line of work not known for its strict adherence to the law or declaration of income. Then there's the debt consolidation and debt collection agencies being run from the same registered address. Seems like a conflict of interest to me. Also regarded as being shady enterprises under some ownership. What do you have to say about them?'

Banks put a thin smile on his face before saying, 'I think you'll find those kinds of references to be historical. As I'm sure you're aware, the businesses you mention have become heavily regulated. Regarding the debt companies, we're licensed correctly through the Financial Conduct Authority. All above board, Inspector, I can assure you.'

Bliss made no direct rebuttal, but instead said, 'And how about your company that does business by buying up properties, often at a figure way below the asking price and with plenty of caveats attached?'

'Is there a question there?'

'There is. I'm sure you're correctly licensed, but it is another business with a shockingly bad reputation, Mr Banks.'

'That's true of many. But not of ours.'

'Of course not. But I misspoke earlier, didn't I? Because in fact you own two such companies.' Bliss glanced down at the notes DC Virgil had prepared for him. 'And our research suggests they are marketed against each other, as if they are rivals.'

'I'm not aware of any law against that.'

'I suppose we'll find that out in due course.'

'Inspector Bliss,' Brian Armstrong cut in. 'I fail to see where this is getting us. Please, if all your questions are going to be like this, I see no good reason for us to be here.'

Undeterred, Bliss continued. 'I'm sorry the pertinence escapes you, Mr Armstrong. The point to them is that we believe Stuart McKenzie's disappearance is related to his business interests. Your client stated that all companies under the Vantage Holdings umbrella were above board, and I'm questioning the veracity of that statement. Each of the businesses I've alluded to have poor reputations, ripe for just the kind of exploitation and abuse I mentioned.'

'The type of businesses you mentioned might well suffer from previously poor standings,' Banks said, his eyebrows angled down. 'But that's not the way we run them.'

'My understanding is that you don't run them at all,' Bliss shot back. 'The car business is run by Mr Nash, as we've already established. I'm pretty sure that if we took a more in-depth look at the others I referred to, we'd find the same thing. You and your partners are the owners. You don't manage them on a day-to-day basis. In that regard, how could you possibly know how above board they are?'

Banks cleared his throat and shifted position slightly before responding. 'Because we have an ethos, and we stand by it. And those we hire to run our companies are fully aware of the principles and standards we expect of them. Honesty and integrity are the mainstays of that.'

Bliss couldn't help but smile at the carefully worded speech. One he was sure Michael Banks had uttered many times before. 'Still… with your hands-off approach to owning companies,' he said, 'you can't know for certain how they are run.'

'All right. For the time being, let's say you're right, Inspector Bliss. If you can prove any wrongdoing on the part of our company managers, I guarantee we will investigate and at the same time open our doors to freely allow you to do the same.'

You're a slippery one, Bliss thought. He'd been right to identify this man as the leader of the pack. Banks knew when and how to erect walls and was equally adept at pulling them down at just the right moment. He was not a nut to crack, but he might yet give something away.

'Moving on to the companies whose names provide no clue as to the nature of the business,' Bliss said, again referring to his notes. 'Do any of them suffer from the same kind of *historical* bad press as those we've already discussed?'

'Nothing comes to mind,' Banks replied, shaking his head.

'All right. I'll highlight a few and you tell me what they are. Let's begin with Russell Benn and Associates.'

'A company we purchased last year. We retained the original business name in order to benefit from the legacy and reputation the previous owners had earned.'

'And it does…?'

'Oh, yes. Of course. The residential and commercial property renting and leasing market is a competitive one, and ours is more than holding its own.'

'So, you are landlords, in other words.'

'If you prefer.'

Bliss inclined his head. 'And that's one you *don't* regard as having a bad rep?'

'Quite the opposite. As I mentioned, its legacy and reputation were its main selling points.'

There was a pattern developing. They could all see it, but only Bliss was throwing shade over the ownership of the companies discussed. He nodded. 'How about Repose? That's a business with a number of properties and telephone numbers attached.'

Banks paused, but maintained his composure. 'I think I can guess what you might say when I tell you Repose is the name for our range of massage therapy operations, sauna spas, and escort services.'

Bliss snorted. 'Yes, I can see why you wouldn't regard them as in any way seedy or dodgy.'

'I think that's perhaps enough, Inspector,' the man's solicitor said. 'My client and his partners freely admit to owning a portfolio of companies. There's nothing illegal about any of them. Cast all the aspersions you like regarding the questionable morality of some, but that's not why we're here. Or is it? I have to ask, because I'm still puzzled as to how any of this connects to the disappearance – if that's what it proves to be – of Mr McKenzie.'

Bliss fixed him with a tight glare of hostility. 'And once again, I'm not responsible for your lack of comprehension. We've spoken about a number of businesses and each of them so far provokes more questions than they supply answers to. Mr Banks initially refused to attend this interview, and only the notion of us digging our noses so far into Vantage Holdings that they turned brown persuaded him to appear. So, then, for the benefit of everyone in the room and the recording, our enquiries have led us to investigate the possibility that Stuart McKenzie encountered trouble of one sort or another, to the point where he was assaulted, due to one or more of his business dealings. We have arrived there because so far, we are seeing no feasible motive emerging from his personal life.'

'Has it even occurred to you that Stu might have been clobbered by a complete stranger?' Banks demanded to know, his voice raised for the first time. 'I mean, it does happen. Or are you simply determined to make your case out to be more than it really is?'

Bliss regarded him closely. The mask had slipped. It might be just a fraction, but a thin strip had definitely opened up. Banks had finally reacted, his steely reserve pricked if not entirely melted down.

'We have,' he admitted. 'And to be honest with you, we haven't yet ruled out the possibility. The full circumstances, however, suggest otherwise.'

'What circumstances are these?' Armstrong asked.

'Our witness to the assault on Mr McKenzie was ex-military. He carried out CPR. By the time he went to get help, he was convinced the victim was dead. If he's correct, a random attacker returning to remove the body makes less sense.'

'I see. And the personal avenues you explored?'

'Ongoing,' Bliss told him. 'Once again, we believe the assault on Mr McKenzie was not random, nor was it in any way personal. We don't know what aspect of his business dealings might be in play here, Mr Armstrong, but we're exploring the possibilities. It's what investigators do. Your client here is not only in business with Mr McKenzie, they are also close, long-standing friends. I'd think he would want to offer us all the help he can.'

'Which is precisely what I am doing,' Banks insisted, throwing his hands in the air.

'You're giving the appearance of helping,' Bliss said quickly. 'But there's also a good deal of avoidance going on, if you ask me.'

'Then be more precise in your questioning,' the solicitor hissed.

With a wry smile, Bliss said, 'With pleasure. Mr Banks, I refer you to my opening question; which of your businesses would you say is most open to exploitation or abuse?'

'And I'll refer you to my opening reply,' Banks said, leaning forward so as to cast a shadow across the table. 'None of them. We employ good people, we do business with good people, we work with good people.'

Bliss squinted. The phrasing felt off. Too carefully worded. Instinct told him Banks had neatly avoided one possible element of the enterprise he ran with his two friends. He thought hard for a few moments before a likely answer fell into place. He nodded to himself, saying, 'What about those you work *for*?'

For the first time, Banks was slow to reply. 'Work for?' he eventually said in a voice laced with uncertainty. 'I don't know what you mean. We own Vantage Holdings and the companies held beneath that corporate banner. People work for us, Inspector. Not the other way around.'

'Really? Are you sure about that? Because if Mr McKenzie had fallen out with somebody who had business dealings with your company, it wouldn't have come tumbling down on him alone. If at all, because unless you all shafted one of your managers or customers, there's no reason for them to come for any of you. No, the only person likely to have the balls and reputation to do that would be someone who has you lot in his pocket.'

'Which, as I said, is not the case,' Banks said, running a hand across his close-cropped hair.

Bliss grinned, shuffled his notes into place. 'That you did,' he said cheerfully, seeing his way through to the next phase. 'Of course, so far we've been discussing your existing businesses. What about a proposed new enterprise, something you're looking to develop?'

'I don't know what you're talking about.'

'Is that so? Our intel must be wrong. I do apologise. So you have no plans to open up a major casino here in the city?'

Michael Banks went rigid, and his face hardened. 'How do you... how could you possibly know about that?'

Bliss arched his eyebrows. 'We're investigators. We investigated.'

The man slumped back and folded his arms. 'I've got nothing to say about that venture. It's nowhere close to being up and running and I refuse to discuss it.'

'But when it is open to customers, I assume it will also be all legal and above board?'

'Naturally.'

'Just another business owned by you and your two colleagues, right? Assuming Stuart McKenzie is still with us.'

'Yes. That's right.'

'Is it, though?' Bliss asked without inflection. 'I know you wouldn't deliberately mislead me, but I could have sworn there was, in fact, a fourth name on your application. A new partner for this particular endeavour. Ah, well, I suppose I must be mistaken. This entrepreneurial stuff is all Greek to me.'

Banks pushed back his chair and shot to his feet. 'I think I've spared you enough of my time,' he said, tight-lipped. 'This will be the last occasion we talk.'

Bliss also stood, offering only a sour look of derision. 'I somehow don't think that's the case. I came into this meeting with an open mind and the problem for you, Mr Banks, is that I've since decided I don't believe you. One of the main benefits of getting people in this room is that you get to see them up close when the pressure is on. Most people don't do well under such scrutiny. I saw a look in your eyes and detected a slight tremor in your voice when I brought up the subject of your new proposed partner. There's something there, Mr Banks. Something you're concerned about. And I'm going to find out what it is.'

THIRTY

RETURNING TO THE MAJOR Crime Unit offices within minutes of each other, all four detectives had questions. Bliss bought everybody a drink and after they'd settled and had time to process their interviews, his thoughts turned to the two weakest links. His eyes flicked between Ansari and Virgil.

'Do either of you have anything solid for us?' he asked.

Both shook their heads, but it was DC Virgil who replied first. 'No certain leads, boss. But Jacob Nash's body language throughout the entire interview was off the chart. He fidgeted like a schoolboy waiting to be punished. Sweat literally dripped from his forehead and he began to stink. Each question caused him to squirm a little more. He offered nothing in terms of his replies, nor did he volunteer any information we don't already have. But if you play back the recording, you'll see for yourself how nervous the man was. He knows something. He has something to hide.'

Bliss nodded and turned to DC Ansari. 'Gul, how did it go with Sharon McKenzie?'

'It didn't. Not that she blanked me. In fact, she was quite open and spoke a fair bit. But when it came to specifics, I got the impression she was genuinely struggling for answers. If you pushed me on it, I'd say she has no clue what happened to her husband nor why. She clearly believes he's still alive.'

It was about what he'd expected to hear. Virgil's experience intrigued him. Nash hadn't exactly been cool, calm, and collected when Bliss and Chandler spoke with him at Platinum Standard Motors, but it sounded as if the man had perhaps subsequently learned something about McKenzie's disappearance that troubled him greatly. It was worth going at him again as he looked the more likely to fall apart. Finally, Bliss turned to Chandler for her feedback.

'Grant Dixon was much the same obnoxious twat as the previous two times we met him,' she said with a grimace. 'A bolshy tosser if ever there was one. Used to intimidating with his build... you all know the type. But I have to say he's no mug. He had an answer for pretty much everything I threw at him, and while I got the impression he was deflecting the odd question or two, he didn't give up anything of note. The more I think about it, the more it came across as a little peculiar. He didn't seem fazed by what was happening, but at the same time I did sense a fair bit of apprehension. Almost as if he had his suspicions but no real knowledge about why or how his friend was missing.'

Reflecting on Chandler's words, Bliss realised he'd come away from his own interview with the same impression. If it wasn't for his gut telling him more than had been stated, he would have described the conversation in much the same way his partner had.

'Okay,' he said, rubbing the scar on his forehead. 'While I'm not convinced that Banks knows precisely what happened to Stuart McKenzie, I get the impression he fears he does. I'm also convinced it's connected to business. Just not quite as I had imagined.'

Chandler frowned and glanced around at the other officers. 'This is going to be interesting. More of your wild speculation, boss, or would you describe it as a Jimmy Bliss hunch?'

Bliss gave a weary smile. 'A bit of both, maybe. Take a look at the video for yourselves and see if you pick up on something the way I did. I can't quite put my finger on it. Was it something he said, a gesture he made, the tone of his voice, or something he neglected to say? Was it the way his body language changed, or something in his eyes? I don't know. But when I pushed him on the instinct I had, I got the reaction I would have expected if I was right. He wanted out of that interview room. So, yes, I do think McKenzie's disappearance is business-related. But equally, I don't think it has anything to do with existing Vantage Holdings commerce.'

'That's interesting,' DCI Warburton said, having earlier entered the office moments earlier to stand at the back without interrupting. 'Can you elaborate on that?'

This is where Bliss knew he had to be careful. Nothing in the crime log could explain how he had come across the information provided by Sandra Bannister. But with Virgil having contacted the NCA and Europol, the story was already out there. Claiming to have acted on a couple of hints picked up from the two agencies, he gradually revealed the link between Hector Karagiannis and the three men who owned Vantage Holdings.

'All of which leaves us where?' Ansari asked. 'It's all still just theories, suspicions and gut instincts as far as I can see.'

Nobody argued.

'I do think we've nudged open a door or two,' Chandler said defensively. 'Jacob Nash is clearly ripe for another crack. If his stress levels are like that at this early stage, how's he going to cope with being put under even greater pressure?'

Warburton agreed. 'Definitely worth more time,' she said. 'And I think we can set aside Mrs McKenzie for the time being. It also sounds as if Mr Dixon might be impervious to our charms. Which leaves us with Michael Banks. Jimmy?'

He gave himself a moment to gather his thoughts together before nodding. 'I've not met Stuart McKenzie, so he may well have been the natural leader. But of the two remaining, Banks is the alpha. He's sure of himself and composed, but I still managed to get to him. I just don't know what it means. I think it's worth pursuing, though. This angle of them doing business with someone outside of their normal scope is something new for us to consider. And this Karagiannis face is somebody to keep an eye on.'

'It's better than having nowhere else to turn,' Warburton said. 'But at the same time, I'm not sure how much further forward it brings us. It hasn't answered any questions, it's just presented us with more to ask.'

'Isn't that normal?' Bliss argued. 'This new lead has only just come to light. We're bound to stumble blindly around at first. Asking questions is what we do.'

'Leaving what as our next move?' Virgil wanted to know.

Bliss thought they could do worse than go back to look at their own ABCs; assume nothing, believe nobody, and challenge everything. In his view, they could discuss theories and hypotheses all they liked, but they were also making assumptions along the way. Assuming McKenzie had been assaulted in connection with a business dealing was just one example he was guilty of. And while it was perfectly logical given the circumstances, it was an assumption, nonetheless. He felt they were fairly secure when it came to believing nobody, as the degree of scepticism regarding the people they had spoken to was pretty high. Which left the team with checking or challenging everything. He asked how happy his colleagues were with that aspect of the investigation.

'I think it might be best to begin by breaking it down into two crimes and two crime scenes,' Chandler suggested.

Bliss was happy with that idea. 'Agreed. Let's start chronologically with the assault on Stuart McKenzie. We have a witness statement, but sadly we no longer have a witness. Any suggestions as to how we move forward from there?'

DC Ansari raised a hand, something she often did out of habit. 'We haven't made a public request for witnesses to come forward,' she said. 'We could also set up notice boards in and around the park asking for people to call in or come to us with any information they might have.'

'We got nothing from the neighbourhood door-to-door,' DCI Warburton said. 'Is an appeal likely to improve upon that?'

'An appeal reaches a wider audience. Members of the public who don't necessarily live nearby but may be regular visitors.'

'Okay. Good.'

'For that matter,' DC Virgil said, 'do we know if anybody returned to the streets surrounding the park to follow up on those addresses where the door-to-door got no answer? I know we currently have Lakeside being completed, but what about the other nearby streets?'

'I can't answer that,' Bliss said, regretting the oversight. 'But it's a good thought. You can check that out yourself, Alan. Gul, have a word with media relations about an appeal. Moving on, forensically I don't see any further developments to come from Roger Craig's overcoat. As for surveillance, I realise we're still short-handed, but I'm told we have additional officers coming over from county HQ later this morning to help out there. Gul?'

Ansari nodded. 'Alan and I have done what we can in the little time we've had to work these actions. I think we all pretty much agreed the other day that this area was unlikely to yield results. That said, there's still plenty to cover. We've yet to chase up cab companies, and there's doorbell camera footage to run down and view. It's just time, boss – or the lack of.'

Bliss took a beat. He had little confidence that they would find a way forward via surveillance footage of any description from any source. The main problem with aggressively attacking that particular angle was the volume of physical resources it consumed. Yet neither was it something they could neglect. Eventually he agreed to put the fresh bodies from Hinchingbrooke on those jobs, and also allocate a couple of uniforms to assist. He instructed DC Ansari to supervise that aspect as well as organising the repeat door-to-door visits.

They were left with the significant matter of phone data to consider. Stuart McKenzie's known mobile had gone offline late on Friday night around the time of the assault. Its data had provided them with no leads. As yet, the missing man hadn't been connected to a second device, but the possibility could not be ruled out. Bliss would dearly love to know if devices owned by Sharon McKenzie, Michael Banks, or Grant Dixon could be traced to the Werrington area that same night, but there was still insufficient evidence for him to have the RIPA request signed off.

After briefly mulling this over with his colleagues, Bliss shook his head in frustration and said, 'I think when it comes to the items we can quickly elevate to actions, we've covered all the bases in respect of the first crime scene. As far as I'm concerned, we're still investigating a murder without a body. Are we in agreement?'

Nods mixed with verbal declarations told him to move on. He reminded them that the two crimes were almost certainly connected, and that he saw no valid reason not to repeat the actions in regard to witnesses and surveillance. They were in the same situation when it came to mobile phones, which was nowhere. Forensics offered the investigation little to go on, particularly in respect of their killer.

'Doesn't this bring us full circle back to our assumptions?' Warburton asked, looking at each of the team in turn. 'We're looking at our witness being murdered two days after the initial assault, seeing that he was initially attacked with some kind of cord around the throat, which matches Roger Craig's description of the incident, and assuming the two crimes are connected.'

'It might be an assumption,' Bliss said, 'but it's a perfectly reasonable one to make. I'd say it's more than an assumption, if I'm being honest. It's a genuine hypothesis based on what we know allied to our experience and plain logic.'

'One you're happy to finish with, Jimmy? This being your final murder case.'

Bliss chewed on his bottom lip for a second or two. 'I could be happier, that's for sure, but I'm fine with our agreed plan of attack. My immediate focus is on this side venture our three amigos were involved in – if I'm right about that. Oh, and Mr Nash, of course.'

He was done talking about it. Discussing the case with team members and other colleagues was a vital cog in the investigative wheel, but Bliss craved action. He badly wanted to pay the man a visit at home in the morning and have him sweat some more.

THIRTY-ONE

AFTER SEEING SHARON MCKENZIE home, Michael Banks joined his two friends in the Fox & Hounds pub at the end of the road. Its gable-fronted mock-Tudor façade lent the building a deceptive age and dignity, having been completely rebuilt in the early 1930s after the original thatched structure had burned down a few years earlier. He found Dixon and Nash in their favourite corner booth, a bottle of Blue Moon sweating on the table for him. He took a long pull of the cold beer before turning to them.

'They know about the Bubble,' he said after wiping his mouth clean. 'DI Bliss didn't mention him by name, but he was probing me about us working with a new partner and said something about how it was all "Greek" to him.'

'Shit!' Nash said, mopping his brow with a tissue. 'I told you all it was crazy to get into bed with a full-blown gangster like Hector Karagiannis. It was bad enough with the diamonds, but at least you could pull out of that whenever you wanted to. As for going into the casino business with the man...' He gave a weary shake of the head before sinking half his pint in one go.

Dixon stared at Nash until the man put his glass down. 'What the fuck has any of this got to do with you, Jacob? It's not your money. Not your risk or reputation.'

'Not with the casino plans, no, but I'm in it up to my neck with the smuggling. Or weren't you listening to me yesterday?'

The larger man flapped a hand at him. 'Yeah, I heard you. Heard you whinge and whine like a bloody old tart. Look, like I said before, you have a minor role in all this. Don't go bigging yourself up and giving it large because you can't stand the heat. Your side of it is not even illegal, for fuck's sake. You bought diamonds from your uncle, which you later sold on to us. A solid transaction. What we did with them afterwards is of no concern to you, nor can you be put in the frame for it. In fact, you're the only one of us in the clear with both the Bill and the Bubble. And why? Because we made sure of it. I don't mean to sound like a prick, Jacob, but this isn't your fight.'

Nash reacted in an unexpectedly aggressive manner. 'Are you fucking kidding me, Grant? You really think Karagiannis is capable of seeing the differences you're talking about? Forget the police. Fuck them. They don't bother me one little bit. But don't tell me I have nothing to fear from that demented Bubble, because it's bollocks.'

Dixon squinted at his friend and leaned closer, glass in hand. 'You've mentioned the man an awful lot lately, Jacob. Yesterday you didn't use his name, but today you're a step further down the line. What exactly did you tell the Bill today? Do they have you wired, mate? Is that why you're so gobby all of a sudden and throwing the Bubble's name around?'

The group had known each other for many years, and while Nash was the one who preferred to remain on the periphery of any business dealings, whether legit or under the table, he was still a friend who was due some respect because of that. Banks reacted quickly before the exchange got completely out of hand.

'Hold up, Grant,' he said, setting his bottle down on the table. 'That was bang out of order. I realise this has got us all rattled, but that's no reason to turn on each other.'

Nash had also fixed Dixon with a piercing glare. 'I can't believe you said that to me,' he barked at him. 'Is that really what you think is going on here? Spilling my guts to old Bill? You think I'm cold enough to be sitting here enjoying a beer with my mates when I'm grassing on them behind their backs? I'm your friend. At least, that's what I thought I was. The way you speak to me sometimes I'm not so sure. But the pair of you closed me down at the golf course and you're trying to do the same here.'

'All right, all right. Wind your neck in,' Banks said flippantly.

'I will do. When one of you tells me what the fuck is going on.'

'We don't fucking know!' Dixon snapped, his voice a harsh whisper.

'Well, it can't be the casino, can it? That's not a done deal. No money has changed hands, nor have any contracts been signed. If it involves the Bubble, then it has to be the diamonds. What else?'

This time it was Banks who rounded on him. 'Has to be… what the fuck are you banging on about, Jacob?'

'Stuart. Remember him? Your other best mate, supposedly. You know as well as I do he's not missing. He hasn't fucked off somewhere to lick his wounds after taking a hiding. He's not living it up on some resort with a bit of skirt. He ain't ever coming back. And I think there's a good chance that your new Bubble friend has got something to do with that.'

Banks took a deep breath. He finished his beer in two long swallows. 'I'm not saying you're wrong,' he finally allowed. 'But I don't know that you're right, either. I mean, I can't think of anyone else who would take a pop at Stu, but it's not as if Hector made any threats. Not that I know of. Grant?'

Dixon shook his head. 'Stu never mentioned anything of the kind to me.'

'There you go. Besides, why just him? If it was the Bubble, why wouldn't he come after all of us?'

'I can think of one good reason,' Nash said, glum-faced and back to blotting sweat patches on his forehead with a handkerchief. He began tapping a finger on the table. 'Hector wants his diamonds. Or the money. Either way, maybe he approached Stu without you knowing about it and it all went pear-shaped. Maybe we're all still breathing because he needs us alive if he's going to get back what he's due.'

Banks closed his eyes and kneaded the furrow between them. His gaze wandered before coming to rest on Dixon. 'We have to consider retrieving those diamonds. And the cash from the sales. We might have to move it all, just in case Stu gave us up before he was topped.'

'No fucking way,' Dixon said, shaking his head. 'Who knows who might be watching us?'

'The police won't be paying any attention to me,' Nash said brightly. 'I'm not a partner. I'm an employee. You tell me where to go I'll get it for you. I'll stash it somewhere nobody will think to look.'

'Are you for real, Jacob? You're right, you're our employee. But why do you think you of all our employees were dragged in for an interview down at the nick today? Because they know we're friends. Old mates. They assume that whatever we know, you know. And they ain't far wrong, are they?'

'How about Sharon?' Banks suggested. 'No way the old Bill will have eyes on her.'

Dixon flushed. 'I don't believe you two. Don't believe what I'm hearing. It's not the fucking police we need to be focussing on here. A man like Hector Karagiannis is going to be all over us like a rash. He'll already know we've been inside Thorpe Wood today. Come to that, he probably knows where we are right now.'

'What are you saying?' Nash asked.

'I'm saying forget about moving our stash. We have to start thinking beyond that. Him getting back what he thinks he's owed is one thing, and yeah, I'm willing to admit it's likely he's responsible for Stu. But it's the police sniffing around us that'll have him squirming at the moment. And we should be, too. Because if he so much as suspects one of us might give him up, Hector isn't going to think twice about the diamonds or his money. He's going to want to keep us quiet, stop us from talking about him.'

'And so we do what?' Banks asked.

'It's not the stash that has to disappear,' Dixon whispered. 'It's either Hector or us.'

*

Jacob Nash decided to drive home afterwards rather than go into the office. He couldn't bear the thought of it; sitting there trying to be casual while all the time he felt he might shit himself. It was better if he buried his head in a bottle of scotch and let the alcohol take him away, however briefly. He'd just pulled up onto his drive and parked outside the garage when he heard a car door slam behind him. Followed by another.

He swivelled, and his eyes snapped wide open. It was the woman and her male companion from the hotel. The two people he believed to be working for the Bubble. The brute who'd threatened to smash his hand with a hammer leaned back against their vehicle, as casual as you like. The woman who'd done all the talking strolled over until she was standing just a few feet away. The dress she wore didn't make her appear any less threatening or more feminine.

'You've had a bit of a day,' she said. 'A nice chat with local Filth, followed by a cold beer with your BFFs. How lovely for you. And why not? You might as well make the most of it while you can. So, tell me, Jacob, what did the boys in blue want with you all?'

Swallowing down his fear, Nash said, 'They think we know more about our mate's disappearance than we're letting on.'

'I see. And do you?'

Nash scoffed. 'Not as much as we'd like to, clearly. And not as much as you, that's for sure. But your boss's name didn't come up at all, so you have no worries there.' When phrased that way, it wasn't quite a lie, just close enough to squeeze a few more drops of perspiration from his hairline. Nobody had actually mentioned Hector Karagiannis by name at the police station.

'My boss?' the woman said, her eyes becoming slits. 'What do you think you know about my boss, Jacob?'

Realising he'd already said too much, Nash tried to walk it back. 'Look, take no notice of me. I don't know anything. I haven't got a clue what I'm saying or even thinking. I'm scared and confused, that's all.'

'Hmm. We might have to return to that at some point. For the moment, tell me what you've learned about the diamonds. You must have some information for me.'

He had to quell the urge to vomit. Confrontation wasn't something he had ever handled positively, but he was well aware that a slip up here might cost him everything. Yet still he came back to what he knew with absolute certainty, and decided it really didn't amount to a great deal. Not enough to take a beating for. The man with the hammer looked as if he might enjoy inflicting pain.

'All right,' he said, lowering his voice though nobody else was around. 'They do still have some of the diamonds. They also have cash from whatever they've moved on so far. Grant and Mickey discussed moving their stash, but decided there were too many eyes on us at the moment. They know somebody is after them. They don't know who, don't know I've spoken to you, but they're suspicious of me, which means they're going to be on their guard from this point on. That's all I know. I haven't got a clue where they're keeping this stash of theirs. I promise you that. I even offered to shift it for them, but they laughed it off. That's it. That's all there is.'

He felt both exposed and pathetic after ratting on his friends.

The woman nodded and drew herself up to her full height, which even in heels didn't amount to much. 'I see. From what you say, it doesn't look as if they're likely to tell you more than they already have.'

Nash was about to agree enthusiastically when he realised what that might ultimately mean for him. It was a trap. If they no longer had a use for him… 'I wouldn't be so sure about that,' he said quickly. 'They're both a bit hyper, but not yet in full panic mode. If they get desperate enough and I can convince them I'm not being followed, I'm the one they're most likely to trust with the location of their stash.'

His tormentor gave a thin smile. 'Okay, Jacob. I hear you. I'll take it into consideration. But let me just say this: whatever rabbit you intend to pull out of a hat, it had better be soon. And it had better not be the Duracell-fucking-Bunny. I'm not known for my patience, and neither is the man I work for. Oh, and my colleague waiting over by the car hasn't eaten any red meat today, so he's all revved up and raring to be let off his lead. The thing is, now that you've confirmed the diamonds still exist along with the cash from whatever they've already punted out, we might yet decide to approach your pals more directly.'

'That didn't work out so well for you when it came to Stuart,' Nash said, almost without thinking. He snapped his mouth shut.

The woman regarded him thoughtfully, as if weighing up his remark. Then she raised a hand as if to slap him again, but this time settled for gently patting his cheek and said, 'By the way, which unit had you in for questioning at Thorpe Wood?'

Nash recalled the lanyard the detective had draped around his neck. 'Major Crime,' he said, adding a doom-laden frown. 'Which means they're not fucking about.'

The woman made no reply. She just nodded and turned away without another word.

THIRTY-TWO

AVING SPOKEN AT LENGTH with a CPS lawyer, a conversation during which he had not pleaded his case with as much enthusiasm as he normally would, they finally reached a charging decision. Bliss immediately contacted Patricia Bell's solicitor and arranged to meet them both in an interview room.

'You'll be pleased to know you're getting out of here,' he told the young girl, whose demeanour remained steadfastly morose. 'You'll be released under investigation. This means that, unlike being released on bail, there's no requirement for you to present yourself here again. However, our investigation is ongoing, and we might want another chat at some point in the future. Do you understand?'

Bell glanced at her lawyer before nodding at Bliss. 'I'm free to go, then?'

'You are. Before you do, I want to say something. First, you'll be pleased to know that Nora has been released from hospital. She and your mother have been moved to a local hotel and are waiting for you to join them. I'm happy to arrange transport for you. I strongly urge you to do that, Patricia. It's not safe for you to return home at the moment. I'm sure you understand why.'

Another sullen nod, then: 'How's Zander?'

'Before I answer that, I'd advise you not to react. Not verbally, at least. I reminded you of the caution a few minutes ago, and I'll do so again.' He gave a nod to the solicitor, who offered an encouraging pat on the girl's arm.

She responded with hands spread. 'Just tell me, please. I need to know.'

'The good news is he's conscious. I called the hospital earlier this afternoon before speaking to the CPS. Mr Hirst seems to have come through the neurological tests better than anybody expected. The bleed to his brain was minor, but I have to say you're extremely fortunate not to be facing a murder charge, Patricia. It could so easily have gone that way. I hope you appreciate the break you've had.'

'I do. But now none of us can go home, which is all my fault.'

Bliss shook his head. 'That's not entirely true. With the stress of everything that has happened, you might not recall this, but your mother was in the process of working out an arrangement for witness protection in exchange for her testimony. That was before your attack on Hirst, of course, but the plan didn't change.'

'But I don't want to be driven out of our home,' Bell persisted, slumping back in her chair and crossing her arms. 'It's not right. They're the ones who did wrong, not us.'

'It's unfair,' Bliss agreed. 'And you're right when you say they are the ones who should be moved on. In an ideal world, that's what would happen. But life doesn't work that way. Besides, I would have thought you couldn't wait to leave behind a home that's brought so much misery into all your lives.'

Patricia Bell looked up at him, her expression drained of any real purpose or expectation. 'I do and I don't. It's my home. Whatever nightmares we experienced there, it's the only home I've ever known.'

Bliss replayed that conversation over and over again as he went to pick up takeaway food. His thoughts turned to Molly, and how she had been driven from her home at such an early age by atrocities he could never fully fathom. He understood the vagaries of life more than most, had learned to accept the downs as well as appreciate the ups, but the ugliness and depravity endured by some was too wicked to even contemplate.

He'd arranged to meet up with Molly and Max at his boat, which was moored just upstream from Orton Mere. The low evening sun cast a light on the *Mourinho* that made its paintwork look more black than royal blue. Molly was already on board by the time he arrived. Max noticed him first and came bounding down the footpath to greet him. Bliss made a fuss of the dog as the Goldador skipped around and between his legs, tail snapping from side to side like a whip. It was touching to see him behave this way, because the early days had been hard on them both. Max's previous owner had been brutally tough on the animal, and it had taken patience on both their parts to forge this new relationship.

He and Molly ate straight from the polystyrene containers the meals had come in. The kebabs were good, and they both washed them down with a beer from his onboard fridge. Molly sat on the side of the boat, her legs dangling over the edge, with the river flowing close beneath her feet. Unlike a lot of kids her age, she didn't have her nose buried in a mobile phone.

'I could get used to this,' she said over her shoulder.

Bliss chuckled. 'I'm sure you could persuade Adam and Fiona to buy a small boat. You live close enough to the marina to get some real benefit from it.'

The couple had fostered Molly when she was moved out of Peterborough due to the threats against her life after she had stabbed a dealer she was running drugs for. They had subsequently adopted a confused, frightened, but spirited young kid, making her a sister for their own daughter, who was a little younger.

'We might live close to the sea, but I don't think either of them is really interested in boats. Besides, won't I inherit this one when you croak?'

Laughing, Bliss shook his head and said, 'You think I'm going to leave anything to an ungrateful brat who does nothing but give me grief?'

Molly pursed her lips and knuckled invisible tears from her cheeks. 'Aw, you know I love you really, Jimbo.'

'You're only saying that because you want my boat.'

'Not true.'

'Oh, really? It isn't?'

'No. I want your boat, your hi-fi, and your record collection.'

'Mercenary.'

'True dat. Seriously, though, this is like some super chilling machine. I love the feel of it bobbing up and down.'

Bliss, who sat on the stern's soft seating area, gave a sanguine nod of appreciation. 'Me, too. I really should do it more often.'

'Do you ever take it out?'

'I have done. And will do again.'

Molly, all gangly limbs, shifted her body around to sit facing him. 'Can't really see you as a Popeye the sailor man type, Jimbo.'

'Not enough spinach, eh?' he asked, flexing his muscles.

'Not in the entire world. You might make a decent pirate, though. Jack Sparrow's much older brother, maybe. The one nobody talks about who spends all day talking to parrots in a home for ex-pirates.' She giggled at her own joke. 'The boat is a nice thing to have, though. A lovely place to come and enjoy. I bet you do a lot of thinking here.'

He nodded. 'Often my best.' He felt her eyes checking him out and knew she saw right through him.

'You thinking about the girl you helped?'

'A little bit. Sorry.'

Molly shook her head. 'Don't be. I would be, too. Even I'm a bit worried about her.'

Bliss cocked his head. 'Oh? How come?'

A deep frown formed on her flawless brow. 'How many miracles are there, Jimbo? I'm not saying this girl is just like me – I mean, there's only one of me, right? – but you came along when I was at my lowest point, and hopefully you've done the same for her. Thing is that, a couple of weeks later, I was on the road to everything I have going for me today. Is she going to be so lucky?'

He shrugged. 'The opportunity will be there. I've made sure of that. But it's up to her to grab it and make the most of it. Just as you did.'

Molly was thoughtful for a while, before saying, 'I sometimes wonder where I'd be right now if I hadn't reached the bottom. What if I'd not lost it that morning and never ended up standing on that ledge? What if I hadn't decided to kill myself on that particular day in that particular place? What would have happened to me then?'

'That's a long and unknown road you don't ever need to travel,' Bliss warned her. 'No good can come of it. I mean, what's the best you can hope for when you start looking too deeply into all the what ifs and maybes? I've no doubt these past few years would have been very different—'

'If I'd even made it this far,' she interrupted. 'I don't think I would have.'

'Okay, but the fact is you have made it and your life turned around for the better. Trust me when I tell you that looking back on what might have been is a complete waste of time and energy.'

Molly seemed to take that on board. 'So, do you reckon this girl will make it?'

He had to think hard about that one. He'd previously linked Molly and Patricia in his head, but the truth was that Molly's life had been so much harder. Whereas she had been used and abused by others from an early age, Patricia's woes were more recent and might not have worn her down to the point where she would rather end it all than go on. In the main, it had been her family who had endured the worst of it, though he was sure she had been through her own form of hell. What he did sense was that this was close enough to the beginning of Patricia's story that he might be able to influence the outcome. Hopefully to the extent that she never had to stand with a bloodied knife in her hand on a wet hotel rooftop, preparing to jump from it.

Bliss offered up a thin smile. 'She has to,' he said flatly. 'I have two final cases and I'm not letting either of them end badly.'

They spoke no more about it. Their topics of conversation included music and Max, his new job and her aims for carving out a career for herself. The gentle undulations of the boat did its job as purple daylight blackened around them. Molly offered to walk Max home, leaving Bliss to tidy things away. After locking up, he threw their waste into a nearby container. As he stepped onto the footpath that ran up to the mere and the spot where he usually parked his car, he noticed a woman sitting on one of the benches dotted along the grass strip between the path and the river. She looked up and smiled as Bliss drew level.

'Nice dog,' she said pleasantly. 'Cute kid, too.'

Molly and Max were long gone, and Bliss hadn't clocked the figure sitting there observing them. He nodded his appreciation, offering a smile that invited no further conversation.

'She yours?' the stranger asked.

Bliss stopped. He turned slowly. Something in the woman's voice set off an alarm bell inside his head. He took a step back, turning to face the figure who had swivelled around on the bench seat to face him.

'Excuse me?' he asked.

'I was just wondering if she was your kid. I see now she's more likely to be your granddaughter. Am I right?'

He ignored the question and spoke bluntly. 'Is there something I can do for you?'

'Now that you mention it, there is.' The woman got to her feet. She was not tall and appeared quite slender, but younger and in much better physical shape than him. If she carried a threat, it was implied rather than overt.

'Don't mind me, I'm a people watcher,' she went on. Her gaze had not shifted from his own. 'If that helps explain my interest. I'm very good at working out what people do and how they live their lives.'

'Is that so?'

'It is. Take you, for instance. To me, you have police officer written all over you. I'm guessing a detective. I'm thinking a Chief Inspector... no, wait, an Inspector. An old-style copper who likes to keep his hand in. One who doesn't mind bending the occasional rule. Am I right?' She followed the question with a conspiratorial wink.

Bliss sized her up. His peripheral vision took in his surroundings, making sure they were still alone. 'Who are you and what do you want?' he asked.

The woman put a hand to her chest. 'Me? Oh, I'm nobody. Seriously, in the grand scheme of things, I'm nobody at all. The person I work for, on the other hand, is a major somebody. A somebody who might as well live on a different planet to us in terms of his influence and desperate need for things to go his way.'

'I'll only ask you one more time,' Bliss said, taking another step closer. 'What do you want?'

'Woah there, tiger.' Her smile switched to full beam. 'Why all the aggression?'

'You brought my dog and my... you brought others into whatever this is. I can't have that.'

'In which case, I'm sure we can work things out between us, Inspector Bliss.'

He said nothing. He stood and waited, his pulse in overdrive and his blood pressure climbing through the roof. He didn't know what this woman's intentions were, but she'd mentioned Molly and Max for a reason, and she had Bliss's full attention.

'Okay.' The woman nodded. 'Let's put a lid on the old testosterone versus oestrogen battle, shall we? We're two grown adults and frankly, we'd look ridiculous getting into a bout of fisticuffs. But here's the thing. I hear via the jungle drums that tomorrow is your last day before you hang up your handcuffs. I'm guessing a man like you has a million and one things to do before waving goodbye, so I have a suggestion for you. More of a request, perhaps.'

'Go on.'

'I'd consider it a personal favour if you left Jacob Nash alone. He's of no use to you or your investigation. Believe me, he is not the missing piece of your puzzle. He's a nobody. A nobody who knows nothing worthwhile.'

Bliss eased his stance, but remained alert. He looked the woman up and down and said, 'If you're confident that he knows nothing worthwhile, then you must have the answers he's lacking. Tell me more. Convince me.'

A smile touched her lips. 'I'm not about to do that, am I?'

'Then why should I take you seriously? For all I know, you might also be a nobody who knows nothing worthwhile.'

She ran a hand through her hair, delicately, as if savouring the moment. 'I understand where you're coming from, Inspector. But you're mistaken.'

'Then if Nash is so unimportant, why are you here warning me off him?'

Her smile became rich with apparent delight. 'That's slippery of you, DI Bliss. But you have me all wrong. I issued no such warning. I'm simply trying to prevent you from wasting your last precious hours as a detective on a man whose presence is leading you astray.'

Hearing trickery in every word, Bliss made slits of his eyes. 'I see. Then if you're being genuine, it suggests to me that my time might be better spent looking more closely at Michael Banks and Grant Dixon.'

The woman shook her head, her tight bob fluttering. 'Not at all. Quite the opposite, in fact. That would make matters so much worse and lead you along the wrong path to the same dead end. But look, allow me to get to the point.'

'I wish you would.'

'Of course. You're a busy man. And while I'm sure a senior officer like yourself is looking forward to a pretty nice pension, wouldn't it be so much nicer never to have to think about money again? If you were to, shall we say, steer the case in a different direction, or perhaps even have it crash into the rocks entirely, we'd be delighted to see that happen. And when we're happy, we can also be extremely generous.'

Bliss weighed up his options. He could arrest the woman, but that would create the kind of he said-she said situation with no winning outcome. It was often better to monitor situations like this from a distance, waiting for your opposition to make the first mistake. Except that he believed she had already made hers.

'You went about this all wrong,' he said. 'See, prior to this moment I wasn't aware of your existence. But now I am. That was foolish of you.'

'I don't agree,' she said, unabashed. 'There are no witnesses to this conversation. For all intents and purposes, it never even happened. And while so far all I've done is offer helpful advice and perhaps alluded to a financial inducement, I can't honestly say things won't go downhill fast if your focus of attention shifts to me.'

Bliss scowled. 'I might have been wrong earlier, but that was definitely a warning, right?'

'You must take it as you see fit.'

'You set your sights on me, I'd say that's fair enough. It comes with the territory. You include others, and you'll find out more about me than you'd ever wish to know.'

The woman's thin smile returned. 'Ah, a shot across my own bows. Well played.'

Bliss shrugged. 'I'm not quite sure where this leaves either of us,' he said.

'Me neither. But we've marked each other's cards. Sleep on my offer, Inspector. One day of misdirection in exchange for a lifetime of fine dining and good living. You won't get a better offer than that. Certainly not from me.'

Bliss cocked his head to one side. He'd kept the conversation going in order to evaluate the woman more thoroughly and thought he might just have her number. 'You clearly don't work for Jacob Nash. I doubt you work for Banks or Dixon, either. A casual observer might think you were trying to steer me away from all three men, but I suspect your true aim is to confuse the situation long enough for you to make your next move.'

'Intriguing. And what next move might that be, Inspector?'

'Ah, well, that I'm not quite sure about. But I'll get there.'

'I do hope not. I've so enjoyed this little chat. It would be a shame to remember it with sadness.'

Bliss rolled his eyes. 'You've been watching too many Guy Ritchie movies,' he said.

'And you have a vivid imagination. Anyhow, this has been an absolute pleasure, but I have to scoot. How about we call it a draw?'

'Why not? And next time you speak to him, please give my best to Hector Karagiannis. Tell him I'm sure we'll bump into each other at some point.'

The woman rubbed her stomach and offered a faux wince. 'Ouch. Low blow, Mr Bliss. Low blow. I still can't help you there, I'm afraid. But I will tell you this much. From what I know of the man, you'll never come within touching distance of Hector. There are plenty of people who are far less friendly and charitable than me out there in a position to make sure of that. But don't worry… the girl and the dog are quite safe. For now.'

'So are you,' Bliss shot back. 'For now.'

THIRTY-THREE

Bliss spent the rest of the evening trying to persuade Molly to return home early. She point-blank refused. He couldn't provide any details, but he made it clear that a threat had been uttered. She wouldn't budge. He then insisted that he would not be able to do his job on his last day if he had to worry about her. It was as if he hadn't spoken.

Despite everything, when he walked into Thorpe Wood station the following morning he wasn't unduly concerned. It made no sense at this stage for Karagiannis's people to make a move against him or those he was closest to. Doing so would only draw the spotlight upon him and his business, and he hadn't been so successful in his illegal dealings by making stupid decisions. If the net tightened, that might present a different level of threat. Bliss would have one eye on that as the day unravelled, and he'd make sure that if things were about to kick off, Molly would have no choice in going back home. He'd see to it personally.

Shortly after arriving at work, Bliss received orders to attend HQ in Huntingdon; his scheduled meeting with the Chief Constable had been hastily rearranged due to the CC unexpectedly needing to be in Cambridge later that day. He left instructions for the briefing with Chandler as DCI Warburton had yet to arrive and headed south down the A1(M). Although he had visited the building at Hinchingbrooke numerous times, on this occasion it felt unfamiliar and somewhat alien. He was just hours away from being a civilian again for the first time in decades, and for some reason that made his surroundings all the more intimidating.

He was shown into Chief Constable Michael Wood-Lewis's office immediately upon arrival, after declining the offer of a hot drink. The area force's boss had access to a better brand of coffee than the rank and file, but Bliss was anxious and had images of himself dropping the cup and spilling his drink across the carpet. It wasn't the man or the position he held that bothered him, so much as the authority the CC commanded. Since agreeing on his new civilian role upon retirement, Bliss had been expecting someone to pull the rug from beneath him. If ever there was a day to do just that and make it hurt, it was this one.

The two remained standing and chatted briefly. Familiar break-the-ice stuff guaranteed to neither offend nor threaten to break new ground. After a few minutes, the office door opened, and a uniformed officer entered with a Nikon camera slung around his neck like Mr T's bling. He also carried an item, which he handed over to the Chief Constable.

Wood-Lewis held up a tastefully framed certificate of service for Bliss to see. The newcomer took a couple of photos showing the pair shaking hands with the certificate being held centre stage by both men before disappearing as quickly as he had come.

'I've handed out more of these than I care to remember,' the CC said as he released his own grip on the frame.

Bliss nodded. 'It must be an excellent way to get to know perfect strangers.'

The moment the words slipped free, he regretted it. 'I'm sorry, sir,' he said. 'That was a cheap swipe, and it was grossly unwarranted. The kind of snide remark aimed at a CC who never steps out from behind the desk to mix with the rest of us. That's not my experience of you, and I genuinely intended no offence. You earned that seat the hard way. The right way, by coming through the ranks.' Bliss shook his head and clapped both hands against his thighs. 'Any chance we could start this again, sir?'

The Chief Constable regarded him closely, before nodding and saying, 'Thank you, Jimmy. That means a great deal coming from an officer of your standing. You can be a cussed sod at times and have caused me more headaches than the combined efforts of every other DI under my command. But I have always respected you. Frankly, I could hardly believe my eyes when I looked at this certificate and saw you'd completed forty years of service. You could have retired ages ago. Yet you chose to stay, and despite us making your exit compulsory, you're still not turning your back on either the police or the public. I'll tell you straight, rather than getting shot of you, I'd prefer to be hiring a hundred more just like you.'

'I don't know about that,' Bliss said diffidently. 'The Job has struggled to accommodate me and my ways over the years. I'm not sure a cotchell of clones of me are what's required these days.'

'On the contrary. It's *these days* that tell me we need more officers in your mould and fewer of the shiny new ideologues. Or perhaps the job itself has changed out of all recognition and the likes of you and me are a dying breed.'

'I think that's probably more true than either of us would care to admit, sir. And in my case, a breed that should have been extinct a decade ago.'

Wood-Lewis shook his head. 'Some might agree. I'm not one of them. And let's consider your legacy. From what I hear, your team members are not so different from you.' He added a sly grin at the end.

Nodding and returning the smile, Bliss said, 'They are, and they're not. You'd be surprised at how often they disagree with me.'

'Vocally?'

'Oh, yes. I encourage it.'

The Chief Constable folded his arms across his chest. 'Sounds to me as if you've done a fine job. They may well be hybrids, but their disinclination to climb the promotion ladder to your own rank suggests they prefer the same kind of hands-on approach as you. There are some people within the force who might regard that as a negative. Not me. While I won't deny we need more detectives at the rank of DCI and DI, we'd barely be able to function without our sergeants and the better constables. If the likes of DS Bishop and DS Chandler wish to remain where they are, more power to their elbows, I say.'

Rather than simply nodding but saying nothing further to encourage the conversation, which was his initial reaction, Bliss offered only an apologetic shrug. 'I agree with you to a certain extent, sir. But I also ask myself if I've held them back. Not by my words, because I've certainly encouraged both to go for it, but rather by my deeds. They see me still loving the grunt side of the job and that has to influence them. I'm hoping my retirement will prompt a re-think. I'd like nothing more than to see one of them filling my shoes in the team at some point.'

'I'm quite sure they all appreciate your qualities as a leader, Jimmy. Strong leadership is not what I remember, that's for sure. You neither, I expect. Those probationary years were a lot tougher than they needed to be. In those days they threw us in at the deep end, so we quickly learned to swim, or we drowned.'

The sluice gates inside Bliss's head opened up and a torrent of memories poured in. 'I think we can agree that's one area of improvement. The good old days were often not so good. It was made an awful lot easier to do the wrong thing, and when you did, you became part of the team. I probably fared better than most because of my old man. In those days, a uniformed sergeant was revered and respected, and most people tended not to take liberties with me because of that. Had it not been for him being a copper, those back-handed inducements and financial rewards for looking the other way might have seduced me.'

Woods-Lewis gave him a look of disbelief. 'I don't get a sense of that at all from looking at your record, Jimmy. I see a man who thinks for himself and stands by his convictions. For a copper, you have the right values of loyalty and bravery, a way of looking at the world that leads you to making the right choices more often than not. But above all else, and the thing that sets the best apart from the rest, you have integrity. That means something to those who look up to you. And to the friends and families of the victims we all serve.'

For the first time in many years, Bliss felt himself blush. 'I'll settle for that as a legacy, sir. Means more to me than any gold watch, that's for sure.'

Laughing, the CC said, 'Not that you get one of those, I'm afraid. But you do leave with your service record, along with my thanks and best wishes. I'm glad you're returning to us as a civilian, Jimmy. You still have plenty to give.'

Puffing out his cheeks in relief, Bliss admitted in a soft voice, 'For a moment when I walked through the door I thought you might be about to revoke the offer.'

More laughter. 'Not a chance. I'm absolutely in favour of utilising the decades of experience retirees bring to the force. Yes, there's always the worry over men and woman being set in their ways and disrupting solid units, but only good can come of you continuing to work with the Major Crime Unit in Peterborough.'

'I'm very glad to hear it, sir.'

'It was never in question, certainly not after DCS Feeley chose to leave us. We'll need a reshuffle, of course, with Detective Superintendent Fletcher and DCI Edwards both moving up and you moving out. But DCI Warburton has already offered her services in a more pro-active role with you having her back as SIO. Should either DS Bishop or Chandler decide to go for promotion after all, we'll still need an interim DI with you gone.'

'I'm sure it'll all click into gear fairly easily, sir. I have to say I'm quite looking forward to the challenge.'

'Good. Then, of course, there's the matter of working unsolved cases. I foresee that being a huge success, much the same as it has been in Cambridge.'

Bliss nodded appreciatively. 'The work they did on Ricky Neave was exemplary.'

'Quite. I'm not suggesting you'll achieve anything quite so spectacular. Thankfully, there aren't too many cases like that out there haunting us. But you'll be kept busy enough.'

'I'm sure I will. Just as soon as I'm done with my final two cases.'

The man fixed him with a look of surprise. 'You're not telling me they're the only open cases you have on the go, are you, Jimmy?'

Shaking his head, Bliss said, 'Far from it, sir. But it just so happens they're my last two and I regard them as the most important on the books. I'm not being given anything new, not so much as being called out to any shouts. So this is it for me, and I have today to put them to bed.'

'And will you?'

Bliss gave a weak smile. 'I genuinely don't know. If not, it won't be for want of trying.'

THIRTY-FOUR

'How did it go?' Chandler asked the moment he walked into the major inquiry room.

Bliss slipped out of his suit jacket and wrapped it around the back of a nearby chair. He explained that it had all gone so much better than expected, and was delighted to admit that the Chief Constable was a thoroughly decent bloke once you got to know him. He finished by saying he'd invited the top man to the retirement bash the following night.

'You what?!' Chandler was beyond astonished. 'You think he'll actually show?'

Bliss laughed at her scepticism. 'No chance. He's decent, not desperate.'

Chandler used hand gestures to urge both Ansari and Virgil to gather round before going over the outcome of their morning briefing. 'In your absence, we assigned me and you the task of revisiting Jacob Nash,' she told Bliss. 'Gul and Alan are going to run down the last of the basic actions, such as checking alibis and doorbell footage. Then we close the lid on those. Essentially, though, during our discussion we kept coming back to potential suspects. Gul?'

DC Ansari gave a disgruntled sigh. 'I know I must sound like an echo chamber, but where are we on applying for the missing phone data? Do we have more on Banks and Dixon than we had before? Enough to make the application?'

Bliss nodded. 'I'll push to get it signed off. The likely connection to Karagiannis has altered the landscape. More so than any of you realise, because I had an unwelcome visitor last night.'

He proceeded to tell them about the woman he'd spoken to down by the river. 'Not muscle, I'm guessing from her physique and attitude, but some kind of go-between. She warned but didn't warn me off Nash, if you know what I mean. Told me he wasn't the piece of the puzzle we'd been searching for; like some female version of Obi Wan Kenobi. And she was also adamant that Banks and Dixon were an even colder trail to follow.'

'Why on earth would this woman approach you directly?' Chandler asked.

The same question had been bothering Bliss since the two had parted company. He suspected the interviews earlier in the day had caused a bit of a flap. 'I think she was there primarily to weigh me up in person and to make an offer she hoped I couldn't refuse – cash in return for me turning a blind eye. The implied threat was also a part of it.'

'I don't like the sound of that, Jimmy.'

'I'm not exactly thrilled by it, but blinking first was a mistake on her part. She's put herself on my radar but has also brought a closer focus to both her boss and our business-owning trio.'

Chandler had a different slant. 'You mention her boss as if you know for certain who it is, but could she possibly be working for them rather than Karagiannis?'

Having already tossed the idea around and found it wanting, Bliss shook his head. 'Unlikely. I certainly didn't come away with that impression. We know these men have business dealings together in the pipeline, and people like Karagiannis don't usually hook up with complete outsiders in such a huge venture. For me, this confirms a connection between them that pre-dates the proposed casino. If pushed, I'd say they stepped out of bounds and Stuart McKenzie took the brunt of the punishment for making a wrong move. Either that or McKenzie had his own little bit of action on the side with the man which went awry. It's all speculation still, but I think that relationship is a weakness we have to exploit.'

They discussed how best to proceed along those lines. Ansari wondered if they should postpone the intended meeting with Nash until they had run down all other possibilities. Her concern, she explained, was that by pursuing the very lead Bliss had been warned about, they might unnecessarily provoke a reaction. Having elected to set aside a final decision until they were done discussing the case, Bliss explored what they knew versus what they believed to be true. He also took them through all that had been done and the conclusions they could draw from the case file as it stood.

'I say we're back to the phone data,' DC Virgil stated emphatically. 'If we can prove either or both Banks and Dixon were in the area of Cuckoo's Hollow on Friday night, then we surely have enough to pull them in. It couldn't hurt to include Jacob Nash in the request.'

Bliss shook his head. 'He's not part of their business, so that won't fly. You're right, though. Having evidence of their lies to us coupled with their presence in the same park in which McKenzie disappeared, would be an ideal situation for us to grapple with. There remains the problematic lack of a body to overcome, but it may not matter if we can turn one of them against the other.'

'I think we need this, Jimmy,' Chandler said. 'Without it, we're struggling.'

'And what if, as I suspect it will, that data comes back only to suggest they were at home where they say they were at the time? If we find no evidence confirming they had anything to do with whatever happened to McKenzie, what or who do we set our sights on then?'

'You think it's more likely to be Karagiannis? Well, not him, but one of his people?'

'In truth, I can't be certain about anything, Pen. For all I know, he contracted one or both of them to do the job themselves.'

Ansari puffed out her cheeks and groaned as she swept back her fringe of hair from her forehead. 'We are going round and round in circles on this. I badly want that phone data, but I'm also wondering if it will only bring us more bad news.'

'Or worse still, equivocal news,' Bliss added. 'As things stand, we can't rule anybody in or out, and the phone data might not change that.'

Virgil caught on, nodding and saying, 'Because the fact that their data says they were at home only means their phones were, yes?'

'Precisely. This is one of those occasions where only a positive will move us forward. But get it done, Gul. I'll make sure it's authorised as soon as we're finished here.'

He was as good as his word. With the request sent, that left Bliss to make a final decision on the actions agreed in his absence. His reluctance to delay speaking with Jacob Nash was obvious; it felt like caving in to the demands made by the stranger who confronted him at the river. His team knew him well enough to accept whatever choice he made and would not doubt his intentions. But he found himself questioning his own processes. His refusal to buckle under pressure could not lead him to making a decisive error by charging into a confrontation with Nash that only made things worse.

'What's your take on Jacob Nash?' he asked his partner when they were alone.

'He reminds me of one of those strips of card we used to slip into the spokes on our bicycle wheels; makes a lot of noise but in the end adds nothing of value. I agree with you when you say he has more to tell us, but my impression is that it will be a whole lot of hearsay lacking any foundation or proof. We might feel better for knowing, but I doubt it will get us anywhere.'

Bliss nodded. 'I'm beginning to suspect the same thing. I just didn't know if I'd been deflected by my encounter last night.'

Chandler scoffed at him. 'Are you kidding me? The stubborn Jimmy Bliss I know would normally do the complete opposite of what he was told not to do, just to make a point. This is a more reasonable you, weighing up your options without erring towards taking aggressive action.'

He accepted his friend's assertions because he wanted it to be true. 'Let's put the alibi checks on hold, too,' he said, grudgingly. 'We can always use the phone data as leverage if it comes back with a favourable result. For the time being, I think we have to be satisfied with the doorbell camera footage and the data when it turns up. If there are leads to be found, we have to hope they'll be in there somewhere.'

Regarding him with overt scepticism, Chandler said, 'The problem is, you will not be satisfied stopping there. Not on your last day. I'm sorry, Jimmy, but this time I don't think we're going to get the result you want by the end of play.'

Bliss shook his head. He pulled out his mobile and said, 'Me neither. But it's not the only op I want to close today.'

*

Detective Sergeant Higgins from the drugs squad had better news for them. After following up on the information Bliss had provided and having taken a personal interest in the cuckooing of the Bell family on his patch, he'd undertaken his own investigation and put out the appropriate feelers. Just that morning he'd received his own positive phone call. The three of them discussed it over drinks and breakfast in the staff canteen.

'The road the Bells live in is too tight for a vehicle surveillance,' Higgins said, slurping tea from a large white mug. 'Wouldn't you agree?'

Bliss did. 'Stone Lane couldn't be a worse vantage point. Besides, the kids around there will know every vehicle owned or used by the people who live there.'

'Right. So, I took a look at the block of apartments opposite. I spoke to my UCO, and we decided that if he made an approach to the residents and got knocked back, it might easily expose him.'

Once again, Bliss was in agreement. The benefit of having someone familiar on the street was outweighed by the potential of the undercover officer being 'outed' afterwards. He smiled, guessing Higgins had carried out the task himself.

The DS nodded. 'I was quick about it. Fortunately, the front doors to the apartments overlooking the Bell house are on the other side of the block, behind locked gates. I only had to get in and out of those without drawing attention to myself. I used a pool van and carried a handful of packages and posed as a delivery driver.'

'I take it the risk was worthwhile.'

Higgins had gathered up pieces of bacon, sausage, and dripping egg on his fork, but he paused before wolfing down the food. 'We got double lucky. Not only did I manage to find a couple who were willing to allow us to run surveillance from one of their rooms, but they're going away for a fortnight starting from tomorrow.'

Bliss made a fist and thumped it on the table. 'Yes! Great work, Hurricane. Seriously, well done, mate.'

Chandler was frowning and quickly raised her concerns. 'Sorry to dampen the spirits, gents, but hasn't the horse already bolted? The Bells are not living there anymore. They're not even going home to collect their stuff, because if all goes to plan, we'll be doing that on their behalf.'

Bliss and Higgins exchanged looks and smiles. 'You tell her,' Bliss said. 'She never listens to me, anyway.'

The DS chuckled and said, 'Penny, the fact that the Bells are not returning home is precisely what will draw those festering turds back to the house. Word will get out that Nora is no longer in hospital and when there's no sign of her, her sister, or their mother, the dealers will be sucked back in. Without them it's a nest without the cuckoos, but it won't stay that way for long because they'll want to use it for as long as they can. Perhaps until they find another family whose lives they intend to ruin.'

Chandler nodded along. 'I get you. And it works in our favour because the surveillance point means you can capture all relevant faces on film.'

'The dealers and the users,' DS Higgins clarified. 'We can confirm which scrotes are nesters and which are casual visitors. Might be a week or two of footage if we get another break. Either way, all of the players will end up on Candid Camera.'

Bliss had to fight down the urge to voice his delight. Having met Frances, Patricia, and Nora Bell, he had a particular affinity for this case. He'd been told his entire career that allowing an investigation to get personal was the wrong way to go about the job. But he'd always taken the opposite view, and it had served him well. His excitement was also soured somewhat by knowing that securing evidence from the surveillance would take time.

And that was one thing not on his side.

THIRTY-FIVE

ETECTIVE SUPERINTENDENT FLETCHER AND DCI Warburton
were looking to arrange a progress update with him, but with
intel coming in from external agencies, Bliss invited his bosses
to join him and the team for a Zoom meeting arranged by NCA
investigator, Gail Roberts. His go-to techie, DC Ansari, set things
up on the eboard in the operational major inquiry room so that
the entire team could be physically present.

Roberts first introduced Interpol's Criminal Intelligence
Officer, Angus Coulter, who was based in Lyon in France. Next
up was EU Organised Crime Specialist, Esmee Vos, from Europol.
As the only member of the team in Peterborough to appear on
camera in the Zoom link, Bliss then gave his rank and name
and thanked everybody for attending. He wasn't a huge fan of
online meetings, but with the cost, time, and travel savings, he
was willing to go along with the arrangement.

'Given you're based in the Hague,' Bliss began, 'let's hear from
you first, please, Specialist Vos.'

'Thank you. And please understand that while we may be
only a little more than 50 kilometres from Amsterdam, there
are times when it feels like a different country entirely. As you

might imagine, we have specialists who spend a great deal of time there and who have acquired considerable intelligence on one Hector Karagiannis. This is only to be expected given the family name, but his links in my country are as extensive as they appear to be in the UK.'

'Do the names my colleague gave you feature in your files?' Bliss asked.

Vos, a pinched faced woman who wore thick-framed spectacles and her fair hair tied back, nodded and even managed to raise a demure smile. 'They are flagged as people of interest. We became aware of them when they started showing up at the Karagiannis casino in Amsterdam around six months ago.'

'What drew your attention to these men?'

'In the main it was the people they engaged with. They dined with the manager, and our intel connected their conversations with the business of running a top-class casino and hotel complex. But they also met with two men of West African heritage whom we have been interested in for some time. While they appear to be employed by the casino, we've never been entirely certain in what role. We believe they are actually in the employ of Hector Karagiannis, and their links to Sierra Leone suggest an interest in diamonds.'

'Aren't they usually routed through Antwerp these days?' Investigator Roberts cut in.

'Indeed they are,' Vos agreed with a firm nod. 'However, some Dutch merchants on both sides of the legal fence have remained in business throughout the various shifts and clampdowns.'

'Thank you, Specialist Vos,' Gail Roberts said, before bringing their Interpol colleague up in the larger window. 'Does this tally with your own information, Investigator Coulter?'

The sandy-haired man with heavy-lidded eyes was already nodding. 'Very much so. We also suspect these African men work directly for Karagiannis despite their salary being paid by the casino which, of course, Hector also owns. We have traced them to several associates in Freetown, Sierra Leone, who themselves have close connections with the Murray Mining Company. Once heavily connected to blood diamonds, that is no longer the case. However, quality diamonds are still being traded, and where there is a source there is also smuggling.'

'Why Sierra Leone?' Roberts asked.

'The quality of the diamonds. They have an international reputation as some of the finest in the world in terms of quality. Those in the know often refer to them as glasses because the best of them are perfectly clear, free of inclusions, and absolutely colourless. Flawless, in other words.'

'I've been wondering if the casino business is just a front,' Bliss said, scanning a printed report handed to him by DC Ansari moments before he'd left the office to attend the meeting. 'In respect of our suspects, Banks, Dixon, and McKenzie, I mean. Because although they made a license application to run this type of casino, we can find no attempts on their behalf to source either land to build on or suitable buildings to acquire here in the city.'

'Perhaps they were waiting on the outcome of their application,' the NCA investigator suggested.

Bliss nodded. 'I'm sure they would ahead of any purchase, but by this stage in proceedings I'd have expected them to have at least looked at acquiring premises or, more likely, land on which to build their new enterprise. As far as we're able to tell, they've done no exploratory work whatsoever.'

'Interesting,' Roberts said. 'And what is it that you believe they are attempting to prevent us from discovering?'

'Our thinking is that they're possibly involved in smuggling. The casino venture explains away any connection they might have with Hector Karagiannis, but there may be little or no substance to it. Our intel suggests they don't appear to be in a hurry to move forward.'

'Are you seeing their interest as a purely financial arrangement?' Esmee Vos asked.

'Not necessarily,' Bliss said. 'These men have a wide and varied portfolio of businesses, but in terms of wealth they are not in the same league as our Greek criminal. I think they are more likely to be smuggling the diamonds from Amsterdam to the UK for Karagiannis. And if I'm wrong about the casino partnership being smoke and mirrors, then the smuggling could be their way of demonstrating their commitment to the man.'

On the screen, Vos nodded. 'To me that sounds plausible. Our information reveals a legitimate interest in casinos. So yes, perhaps your three men are on the fringes of both.'

'We can apply some pressure at our end,' Intelligence Officer Coulter said. 'See what more we can learn from Sierra Leone. I'm not hopeful because I suspect the Karagiannis family has their illegal dealings compartmentalised. But we have people in place who can dig a little deeper. How about over there in Amsterdam, Specialist Vos?'

'Absolutely. I wouldn't want to spook anybody at this stage, but there are people we can lean on if that's the way we all decide to go.'

'How about the NCA?' Bliss asked. 'Any room for manoeuvre with your investigators?'

Gail Roberts nodded, pushing her glasses back up the ridge of her nose. 'I can but try. From everything I've been able to glean so far, the smuggling is a minor aspect of the family business. In a way, it's traditional, like a family heirloom handed down to each subsequent generation.'

The conversation went on, but less than ten minutes later the meeting was over and the digital screen closed down. 'Are we in as much gridlock as it appears, Jimmy?' DSI Fletcher asked.

It pained him, but he nodded, saying, 'We are no closer to identifying the killer. Our number one theory is still that we're looking at a double murder committed by the same unknown individual, but none of our usual procedures are shedding any light.'

'What are you waiting on currently?'

'The phone data you signed off on earlier, plus additional doorbell camera footage. We're still sifting through videos we already have, plus there's a couple we've yet to get hold of because the owners are or were away.'

'I sometimes wonder if we rely too much on technology.'

'I sometimes wonder if we'd solve any cases without it.'

'And the Bell case?' Fletcher asked.

Bliss updated her and Warburton on the surveillance arrangements and Zander Hirst's condition.

'Patricia Bell has been released pending further investigation,' the DCI herself confirmed. 'We'll revisit that as soon as we know Hirst's prognosis, but from what I understand he's going to be fine.'

'And do we have any confirmation in relation to him being the father of Nora Bell's child?'

'No, we don't,' Bliss replied, his disappointment evident. 'He's been in no fit state so far to interview or make a request for his DNA, not that he's likely to give it up voluntarily. I'm having a chat with the CPS later today because I'm trying to put together an arrest package. Immediately prior to our Zoom meeting we had some minor progress, in that both Frances and Patricia Bell identified Hirst as one of the chief instigators of the cuckooing and for dealing drugs from their house. As you might imagine, Nora Bell is being treated gently and sympathetically, but moments before we gathered here, we learned that she recognised Hirst as one of the boys who visited the house. From what we're able to discern, he spent time in her room playing games as she thinks of it… but, then, so did several other boys.'

Superintendent Fletcher groaned in the back of her throat, making it sound more like a low, primal growl. Her features became rigid and the knuckles of one hand turned white.

'Are we really saying this poor girl was raped by any number of these sick bastards?'

'It's beginning to look that way, yes.'

'The poor little mite.' She looked up at Bliss. 'I want the fuckers, Jimmy. I want all of them. Every single one of the pricks who so much as touched her.'

'You're not alone there,' Bliss said, wishing for all manner of violence to be foisted on the molesters and rapists.

As if she'd only just remembered his status, Fletcher sighed and said, 'I'm so sorry, Jimmy. You, of course, won't be running either investigation after today.'

'Actually,' Bliss said, sitting up straight. 'I wanted to have a word with you about that.'

'Oh?'

'Today is only nominally my final day due to shift patterns and annual leave owing to me. Contractually speaking, I needn't leave for another nine days. I'd therefore like your permission to forgo my holidays and stay on both cases.'

The DSI grinned. 'I'd already worked all that out. If you hadn't volunteered, I'd have asked. I thought you might want to see these through to the bitter end.'

'You know me too well,' Bliss said, chuckling. 'Which probably means one final week is long enough. When I become too predictable, it must be time to call it a day.'

'Nonsense. You'll be greatly missed, Jimmy,' Fletcher assured him. DCI Warburton nodded and concurred with their boss. 'I only hope you can put these to bed in the time you have left.'

Bliss stood and looked at the two women. 'Believe me,' he said. 'It'll be my genuine pleasure.'

THIRTY-SIX

I F SHARON MCKENZIE WAS surprised by his visit, she was at least polite enough to hide it. For Jacob Nash, she was his last refuge. He wasn't going to prise more out of either Mickey or Grant, which left Stu's wife as the only other person who might know where her husband kept the remaining diamonds and cash. After paying his respects and having a stab at offering all the encouragement he could muster, he got down to the business at hand.

'I had a few drinks with Mickey and Grant yesterday,' he told her. 'To tell the truth, Sharon, we're all still reeling with shock. We spoke for ages about how we might be able to help you both, but we came up with nothing. Well, almost nothing. See, the thing is, they remembered Stu mentioning something about having a little hidey-hole.'

'A what? What are you talking about, Jacob?'

The two of them had never gelled. She accepted him because he was one of her husband's friends. He accepted her because she was his friend's wife. But he had always felt that she looked down on him, especially in comparison to how she treated Mickey and Grant. And he knew that the distance she insisted on keeping between them owed much to him being a mere employee.

Forcing himself to smile, Nash said, 'You know I enjoy nothing more than pottering away in my shed, right? I think this hidey-hole they reckon Stu has is his version of that.' He shrugged and stretched the smile further. 'No big deal, really. Just a place to hang out on your own to do some thinking. Come on, you must know what I'm talking about. He had to have discussed it with you. I bet you tore into him about having somewhere to escape to.'

McKenzie's face stiffened. 'Are you saying my husband needed to escape from me and the kids? Is that what you're telling me, Jacob?'

He shook his head. 'No, not at all. It's not a question of needing to, Sharon. It's just something we men do. We all have our own version of a man-cave. It doesn't really mean anything.'

'It might be something you do,' she said gruffly, 'but my Stuart has no need of such a place. Besides, don't you all get enough freedom when you go away on your long weekend jollies?'

'I don't get to go on all of them,' he countered. 'So maybe that's why I have my shed. And besides, it's about having time to yourself, not spending it with others.'

McKenzie spread her hands. 'Why even bring it up? Are you suggesting he has one of these… man-cave places or whatever you call them and has been hiding away all week for whatever reason? What nonsense.'

Nash thought quickly. 'I agree,' he said. 'That would be nonsense. No, what I'm saying is, he might have gone there and… I don't know, had a fall, an accident of some kind. All I was thinking is that if you knew where it was, I could go over and check it out for you.'

It made perfect sense to him. It felt like a safe, logical story. But Sharon merely rolled her eyes at him and said, 'I'm sorry, Jacob. I know you mean well. But if Stu had a place like that, I would know about it. He doesn't have to hide anything from me. No, you're barking up the wrong tree with this idea.'

Nash felt crushed. He saw his last chance to obtain worthwhile information vanishing before his eyes. 'Are you sure?' he asked, barely managing to keep from pleading with her. 'I mean, you don't seem to be even contemplating the idea.'

'That's because I'm certain,' she said in a clipped voice. 'I don't need to consider it. I know my husband. Certainly more than you do.'

*

When he ended the telephone conversation, Grant Dixon glanced across at Michael Banks and shook his head. 'That was Sharon,' he said. 'You want to guess who just paid her a visit?'

Banks looked up and shrugged. 'I've no idea. David Beckham? Tom Cruise? How about Dame Judie Dench?'

Dixon knocked back the remains of a large scotch he'd been nursing when he took the call. 'I'm serious, Mickey. Jacob has just been round there. He gave her some old bollocks about being keen to help find Stu, but all he kept banging on about was man-caves and whether she knew where Stu's was. Suggested maybe he'd gone there last weekend and had some kind of accident. Being the kind soul he is, he volunteered to check it out for her, to make sure Stu wasn't lying there injured.'

Banks frowned. Took a swallow of his own drink. 'That fucking toe-rag. He's after the diamonds and the money. Fuck it, Grant! Why the bloody hell did Stu have to go and tell fucking Jacob all about it?'

'I don't know. Maybe he felt bad about keeping him on the outside too often. Anyway, Sharon sent him off with a flea in his ear. Told him Stu had no such place. She genuinely doesn't seem to know about it.'

'Which means Jacob still doesn't, either.'

Dixon chewed on his bottom lip for a moment, then said, 'You reckon he's after it for himself? You think all his old chat lately is about finding our gear and having it away?'

Banks shook his head, sneering. 'Come off it, Grant. You're giving him too much credit. Jacob is a decent enough bloke, but he's a worker drone. He doesn't have ideas of his own.'

'So, what then? You think he might be working for the Filth? You think they turned him when he was interviewed?'

'I don't know, mate. But even if he was, so what? I mean, what can he tell them? He doesn't know anything. Sharon couldn't provide him with any information because she doesn't have a clue herself. And we're not going to tell him.'

'All right. So, what are we going to do about him, then? If he's working against us, then the least he deserves is a smack or two. Maybe even more.'

'No, nothing like that, Grant,' Banks said, this time with a smile. 'Let him think he's getting closer and let them think he's doing a job for them. Meanwhile, you and me will sit tight. We have a while before we need to move our gear elsewhere. We'll just bide our time, mate.'

'Shame. I really want to thump him for this.'

Banks laughed. 'Yeah, I know you do. You and him have never been quite as close as both of you are to me and Stu. But don't worry about Jacob. He can't hurt us.'

'Maybe he can even help us,' Dixon said, scratching at his unshaven chin. 'After all, we can feed him whatever bullshit we like. We steer him and the Bill in one direction, while we sneak our gear out the opposite way. Might as well make some use of the fat bastard.'

'That's not a bad idea,' Banks said. 'We'll let things cool down first. Like I said, we wait it out. One way or another, the situation is bound to sort itself out.'

THIRTY-SEVEN

WHAT OUGHT TO HAVE been his final briefing became a stay of execution for Bliss. His colleagues were delighted to learn they had more time with him at the helm, but he also got a sense of the renewed burden he had placed upon them. It had always felt like a stretch for the team to close two new investigations in less than a week, and as Friday evening had drawn closer the atmosphere had changed to one of acceptance that they were not going to get it done. His decision to work out his days had put them all back on the clock. With this in mind, he'd done his best to end the day on an upbeat note, and had wished everybody a good weekend, hoping to see as many of them as possible at his leaving do.

A leaving do that could not have gone any better.

Bliss was only part way pissed – that is if part way equalled a hundred percent. He was feeling no pain, but that was due to more than the alcohol sloshing around in his bloodstream. He was also experiencing the kind of mellow contentment he hadn't enjoyed in many years.

When entering the restaurant and function annexe of his favourite Windmill pub a few hours earlier, he'd been overwhelmed by the reception that greeted him as he came through the door. Cheers rang out all around, and the warm applause went on for what felt like ten minutes. Familiar faces welcomed him with genuine affection, and he was particularly delighted to see a fellow recent retiree Lennie Kaplan, plus a beaming Olly Bishop, stuffing their faces at the enormous buffet table.

Bish's gift had cracked him up. He'd eagerly unwrapped what he could already tell was a framed object the way a child might shred Christmas wrapping paper. Assuming it would be a photo, he roared with laughter when he saw the item. Behind a pane of glass set into a quality oak frame was the front cover of a programme commemorating the 2021 FA Cup Final at Wembley Stadium. Bliss's beloved Chelsea were enjoying a run of appearances in finals, but on this occasion it had been Olly Bishop's Leicester City who ran out winners by one goal to nil. In truth, Chelsea had done well to get nil on the day, and yet a week later they'd beaten Manchester City in Porto to lift the Champions League trophy. As a wise old sage of the game and an ex-Chelsea legend had once said, football was a funny old game.

Chandler's own surprise present had been a little more subtle. A year's subscription to *Koi Talk* magazine, a publication Bliss had once mentioned as being possibly the worst in the whole of the fish-keeping genre, was inspired devilment on her part. It also brought that great smile of hers to the fore. A smile he adored and could always bring to mind whenever he shut his eyes in need of a boost.

The main gift from the unit was a stunner, though. An eighteen-year-old Macallan Sherry Oak single malt whisky, presented to him in a purpose-built velvet-lined box with brass hinges and lock by the new Detective Chief Superintendent herself. He had guarded his bottle of scotch for the rest of the night like it was a

Faberge egg. He'd rejected two bribes and one failed attempt at distraction, and nobody was prising the bottle from his hands.

But they saved the best for last. DCI Warburton handed over his Bliss Pissed-Ometer, the creased and aged cardboard having been signed by every member of the team prior to it being framed. It had depicted his moods, ranging from 'Grumpy' to 'Apoplectic' since his first year at Thorpe Wood, and he was touched by the thoughtful gift.

'Thank you so much for this,' he said as the resulting laughter died away. 'But to top it off, you can tell me which one of you childish bastards has been responsible for moving the pointer on this bloody thing across the years.'

More laughter followed, and after a moment of hesitation, Chandler took a step forward. 'I'm Spartacus,' she said.

Before Bliss could respond, DC Ansari also stepped up to say, 'I'm Spartacus.'

Then Bishop. 'I'm Brian, and so's my wife,' he cried, quoting from the Monty Python film *The Life of Brian*.

He was swiftly followed by Alan Virgil and even DC John Hunt, before finally Diane Warburton herself.

'Et tu, Brute?' Bliss said to her with mock disappointment. 'Et Tu?'

As the night wore on, Bliss found himself standing by the main window staring out at the night when Chandler popped up alongside him to link arms. Leaning into him, she said, 'Hazel would have been so proud of you tonight, Jimmy.'

It was as if his best friend had been reading his mind. His late wife had been at the forefront of his thoughts since the start of the festivities. Bliss wondered what she would have looked like celebrating here with him tonight had a stalker with a depraved mind not cut short her life. He was as certain as he had been about anything that Hazel would have remained slender and elegant despite the years chipping away at her, yet with the same sense of fun and a penchant for mischief that he had adored. He gave a reflective smile. 'You think so?' he asked, not taking his eyes off the crescent moon.

'Of course she would, you doughnut. And you know what else? Instead of tossing that framed certificate of service into a box or burying it in the back of a cupboard like you probably will, she would have hung it where everybody who came through your front door would see it. And you should do the same because it's a hell of an achievement, my friend.'

Nodding absently, Bliss said, 'I wish you'd had the pleasure of meeting her, Pen. You two would've got along famously.'

Chandler rested her head on his shoulder. 'You don't think she might have been a teensy bit jealous of you and me? I mean, not that anything ever really happened between us, but you can't deny how close we are.'

'I know. But that's what my amazing wife would have loved about you. The fact that you have my back, that you're always there for me. She'd've been the first to embrace you as my work wife. No, Haze didn't have a jealous bone in her body. She knew how I felt about her and that was all she needed.'

Silent for a few seconds, Chandler gave a gentle sigh and said, 'It's a beautiful thing that you had with her, Jimmy. Some people search all their lives and still never find that kind of relationship.'

'I know. I'm a lucky man. To have had it and lost it is hard, but the thought of never having had it at all… no, I'd rather live with the pain and emptiness. That's why I have no regrets. But the one thing wrong with your theory about her being proud of me tonight is that if Hazel and I were still together, I'd never have served forty years in the Job. I'd have retired yonks ago to spend more time with her instead.'

Chandler loosened her grip and took a small step back, looking him up and down. 'For a man with such incredible insight when it comes to other people, you're crap when you turn that focus on yourself. Jimmy, even if you and Hazel were still together, you'd have been retiring this year anyway. It might not have been here in Peterborough, but wherever you'd ended up you'd still have served the same amount of time as a copper. That's just who you are, and from what I know about your late wife, she would have supported your choices all the way.'

Bliss turned his head, his face wreathed in smiles. 'Thank you for that, Pen. I needed to hear it. But let me do you a favour in return. Let me badger you one last time to go for promotion. I want to see you running the team. What's more, they want it, too.'

'I don't know if I can, Jimmy.'

'Of course you can. You're primed for it.'

Chandler shook her head. 'No, I don't mean it that way. Look, I didn't want to say anything to you before, but the truth is I'm not sure if I'll still be around.'

'What? Why not?'

'Because Graham is thinking of taking a job in Brussels and he wants me to join him there.'

'He does?'

'Yes.'

Bliss stared blankly at her before frowning and saying, 'In that case, I have just one question for you.'

'Okay. Fire away.'

'Who the fuck is Graham?'

Chandler rolled her eyes. 'Graham. My Graham. Shrek, you moron!'

The penny dropped; her boyfriend. 'Oh. *Oh*. Things are that serious between you, are they?'

'I don't know. They could be.'

'But what would you do if you joined him?'

'There's always Interpol.'

He felt suddenly deflated, crestfallen at the idea of Chandler no longer being with the unit. 'When do you have to give him an answer?' he asked.

'I have a few weeks. He's not made up his mind about the move. He has a deadline at the end of the month, by which time I have to have an answer for him.'

'And you're actually considering it? Leaving the team. England. What about your daughter?'

'Anna is one of the reasons why I didn't give him an immediate answer. It'll be especially difficult now that she's decided to stay here in the UK rather than return to Turkey.'

'And the other reasons?'

'Too many to list, Jimmy.'

'I didn't realise you thought enough of him to uproot your entire life to go and live with him in another country? I mean, you do know how close Belgium is to France, don't you?' Bliss gave a mock shudder at the thought.

Her smile, it seemed to him, was uncertain. 'That's one of the other reasons,' she said. 'Because every time I ask myself the same question, my answer changes.'

Bliss breathed in slowly. 'Oh. I see. Obviously, it has to be your decision, Pen. Just don't worry about including me or any of us or our feelings in the decision-making process. For one thing, we don't even like you, so the truth is we'll be glad to see the back of you.'

Chandler flicked two fingers at him and blew a nasty-sounding raspberry. 'You make me wish I'd not been nice to you after all.'

He laughed. 'It made for a pleasant change.'

They were joined by Molly, who had mingled with the guests as if she had known them all her life. Bliss's work family had become hers also, extending their own relationship further still. He picked up his mood as Chandler returned to the main group, still stunned by her revelation.

'What do you think?' he asked, turning to take in the whole room and the people in it. 'The team did me proud with this fantastic do.'

Molly gave him the kind of withering look Chandler had only moments before. 'The *team* didn't arrange all this. It was Penny's job. She made sure of it. I'm telling you, Jimbo, I can't believe you haven't nailed that one yet.'

Unable to help himself, Bliss laughed at her crassness. 'That's my partner you're talking about.'

'So? She's a sort. You missed your chance there, Jimbo.'

Bliss shrugged it off. 'I'm not saying we don't have chemistry and a special kind of bond, but these days it makes me feel as if I'm thinking about my sister and my best friend rolled into one. No, if we ever did have a moment, we left it behind us where it belongs.'

His mind went there, though. The flirting, the thinly veiled remarks, the smouldering kiss on his doorstep when they were both three sheets to the wind. What stopped things from going further was their deep respect and friendship, something neither of them wanted to risk losing for the sake of a physical encounter. Bliss had no regrets, and he knew Chandler felt the same way. What they had was pure and untarnished, something he would always treasure because it was so hard to find.

Before the night was over, there were three further speeches. The first from Diane Warburton, who used her wit and charm to great effect. The deep affection she held for him was apparent, and more than a few tears were shed as she wound it up by insisting the second phase of her career would have been impossible without his efforts and support. Then it was the turn of Marion

Fletcher, who herself had received a rousing cheer for her promotion. The last to voice their appreciation was Olly Bishop. With surprising good humour, he negotiated his own current status, and thanked Bliss for doing what he himself lacked the courage to do. Stepping back and regaining some perspective was, he insisted, already proving to be a positive experience. He went on to thank his boss for being the best mentor anyone could have and claimed to be a better police officer and a better man for having Bliss as a leader. That this was all said in front of Michael Wood-Lewis came as a major shock to everyone else in the room, but the Chief Constable stayed long enough to have a drink and a chat with many of them.

As one by one or couple by couple the partygoers drifted away, Bliss reflected not just on the night but on his career as a whole. Bishop's breakdown bore testimony to how tough a career policing could be. It whittled away at a person sliver by meaningful sliver. It devastated relationships. It brought some to ruin. He'd never considered surviving that to be about mental strength or character, more about having the ability to divert the darkest, soul-sucking moments of the job into subsidiary channels that fed the furthest recesses of the mind. If you were capable of keeping them locked up in the dark without shining a light on them, it gave you a better chance of coping with the daily rigours and devious minds encountered.

An easy thing to talk about, but never quite so simple to accomplish. He'd lasted forty years in the job because he was one of the lucky ones, Bliss reflected. He only hoped his luck would hold for one more week.

THIRTY-EIGHT

JACOB NASH'S RUSTY SHERIFF'S badge stung like a bastard. For days, his digestive system had been in a state of disorder. Whatever he fuelled himself with at one end came out either the same way or in the worst case of the runs since a gastrointestinal infection back in his youth. The stress of his current situation caused knots of anxiety to twist his stomach, leaving his intestines feeling as if a coach load of clowns had each created a balloon animal with them.

Pressure was coming at him from so many directions he didn't know which way to turn. Mickey and Grant were giving nothing away, no matter how much he probed. He was sure they were on to him, or at the very least had become suspicious of him. He knew he'd been asking too many questions. He felt the rank odour of betrayal oozing from his pores whenever he broached the subject of the diamonds and Stuart. Not forgetting the man's wife, who was either the best liar he had ever encountered, or completely ignorant about any secret stash.

The woman who had demanded answers from him brought him out in cold sweats every time he thought about her. She was clearly a serious villain in her own right, but the brute with the tools who had followed her into the hotel room did not look the type you could barter with, either. If he had his instructions, he was willing and able to carry them out. Just the thought of the kind of damage that hammer was capable of had left Nash weeping like a baby and begging for a chance to make things right. That he'd failed to do so injected another jagged shot of terror into his bloodstream. What else might appear from the inside of that bag of delights after his bones had been pulverised? Pliers for pulling nails? A drill to put holes in his kneecaps? Knives to slice open his flesh?

Yet the threat of physical violence was only part of the nightmare he was facing. The underlying fear associated with his recently acknowledged affection for young men and perverse sexual pleasures being exposed was, perhaps, the worst of all possibilities. If these maniacs did not kill him, he'd eventually recuperate from whatever wounds they might inflict. In time, he might even forget the pain they'd caused. But he would never recover from being outed as a deviant. It didn't matter if his interest in the more sculpted male body doing unspeakable things to him was socially acceptable these days. The simple fact was, if word got out, he would at the very least lose his family.

But what was he to do?

Every time he enjoyed even the slightest period of isolation, his thoughts turned to how he might extricate himself from the situation he had become embroiled in. Having considered several avenues, he had subsequently reduced them to just a single viable possibility. He was neither big enough nor tough enough to go at Mickey and Grant with threats and a show of intimidation, to somehow force them into revealing the whereabouts of the diamonds and the proceeds from their sales. Which left giving up his friends to the police. Throwing himself at the mercy of the investigating officers by striking a deal that would see him immune from prosecution in exchange for what he knew, was the only path left for him to travel.

Yet in addition to the constant fretting, Nash mentally laid into himself for being so weak. A real man would refuse to buckle. A real man would stand up to these people. He was a human being, after all, not a butt for Grant's jokes and the woman's passive aggression. Yet here he was, hiding away in his garden shed, cutting himself off from his wife and children in case his terror somehow managed to transfer itself to them or spill over into a gushing confession.

And what about them? Would that be the next threat? After working on him with their tools and getting the same response because he had nothing more to give them, would those monstrous villains shift their cold determination to his family? His heart broke at the thought, because in his mind he'd done nothing to deserve this. Not when it came to the smuggling, at least. As for his other inclinations, even if it was wrong for a married man to indulge himself in such a way, and even if he deserved to be punished, that should not extend to others in his social circle.

Nash cupped both hands to his face and drew them slowly down, folds of flesh undulating as he pulled it through his fingers. He wept for the third or fourth time in the past hour, snivelling wreck of a man that he was. He was disgusted by himself. Perhaps he didn't deserve to live.

Perhaps he didn't deserve to live...

Now there was a thought. The only way to kill all birds with a single stone, so to speak. The woman wouldn't come after his family if he was dead. Exposing his proclivities and the seedy way he had gone about procuring sex from another man wouldn't make sense, either. As for whatever Mickey and Grant were thinking, what they might decide to do if they acted upon their suspicions, none of that would matter if he was no longer around.

He didn't want to die, had never considered taking his own life until moments ago. But there was a lot to be said for the idea. When you were gone, you were gone, and absolutely nothing that happened afterwards could possibly affect you. And if he could make it look like an accident, his family would be taken care of in terms of insurance policies.

Is this really what it's come to?

Is this all that I have amounted to?

Life wasn't fair, but that was news only to complete morons or the terminally arrogant. In general, he'd led a decent life. He was a beloved figure to many. If his demise was deemed to be accidental, then people who cared would mourn him as he deserved. For the most part. How to end it all was the real question? A car accident was by far the most feasible method. But a collision that might instead leave him disabled, perhaps a quadriplegic, was not something he could possibly risk. If he opted to bow out that way, he had to make sure. It had to be all or nothing.

And it had to be immediately, before he lost his nerve.

Pulling himself together and wiping away his tears with the palms of his hands, Nash heaved himself out of his folding travel chair and pulled open the shed door. If he took action immediately, allowing himself no time for further thought, he might just get away with it. Still silently weeping, he started to turn towards the path leading around the side of the house.

Which was when some base instinct sensed movement in the darkness a split second before he felt a heavy blow to the back of his head and everything went black.

THIRTY-NINE

HIS HEAD BANGING, THROAT parched, and stomach queasy from the aftereffects of alcohol, Bliss had just waved Molly off at the railway station when he took a call from the control desk. The message relayed from the drugs squad at Thorpe Wood was to call DS Higgins as a matter of urgency.

'Did you know one of your supposedly protected people was roaming free?' Higgins asked in lieu of a greeting.

The frown Bliss had already been wearing deepened, and if it were possible his head began to thump harder still. 'My supposedly... you mean the Bells?'

'Yes. More specifically, Patricia Bell.'

Bliss couldn't understand why he'd not been informed. A protective detail should have had the family under observation at all times, so for one of them to slip away unnoticed was a serious breakdown of procedure. Any argument over who had dropped a bollock could wait, he decided, suddenly understanding why he was hearing about it from DS Higgins.

'She's gone home, hasn't she?' he said. 'Your surveillance team spotted her.'

'Just over an hour ago. I spoke with them before I put out the message for you to call me. We're wondering if we ought to stick or bust with the surveillance. Her returning to the house might give our dealers some pause.'

Bliss rapidly weighed the pros and cons. 'She's only been back for a short time. We can't be certain she's home for good.'

'Agreed. Our problem is, if we call and ask what the fuck she's doing there, we give away the fact that we have eyes on. I think we'd all rather she wasn't aware of that.'

'Definitely not,' Bliss said. 'But we were always bound to find out that she'd skipped from the hotel. I could call her. If she answers the phone, I can ask where she is and hope she's honest with me. Then I can grill her about her intentions.'

'Sounds like a plan, Jimmy. Sorry to ruin your Sunday, but as mine has been I thought I'd share the pain around.'

Bliss grunted and jokingly told Higgins where he could stick his pain. He then called Patricia Bell, who surprised him by not only picking up, but also immediately going on the offensive. 'Don't bother having a pop at me,' she told him bluntly. 'I just decided I'd had enough of being afraid. I've agreed to leave the city with my mum and Nora to start a new life together somewhere far away from this shit hole. But there's no way I'm going with my tail between my legs. What I did to Zander was payback for what he did to my sister, but I wanted to give them all a big 'fuck you' for the misery they put us through.'

'What does that mean, Patricia?' Bliss asked. 'Where are you?'

'The last place they'd expect to find me. At home.'

He gave it a moment, allowing enough time for the news to sink in should it have come as a shock to him. 'Is that the wisest course of action for you to follow? They not only have their sights set on you, they probably also have plans for your house as well.'

'Yeah, well I'm here, so let them try.'

Keeping his voice neutral and even, Bliss said, 'While I understand the impulse, did it occur to you that they might not care?

Or that all you've done by going home is present them with a stationary target? Look, we can't force you to comply until you've signed the relevant documentation, but neither can we spread ourselves to put protection in place outside your house as well.'

'Good.' Her determination and spirit became clear in that single word. 'I want them to come. I want them to know I'm here and fronting them.'

'Patricia, these people don't fuck around. I'm not talking about the local grunts who used your home like a drugs dispensary, or cycle around the streets thinking they're so bloody hard. Neither Zander Hirst nor his mates bother me a great deal. But remember, in addition to raping your sister, he was dealing drugs. And dealers have suppliers. It's the faces he works for who concern me more. They will not give a shit about your one-woman protest group.'

'It's just for a day or two,' Bell argued. 'We were told the legal stuff is going to be prioritised and we'll be out of here by Tuesday or Wednesday at the latest.'

Bliss sighed. He knew he wasn't going to convince her, but he gave it one last try. 'Like you say, it's only for a couple of days. Is it really worth the risk for so little reward?'

Her emphatic answer prompted him to offer a few safety tips before he put in another call to DS Higgins. Following the update, he sought permission to join the surveillance. It wasn't his team's operation, so he couldn't just turn up and expect to be welcomed with open arms. But Higgins understood and gave him the go-ahead.

'There is just one problem, Jimmy,' he said. 'Her presence there might fuck up our op in other ways. If she draws a crowd and things start to turn ugly, you're not going to just sit there and let them dole out a punishment, are you?'

'Of course not.'

'Right. Neither would my people. So, if it kicks off and you all go steaming in to protect her, that's our entire operation down the pan. You certain there's no way you can shift her out of there, mate?'

'She's staying put, Hurricane,' Bliss confirmed. 'But if I get a sense that the wind has changed, I'll give her another bell and try to persuade her one last time. I can't very well go in and drag her out by the scruff, but I will apply a bit more pressure. Truth is, I admire her taking a stance.'

'Well, let's make sure we can all appreciate her after a successful outcome, shall we?'

Stone Lane was only a couple of minutes from the railway station. Bliss parked a few streets away and walked the rest, hoping to make his arrival less obvious. At the gated entrance to the apartment block, he used the code Higgins had given him to gain entry. He then made his way around the back and up a flight of stairs to their surveillance location. Today it was staffed by two constables, DCs Ryan Stotter and Pete Garroway. Neither appeared to be put out by his presence. If anything, they were more nonplussed by his willingness to give up a day off.

In the living room, the team had set up a video camera and a still camera on tripods, both trained on the street below with the front garden and door to the Bell house their centre focus. They also shared a pair of binoculars and log sheets attached to a clipboard. Bliss flipped back through the list of observations over the entire twenty-seven hours of surveillance notes.

'Nobody's taken the bait so far, then,' he observed. 'No interest at all in the place from what I'm seeing here.'

DC Garroway looked up from the video camera viewing screen. 'Nothing doing,' he said. 'The Bell kid made a bit of a show of coming home, lingering on the doorstep taking a good look around. As far as we could tell, nobody was close enough to clock her, but there could have been some kids further up the street beyond our field of vision. Or somebody might have spotted her as she made her way here. If they had, we'd have expected some early movement, even if it was only some vague sniffing around. But as you can see from the log, none of those who passed by so much as paused or glanced in the direction of the Bell property.'

'It'll come,' Bliss said confidently. 'It has to.'

They continued to wait. And wait. The sun set rapidly, and the afterglow seemed to last barely a few minutes. As time ticked away so Bliss felt increased tension setting in. With Patricia Bell on the plot, he wondered if he ought to be doing more by way of additional surveillance and security. The case the drugs squad hoped to make against the dealers was nothing to do with him, but in terms of the young woman and her family, his concerns lay in keeping them safe. If something went off, he felt certain that the two detective constables with him would react as he would, regardless of what it did to their operation. But would the three of them be enough if the crew came mob-handed?

Or armed?

One of the tips he had given the girl was to leave a light on and the curtains open from the moment darkness descended on the street. He wanted to make sure they had eyes on her as well outside her home. He had a moment of panic when the living room light winked out, before recovering his breath as soon as the bedroom became illuminated. He'd reminded Bell she was being watched, so to keep her wits about her and remember to get changed in the bathroom or at the very least out of sight. To his relief she did appear to be following his advice, and the street itself remained quiet.

Bliss had pretty much commandeered the binoculars. During one of his sweeps of the street and the Bell property, something nagged at him. He couldn't quite grasp it at first, but quickly felt his shoulders and neck beginning to tighten. A familiar tingle as hairs rose on his arms and nape raised red flags. He made the same observational sweep three more times before feeling the same kind of nag intruding into his consciousness.

Police officers tend to listen to their instincts telling them something is not quite right. Bliss was no exception. He trusted his gut feelings, and his prickling flesh insisted he do so once again.

But what had he picked up on? What was out of place?

He squinted and ran it back. Both eyes flew wide open again as he realised what he had noticed. The downstairs front window had blinds rather than curtains, which Bell had dutifully left open. The individual slats were made of thin strips of plastic, lightweight and flimsy. He knew that the first subliminal alert had been triggered by the shutter momentarily fluttering sideways. The meaning behind the sudden movement hadn't immediately dawned on him, but the second time around it registered more fully and the logical question sprang to mind: what had caused them to shift in such a manner?

Bliss worked the problem. Patricia Bell hadn't left the bedroom, which meant she hadn't touched them. So how on earth had they moved? They hadn't parted as if somebody was trying to peer through, more flapped as if… as if disturbed by a passing breeze. A breeze caused by what, though? Bell hadn't left the room upstairs, so she had neither opened nor closed a door. But hers wasn't the only door in the house. What if somebody had been waiting inside? No, not likely, because they couldn't possibly have known when or if she would return. But what if they had both entered and subsequently exited the house from the rear? That would explain the two disturbances of the window blinds.

He set the binoculars down on the windowsill and brought up Google Maps on his phone. He typed in STONE LANE MILL-FIELD and set the view to Satellite, which brought the area to life from above. He swiftly tweaked the image to zoom in and quickly spotted something he'd hoped not to see. At the end of the Bells' back garden sat an attached garage, the entrance to which was situated in a long, narrow driveway that emerged onto Lincoln Road.

If somebody had access to the garage, they also had alternative access to the house.

Bliss reacted as if scalded. 'Call it in!' he cried, startling his two companions, who both peered up at him as if he were having a fit of some kind. 'Somebody's inside the house!'

About to turn and run for the front door of the surveillance flat, his peripheral vision became aware of an aggressive flickering. He turned his head and blinked twice, focussing his eyes.

There it was again.

An orange blush, blooming and dying in a continuous festival of movement. Shimmering like candlelight, only much more significant and deadly.

'Jesus!' Bliss said, his heart plunging as if he were trapped in a falling lift shaft. 'The house is on fire. Get everybody here. Now!'

FORTY

BLISS RACED FOR THE apartment door and made a call on his mobile at the same time. When Patricia Bell picked up, he spoke calmly although his head was reeling with all kinds of dreadful possibilities.

'This is DI Bliss. Listen to me and do exactly as I say. Somebody has been inside your home, and they've lit a fire on the ground floor. I'm close by and I'm coming, but you have to do something before I get there.'

'What? What are you telling me?' Bell cried, her voice pitched high and seemingly uncomprehending.

Bliss shouted this time to cut through the girl's panic. 'Just listen to me! Is the bedroom door closed?'

'Yes. Yes, it's closed.'

'Okay. Touch the handle. If it's warm, then don't open the door. If it's cold, crouch low and open up just enough to see out into the passageway. If you don't see flames, go to the landing at the top of the stairs and tell me if you have a clear path down and out to the front door.'

'But—'

'Just do as I tell you!' Bliss roared into the phone, the time for niceties long past.

He was dashing down the stairs to the rear of the building. His mouth was bone dry and his pulse raced. By the time he'd reached the bottom, Bell was back on the line, hysterical and almost out of control. 'I got out, but the flames are right at the foot of the stairs. I'm trapped! Please help me! Help!'

Bliss didn't have to imagine the girl's terror; it was all too evident in her voice. 'Okay, okay. Calm down and listen to me again,' he said, reeling in his own rising anxiety. 'Go back into the bedroom. Close the door and stuff something along the bottom of it to plug the gap. Then I want you to open the window and wait for me.'

He burst through the wrought-iron gate and sped across the road without checking it for traffic. His heart hammered and blood rushed through his head. He saw Patricia Bell appear at the window she had thrown open. Her face was twisted with terror.

'Okay,' he called out, staring up at her and pulling the phone away from his face. 'Listen to me closely. Slowly edge yourself out onto the windowsill, shift your body around and start lowering yourself down until you're hanging there by your fingertips. Then just release. I'll catch you. I promise I will.'

At most I'll steady your fall and we'll both end up sprawled out on the ground, he thought, but didn't say. Still, it was better than her staying rooted to the spot. Only that's precisely what Patricia Bell did.

'No. I can't!' she cried, a look of utter desolation moulding her features into a grim mask. 'It's too high. I'll break something or smash my head.'

'Not if you hang down as far as you can before you let go,' he said urgently. 'Believe me, it always looks further down from up there. By the time you hang over the edge, there'll be hardly any distance to drop.'

Bell crouched, forcing herself into a pleading position, hands clasped together to her chest. 'I can't!' she screamed, imploring him to understand her plight. 'I just can't!'

The girl was petrified, and her inability to do as instructed left Bliss with no option.

'Fuck it!' he cursed beneath his breath. 'All right. Stay where you are. I'm coming for you.'

He caught the sound of pounding feet approaching fast. Stotter and Garroway joined him in the front garden, both officers keen to know what they could do to help. He turned to them and laid out his revised plan. 'One of you climbs up onto this lower windowsill, the other stands behind and gets ready. I'm going to lean out and lower her down to you.'

'You're going to do what?' DC Garroway said. He shook his head. 'There's no way you're going in there, Inspector.'

'I don't have time to argue,' Bliss shot back, setting his jaw. 'More to the point, neither does she. You two just brace yourselves.'

He gave neither of them time to respond. Without another word, he shifted sideways and ran at the front door. It took him two hard kicks to force the lock open, and he was grateful that the drugs gang hadn't reinforced it. The sight that confronted him in the hallway almost broke his resolve; the fire had been set close to the foot of the stairs, and the flames had spread to the wallpaper and carpeted flooring. The banister newel post had begun to smoulder, and as the flames climbed higher up the stairway wall the black smoke was beginning to roil beneath the high ceiling. The oxygen he'd added by smashing the door open momentarily fuelled the fire and prompted it to rage harder.

Snapping himself out of his momentary stupor, Bliss darted towards the fiery gateway almost obscuring the staircase beyond and leapt for all he was worth, aiming for the fourth tread from the bottom. He hit it hard, and a sharp pain shot between his right knee and ankle. Stumbling and losing the battle to regain his balance, Bliss snatched a hand back from the hot banister rail but somehow managed to steady himself by grasping hold of the tread closest to his free hand. He glanced back to see if he'd managed to avoid the licking flames, a sense of relief surging through him when he saw his clothing had not been ignited.

He scampered up the steps, feeling another stab of pain in the ankle that had buckled when he'd smashed into the staircase. The smoke he swallowed burned the back of his throat and immediately forced him to cough. It was becoming increasingly harder to see, but Bliss picked up speed on the landing and exploded into the bedroom, inside which he found Patricia Bell cowering on the floor beneath the window. He slammed the door closed behind him, used his feet to rearrange the clothing the girl had stuffed into the gap, before striding across the floor towards her.

'Okay,' he said, knowing there was no time for delicacies. 'That fire is getting worse and any time soon you won't be able to breathe out there. So one way or another you're going out of that window. My two colleagues are waiting for you, and what I'm going to do is lower you down. There'll be no fall whatsoever if I do that. I'll just be passing you from my hands to theirs. Okay?'

Bell was sobbing furiously, close to hyperventilating. She was in a state of acute shock, and Bliss realised he'd have to snap her out of it to make her compliant.

'Patricia!' he yelled, the smoke in his lungs making his voice sound harsh. 'Cut it out! You either do this or you die in here, and I'm not waiting around for you to decide. You hear me?'

Through her whimpering and mental torment, something registered. She nodded and her wide, round eyes fixated on his.

He gave a grim nod. 'Right then. Let's do this.'

Bliss gripped the girl's upper arms, and helped her first kneel down upon and then swivel around on the sill. He guided each leg in turn over the edge. 'Okay,' he said calmly. 'Keep your eyes on me. You hear me? Just focus on my face. I'm going to switch my grip to your hands, at which point we'll bind them together as tight as we can. When we're both set, I'll start to lower you. It might feel awkward until you're perfectly horizontal, but then you'll notice the tight connection between us and by the time I've extended out and down, my colleagues below will be grabbing hold of your feet and legs. All good? Let's do this.'

He took his time. The door would keep the smoke and flames at bay long enough, provided the girl didn't panic and refuse to go. But with each passing minute the shock had deepened, and he thought he could get her to do anything he wished at that moment. Easing through the procedure stage by stage, he leaned out until her full weight pulled him into the ledge where it formed a rigid barrier against his lower stomach. Ignoring the pain and the wrench on his arms, he inched further over while keeping one foot pressed against the bedroom floor. A burning ache spread across his shoulders and neck, and as it reached the limit of his endurance he felt the burden lessen and heard a shout from DC Stotter below.

'We've got her. She's okay. Now get your arse down here and join her.'

Bliss didn't need telling twice. He clambered out of the window, twisted his body around, grasped hold of the sill, and lowered himself until his fingers started to tremble. Then he released and let himself fall. DC Stotter both steadied him and prevented him from hitting the ground with the full force of his momentum. A jolt of pain shot between his ankle and his knee for a second time, but he was safe.

They both were. As the fire inside the house continued to roar.

FORTY-ONE

LTHOUGH HE WAS NO longer on the shift roster and therefore not expected in at any particular time, Bliss nevertheless called the station early on Monday morning to tell them he'd be late. He left word for DCI Warburton and DS Chandler to handle the first briefing of the day, and that he'd catch up on any actions upon his arrival.

He'd had a bad night after getting home late. The aftermath of the fire had taken its toll long after the scene had settled down; which in itself had been a protracted experience. After climbing down from the first-floor window, he quickly became aware of how many neighbours had been drawn to the flames like moths. Many of them wore looks of genuine concern, while others stood gossiping and pointing fingers. Bliss made a mental note of the younger faces standing back in pockets of darkness laughing and joking as the sound of sirens rent the air.

Having sent Patricia Bell off in a traffic car to join her family soon after a paramedic had given the girl the all clear, he'd waved away the same emergency worker who was desperately trying to check him out. Bliss waited alongside the two surveillance officers for Higgins to turn up for an initial post-incident debriefing; it was as important for the police to provide early witness statements as it was for members of the public. Upon his arrival, the DS was clearly frustrated at having an op blown, but once the series of unfolding events had been explained he accepted the situation for what it was.

Bliss had stuck around solely to cough his way through a verbal statement, including the decision to enter a burning property. None of his colleagues at the scene took him to task; that would be the role of a more senior officer, and he knew that wasn't going to happen in his last few days. Besides, most of them would have done exactly the same thing had they arrived first.

Hanging his head, Higgins said, 'I can't believe we missed the way in from the rear. My only excuse is that this op was put together rapidly, and in truth we were only expecting to observe foot traffic related to drugs.'

'Don't blame yourself,' Bliss told him. 'You're right. You were set up to watch comings and goings, not waiting for some prick to burn the house down.'

'I know. But I still feel like shit about it.'

Bliss knew all about self-blame. In this instance it was unwarranted, but he knew Higgins would feel bad about it for a while.

By the time he eventually reached home, he was beyond exhausted. The mental and emotional fatigue was every bit as draining as the physical. His painful knee and ankle were not the problem. Nor the cough. The massive high of his retirement party had subsequently collided with the intense low of somebody setting fire to the Bell home while he and two colleagues were watching the place. The combination of the two and the fierce clash of emotions it prompted worked hand in hand to bring him down. He had time only to let Max out into the back garden, apologising to the animal for not going out for a proper walk. Once he'd dragged himself upstairs, Bliss threw himself fully clothed and face first onto his bed, where he remained until shortly before 4.00am.

He'd awoken to a spinning room, ears full, tinnitus raging with pulsing screams and coarse popping sounds; symptoms he recognised and reacted to in an instant. He barely managed to make it to the bathroom before vomiting. On his knees with his forehead pressed against a tiled wall, he waited out the discordant rush of vertigo, accepting the result of his inattention to the care and management of his illness over the past week; a regular theme since his diagnosis. Sometimes he got so swept up by an investigation that he forgot to attend to his own physical needs, but these lapses always caught up with him in the end.

The extra few hours he spent at home recuperating did him some good, and by ten-thirty he was back at Thorpe Wood and looking forward to gaining traction on both cases. He first sought out Penny Chandler and asked her to catch him up with the morning's progress so far.

'I'm pleased to say we have had some,' she told him eagerly. 'Additional doorbell camera footage came our way from a householder who'd been away. Phil's going through it as we speak.'

He turned to look across the room. DC Gratton had returned to work that morning and was beavering away at his computer. 'Welcome back,' Bliss said, striding towards him. 'I trust you and your betrothed had a good holiday.'

The DC looked up from the monitor and gave a wide smile. 'We did, thanks. Plenty of sun, sand, and... Sangria.'

'Yeah, I was thinking you didn't look very tanned,' Bliss observed drily.

'I'm a shade person.'

'In that case, you should've stayed here. The clouds offer loads of shade. Oh, and thanks for my leaving present. Inspired, mate.'

Gratton's gift had been a large caricature sketch. It depicted Bliss sitting in his garden, a pint of Guinness in one hand, a tumbler of whisky in the other. He wore headphones and his eyes were closed, his parted lips offering up the lyrics to a popular Steely Dan song. By his feet, the Koi in the pond sported pained expressions, their fins wrapped over their heads as if pressing them against their hidden ears to ward off his strangled and tuneless vocals.

'You're welcome,' Gratton replied. 'I'm only sorry to have missed the party, though I'm pleasantly surprised to see you still with us.'

'Cheers. You got anything for me?'

'As it happens, I think I have. Not sure what to make of it, but this might be what you've all been waiting for.'

Bliss leaned in to peer at the monitor. 'Show me what you have, Phil,' he said.

Gratton indicated the image he was fixated on. 'This is the most recent doorbell camera footage. The homeowners have been away, but they read the message we stuffed through their letterbox and checked the night in question. Their camera is motion-activated and seems to be more sensitive in the dark. So while we don't see the vehicle I'm about to show you as it arrives, here's what we do have later on that night at 9.21pm.'

The DC clicked on the mouse to allow the film to run through. It revealed a light grey or silver car with its lights on. The image wasn't good enough for them to distinguish the driver, but a few seconds later a bright white glow appeared at the back of the vehicle, at which point it reversed off screen to the left. Bliss recognised it as a Ford Focus.

'At this point, the camera switches off,' Gratton said. 'But the next clip comes just a couple of minutes later and as you'll see...'

The same car flashed across the monitor, left to right.

Bliss nodded and stroked his chin. 'Okay. I grant you these are unusual movements, but whether they're suspicious or not remains to be seen. Have you checked with the house owner to ask if this vehicle is known to them?'

'I have, and it isn't.'

'Interesting.' He arched his eyebrows. 'And judging by the child-like grin on your boat, I can see you have more for me.'

Gratton did. He switched to GoogleMaps and shifted the mouse pointer. 'This is where the car was parked. Reversing would have taken it off the grass verge and onto these tracks leading into the park close to the path and the first shelter of trees not far from the bridge. The second time we see it, the car is heading out of the close. There are only two ways it could have turned once it hit the junction with Fulbridge Road. Unfortunately, there's no CCTV or ANPR close to the scene, but although the plate wasn't captured on the footage, at least we do have a make, model, and approximate colour to search by. That's my next job.'

Despite the lack of firm details, Bliss was buoyed by the breakthrough. He felt the rigours of the previous day abandoning his mind and body, leaving him feeling renewed and ready to tackle what came next. He sensed this was an important moment. If things went their way, they'd reach a tipping point, where once the shift beneath their feet began, it took on a life of its own and became an unstoppable avalanche.

He clapped his hands together, drawing the attention of the entire unit. 'We have movement,' he said, relaying the fresh information. 'One final push, people. Let's be ready for anything.'

As he grinned and turned to Chandler, his phone rang. It was the hospital. His request to draw a DNA sample from the foetus Nora Bell was carrying had been acted upon as her doctors had met and concluded she was in the eighth week of her pregnancy. Together with swabs from her own cheeks, they could make progress on the investigation into who had raped the young girl and fathered her child. Frances Bell had authorised the procedures from her hotel room.

'I'm nipping off to have a word with Zander Hirst,' he told his colleagues. 'I won't be long.'

'You need company?' Chandler asked.

Bliss shook his head. 'Not this time, Pen. It's a one-person job. I'm not expecting miracles, but let's test the water while we know exactly where to find the little fucker.'

The look she gave him was one of deep concern. 'If you say so. How are you doing after yesterday's scare?'

'I'm fine. Coughed up some ugly black gunge last night, but all good, thanks.'

'I won't ask why you did it. I like to think I would have done the same things in your shoes.'

'I've no doubt you would have. And it all worked out fine. I'll see you when I'm done with our deviant patient.'

He wasn't feeling at all hopeful when he entered the ward in which Zander Hirst was being cared for since his move down from the Major Trauma Centre. But with the young man fully alert and on the verge of being discharged from hospital, Bliss wanted to tackle this third stage of the identification process himself.

The lad and his parents had been told by the family liaison officer assigned to the assault victim to expect a visit from a detective, and as expected, their glares turned instantly hostile when Bliss brandished his warrant card.

Zander Hirst was nothing if not direct. 'What do you want with me?' he said, his tone frosty and aggressive. The boy was lean, his face pockmarked with acne scars.

'Two things,' Bliss replied. 'First of all, I'm here to tell you that prior to your discharge two of my colleagues will visit you to complete a formal statement in relation to the assault on you.'

'Yeah, by that bitch Patsy Bell,' the lad sneered forcefully. 'You better bang her the fuck up, man.'

Bliss told him to save any outbursts or details for another time. 'The other reason I'm here is to ask if you will submit to a DNA test. It's a simple procedure, requiring a quick swab of the inside of your mouth cheeks. It'll take no more than a few seconds.'

'My son's doing nothing of the sort,' Zander's father said, shooting to his feet. 'I know our rights and you can't force him to.'

Bliss turned to the man and said, 'That's correct. Not even if I arrest him, which I'm perfectly willing to do. But at this stage, we don't need to go that far provided Zander agrees to the test willingly.'

'Arrest him?' Zander's father was outraged by the suggestion. 'He's the bloody victim here.'

'Of the assault? Yes, quite possibly. That's being dealt with by my colleagues and is not why I'm asking for your son's DNA.'

'Well, I don't care what you want it for. He's not doing it.'

'Your son is of legal age to make that decision for himself.' Bliss turned to the young man sitting propped up against a stack of pillows wearing a Peterborough United shirt, training bottoms and white socks. 'Well?' he asked.

'Tell me *why* you want my DNA?' Hirst demanded to know, folding his arms across his chest. 'And what's all this bollocks about arresting me?'

After a short pause, during which he made a point of glancing at Hirst's parents, Bliss said, 'You want me to explain myself here and now, with them here?'

'Yeah. Whatever. I don't care. I ain't done nothing wrong.'

Bliss abhorred the use of double negatives, but for once he kept his thoughts on the subject to himself. 'Very well. Zander Hirst, an allegation has been made against you and we suspect you of having penetrative sexual intercourse with a minor. Due to the girl's age and medical condition, we don't believe she was able to consent, so we're dealing with the matter as rape. As a consequence of that rape, the girl in question is pregnant. A DNA test will tell us if you are the father as has been alleged.'

He shut down the angry retorts and frenzied exclamations from both parents. Angling his body away from them and engaging the lad only, he lowered his head and said, 'You still say you did nothing wrong, Zander? Then prove it. Go on, be a real man.'

At the end of a long career during which he had witnessed just about every kind of reaction from suspects, this one still had the capacity to surprise him. He could scarcely believe it when Hirst not only nodded in agreement but did so with a beaming smile on his face.

'I told you, I ain't got nothing to hide. Do your swab, mate. But tell me something first. Is this why that soapy bitch smashed me over the head with an iron bar? Because she thought I'd put her mong sister up the spout?'

Bliss resisted the urge to wrap both hands around Hirst's throat and squeeze until the little prick's face turned blue. 'Save all that for later,' he said through teeth that almost refused to part. 'Please just confirm that you are agreeing to the DNA swabs being taken.'

'Yeah. Do it. Get it over with. And then you can all leave me the fuck alone.'

Both curious and suspicious, Bliss couldn't help but ask one more question. 'Are you going along with this because you're hoping the DNA won't come back as yours or because you genuinely had nothing to do with this young girl?'

Zander Hirst gave the question some thought. 'Because I'm innocent,' he said. Then he frowned, half closed one eye and seemed to consider his response, before breaking out into another huge grin. 'Or maybe it's because if I was to do something like that, I'd be clever enough to wear a condom.'

Bliss felt his expression freeze. How were monsters like Hirst created? Creatures with no conscience or empathy. The kid smiled again and threw in a wink this time. 'Either way,' he added. 'You'll never know.'

FORTY-TWO

BLISS HAD SELDOM SEEN his partner so incandescent with rage after he told her about his hospital visit. 'Seriously, Jimmy,' Chandler said. 'Can we hire someone to beat the shit out of him when he's back on the streets?'

He laughed and said, 'We could always do it ourselves. Finish the job Patricia Bell started.'

'You've had worse ideas.'

He understood she was merely venting. Chandler talked a good game, and her fury was genuine and fierce, but she would never cross that line. Not even for a complete scrote like Zander Hirst. He, on the other hand…

'The little halfwit was so smug about it,' Bliss continued. 'And all while his mother gazed adoringly at her little soldier and his father stood there chuckling at his son's antics. When he clocked me looking at him in obvious disgust, the man just shrugged it off.'

'Did you say anything?'

Bliss nodded. 'I said, "Boys, eh? One minute they're kicking a ball around in the back garden or playing conkers and the next they're raping disabled children." I might as well have saved my breath. He just carried on standing there like the useless fat lump he is. Is it any wonder his kid turned out to be such a worthless piece of shit?'

Chandler swallowed down her anger and somehow raised a thin smile. 'Well, at least we've made some headway in your absence. Some good news to wash away the foul taste of your experience.'

'Did Phil come up trumps?'

Nodding, she said, 'He did. With bells on. He's off checking something else out, but wait until you hear this. The silver Focus is owned by Platinum Standard Cars.'

'What?!' Bliss was incredulous. 'Are you telling me this motor is sitting on their forecourt?'

'Not quite. Phil called Jacob Nash earlier to ask about it. He wasn't in the office, but that dozy twat you and I saw when we paid them a visit told Phil it was one of their courtesy cars.'

Bliss sighed and put a hand to his head. 'I can't believe the motor we wanted to trace was under our noses all the time.'

'I know. So... ah, here's Phil now. He can do the honours.'

DC Gratton had just returned to the incident room. He quickly explained that he had also asked Natalie, the Platinum Standard Cars receptionist, for a complete list of vehicles owned by the company. She had muted the call for a few minutes and when she came back to him, reeled off the details of their motors up for sale, plus two more courtesy cars and a van.

'So, here's where it gets even more interesting,' Gratton said, enjoying his moment in the spotlight. 'We got this far because a silver Ford Focus was picked up by an ANPR camera on the A1(M) just outside Stamford at 9.57 that same Friday night. That gave us a plate, which in turn led to Platinum Standard. I followed up by going through CCTV at the Stamford junction and was able to pick up the Focus again on the road leading out to Ryhall. It didn't reappear on the next available camera, but even so, we have a rough idea where it must have stopped. No sighting of it after that on ANPR, but the Ford is new enough to have GPS, which means that once we get our hands on its data we'll be laughing.'

'Well done, Phil,' Bliss said. 'That's bloody good work, old son. Did you get a RIPA request signed off?'

'Yep. All done. With an urgent rush alongside it.'

'Good stuff. But here's a thought… what if this wasn't the first or last time one of them used a courtesy car for something like this? Add a note to the request for the GPS data stored on all their not-for-sale motors.'

With Gratton enthusiastically working on the action, Bliss pulled Chandler, Ansari, and Virgil to one side. 'I didn't see this coming,' he admitted, feeling a little breathless. 'I have to say, I'd pretty much dismissed Banks, Dixon, and Nash from my thoughts concerning what might have happened to McKenzie. My money was on Hector Karagiannis. It seemed likely to me that it all centred around a diamond smuggling operation that ended up disastrously somehow. Tell me honestly, were any of you as convinced as I was?'

All three nodded and DC Virgil said, 'I think we all agreed it was the most likely hypothesis so far, boss. I don't think you or we completely disregarded that trio, but the connection to the diamonds and a genuine gangster known for casual violence seemed like the best option.'

'Thanks,' Bliss said. 'I can't say I've felt entirely sound in my judgement of late, but that makes me feel a bit better. Even so, where does this leave us?'

'Have we checked out their alibis for Friday night?' Ansari asked.

Chandler shook her head. 'As far as I know, Nash wasn't asked for one because he was never in the frame. Banks and Dixon told us they were at home, but at the time we first spoke with them they weren't suspects, either. Given we were short staffed and so busy, nobody has had time to speak with their wives to confirm.'

'I made the decision to set that action aside,' Bliss said, though he didn't think it would take them further. Family alibis were notoriously unreliable. 'But let's get that done as soon as. What else?'

DC Virgil thought he'd spotted a lapse. 'All along, we've worked under the belief that whoever assaulted Stuart McKenzie also murdered Roger Craig. So surely we need their alibis for Sunday night as well.'

'True, but same result, I suspect. Their wives will be well coached by this time.'

'This might help,' said DC Gratton, rejoining them. 'In the early hours of the morning two Saturdays ago, the van registered to Platinum Standard was picked up by the same ANPR camera on the A1(M). I was then able to follow its path, which took it towards Stamford in the same direction as the Focus did on the Friday night.'

'None of them live out that way, boss,' Ansari said. 'So why would any of them be out there, especially in the early hours? What's in that location to draw them?'

'I had a quick look at GoogleMaps,' Gratton said. 'Once you get through the residential properties there are various sports grounds and fields, with some farmland between there and Ryhall itself. But there was one place that caught my eye, and that was a storage facility.'

'Now you're talking,' Bliss said. 'That sounds promising.'

'Exactly what I thought, boss. Though the open land is also interesting. I mean, if we're looking at one of them disposing of McKenzie's body, it has to be a viable option.'

'You're not wrong. And Phil, well done again. This feels like something solid for us to get stuck into.'

Gratton smiled. 'Thanks, boss. The GPS data is going to be crucial.'

Bliss agreed and felt a churning of excitement brewing inside his stomach. 'In the meantime, let's consider the likely scenarios,' he said. 'If it's the storage area, what does that suggest?'

Chandler took the chance to say her piece. 'If we're right about the two visits and the first was to dump McKenzie's body, then what's the second journey about?'

'And why the change of vehicles?' Ansari asked.

Bliss responded with the first thing that came to mind. 'The second visit was to bring something bulky to put the body in, hence the need for a van.'

DC Virgil nodded. 'That fits. If they didn't mean to kill McKenzie, then they wouldn't have been prepared to bury him. Maybe whoever did it drove the body out to an area they knew and left it somewhere, just to make sure it was hidden from view, then came back, loaded up the van with tools and maybe a sheet of tarpaulin and some rope… that kind of thing.'

Bliss gave that some thought. It made sense. While it was more time-consuming to make two trips, it was the safer option to get rid of the body as soon as possible. He followed the idea through and realised they were missing something crucial. 'Hold on a moment. Why did neither vehicle get picked up by the camera on their way back?'

'Perhaps they took a different route,' Ansari suggested.

'No, it's much simpler than that,' Gratton told them. 'The cameras don't share the same pole. They're in different locations. And the southbound camera is on the northern side of the junction, which means it couldn't pick up the vehicles if they came back the same way. I checked.'

WHAT DIES INSIDE US

'Fuck me, you're on the ball today,' Bliss said with an appreciative laugh. 'That holiday clearly did you the world of good. This detecting lark is a piece of piss for you at the moment.'

Gratton shrugged. 'I reckon my mentor must be rubbing off on me, boss.'

'Well, I like to think I can occasionally inspire people.'

'Oh, no I meant Penny. Sorry, boss.'

When their laughter subsided, Bliss handed Chandler his bank debit card and got her to make a Deliveroo order from Five Guys for cheeseburgers and fries all round, together with soft drinks of choice. They used the estimated forty-minute waiting time to get stuck back into work. Bliss ran through their approach once the GPS data had come through. He suggested putting surveillance teams on Banks, Dixon, and Nash. If one of them headed out towards Stamford, the watchers would follow in the hope of catching them in the same location as Stuart McKenzie's body. If not, they'd analyse the vehicle data to see precisely where it led them.

As a group, they debated whether they'd have enough to make arrests, ultimately agreeing it was too soon to make that call. They'd need to be patient, and as nobody else looked to be in imminent danger from any of the three men, the team could afford to wait for a better opening. Discussing the many ways in which Operation Sandpiper might steer them, each contributed in terms of suggestions and observations. Plans were made depending on where the different paths led.

After lunch, the unit dispersed into their usual partnerships, except for DC Ansari, who stuck close to Bliss and Chandler. Bliss reported to DCI Warburton and the new DCS, Marion Fletcher. He also arranged for surveillance specialists to locate and stick to Michael Banks, Grant Dixon, and Jacob Nash. Later, with his mid-afternoon cup of hot chocolate still steaming on his desk,

Bliss took a call from the DS leading the watchers. Banks and Dixon were under observation, but of Nash there was no sign.

'His motor is parked outside his house,' Detective Sergeant Reynolds confirmed. 'So's his wife's. My team caught sight of her in the garden, but they've yet to lay eyes on him.'

Bliss thought about it and quickly made a decision. 'I'll give him a bell. Tell him we want a chat sooner rather than later. If I can persuade him to come to HQ, you can pick him up from there.'

When Nash failed to answer his phone, Bliss left a message asking him to call back as a matter of some urgency. He then asked DC Ansari to see if she could trace his device, which was picked up by a phone mast close to the vicinity of his home address.

'Has he had any messages or calls today from either Banks or Dixon?' Bliss asked.

A few keystrokes later Ansari came back with an answer. 'Nothing, boss. He had one from Platinum Standard, presumably the receptionist trying to find out where he was. But that didn't last long enough for them to have spoken.'

'Voicemails?'

'Yes. Three, no, four from the same number. And… yeah, they're all from his wife.'

'His wife?' The information had taken Bliss by surprise. 'So maybe he's not at home after all.'

Ansari nodded. 'Sounds likely. You want me to play the voicemails?'

Bliss gave the nod and Ansari slipped on her over-ear head-phones. Half a minute later she swivelled in her chair. 'His wife is looking for him, Jimmy. She left her first message late on Saturday night. She sounded pretty casual asking where he was and what time he'd be home, complaining about him leaving the house without a word. The next was early yesterday morning, and this time she's clearly angry with him. In the last two, again left yesterday, she sounds concerned about his welfare.'

'Has he done a runner or is he also missing?' Chandler asked what they were all wondering.

'Let the surveillance team know, Gul,' Bliss said after clearing his throat. 'Tell them to stand by as we need to give this some urgent thought.'

No sooner had he issued the command than DC Virgil shot to his feet on the other side of the room. The young officer pirouetted on the spot and came bounding across the floor. 'Boss,' he said, his cheeks flushing red. 'I just got DNA confirmation from the lab. We know who the father of Nora Bell's baby is.'

FORTY-THREE

N OT HAVING A DIRECT line-of-sight observational post was immensely frustrating for a surveillance team. Without the benefit of an ideal position, they had to rely on experience and ingenuity, together with a knack for making the most of any good fortune that came their way.

Along the short length of the close on which Michael Banks lived, not a single vehicle was parked either on the kerb or the grass verges. Assuming that was usual and expected, Detective Sergeant Tom Reynolds was faced with an immediate operational decision. The usual play was to move some kind of utilities vehicle into position, but when looking at the plan of the location he realised it would be too close and far too obvious, and likely to prompt neighbours to question their presence. But he noticed a streetlight immediately opposite the entrance to the street and smiled to himself. He then ordered a team to park up by the tall post and for one of his officers to remove the casing to expose the electronics and pretend to be running a diagnostic check while a colleague remained in the back with a camera trained towards their target area. In addition, he had a motorcyclist circling the local roads ready to move into a following position the moment

Banks was seen leaving the property. This would allow those with the van to clear the area and follow at their leisure.

That was the plan, at least. And less than an hour into the operation, it was put to the test when Michael Banks's Audi nosed its way out of the gated drive. The officer inside the van trained binoculars on the vehicle and confirmed Banks as the driver while alerting the motorcyclist to be ready for the SUV to emerge onto Bretton Way, from which it could go only south-bound towards the Thorpe Wood Interchange roundabout.

With perfect timing, the motorcycle tucked in behind, the rider relaying information to his colleagues. On the A47 Soke Parkway where it met the A15, the van took over as the primary vehicle. It followed Banks further east until the Audi turned left at the Dogsthorpe Star Pit. The van driver immediately called up the bike to take the lead again while it continued on, intending to find a way to eventually draw level or perhaps get ahead. Reacting to transmitted directions, the van hung a left at Eye Green and took narrow minor roads in the general direction that would eventually bring them close to their colleague's location.

When the Audi stopped at the beginning of Turves Drain on an isolated patch of land, the motorcyclist issued a warning for the van to hold back as there was no obvious point for it to secrete itself.

'I'm keeping my distance but have eyes on,' DC Marsh said across the operation team's communications. 'Target is stationary but remains inside the vehicle. He's alone, but this looks like a meet. Be aware of an unknown vehicle about to enter the plot. Keep well away because if you find me on the map you'll see there's only one way in and out. I've secured my bike behind a row of heavy gorse bushes, and I'm making my way along behind them to get a bit closer. I won't get near enough to hear anything, but I'm secure here. I'll take video and stills.'

Back at the team's control centre, Reynolds was focussed on the GoogleMap view of the area. Marsh was spot on – there was no way anybody else could get close. Analysing the surrounding area, he weighed up his options before directing the van to sit tight on White Post Road as close to the junction with Green Road without drawing attention to themselves. Given these were the only two routes out for the Audi and whoever Banks might be meeting with, he considered themselves covered. But he was also interested in the meeting itself and put in a call to DI Bliss.

'What do you need me to do?' he asked, having explained the situation. 'I can focus our attention on Banks and bring in a team to pick up the newcomer when they leave. But I can spare only one team in one vehicle. Sorry, but that's all I have at my disposal unless you want in on it.'

'Thanks, Tom,' Bliss said with enthusiasm. 'I'm about to make an arrest unconnected to this operation, but I'll get DCs Gratton and Ansari out there. Put them and your spare pairing on who-ever Banks meets with and leave the others in place to focus on your priority target.'

Less than five minutes later the van driver noted a Range Rover gliding past heading in the right direction. Shortly after-wards he confirmed it had not turned onto Green Road and looked as if it was about to join Michael Banks. The registration number came back to a company name, which DS Reynolds ordered looking into. Meanwhile, Marsh, still tucked behind the dense bushes, let everybody know that the newcomer had pulled up alongside the Audi. Its driver, a woman who looked to be in her mid-forties and who wore a purple suede jacket, and Banks exited their vehicles at the same time. The two talked for just under twenty minutes before leaving the way they had come.

Banks drove back into the city, pulling up in the car park adjacent to the Gordon Arms pub in the shadow of the Nene

Parkway flyover in Orton Longueville. Prior to that, the team surveilling the home of Grant Dixon piped up to alert others that their target was on the move. They followed him the short distance to the same pub. Reynolds ordered a male officer from one pairing and a female officer from another to enter the Gordon Arms and sit on the two men. He relaxed, knowing he didn't have to either advise or warn them further when it came to this aspect of the job. Both officers were hugely experienced, and this was their meat and drink.

Meanwhile, the Range Rover ended up parked on the road outside the Haycock Manor hotel in Wansford, to the west of the city. The driver had gone inside, and shortly afterwards both Gratton and Ansari were at the bar sipping soft drinks in an ideal location to keep an eye on the entrance.

The team inside the Gordon Arms reported back. They were unable to hear the details of the conversation that took place between Banks and Dixon, but at one point it had become animated, and Banks had raised a hand to quieten his friend. They had two pints each before heading off back to their respective homes.

After an hour loitering at the bar, DCs Ansari and Gratton returned to their vehicle having not laid eyes on the woman who had earlier met with Grant Dixon.

Of Jacob Nash there remained no sight.

FORTY-FOUR

THE MOMENT PETER ALINSON opened his front door, Bliss could tell from the man's distraught expression that he knew exactly why the two detectives were standing on his doorstep. The social worker moved back into the hallway of the ground-floor flat, his shoulders collapsing beneath the weight of applied knowledge.

'How?' he asked simply as they made their way into a small, square living room devoid of style or charm.

'DNA,' Bliss said, positioning himself in the doorway.

A deep frown revealed the man's confusion. 'But my DNA isn't on record anywhere. I know that for certain.'

'True enough,' Chandler confirmed with a sharp nod. 'But you have a brother, Mr Alinson. Jake. And his DNA *is* held in our database following several arrests down the years.'

All remaining air escaped Alinson in a single, lengthy exhalation. He fell into a tired-looking armchair, shaking his head disconsolately. 'Of course. Dear old Jake. My long-estranged and troubled sibling. The gift that keeps on giving.'

'Naturally, his DNA is not a direct paternal match for the sample we took from Nora's baby, but it was close enough to suggest a brother might provide the connection we were looking for. Imagine our surprise when your name popped up in our enquiries.'

The man jerked his head up, renewed hope in his glazed expression. 'But without my own DNA, where does that leave you?'

'I can answer that,' Bliss volunteered. 'Peter Alinson, I am arresting you on suspicion of the rape of Nora Bell. You do not have to say anything. But it may harm your defence if you do not mention when questioned something which you later rely on in court. Anything you do say may be given in evidence. The arrest is necessary to protect a child and to allow the prompt and effective investigation.'

He usually left making arrests to other members of the team, but if this was to be his last, then it was at least a memorable and important one.

Not long earlier at Thorpe Wood, Bliss had argued for the rape charge. DCS Fletcher and a CPS lawyer had concerns in respect of Nora Bell's participation in the act itself. They reasoned that Alinson might try to claim consent and therefore expect a lesser charge of sexual activity with a child and not rape, but he cited the girl's diminished capacity due to her medical condition, and her resulting inability to give proper consent. They had subsequently agreed to charge accordingly and put their faith in the CPS later making it stick.

Chandler beckoned the shattered man back to his feet and immediately cuffed him. As she slipped them over his wrists, she whispered softly in his ear, 'You are one sick individual. You betrayed the very child you had a duty of care for.'

'To be precise,' Alinson declared loftily, 'that duty of care was to Frances Bell. My remit might have extended to her children, but Nora Bell was not specifically named.'

'You think that's going to matter with the Nonce Finder Generals waiting for you inside?' Bliss said to him. 'You have heard of them, haven't you, Peter? You'll find them lurking in most prisons, especially Cat A. To be blunt, they're a bunch of angry men with pent-up rage who simply don't give a shit about anything or anyone, and who get their kicks by torturing perverts like you. Raping a kid is bad enough, but when they learn that kid was also disabled… I can only imagine the things they'll take great pleasure in putting you through.'

From nowhere, Alinson found a reserve of courage. Enough to stand his ground by sticking out his chin and saying, 'Even if I did what you say I did, and even if I'm convicted of it, I'll make sure I'm in a segregated unit or wing, don't you worry about that. I'll enrol on a training programme and be a model prisoner.'

Bliss met his cool gaze. 'You think there aren't different categories of sickness even inside the nonce units? Admittedly, most of them won't be bothered by the rape of a fourteen-year-old, but for some the kid being disabled might just be too much to stomach. And even if they are all as twisted as you, prison procedures can get sloppy. I'd be astonished if you didn't encounter an ODC every now and again.'

He saw the query in Alinson's frown. 'An Ordinary Decent Criminal,' he explained. 'The word will spread among them about you, Peter. And the Nonce Finder Generals will carve out a way to spend some time alone with you.'

That was the last any of them spoke until Alinson was booked in at the custody suite, Bliss repeating the charge for which the man had been arrested. After processing, Bliss and Chandler grabbed a hot drink while they waited for legal representation to arrive.

'Is that true what you told him?' Chandler asked as they made their way upstairs from the canteen. 'About the Nonce Finder Generals, I mean.'

Bliss grinned and shook his head. 'I don't know if their little club has a formal name or a membership list,' he said with a chuckle. 'But whatever category prison he winds up in, I want him to live in fear of meeting the wrong bloke at the wrong time in the wrong place. I only hope it happens sooner rather than later, because if ever a monster deserved a bloody good hiding, it's Peter-fucking-Alinson.'

DC Virgil had been updating the crime logs and answering phones while he held down the fort in charge of a team of civilians and uniformed officers. Bliss bought him a coffee from the vending machine out in the corridor, after which the newest member of the unit took a couple of swallows of his drink while he composed himself.

'There's a lot to update you on,' he admitted. 'What do you want first?'

Bliss gave him the nod. 'Sounds good. Where are we on surveillance?'

Virgil coughed into his hand. 'Gul and Phil are sitting on the hotel in Wansford. They're due to be replaced within the next ten minutes or so by a pairing from the surveillance team and will head straight back here afterwards. Banks and Dixon are tucked up at home for the time being. It's fair to assume they met at the pub to discuss Dixon's earlier meeting with Range Rover Woman.'

'Speaking of whom,' Bliss interrupted, 'do we have an ID on her yet, Alan?'

Virgil shook his head. 'Not so far, boss. I'm still chasing up the company that owns the vehicle.'

'Description?'

The DC consulted his notepad. 'Average height and build, shoulder length hair, most likely in her forties and wearing a purple suede jacket.'

Bliss thought back to the woman he'd confronted on the towpath by the river. He still felt some lingering anger over her mention of Molly and Max. 'I think she'll probably end up connecting back to our Greek gangster, but confirmation would be good. I'd like to know her name and address, if only to pay her a surprise visit at some point.'

'I don't think we'll get that from the surveillance, boss. Gul did some discreet checking while she and Phil were having a drink in the bar and confirmed the woman is staying at the hotel under the same company name her wheels are registered to.'

'Okay. In that case, let's have Gul and Phil rejoin us and tell one of them to call off the surveillance. Might as well free them up in case we get movement from either Banks or Dixon.'

'I'll do that and then chase up the company and ID of the driver as soon as I'm done here. Next, I have some good news. We have been granted the authority to access vehicle GPS data and phones. It all came back in a single hit, so we're good to go if I can get some help to sift through it all.'

Bliss nodded. 'No problem. Grab however many people you need. One more thing before you get stuck into that. Did you happen to run those not-for-sale motors through ANPR to see if any of them were picked up by the same camera this past week?'

'The check I ran was right up to the time of my search, boss. No further hits. Why, what's on your mind?'

Bliss grimaced. 'Jacob Nash. We can't locate him, so I was just wondering if one of our suspects had made a run to Stamford over the weekend.'

'You think they've taken him off the map?' Chandler asked, seemingly surprised by the implication.

'I wouldn't rule it out,' he said with a shrug. 'Either that or he may be on the run.'

'I guess. And why hasn't his wife reported him missing?'

'Who knows with these people?' Bliss said. 'But you can bet she called either Banks or Dixon when she got no response to her voicemails, so perhaps they pacified her. Either way, he's still not been spotted, so I'm not going to discount anything at this stage. And that includes the possibility of him being murdered.'

FORTY-FIVE

BLISS LEFT THORPE WOOD later that night as satisfied as he could be about the way the day had panned out and happy with the plans agreed upon for first thing the next morning.

The interview with Peter Alinson had gone better than expected. Confronted by the DNA evidence, he was in no position to complain about the arrest. As anticipated, however, following his meeting with a duty solicitor, he confessed to having sexual intercourse with Nora Bell but denied rape on account of her giving consent.

'She and I spent more time alone together than was perhaps advisable under the circumstances,' he admitted. 'But you've met her. Physically she is no child and believe me she enjoyed the attention. I confess I was drawn to her and flattered by the interest she showed in me. Frances and Patricia trusted me implicitly, and on occasion I volunteered to give them both some respite by agreeing to look after Nora for an hour or so. One thing led to another. I realise I took advantage of the situation, which was wrong of me. But if at any point I had given thought to her age, I would of course not taken things any further. The thing you have to understand is that when we were together, I never once considered her to be a child.'

'Physically, I can understand why,' Bliss told him, biting down on the many truths he would have preferred to ram home. 'But every time she spoke that must surely have jolted you back to reality. Looking like she's in her late teens is one thing, but her behaviour and manner of speaking is that of an eight-year-old. How could that not have dented any initial allure?'

'I truly never saw her that way,' Alinson said.

'So, you simply considered it the acceptable thing to do? Having sexual relations with this young girl.'

'I told you, I never thought of Nora like that. Here was this attractive teen who was warm and inviting and who clearly found me attentive and exciting. It was impossible to resist under those circumstances, especially as we had already formed a close bond.'

'One that you exploited.'

He made no reply.

Bliss took a breath, hoping to keep calm. 'And it never occurred to you that you might need to use protection.'

For the first time, Alinson's cheeks reddened. Having sex with an underage girl seemed not to have embarrassed him, but slipping up on using contraception did. It made Bliss fume all the more.

'Ah, there you have me,' the man said, as if he were guilty of nothing else but this single oversight. 'I freely admit the sheer excitement overwhelmed me on a couple of occasions. I did use a condom before and since, but I admit to being caught up in the moment once or twice. That's what a body like that can do to a man.'

'Thank you for confirming the regular occurrence of your sexual abuse, Mr Alinson,' Chandler said, unable to disguise her revulsion.

From that point on, the demonstrably chagrined child rapist chose to make no comment to most of their remaining questions.

His argument for the lesser charge was refused, rape being confirmed along with a request for Alinson to be held on remand pending trial.

Disgusted by the man and feeling as if they needed showers to wash away his taint, both Bliss and Chandler were nonetheless delighted to have the repugnant creature off the streets.

Returning to the team for a final catch up, the GPS information from the vehicles had been illuminating. The courtesy car run on the night Stuart McKenzie went missing had completed its first journey at the premises of a company called Lincs Storage on the road leading to Ryhall. It was there for just shy of five minutes before heading back to the yard in Fengate. Shortly afterwards, the company van made a brief trip to a second storage company at the other end of the Fengate industrial centre before proceeding to the one close to Stamford. It remained there longer this time, but after twenty minutes it also made the return journey.

Some of this they already knew, but the team was further enthused by the records showing a second round-trip journey at the approximate time Roger Craig was murdered. On this occasion there was no visit to Stamford, just a trip logged between Fengate and Werrington and back. Finally, there had been a fourth and equally revealing drive taken by the same van just two days ago. The GPS records graphically revealed the route it had followed out of Fengate before stopping off in the village of Glinton close to a property they knew to be Jacob Nash's home. It then continued to the same storage facility in Lincolnshire, taking a route that avoided the A1(M) and therefore also avoiding the ANPR camera. The team drew the inevitable conclusions from that specific item of data.

Nothing from relevant phone records matched, but none of them were truly surprised to discover that the killer had opted to leave their mobile at home. Firstly, to go about their business without anyone being able to track or confirm where they were, but also with the intention of establishing an alibi should anything not go to plan. In spite of this, the evidence not only convinced Bliss he had been right to suspect what had happened to Nash, but also persuaded every member of the team that they had enough to make arrests.

Bliss let everybody go on time, reminding them of their early start the following day. He remained behind to arrange back-up units to rendezvous at the station at 5.30am the next morning with the expectation of making 6.30 arrests at the homes of both Michael Banks and Grant Dixon. With authorisation from above, he felt calm and relaxed as he drove home.

He took Thorpe Wood Road before slipping down onto the Nene Parkway, easing across the river before taking the next slip road down to a mini-roundabout and then turning right onto Oundle Road. The light at Orton Mere turned red as he approached. Bliss activated the Mondeo's handbrake, slipped off his seatbelt, exited the car, walked back the way he had come past two other vehicles, before hammering the side of his right hand on the roof of a grey Range Rover.

'I've had a change of mind,' he said to the driver as the window slid effortlessly down. 'Instead of going home, I've decided to visit the same place where you and I enjoyed a lovely chat the other day. I suggest you join me there.'

With that, he went back to his car and with the lights having turned green and horns blaring from behind, he used a gap between oncoming traffic to make a right turn. He came to a halt in Orton Lock car park close to Osier Lake. After locking up, he cut across the railway tracks, strolled by the mere and headed along the path leading to the mooring points.

A couple of minutes went by. At first Bliss wondered if he might have scared the woman off, but the next time he looked up he saw her appear from behind the hedgerow and amble towards him as if she had not a care in the world.

'I was hoping to bump into you again,' Bliss said, keeping some distance between him and Range Rover woman.

'This encounter isn't exactly by accident,' she said without rancour.

'No, I didn't think your surveillance technique could be quite that obvious. And you're a brave woman to confront me a second time on your own, I'll give you that.'

The woman, both hands wedged deep into the pockets of the same purple jacket, gave a languid shrug. 'Really? You think so? In what way, might I ask?'

Bliss steadied himself, reining in his anger. 'Because the last time we spoke you made veiled threats against my companion and my dog. I don't usually allow people to get away with that. And certainly not for a second time, if that's what your intention is.'

This time Range Rover woman nodded. 'I can empathise with that. But just so's we understand each other, Inspector, if there was a threat it was by implication only. And deliberately so. I wouldn't have carried through on it.'

Bliss wasn't so sure. He raised his head, met the woman's unswerving gaze. 'Not personally, perhaps. But you might have ordered it done.'

She shook her head, her bob falling perfectly back into place afterwards. 'No. Not on this occasion. I prefer to avoid involving children and animals altogether because it tends to make people emotional and unreasonable. Those are two things I steer clear of if I can. Besides, I was genuinely trying to keep you off balance long enough for me to take appropriate action elsewhere.'

Bliss angled his head to one side. 'I see. You were looking to buy time. To have me rethink my strategy, hoping it might work in your favour. Tell me, whatever your name is, are you the reason Jacob Nash is missing?'

This brought to her face a look of interest rather than the anxiety he'd hoped to see. 'So, he *has* gone AWOL?' she said pensively. 'I guessed as much. In fact, that's the main reason I'm here, Inspector. I can see why you might think I'm involved, and I can also understand why you had people following me earlier this afternoon. But I'm here to tell you one last time you're being steered in the wrong direction.'

'Is that so?' Bliss cocked his head and tensed. If things were about to get physical, he wanted to be fully prepared. 'Tell me why and how. Explain yourself if that's why you're really here.'

Range Rover woman rested a lilac fingernail against her lips and had a quick look around before replying. 'You suspect I am in some way connected to the disappearance of both Stuart McKenzie and Jacob Nash. Not true, Inspector. In either case. I freely admit to having words with both men prior to them going missing, but I took no further action beyond our conversations.'

'That doesn't bode well for Grant Dixon,' Bliss said. 'You spoke with him today, so when might we see him go missing?'

The woman studied him for a second or two before smiling. 'Like I told you, Inspector Bliss, my interactions with these men amounted to a bit of verbals only, you understand? Nothing physical. No violence whatsoever. What your people observed earlier today between myself and Grant Dixon is all that you would have seen pass between me and the other two had you been following me at the time. Now, I'm not about to embarrass either of us by suggesting warnings were not given, nor that our efforts might well have stepped up several gears had these men not vanished off the face of the earth when they did. But whatever happened to them had nothing to do with me. Or my boss, for that matter. Believe me or don't believe me, but it happens to be the truth.'

Bliss squinted at her. 'Why would you bother seeking me out to tell me that?'

The question drew a second thin smile. 'Because I could do without you and your colleagues taking any further interest in me. More importantly, so could my boss. I may not be able to point you in the right direction, but I'm here to impress upon you that you are heading the wrong way as things stand. I'm sure none of us wishes to be inconvenienced by you continuing to do so.'

Bliss quickly assessed the situation. It felt right but could just as easily be wrong. 'You say you would prefer us to have no interest in you, but the fact is we had no idea you even existed until you put yourself in the frame.'

The woman shook her head dismissively. 'The point is you would have. Eventually. You know about my boss, and you're starting to look closely at him. It's my job to ensure that doesn't continue, and I take my responsibilities seriously.'

'So, your only connection to these men, your boss's only connection to them, is the proposed casino. Is that what you're telling me?'

She regarded him with a mixture of surprise and appreciation. 'I don't recall telling you who I work for, Inspector.'

'You didn't. But let's just say for the sake of argument that I'm right. If your boss is who I think he is, your connection to these men involves the new casino and nothing more.'

'It does. If, that is, my boss is indeed the person you think he is.'

'And you expect me to believe that?'

'I don't.'

'Uh-huh. And are you going to tell me what you spoke about with McKenzie, Nash, and Dixon?'

'I'm not.'

Bliss huffed and shook his head in irritation. 'Well, this *has* been informative. We must do it again sometime.'

The woman raised a hand to quell the protest. 'All right, all right. Let me play along and assume for the moment that what you say is true, but remember, I admit nothing. Our business with them may have run into a bit of a stumbling block. There might have been one or two disputes and disagreements along the way. That would not be unusual in our world.'

'Okay,' Bliss said, remaining watchful. 'Say I accept that. It doesn't explain why you had words with Jacob Nash, because he is not part of the proposed casino enterprise.'

After a slight pause, the woman replied, 'You are incredibly well informed, which is of some concern, I have to say. However, if you'll allow me to speculate as part of this little game of Cluedo we're playing, Mr Nash may have been acting as a liaison on behalf of his friends. Much as I do for my boss. That could explain why he was involved. But once again I must insist if either of them has come to harm, it has nothing to do with us.'

It was Bliss's turn to smile. 'Oh, we already knew that.'

Range Rover woman tried her level best to disguise her disbelief but failed. Bliss saw the truth flicker in her eyes, a slight pulse of the left cheek. 'Is that so?' she muttered, clearly distracted.

'It is.' Bliss was starting to enjoy himself.

'I'm surprised to hear that,' she admitted. 'But it does suggest you do know who *is* responsible.'

Bliss slowly nodded. He pulled his jacket tight to his chest and passed closer to the woman as he started making his way back to the car. 'If I were you, I'd stay tuned,' he said. 'I have a feeling you'll find out sooner than you might have expected.'

FORTY-SIX

THAT EVENING FELT AS if it defied all logic by becoming warmer as it went on. The lunchtime burger and fries had filled Bliss enough that he dined on dry cereal coupled with a pint of Guinness. He spent some time in the garden, eyes on the Koi and goldfish, while his hand gently massaged Max's head. The dog barely shifted, seeming to enjoy the feel of human contact, which hadn't seemed likely when the two got to know each other at the Wood Green animal shelter in Godmanchester.

When the night eventually set in and it began to cool, the pair moved indoors. Bliss wasn't in the right frame of mind for TV or a film, so he spent some time flipping through his vinyl collection. Then he remembered that Molly had installed Spotify on his television. He switched it on, ran the app and scrolled through the playlists she had made for him. He settled on Postmodern Jukebox, who covered songs by other artists but in a completely different style. The band utilised the wonderful voices of a whole range of female vocalists, and he had become particularly fond of their version of Radiohead's *Creep*, featuring Hailey Reinhart, and Aerosmith's *Dream On*, the soaring vocals beautifully performed by Morgan James. He loved the retro feel with jazz undertones and lost himself in the pleasing melodies while admiring the range and tone of the singers. The upbeat Toto song, *Africa*, pulled him out of his reverie long enough to reflect on other matters.

By the time Bliss had left work, Peter Alinson was awaiting transportation to the city's own Category B prison where he would spend his custodial remand before most likely being transferred to Perry in Cambridgeshire, if found guilty. HMP Littlehey was the largest sex offender prison in the whole of Europe, and Bliss had no doubt Alinson's request for segregation from even his own kind would be granted. If he made it that far. Peterborough's prison was well run, but procedural loopholes were there to be exploited by the ruthless and determined, and he very much hoped at least one such villain would make his feelings towards a child rapist known.

Thinking back to the plan devised for the following morning, Bliss was confident of the swift and relatively confrontation-free detainment of both Banks and Dixon. Although he believed one of them to be a killer, neither was known to have form for violence and were considered low risk in relation to the possibility of firearms use – if the intelligence was accurate. Taking them early in the morning would hopefully find them sleeping, or at the very least dazed and confused by the sudden rush of police officers into their home.

The interview element had been discussed at great length. The decision they all agreed upon was to have DCs Gratton and Virgil in with Michael Banks, leaving Chandler and DC Ansari to tackle Grant Dixon. Bliss and DCI Warburton had elected to watch via a feed to monitors in an adjoining room. He ran the various plays through his head, imagining the conversations that were likely to take place – if at all. He assumed neither man would comment other than when advised to do so by their solicitors.

The team had spoken at length about this aspect, drawing no conclusions. It was unlikely that either man had criminal lawyers on retainer, though both had successfully used them in the past. His best guess was that they would probably go with the same separate companies, if not the exact same briefs.

Bliss and his colleagues had been even less certain about the potential outcome at the end of the custody period. The evidence was clear, suggesting one of the two men had lost control of an already bad situation. They had used vehicles registered to the car sales company they owned to visit the storage facility outside Stamford. They had done so on three separate occasions. The first and third journeys were closely connected by timeline to the disappearance of both Stuart McKenzie and Jacob Nash. The second remained unexplained, though Bliss still believed the van had been used to transport something large.

Yet what troubled the team was the disconnect between the vehicles, the journeys made, the storage facility, and the two men about to be arrested. Their alibis for the first of those vehicle trips in the courtesy car had them at home with their families. Their phone records appeared to back up their accounts. The same phones suggested they were also at home when the other trips were made. Had the data revealed otherwise, it would have given the interviewing pairs something to go at both men with, despite providing no actual evidence of their involvement. Likewise, the phones being static in Bretton did not mean either of the men were not elsewhere at the time.

It was a grey area. If both Banks and Dixon kept their heads and listened to their solicitors, the case against them would remain circumstantial. Having met them, Bliss had no expectations of either a confession or the pointing of fingers against the other. His team needed additional evidence, the thought of which led him in one direction.

Troubled by the way his mind had begun to twist things negatively, Bliss jumped into the Mondeo and headed north towards Stamford. He took the A1(M) route, knowing his pool car would be recorded by the ANPR camera. It took hardly any time at all before he found himself parked outside Lincs Storage. Behind the secure walls and gated entrance, he spotted rows of containers stacked side-by-side, each large enough to store a moderately sized vehicle. A large two-storey structure off to the left of the compound suggested there were further, smaller containers inside the warehouse-like building. As he stared vacantly at the facility, a troubling thought occurred to him: what if either McKenzie or, more likely, Jacob Nash wasn't dead? What if neither man was? Concentrating on Nash, Bliss considered the very real possibility that the man had simply been spirited away and dumped inside the container, perhaps tied up and gagged to prevent him from creating a commotion. Leaving him to die slowly in isolation was surely easier than murdering him and then secreting his corpse.

In films and on TV shows, he'd often heard the term 'exigent circumstances' bandied about, but there was no such recourse in the UK. His friend in this case was Section 17 of the Police and Criminal Evidence Act. It opened the way for him to enter the unit and carry out a search without warrant on the basis that he believed life and limb were in danger and could potentially be saved by his actions. It was one of those 'begging for forgiveness afterwards rather than asking for permission beforehand' situations, and Bliss had always enjoyed the implied leniency the saying had afforded him in the past.

Without further internal debate, Bliss threw open the door, locked up and ran across the road. On one wall by the gates was a keypad panel, which he assumed customers used to gain entry as they pleased. Beneath it was an intercom, with a large button for him to press. He did so, and when he heard a slightly garbled voice asking what he wanted, he held up his warrant card so that it could be seen by a CCTV camera mounted on the other side of the wall. He explained who he was and why he was there. After a brief exchange, during which the woman at the other end of the system appeared to become more confused, a buzzer sounded and a side gate in the same wall clunked as it released its lock. Bliss entered and trotted across to the only illuminated building he could see. As he closed in, a door opened, and a woman dressed in navy blue came out to meet him.

'Sorry, Inspector,' she said, offering a bright smile. 'I couldn't make out half of what you were saying. May I please just see your ID again?'

He showed her his credentials and began to explain one more time and in greater detail. 'I have reason to believe there might be one or possibly two men being held in one of your containers. I have no warrant to show you that will allow me to carry out a search, but Section 17 of PACE allows me to use my discretion if I am convinced that a life is at stake. In this case I do, and I would like to effect entry.'

The woman had initially gasped and clutched both hands to her chest, but as he went on, she began to nod and relax at the same time. 'Not to worry, officer,' she said. 'I've worked security here for over ten years, so this is not the first time I've had Section 17 thrown at me. Tell me, do you have a unit number or name for me?'

Bliss took a breath. 'What's your name, please?'

'It's Davina. Davina Redwood.'

'Okay, Davina, here's the situation. I don't have a name or a number. I can provide you with three possible names if needs be. However, I can point to the precise time the unit was last accessed. If your system works the way I hope it does, the code used to gain entry will include the unit number.'

'Well done.' Redwood flashed a wide smile. 'If you can give me the date and time, then I can tell you which code was used, and from that I'll be able to extrapolate the unit you wish to search.'

Bliss's habit in recent years was to use his phone to photograph relevant screenshots from the case file. He knew he had the GPS data provided by DS Virgil and quickly brought up the gallery. It took only five sweeps sideways to find the image he required. By then he and the security officer had walked across to the building she had emerged from. Seconds later, they were in her office. He gave her the information she needed. No more than a minute had passed before she looked up, her wide smile back in place.

'You want unit 278. It requires both the code entering into a keypad and an actual key to fully release the locking mechanism. I'll come over with you.'

Faltering, concerned about the woman's reaction should they discover two dead bodies inside, Bliss tried to persuade her to give him the skeleton key and the code, leaving him to take care of it himself provided she told him where to find the unit. But Redwood was having none of it; something about her job and her responsibility.

Thankfully, the container was close by. The night was still and silent, their footsteps loud, echoing off the steel structures on either side of them with a metallic clang. As they walked along one of the rows, Bliss thought of a question he ought to have asked. 'Did you happen to get a look at the name of the person renting the storage space?' he asked.

A third smile, accompanied by a knowing nod. 'I did. No flies on me, Inspector. You mentioned before about providing three names. What are they?'

Bliss saw no harm in playing along. 'Michael Banks, Grant Dixon, or Stuart McKenzie.'

Redwood's brow furrowed. 'Hmm. Close, but not quite. The name came back as Sharon McKenzie.'

Of course. It made perfect sense. The man had provided a further layer of security and deception by renting the unit in his wife's name. When they reached the unit 278, the security officer used her key and tapped in the code, but Bliss had her take several paces back as he rolled up the shuttered door. A striplight flickered on automatically, and with the entrance fully open he saw shelving units ranged along both sides of the container. Most were bare, but two of them held a number of cardboard boxes, and on another he spotted a cabinet containing several drawers. Thankfully, there were no bodies on display. But what drew his attention most of all, while at the same time sending a chill racing down his spine, was a chest freezer sitting on the floor at the far end of the container.

It was plugged in, and it was humming.

Bliss looked back over his shoulder at the security officer. 'Stay here,' he said. 'I mean it. Don't come in with me, as you might contaminate a crime scene.'

Redwood nodded; she knew how it went. His mouth felt dry as he walked over to the freezer. He drew in a deep breath, releasing gradually as he gripped a built-in handle. He gave a sharp tug to break the seal before slowly raising the lid. He already knew precisely what he would find inside, yet that didn't prevent him from recoiling as his gaze came to rest on two frozen dead bodies.

FORTY-SEVEN

Bliss summoned the entire team into work, but his first call was to DS Olly Bishop. 'It's your choice entirely, mate, but I thought you might want in on this,' he said simply. 'I couldn't deny you the opportunity.'

They worked through the night. Bliss postponed examining the storage container until the crime scene investigators were done. Rather than wait around aimlessly, he put everyone to work on a case review, seeking any other aspect of the job they might need to complete before carrying out the scheduled arrests. Before leaving Lincs Storage, he had Davina Redwood search through gate security footage, looking to locate video of the van and courtesy car drivers. When he found what they were looking for, he then arranged for the files to be sent to DC Ansari's email address, though he was unhappy with the outcome.

In the early hours of Tuesday morning, with the team gathered in the incident room, Bliss outlined their dilemma. The main problem they had was in identifying which of the two men was responsible, though it was still possible that both were culpable. Picking that apart wasn't going to be easy, so in addition to gathering evidence they also revised the strategy for the interviews based on the evening's findings. When the time came to roll, they were more than ready.

At 6.30am, both Michael Banks and Grant Dixon were in bed at home and disturbed from their slumber by hard thumps on their front door. Neither man resisted and their arrests went off without a hitch, though the officers involved were forced to endure the sharp end of vitriol spat by two enraged wives. Little more than two hours later, the pair were ensconced with their respective solicitors, and thirty minutes after that they were ready to face their first grilling.

Based on additional evidence discovered shortly before the arrests were made, Bliss opted to have the initial interviews run simultaneously with his colleagues sticking to a specific order of questioning. Depending on what was said inside the respective rooms, the interviews would then be suspended, allowing time for the suspect to talk with his solicitor but mainly to provide Bliss and his team with the opportunity to discuss the next phase.

Gratton and Virgil conducted a perfect interview with Grant Dixon, following the revised strategy to the letter, using the pre-prepared questions, and responding with follow-up queries seeking confirmation or clarification. There were different methods to utilise when interviewing. Sometimes you hid your trump card behind a myriad of non-related questions designed to catch the suspect out in a lie. On other occasions, you played it immediately in an attempt to unbalance the person sitting in the chair opposite. Neither approach was right or wrong, you just went with the best fit based on the man or woman being prompted for answers. In this case, Bliss had decided his team should lob a few easy questions out there before quickly moving to the location where two bodies had been stored in a chest freezer.

Bliss looked on with mounting anticipation as DC Gratton asked Dixon to tell them what he knew about Lincs Storage. The man's reaction was one of alarm, his response instantaneous. 'No comment.'

'Your friend and business partner, Stuart McKenzie, rented a storage unit there in his wife's name. What can you tell us about that?'

Same reaction.

'I'm surprised, Mr Dixon,' Gratton said amiably. 'These are soft questions. Easy enough to answer without implicating yourself. You either did or did not know about Mr McKenzie's storage container.'

'No comment.'

DC Virgil opened up a wallet folder and took out a series of 25x20mm photographs. Looking on, Bliss tensed; this was the final piece of evidence his team had earlier managed to dig out. On the screen, Virgil laid one of the photos face up on the table. 'Take a look at this still image, Mr Dixon. You'll see from the registration plate that the first is a courtesy vehicle owned by Platinum Standard Cars, which is one of your companies. Is that correct?'

Dixon leaned over to whisper in his solicitor's ear, who hid her mouth behind her hand when replying. It was all a bit of a charade, as Bliss knew his two detectives would be able to hear what was being said from the other side of the table.

'That's one of the companies I co-own, yes,' Dixon admitted.

'Which makes it one of your vehicles.'

'I don't know them all off by heart.'

'Fair enough. We have confirmed the details, and this vehicle *is* owned by your company.'

'One of my companies' Dixon sniffed and wriggled in his chair.

Virgil flipped over a second sheet. 'Indeed. And in the next photograph, you can clearly see that same vehicle. This still is taken from a camera located by the gate leading into the grounds of Lincs Storage. It was taken on the night of Friday 22nd April this year, less than two weeks ago. Tell us why you were there that night, Mr Dixon.'

Bliss leaned closer to the monitor. Grant Dixon looked genuinely bewildered, and more than a little concerned by what he was looking at.

'Are you trying to say that's me behind the wheel?' the man said, raising his voice and thrusting a finger at the photo.

'Are you saying it isn't?' Gratton asked.

'Too bloody right it isn't, pal.'

Bliss felt excitement build inside his chest. The image showed a figure with their head down, wearing a peaked cap, their jacket collar pulled up around their neck. It was the shot that had earlier caused Bliss's consternation and doubt. But without any hesitation he smiled, knowing what was coming next.

The third shot revealed the same car, only this time the cap had been removed, the collar turned down, and the driver's face was both upright and clear.

'Drivers in the UK have become so fixated on yellow speed cameras,' DC Gratton said, 'that they've become almost desensitised to those designed to observe traffic flow. They barely notice them any longer because they're not there with the intention of providing a means to prosecute motorists. But a colleague of ours happened to spot one of these cameras on their way over to Lincs Storage last night, and as it's nearby, she thought it might provide us with some useful information. She was right, wasn't she, Mr Dixon? Because this still taken from that very same camera was shot less than thirty seconds after the same vehicle left Lincs Storage. While I admit we didn't get a good look at the driver on his way into the facility, this one provided a much clearer view moments after it left. And if you look closely, I think you'll be able to tell us who that is sitting in the driver's seat.'

*

In a room two doors along the same corridor, Chandler was about to turn over a copy of the same photograph. She didn't use the same spiel as Gratton because that had mostly been unrehearsed, but she did ask the same question the moment the image was revealed.

When the suspect said nothing, she prompted him. 'It's not a difficult question to answer. We can all see that's you behind the wheel, Mr Banks.'

Chandler then proceeded to lay down several more shots. 'This is you in the company van going to Lincs Storage, and this is you driving away again. As you might imagine, we have every relevant image of your comings and goings over the past couple of weeks. In addition...' Chandler took several sheets of paper out of her own wallet folder and set them on the table alongside the photographs. '... we have GPS tracking data to match every single one of these journeys. Perhaps the most telling is the one you took on Saturday night. You collected the van from your yard in Fengate, from there you drove to Jacob Nash's home where the vehicle was stationary for quite some time before moving on to the storage facility, from which it then returned to the yard. All this is telling because Saturday was the last night Mr Nash was seen or heard of until my DI discovered him inside a freezer cabinet that stood in one of the container units at Lincs Storage. Now, Mr Banks, what can you tell me about everything I've just said?'

Fully absorbed, Bliss looked on and listened closely, switching between the two interviews. Inside IR3, Grant Dixon was not holding it together at all well. He had reacted adversely to seeing his friend in such a compromising situation, but also with the knowledge that the police had access to the unit. Bliss understood the man's reaction, because word had come back from DC Virgil of a major discovery. Inside the boxes that had been sitting on the shelves, they had found sealed packs of cash, amounting to hundreds of thousands of pounds, while the cabinet drawers had been choked with diamonds.

Dixon continued to protest his innocence, and Bliss found himself close to believing the man. But things were very different in the other interview room, where Michael Banks remained cool and calculated. He was no longer commenting on anything. Bliss sensed both Chandler and Ansari were becoming frustrated when his partner switched to a topic the two of them had discussed earlier.

'Mr Banks,' she said with a resigned sigh. 'Have you heard of POCA?'

The man merely shrugged, a gesture Chandler mentioned for the recording device. 'POCA,' she went on, 'is the acronym for the Proceeds Of Crime Act. Fundamentally, it allows us to work together with the Crown Prosecution Service to recover proceeds of crime assets, mainly by way of confiscation. All we really need to prove is a criminal lifestyle, and that somebody benefitted financially from criminal conduct. More importantly, the burden of proof is on the balance of probabilities, all of which essentially sways things in our favour. It would be difficult to prove that you benefitted from the murders of Stuart McKenzie and Jacob Nash, but unless you're some kind of psycho who gets off on killing, I suspect you had your reasons. I don't know about you, Mr Banks, but I reckon we have a good chance of building a case against you in respect of, say, diamond smuggling and the proceeds gained from the selling of those diamonds. Do you have anything you'd like to say to me about that?'

He didn't. Or if he did, he kept it to himself.

Chandler smiled and nodded. 'The reason I mention POCA is that we can go one of two ways from here. If we receive adequate cooperation from you, Mr Banks, then we may be disinclined to push for confiscation and recovery. However, if you continue to say nothing, then we might well decide to put all our spare efforts into it.'

'DS Chandler,' Banks's solicitor said in a gruff manner. 'You're treading a fine line here between making an observation and making a threat. My client has a right to make no comment to any question you put to him.'

'I don't agree at all about the line I'm walking. I'm merely pointing it out. And to explain the process further, should we divert our attentions to POCA, we might reasonably assume that any and all of your client's assets were ours to confiscate, as he and his family could have benefitted from the proceeds of his crimes in any number of ways. Off the top of my head, I'm thinking everything in their savings accounts, the house – in fact any properties either of them own – and of course their cars and luxury items such as watches and jewellery, coins, perhaps even some fine wines. Most distressing of all, POCA can be hard on the families left behind while the real criminal rots in prison. But perhaps they have good friends who might offer them a roof over their heads.'

Bliss's admiration for Chandler was boundless. He'd forgotten how masterful she could be in the interview room. Her intelligence coupled with ruthlessness and a great eye and ear for detail made her a force to be reckoned with. He could see Michael Banks's confident exterior beginning to crumble as his partner's words drove home with the brute force of an ice pick.

Most criminals he knew accepted their own fate as part of the game they played. What tended to hurt most of all was the effect on their families. Inside that room, Michael Banks was being made aware without being told that if he broke his resolve to tell the police everything, then his family might yet be allowed to enjoy their comfortable lives, albeit without him for the next few years. However, if he continued to say nothing, his wife and children were likely to lose their home, their money, their influence, and their dignity. Hard enough when a wife loses her husband and children lose their father to a lengthy prison sentence, but much harder still when they are suddenly stripped of everything they have and are forced to start life all over again with absolutely nothing.

Bliss held his breath as the interview room fell silent. Chandler and Ansari refused to break that silence first. Eventually, Michael Banks drew himself upright in his chair and said, 'What is it you want to know?'

FORTY-EIGHT

AT THE END OF what proved to be a long and exhausting day, Bliss invited everybody to The Woodman and put his debit card behind the bar for the rest of the evening, all drinks for his colleagues on him.

Banks had confessed to everything they demanded of him. Stuart McKenzie, he had explained, was greedy and untrustworthy. It was McKenzie who had slowed the casino progress by demanding the three of them take more than a quarter share each. McKenzie again who had initially propositioned and then badgered his two close friends into switching the diamonds when Banks and Dixon were happy enough with their cut of the smuggling deal. And it was also McKenzie who had sold some of the gems after making a transaction without first consulting either of them. Concerned by the man's increasingly cavalier attitude to the business and his partners, Banks had summoned McKenzie to a face-to-face confrontation.

When he tried to insist that he'd had no intention of hurting McKenzie that night, it was DC Ansari who pointed out that Banks's use of the courtesy car rather than his own vehicle indicated otherwise.

'Okay, so maybe I thought it might turn violent,' he admitted. 'I don't know for sure, but anyone will tell you how aggressive and unpredictable Stu could be. I decided not to use my own motor just in case things got out of hand. I admit I didn't want to be traced to the park that night, but I honestly never meant to kill him.'

Chandler had scoffed, openly mocking him. 'Do you realise how lame that excuse sounds to us?'

Banks shrugged off her comment, instead going on to explain that the disagreement between the two men had started with harsh words before swiftly evolving into a pushing and shoving match. It was McKenzie who threw the first punch, Banks claimed. He had reacted in kind – *'with a length of cord you just happened to be carrying in your pocket'* Chandler reminded him – and had subsequently lost control of his temper and the situation.

Yes, he had scarpered but tucked himself out of sight close by as the dishevelled figure came running out of nowhere at the other end of the pathway by the trees. Banks had looked on, hanging around to see what happened next, before acting the moment the stranger turned to run off in the opposite direction. Without any conscious thought or aim in mind, he hoisted McKenzie's body over his shoulder and then carried him back across the bridge and into the trees. There he set the body down close to the exit, fetched the car, bundled his friend into the boot, and drove off.

He knew all about the storage unit, well enough to know the code, and had already found the key to the container in McKenzie's pocket. In that moment of uncertainty and near panic, it felt like the perfect place to dump the body and buy some time to gather his thoughts. After disposing of his friend inside, he realised he couldn't keep the body there indefinitely. Eventually

Sharon would report her husband missing, and when he failed to reappear, and she began to get Stuart's affairs in order, she was bound to discover the existence of the unit. She'd soon get it opened up to find out what her husband had been storing there. Banks thought he had a couple of weeks or so, perhaps a little longer, before he had to strip the container of everything. In the meantime, he didn't want the body to start stinking the place out as it rotted, so he drove back to the yard, exchanged the courtesy car for the van, collected an old freezer he'd been keeping alongside other white goods in one of his own storage containers, then transported it back to Lincs Storage and dumped his friend's body inside.

'That proves I didn't plan any of it,' Banks said. 'Or I would already have had the freezer set up in the storage unit.'

'And Roger Craig?' Chandler had asked.

'Who?' Banks looked up at her beneath hooded eyes, puzzled by the question.

'The homeless man.'

'Oh, him. Yes, that was a pity. The thing is there, I couldn't possibly know what he had seen or not seen. I didn't have a clue how much of the fight he had witnessed, or how much of a description of me he might be able to provide the police with. I realised there was no way I'd be able to do anything about it that night, but neither could I allow him to pick me out of a lineup.'

'We don't do things that way here anymore,' Chandler told him. 'We're a bit more high-tech and sophisticated these days.'

Banks continued to quibble and obfuscate, but ultimately he confessed to murdering Roger Craig. He'd arranged for an acquaintance to follow the homeless veteran from the moment he was taken by the police from the park to Thorpe Wood, and had decided to take action upon hearing the witness had returned to his previous spot among the Cuckoos Hollow trees.

'I caught him unawares,' he admitted. 'If I hadn't, he might have fought me off. He reacted quickly enough to prevent me from using the cord, but he couldn't fend off the machete I'd brought with me as a backup.'

Chandler and Ansari both later mentioned how cold and almost detached Banks was when he spoke about committing such an evil act. They found it chilling, as had Bliss while he sat enthralled by how the interview was unravelling. Banks seemed not to find anything wrong with carrying a length of cord around with him, and had been nonchalant when admitting to being armed with a serious bladed weapon.

When asked about Nash, Banks closed his eyes and gathered himself for a few moments. For the first time, he became emotional, a reaction that appeared to be genuine. 'The bloody fool was asking too many questions and acting strangely around us. Even for him. Me and Grant were convinced Jacob was trying to prise information out of us. We just couldn't decide if it was for you or somebody else.'

He went on to tell them in detail about the way he had ambushed Nash as the man came out of his garden shed, before eventually throwing him into the freezer on top of McKenzie's frozen corpse. On that occasion, the cord had worked effectively and quietly following the initial blow to the head. When pressed extensively on the matter of diamond smuggling, he admitted to the offence but refused to say a word about their partners at either end of the deal.

'Keeping quiet this time is about life and death,' he told them. 'Not losing houses and savings accounts.'

They knew precisely what he meant. Ratting out a major villain carried a far greater punishment than any the police might come up with. The two detectives decided at that point to break and discuss the outcome with Bliss and DCI Warburton. The four of them later chose not to go back at Banks about the smuggling. It wasn't why he'd been arrested, and they were not inclined to charge him with the offence at this stage, knowing it was something they could return to at any time in the future.

Taking a few minutes to himself, Bliss shut the door to his office and sat at his desk with the chair turned towards the room's solitary window. Outside, another warm day had been made humid by the showery squall passing over the city and spattering the window pane. His thoughts turned to Roger Craig, a decent man whose death was so unnecessary. While Bliss was happy to have solved the man's murder, and that of Stuart McKenzie and Jacob Nash, he shook his head in dismay at the callous disregard for life displayed by Banks. Nonetheless, he found comfort in having achieved a measure of justice for the three lives lost.

He made a quick call to Sandra Bannister, providing the reporter with a heads-up while offering only the basic details. He told her nothing that wouldn't eventually feature in forthcoming media reports and online releases, but she had earned the head start on her counterparts with the information she had provided about the casino application.

'Is that it for you now?' she asked him.

'I'm afraid so. I'll feel naked without my warrant card, but at least I still get to work cases.'

'I'm glad to hear it, Jimmy. You know where I am if you need my help.'

They said their goodbyes, and Bliss heard the same amount of emotion in his own voice as he heard in hers. Their relationship hadn't always been an easy one to navigate, but it had never been less than rewarding.

As for the Bell family, Bliss was far less pleased. How their relocation would work with the eventual trials of Alinson and whoever else might ultimately be charged with raping Nora, he couldn't imagine. But at the very least, they would all benefit from the fresh start offered to them. His heart broke every time he thought of the poor kid, and the stark, horrible choices facing her and her mother. Terminating the pregnancy seemed like the most pragmatic and kind thing to do under the circumstances, but it wasn't an easy decision to make. Not for any of them. He hoped they would find some kind of peace in their new lives after enduring so much misery and torment in this one.

...OR THE END OF THE BEGINNING?

ATER THREE OR FOUR liveners at the Woodman, Bliss invited everybody back to his place for a few more. He even offered to pay for cabs. Nobody refused, and as a team they celebrated their victories into the early hours. Shortly before the impromptu party broke up, Warburton spoke to him about Range Rover woman and her Greek paymaster. Bliss's response was to shrug and remind the DCI they were no longer his problem, though his final piece of advice was for her to make pursuing the matter a priority in the coming weeks and months.

Eventually it was just him and Chandler remaining, and when she also decided time was up, she texted her boyfriend to ask for a ride home.

The pair waited for him by the open doorway, taking in the fresh air beneath the vague glow of a nearby streetlight. Out of nowhere, Bliss gave a snorting laugh, which became more of a juvenile snigger. 'I'm more than a little bit sozzled,' he said.

Swaying slightly, Chandler refocussed her eyes a couple of times before saying, 'I can see that. I think I might be as well.'

A sly grin spread slowly across his face. 'The last time we stood here like this is still seared upon my memory. You're not going to want another snog, are you?'

'Uh-uh. No danger of you taking advantage of me again, pal.'

'Me? The way I remember it, you were all over me and planted your lips first.'

'If I did, it was only to shut you up. Plus, if I recall correctly, you were about to do something stupid and dangerous.'

'But you didn't stop me. You still let me go.'

'As if I could have stopped you going anywhere that night. Once your mind is made up, Jimmy, you can be a stubborn old bugger.'

He nodded. 'So I've heard.'

Chandler flapped a hand. 'Anyway, good old Shrek will be here at any moment, so no getting revenge with a sneaky smacker of your own.'

He held up both hands. 'I hear you loud and clear. I'll keep my hands and my lips to myself. And speaking of the Shrekster, have you made up your mind about moving away with him?'

'Nope.' Chandler jabbed a sharp fingernail into his chest. 'And don't you go saying anything to him about it, either. It's my decision. Not his. Not yours. Mine.'

Bliss let it go. Other than to say one last thing. 'After your performance in the interview room today, how can you even think about leaving us?'

Chandler shrugged and shook her head. The night had become cool, and a light breeze caressed their skin. It seemed to invigorate his friend. Still unsteady on her feet, she suddenly froze and then turned to face him as he took a step backwards.

'What?' he asked of her raised finger.

'I just realised something new about you.'

'On the way out of the door? Really? What is it, you like the chrome handle?'

'No. Don't be a plonker all your life. I'm not quite sure what to make of it yet, but I think I've caught you out, old timer.'

'So, you're certain you discovered something new, but at the same time you don't know what it is. You *are* drunk, Pen.'

Chandler brushed past him and staggered back into the living room. She nodded to herself and said, 'I was just thinking to myself how much more homely this lounge looked with the sofa here as well as your two recliners.'

He shrugged. 'So what? You've seen my sofa plenty of times since I bought it.'

'I know. You got it when you and Emily were taking things seriously. But it's not the sofa that pulled me up short.'

'Then what is it? Honestly, Pen, I'd have more luck getting the head of an armed gang to spill their guts.'

Up came the finger again. This time it wagged. 'Oh no, you're not putting me off the scent. You know what I'm talking about, don't you?'

'I genuinely don't have a Scooby.'

'Yes, you do.' Her mouth became a huge 'O'. Then she reframed her face to raise a wide grin of satisfaction. 'And now so do I, and I can't believe I missed it all these sodding years. I saw your expression change when I mentioned the recliners. The *two* recliners, Jimmy. I fully admit to being three sheets to the wind, so forgive me if I'm wrong, but a man who supposedly shuns visitors and prefers to be on his own doesn't buy two of those beauties when he moves into his new home.'

Bliss peered closely at her and blinked. Then turned and swept a hand towards the recliners. 'It's just a chair. It'd be rude not to have a second one if I did happen to have the occasional visitor.'

'Yes. But not two expensive recliners like that. You'd buy something that nice for you to use, and some old shitty armchair, uncomfortable, with springs poking out, for any chance visitors. You wouldn't have two luxury recliners lined up alongside each other facing your TV and stereo. That's a couples thing, and you're not part of a couple. Or were you thinking you might pull one of your Koi?'

He laughed that off. 'So, what exactly are you suggesting in your own inim… iminitable… inimini… your own sweet way?'

Again with the finger. Chandler had a habit of getting quite pointy when she'd had a few too many. 'That's the part I haven't worked out yet. But I will. Now that I've noticed it, I won't be forgetting about it in a hurry.'

Bliss snorted and shook his head. 'If it's taken you all this time to notice, you must be a pretty piss-poor detective.'

'Whatever. But I see you now, Jimmy Bliss. Just you wait until I figure it all out.'

'I'm already closing in on sixty, Pen. Judging by your miserable sleuthing skills, I won't live long enough for the bulb to light up above your head.'

'Okay. Okay, let me give it a stab,' Chandler said, slurring her words. She giggled at what she had said. 'I don't mean stab the recliner because that would be cruel. I mean, let me have a go at working it out. So, let me think. You bought two recliners because you… because you hoped you'd eventually have somebody sitting there alongside you. Am I right? Am I?'

He blinked a couple of times, struggling to keep her in focus. 'How about you let me sober up and I'll give you your answer in the morning?'

'Are you still coming in? You don't need to. We can easily wrap things up from here.'

'No, I'll be in. I want to go over a few bits and pieces with the big cheeses. Plus, I have paperwork to complete and my warrant card to hand in. I'll be late, though.'

She gave a sympathetic smile. 'You think you might be suffering from a hangover when you wake up?'

Bliss shook his head. 'Probably, Pen, but that's not it. Roger Craig is being cremated in the morning. Bish and I are both attending.'

'Oh. I'm surprised his body has been released before the inquest.'

'We didn't need to delay. We have more than enough on Banks with McKenzie and Nash.'

Chandler let it go, but not before admonishing him not to call her 'Pen'. After finally seeing her off, Bliss closed the front door behind him and walked slowly back towards the living room. He stood on the threshold, leaning against the frame staring down at the reclining armchairs. Even pissed off her trolley, Chandler had nailed it. He couldn't remember having those precise conscious thoughts, making the decision to purchase both chairs for the reason his friend had declared, but he knew she was right all the same. He hadn't returned to the city intending to remain alone. Without being aware of it, he must have planned, or at least hoped, to share his life eventually with a special someone.

From the outside, he knew it might seem as if he had failed in that objective. And yet while that second chair had for the most part stood empty and unused, wasn't sharing his life with a special someone precisely what he had done? Not just once, but on several occasions.

Did Emily not count?

How about Molly?

Even Chandler herself?

All three of them special to him in their own way.

Perhaps not for the reasons or for the duration he had envisaged when purchasing the chairs, but moments to treasure all the same. Many of them.

And sometimes, Jimmy Bliss thought with a smile of satisfaction, moments were all you needed.

AUTHOR'S NOTE

I WROTE THE VERY FIRST draft of **Bad to the Bone** (DI Bliss #1) in 2005, which means I've lived with Jimmy inside my head for 18 years. That of course was a pivotal book because it launched a series. **If Fear Wins** (DI Bliss #3) was also key because for me it is the book in which the characters and the series really took off inside my head. (DI Bliss #6), **Endless Silent Scream**, was also crucial for two reasons: it was the first book after leaving my publisher, and it introduced a significant recurring character in young Molly. For a while, **The Autumn Tree** (DI Bliss #8) stood out from the rest because I considered it to be my finest novel to date. Indeed, my concern at the time was that I'd never be able to match it. More recently I've come to appreciate the books that followed, but that one still resonates with me.

And now here we are with another pivotal moment in the series with **What Dies Inside Us** (DI Bliss #11), because with this book we have reached the end of one chapter in Jimmy's life and career. But happily, not the final one. Because, thankfully, while his time as a police officer is at an end, his time with the police is not. Jimmy will return in **Something More To Say**, (DI Bliss #12) in 2024. I couldn't be more delighted to have discovered a way to keep the series going while at the same time making huge changes to Jimmy's story. He's become a major part of my life, and I hope he's had a positive impact on yours, too.

Tony
October 2023

ACKNOWLEDGEMENTS

LET ME BEGIN WITH Graham Bartlett, fellow novelist and police advisor. Late in 2022 he and I were on the same panel at a literary event, and over a meal afterwards conversation turned to Bliss. I mentioned that he was due for retirement and that I'd considered having him work cold cases, but that I wasn't entirely satisfied with that idea. Graham then told me the police were using experienced retirees as civilian Senior Investigating Officers, and my immediate response was to work the notion of him doing both jobs. After seeking further advice and confirmation from Graham, I knew this was the way I wanted to end Jimmy's story – with new colleagues investigating old cases, but also working with his usual team and current major crimes.

A big thank you also to my wonderful cast of regulars: my editors, cover designer, typesetter, beta readers, Facebook group, ARC readers, regular readers, bloggers, and the usual array of supporters. You have all made a valuable contribution in one way or another to the Jimmy Bliss journey. For that, both he and I offer you our sincere gratitude.

Best wishes.
Tony

Printed in Dunstable, United Kingdom